MW00577837

KEY CHANGE

COMMON THREADS BOOK #3

HEIDI HUTCHINSON

Heidi Hutchinson

WWW.SMARTYPANTSROMANCE.COM

COPYRIGHT

This book is a work of fiction. Names, characters, places, rants, facts, contrivances, and incidents are either the product of the author's questionable imagination or are used factitiously. Any resemblance to actual persons, living or dead or undead, events, locales is entirely coincidental if not somewhat disturbing/concerning.

Made in the United States of America

Print Edition

ISBN: 978-1-949202-68-7

DEDICATION

to Charlie
you are my gift

PROLOGUE

ASHTON JAMES BARES ALL AT NMA

"It's all fun and games until your tits come out—then it's a party!" Ashton James was quoted as saying on the red carpet just hours before she had to be removed from the evening's activities by local police.

Party indeed.

Backstage video has surfaced of the pop music bad girl's bizarre altercation at the National Music Awards over the weekend.

CelebX originally broke the story that Ashton James, stripped naked and threw punches backstage before having to be escorted out by police.

Ashton James, known for her outspoken and abrasive personality, had been nominated for three awards that evening, including album of the year. She was slotted to perform during the show but sources reported that she never showed up for rehearsals and her set was scrapped.

Witnesses claim to have seen her arguing backstage with her longtime manager, Terrence Shields, right before she announced the winner of Best New Artist (Zara Lorna).

When Album of the Year was presented to Michelle Keith, a clearly intoxicated Ashton James stormed the stage and physically attacked the album's producer, Coach Riley. Security intervened, carting Ashton away.

New video provided by an anonymous source shows Ashton backstage arguing with several unnamed persons. The argument quickly escalated when Ashton removed her dress and shoes, and began throwing punches.

Police were called to the venue, but no arrests were made.

Attempts to get a statement from Ashton James' publicist have gone unanswered. Terrence Shields and the National Music Award Association also declined to comment.

CHAPTER ONE

HOW I ROLL

HANNAH

The hardest part about reinvention?

The motherfucking paperwork.

Hannah's left eye twitched involuntarily. She shoved her glasses to the top of her head and rubbed her face with both hands.

The glasses weren't prescription. They were large, boldly framed, blue light filter glasses that she only wore for work and in public.

They were absolutely hideous and she loved them.

Most of her wardrobe consisted of blacks, grays, and boring.

At first it hadn't bothered her because boring meant invisible—which was the entire point.

But after a few months she began to incorporate ugly things into her wardrobe daily.

Personal experience and subsequent observation confirmed her theory—ugly was a different kind of invisible.

Taking a deep breath, she reread the text she'd received and stifled the sigh.

It was from a number not saved in her phone; therefore it could only be one of four people. The context of the message narrowed it down to one.

Unknown: Two more things popped up this week. Meet me in the usual place at the usual time.

She tapped out her affirmative and slipped the phone back into her bag. She probably wouldn't get fired if she got caught breaking the rules, but she also didn't want to attract any extra attention.

Lowering her glasses back onto her face, she unmuted the headset.

The customer was still yelling, but Hannah sensed it was coming to a close.

At least she hoped.

"Have you disconnected the surround sound?" Hannah asked when the woman paused to take a breath.

"I already told you!" Ms. Fairbanks shouted. "I don't know what you're talking about!"

"The surround sound will be connected at the—"

"Repeating yourself isn't going to do me any favors, you little hot dog. What I really want is to speak to your supervisor!"

Hannah scrunched her nose and silently bared her teeth at the computer monitor. This would be her second supervisor referral this month. One more and she'd get a written reprimand.

"Absolutely. Please hold."

Hannah pressed the button on her headset, suspending the call.

She hadn't even had a chance. Ms. Fairbanks had been on hold for thirty-seven minutes before she'd ever gotten to Hannah's line.

Which meant that she'd had an extra thirty-seven minutes to stew in her distress.

The distress being that her surround sound was fucked up, but she thought it was the television. Hannah had tried to talk her through resetting the system, but it hadn't worked. Nine times out of ten, it was user error. But the user wanted very badly to yell at someone for it.

Enter Hannah.

For eight hours a day she took calls from people who couldn't get their shit to work. She'd run through the troubleshooting script so many times, she could program televisions in her sleep in four different languages.

But that didn't mean the person on the other end had to listen to her. Or be nice to her. Or even kind of respect her.

And Hannah was fine with that.

Mostly.

Respect wasn't something she expected from faceless strangers.

She couldn't say the same for her coworkers. They always took being bitched at so personally.

Hannah didn't give a shit.

And she wasn't paid to give a shit.

Speaking of…

"I have a request for a supervisor," she spoke into the headset.

Collin swore under his breath before taking the call.

See, Collin *did* get paid to give a shit. So he was usually pretty pissed off.

Part of her sympathized with him, but that's why he made the big bucks and she made minimum wage.

Hannah glanced up in time to see the time clock hit the fifteen after mark and she logged out.

Some people stayed late. Super late. Trying to hit numbers and reach records that might reward them with a gift card to a sports bar downtown or a plaque with their name on it in the break room. Some were working their way up to middle management so as to leverage the promotion and get hired out of the cesspool that was Superior Electronics Inc.

Not Hannah, though.

Nope.

She was more than content working in the customer service call center of the mediocre television manufacturer. They didn't suck. And she couldn't really ask for much else.

She'd wanted a job where she could be invisible but productive and leave at the same time every day. It wasn't food service and she didn't have to interact with people face-to-face too often. She was paid on time and she could leave work at work instead of it being her entire life.

Though she knew she'd lucked out with her locked in schedule.

She'd heard what her coworkers whispered about her. Having a consistent daytime shift when the others had to rotate meant they assumed she'd slept with someone at the top somewhere to get what she wanted.

Which, hilarious.

Hannah had no issue being labeled the "office slut" so long as it meant they left her alone and no one tried to be her "friend."

Though she often wondered what it would be like to sit with her coworkers and swap best and worst call stories, talk about their day, share personal information about their lives…

But it was too risky.

She couldn't make any close connections for two main reasons. First, she'd have to lie. And no healthy relationship could be established, let alone survive, without honesty. Second, telling the truth would be the kind of distraction that could harm Piper.

And protecting Piper was rule number one.

"Hey, Hannah."

She nodded at TJ as she slid on her generic black coat and buttoned it up to the top.

"Do you have plans for lunch tomorrow? I was thinking of going over to Wylde Pub. Would…" TJ cleared his throat and shifted on his feet. "Would you like to join me?" The question came out like a squeak.

Hannah pulled her knit cap over her head, covering most of her long dark hair, the rest of it tucked inside her coat.

She didn't know TJ outside of the fact that his cubicle was two down from hers and he sometimes smelled of cigarettes. She suspected he only smoked when nervous because she could smell it now.

Ah, vices.

Everyone had them, but no one talked about them.

A person's private shame.

She could relate.

She slung her bag over her shoulder—not a purse, more of a cross between a messenger bag and a small backpack—and secured it to her person as she contemplated how best to decline his invite.

"I appreciate the offer," she said quietly with a small half smile. "Maybe some other time."

But probably never, she added internally.

"O-oh." TJ shifted, not sure how to proceed.

Had that been mean?

Hannah replayed her response again. He'd asked a question and she'd answered. She didn't snort or laugh in his face. She also hadn't commented on his clothes or hair or posture. In fact, she hadn't even *thought* of any insults that had needed to be stifled.

Hey! Growth!

She hadn't been mean! (Internal high-five!)

But rejection was awkward. That's probably what he was feeling and why he couldn't meet her eyes anymore.

Was that unprompted empathy for a stranger she was experiencing?

Whoa. Big day for Hannah.

"See you tomorrow," she said, trying to soften the moment and also end the conversation for both their sakes.

TJ nodded, the tips of his ears turning red.

Man, that sucked.

For him.

That had actually been kind of a cool moment for her and what she'd been working on. But TJ was probably feeling the opposite of cool.

Hannah exited the building, and the cold, crisp air of an early Chicago winter blasted through her thoughts and had her refocusing to the next part of her day.

Her favorite part of the day.

In the beginning, riding the train to and from work had been… uncomfortable. She'd had to battle huge spikes of anxiety. But she'd pushed through and now her daily train ride was just another part of the routine.

She recognized the usual commuters even though she didn't interact with them. Not directly.

A smile for the toddler balanced on her mom's lap; saving the seat for the grumpy man with a WWII emblem on his hat; making room for Napoleon the service dog and his handler.

Small occurrences that she had become accustomed to and had fit into her comfort zone.

Being able to recognize everyone around her added to her sense of security. If ever anyone new showed up, she knew how to avoid direct eye contact and which stop to get off in case they tried to follow her.

But the likelihood of that happening grew smaller with each month that passed, and her life was relatively undisturbed.

She was surrounded by people all of the time. They were in her life in a safe and careful way. But not in a way she might hurt them.

Because she would hurt them.

It was just in her nature.

So, she stuck to the routine.

And the longer she kept the routine, the more space existed in between who she was and who she was becoming.

The routine was the key.

A necessary evil for humans to maintain healthy and balanced lives.

(Even though Hannah had watched several true crime shows that argued it was a set routine that had led to the victim's grisly murder.)

And where did her routine fall on the spectrum of healthy and balanced?

Good question.

One she asked herself at least once a day.

She was somewhere between life and death.

The ever-important middle space.

The subway lurched through the stop before hers and she moved closer to the exit.

Routine and rhythm had been natural skills she'd been blessed with and had continued to cultivate her entire life.

It had been an invaluable skill in her previous life—the one of which they did not speak.

And now it kept her on track.

Kept her clean.

Well...clean-*ish.*

She doubted she'd ever be truly clean.

But clean enough would work just as well.

When the subway stopped again, she was already at the door. Then she was on the platform and moving with the small crowd to the CTA exit, where she would continue on her usual route to the sidewalk and on to her apartment. First thing she'd do when she got home was take off her bra. Then make dinner for her and Piper, do a load of laundry, and shower before bed.

Maybe some meditation before she went to sleep.

Which was so different than it had been a year ago.

Being alone with herself in the beginning had been terrifying.

Too many nights she had ended up just watching anything she could find to keep her mind occupied and keep herself from thinking about *all the things.*

Running away from reflections and echoes.

But these days there was less running and more rumination.

She kept track of heartbeats, home-cooked meals, steps to her door—the first place she'd ever called home.

She tried to keep the things that mattered at the forefront of her mind.

Her determined stride toward the CTA exit was interrupted when a sound hit her ears. She was so startled by the intrusion she stopped short.

A clear tenor voice permeated the din of other buskers and CTA passengers. It was accompanied by an acoustic guitar that picked its way through the melody instead of strumming along, creating two singers out of one.

The person behind her collided with her back and pushed off her to go around without so much as an apology.

But Hannah was too caught off guard by the song to care.

She tilted her head in the direction of the music and moved toward it.

Her stomach clenched with the deviation from the routine, but she had to at least answer one question.

Who would be singing *this* song?

Her eyes scanned the buskers on the platform, her experienced ear picking through the sounds until she found what it was that had caused her pause.

The busker wasn't new.

A young man she had passed more times than she could count. Probably in his late teens, *maybe* early twenties. Brown, glossy hair, square jaw that hadn't finished revealing its future glory, fingerless gloves, strumming a used but lovingly cared for guitar. His jeans were clean and so was the gray hoodiethat accompanied his "starving musician" look.

She paused in front of his open guitar case and listened to a song that was more than familiar to her.

Chills raced over her arms and she was glad to be wearing thick layers.

More than just straight covering the song, he'd sped it up a half step and switched the pronouns, putting his own stamp on it.

The song picked up in intensity at the bridge, and Hannah smiled to herself because she'd always loved this bridge and she'd never heard it sung with such conviction.

Again. Chills.

Ooh, I'm over my head
Trying to be clever,
My heart is underfed
Because my love doesn't matter.
And you say that you need me
But you're giving hope to things that can never be...

If I kiss you with my eyes closed tight
I know our bed won't be cold tonight,
I always get lost in your lips,
And my world, my heart
Is yours to twist.

It was a song she hadn't heard in a long time. One she'd recorded on her first album.

Shit, it felt like a million years ago.

One of the rare songs she'd written herself that had been green-lighted by the studio.

Also, one of the last times she even tried to put her own work out there.

It had never been an audience favorite.

To be fair, it had a different sound to the rest of her stuff. It was more introspective and deeply personal.

Having it rejected en masse had been enough to teach Hannah that her heart wouldn't get her what she wanted.

But her ambition would.

And it did.

Her ambition also got her herpes.

But that was another thing entirely.

The song finished and the busker fluttered his overly thick eyelashes at her with a small smirk.

Now was the part where she would slip a few dollars into the guitar case.

And she would.

In a second.

"Interesting song choice," Hannah remarked flatly.

The young man's eyes sharpened on her, and the skin around his mouth tightened as he looked her over.

She wasn't worried about being recognized.

It hadn't happened in ages and she had done a fairly decent job at changing her trademark "look." The fact that she was mostly covered, even wearing glasses when she didn't need them, definitely helped her feel bolder.

Though engaging a musician in a conversation about one of her own songs put her at a certain risk and her heart quickened.

Oh boy.

That felt good.

It was a small shot of adrenaline in a body she had been keeping as bored as possible.

A bland routine. A life with no surprises. That's what she had successfully designed and maintained.

"You know it?" the busker asked with a suspicious tilt of his head.

"A forgettable song on a forgettable album," she responded.

She wanted to tell him that his rendition was world-shifting. That his style and spark were fresh and bright, and she could make a phone call and change his life.

But she wasn't going to do any of those things.

Because more than his life would change.

And Hannah had priorities.

He huffed a harsh laugh and shook his head, his long bangs swinging into his eyes. He pushed them back with one hand. "Disagree."

He held her eyes unflinching but didn't expound on his opinion.

Hannah's lips twisted to the side as she tried to fight the smile creeping into her expression. She dropped a five into his case and pursed her lips.

"Get some better material, kid." She lifted her chin and walked away.

When she hit the steps, she heard his clear voice singing the song again.

Little shit.

Hannah snorted a laugh and jogged up the steps to the street.

Now she had a story to tell Piper at dinner.

But first she had to hurry to her clandestine meeting before her contact thought something had happened to her and called in reinforcements.

* * *

The doors to the elevator slid open revealing one Alex Greene.

He had a laptop balanced on one hand while he used the other hand to type and scroll rapidly.

He glanced up through thick eyebrows and even thicker black glasses.

Hannah's gaze bounced from him to the intimidating man taking up the other corner of the elevator.

"Gentlemen," she greeted, stepping inside.

Quinn Sullivan pressed the button to close the doors.

The elevator moved smoothly between floors for a few seconds before Quinn hit the emergency stop and the lift came to a halt with a bounce.

This was their chosen office, their meeting place, their secret tree house.

Quinn had an actual office with real security in a high-rise with all the bells and whistles.

But when Hannah had first met with him nearly two years ago, she'd felt overly exposed in the shiny building with all the windows.

He'd compromised and they'd moved their meeting places all around the city until he'd convinced her to move into the building he owned (and also lived in). That's when the service elevator had been employed as their new office.

It had been Alex's idea.

Something about the heavy, reinforced steel, and the obscure location making it "safer" than meeting out in the open.

His paranoia was reassuring to Hannah, who had been afraid she had been taking it too far.

But nothing compared to how Alex Greene operated in his day-to-day life. And because of that, she knew she could trust him to keep her invisible.

"Two things showed up this week in my search that I thought should be addressed," Alex started right in without saying hi or even nodding in her direction. Again, another trait she appreciated.

He turned the laptop screen to face her.

"Your name appeared in a writing credit in the Double Blind Study box set scheduled to release next year. So far, it's caused minimal waves in the fan chats. Most people hate you too much to care where you are."

Hannah shrugged, because, no shit.

And leave it to Luke Casey, her ex and lead singer of the famous rock band, to remind her of a time in her life where she had tried and failed in spectacular fashion.

She knew without Alex telling her what song it was.

She and Luke had written it together in the early days, before all the fuckery.

"It's for something called…'Somewhat Alive' and the band has asked you to rerecord your vocals for that.

"Also, for some reason your name was listed as a topic for a behind-the-scenes episode on a web series that launched last month. The episode has not been given an airdate, but the title is 'Where Are They Now?'"

"Huh?" she asked.

He turned the laptop back around and clicked rapidly while speaking. "From what I've been able to find, it doesn't seem that they actually *know* where you are, but they're using your image as clickbait."

Hannah shook her head in an attempt to straighten out the information that had been fired at her.

Clickbait wasn't a new tactic. And Alex's instincts were usually spot-on for things such as this, so she trusted him that it wasn't anything else.

But the vocals on the DBS track?

"What do you want to do about Double Blind Study thing?" Alex asked without looking up from his screen. "So far, the official stance has been that you don't really do that anymore. I had Sandra pose as Melanie, your personal assistant, in case anyone asks. She told them no, but they've continued to send emails and call the dead line."

The dead line was one of the first things Alex had set up for her. It was exactly what it sounded like: a phone number that went nowhere. That and a vague email address were all that remained of her previous career.

No publicist, no manager, no entourage.

Just her and these two weirdos in an elevator.

Her gaze bounced between Quinn and Alex.

"What if I want to think about it for a minute?" As the words left her mouth, she felt rather than saw Alex's disappointed scowl. He loved to say no to people obsessed with their own self-importance.

Alex stopped typing and leveled her with his intense stare. "What's there to think about?"

So. Much.

But all that came out was, "It's complicated."

Alex's scowl deepened, and he opened his mouth to say something when Quinn got there first.

"Think about it for a couple of days and get back to us."

She nodded her thanks and pressed her lips together. If they were waiting for her to open up and share any of those complications, they were going to be in that elevator for a long time.

Quinn must've sensed that because he tilted his head slightly and rocked back on his heels. "How's the job going?"

"Boring. Just like I wanted," she replied with a smirk.

He studied her with his all-seeing gaze and she fought the urge to look away.

"Maybe you should think about getting a hobby," he suggested after a beat.

This was Quinn's way of saying he cared. He got bossy.

Which was honestly adorable.

Add his dangerous good looks and driven personality and Hannah would be all about rearranging some of her current priorities.

But Quinn was happily head over elbows in love with his wife. He was also very protective of her, which was probably why even though they lived in the same building, Hannah had never seen her. Which added to his appeal in a very different way.

"Yeeaahh," she drew out with a thoughtful squint. "The last time I had a hobby, I tried to recreate the Sistine Chapel on the ceiling of my *very* expensive New York City apartment."

"I didn't know you were a painter," Alex remarked. "How did it turn out?"

"Well, since I'm not a painter and just an ambitious alcoholic, not well."

Alex barked a laugh and quickly silenced himself.

Hannah smirked.

"Alcoholism isn't a hobby," Quinn reprimanded coolly.

Hannah rolled her eyes. "Yeah, I know. I was trying to be funny about it."

Quinn's lips twitched and he disengaged the emergency stop. The elevator began moving, bringing their secret rendezvous to a close.

Hannah's eyes flicked over Alex's knit cap that adorned his head. She'd seen it before but always failed to ask about it.

"I like your hat," she said, a strange feeling circling in her chest with the small compliment.

"Thanks. My wife made it for me. She knits." A slight blush touched Alex's cheeks.

"Hmm," Hannah remarked as the lift came to a stop at her floor. "Maybe I'll take up knitting. That's a safe hobby, right?"

* * *

"He's the killer."

"Who?"

"The building manager."

"No way."

Hannah shrugged and shoved a forkful of noodles into her mouth.

It was Stir-Friday. Sesame chicken and *Hawaii 5-0.*

Another part of the routine.

But truth be told, probably Hannah's favorite.

It was the one night a week where she didn't make Piper do her homework and they had "family time."

How weird was it that Hannah had a set routine let alone a designated "family night?"

Super weird.

Eighteen months ago, she would have never predicted this.

How could she?

But here they were.

She glanced to the end of the couch where the twelve-year-old sat curled up, devouring her own bowl of noodles and stir-fry.

Even though the run-in with the busker singing one of her songs had set off a flurry of memories and "what-ifs" throughout the evening, nothing in the world could get Hannah to change what she'd gained all those months ago.

Piper dropped her fork in the bowl with a gasp. She turned her wide eyes on Hannah—striking blue eyes that matched Hannah's own. "How did you know?"

Hannah chuckled but didn't reply.

"Whatever. One of these days I'm gonna figure out how you're cheating, and then we'll see who the smart one is," Piper grumbled without any real ire.

"Not cheating. I'm just that good," Hannah teased with a single shoulder shrug.

Piper sighed and stood up. "Is there more?"

"Yep." Hannah nodded. "Made extra. Thought you might be hungry tonight." She watched the preteen shuffle into the kitchen of their luxury apartment.

At first, the swanky accommodations had been a source of contention between them.

Piper had been raised in a lower income home and she wasn't used to high-end living. She had thrown it in Hannah's face multiple times a day for those first few months.

But Hannah couldn't risk their security just to make the young girl more comfortable.

It was an unfortunate but expected residue of her previous life.

Still, Hannah compromised in all the places she could. The décor was modest, even minimal. Clothes, shoes, accessories were as middle-class as she dared. Piper had her own mobile phone, but it was a basic design. There was only one computer in the home and it was used in a shared living space.

Hannah had learned as much as she could from parenting blogs and books recommended to her by their family therapist.

Was she doing it right?

Probably not.

But she was trying as hard as she could.

And that had to count for something.

She hoped.

She hoped so hard some days she was positive that her hope was the only thing getting her to the next day.

"How was practice today?" Hannah asked.

Piper had decided to join the basketball team at her new school.

Hannah wasn't a "sports person," but she didn't try to discourage the younger girl from doing something she was interested in.

"It was okay." Piper returned to the couch and frowned at the floor as she thought.

Hannah waited, having learned that as soon as Piper sorted

through her thoughts, she'd share. But pressuring her often meant Piper second-guessing herself and internalizing too much.

As the only parental figure in Piper's life, Hannah was bound and determined to be a positive one. Which was why she'd been going to both family counseling and individual therapy for a year. And would continue to go indefinitely.

Because if she failed at this guardian gig, it wasn't going to be from lack of trying.

She would try the fuck out of it.

With everything she had.

"The other girls don't seem to like me that much," Piper finally confessed.

Hannah swallowed, a heavy weight settling in her stomach.

Her first instinct was to ask her if she wanted her to "fuck 'em up."

But that probably wasn't good advice for anyone and especially not a seventh-grader.

But *most* especially, not Piper.

Piper was good and clean and pure and nothing like her older sister.

They shared nearly identical facial features—same dark, nearly black hair, pouty lips, high cheekbones, severe blue eyes, thick eyelashes, perpetually sun-kissed cheeks. But where Hannah's body was that of a fully formed (and enhanced) woman, Piper was gangly and flat-chested—puberty having decided to wait a little while.

More than likely due to the emotional stress of the past couple of years.

Which was another contributing factor to Hannah's determination to make Piper's life as secure and stable as possible.

Still, Piper was a gorgeous girl.

And being pretty in middle school had its drawbacks.

Especially when it was paired with a sweetness like Piper's.

Misplaced jealousy could make girls be horrible. And Hannah knew that from experience.

But not from Piper's side, from the horrible side.

Hannah wasn't sure what to say in this situation. Then Piper turned those blue eyes on her, wide and worried.

"I just wish I could make a friend, you know? Just one."

Hannah bit her bottom lip and quickly set her bowl aside. She opened her arms to the younger girl and Piper crawled across the couch to settle against her big sister. She curled into Hannah's side and fixed her eyes on the television and continued to eat her dinner.

Hannah wrapped one arm around Piper and stroked her dark hair back as she pressed her lips to Piper's temple.

"Oh, beautiful girl," Hannah murmured. "I wish that for you too."

Piper deserved a happy life with beauty and good friends.

She didn't deserve Hannah Lee James, formerly Ashton James, as a guardian.

But here they were.

* * *

JOHNNY

"You're late."

The front door closed with a slam.

"I know," Shawn sighed. "It was a choice."

Johnny Enamorado Torres smirked at his little brother's reply and flipped the pancake.

Perfect.

Just like the last two.

"Pancakes for dinner?" Shawn questioned as he removed his

jacket and tossed it over the back of the couch. "Is this one of those things I'm not supposed to tell Mrs. Grayson?"

"Tell her whatever you like," Johnny replied. "But if she takes you away from me, there won't be any studio time in your future."

Not that it mattered. The seventeen-year-old would be eighteen in less than a month. So Mrs. Grayson could suck it at this point.

But still, just the mention of their assigned social worker had his stomach trying to tie itself in knots.

Mrs. Grayson was a decent enough person. But she represented a system that hadn't exactly made their family life easy.

Johnny was looking forward to putting that part of their lives firmly behind them.

The silence that followed his statement had him looking over his shoulder to see if Shawn had heard him.

The younger man stood with his mouth agape, arms lax at his sides.

Yeah, he'd heard him.

"You got it? It's finalized?" Shawn finally asked. "All the papers have been signed?"

Johnny took a deep breath, feeling the pressure of pride and terror in his chest, pushed it aside, and kept his voice steady.

"Why do you think we're having pancakes—oof!"

He was slammed in the back with Shawn's hug.

Johnny closed his eyes as his lips curved into a smile. Hugs from this kid had always hit him much deeper. All the way into his heart, a part of him he only felt when Shawn was involved. His soul, maybe?

It was warm and huge and powerful.

And it made Johnny feel blessed.

Not #blessed.

But as if a power higher and greater than any in this world had looked at him for a moment and he'd found favor.

He cleared the emotion from his throat. "Set the table for me, would ya?"

Shawn chuckled and let him go, moving toward the dishwasher. He began unloading the dishes they'd need to eat.

There were only a few things that Johnny had decided were important when Shawn had come to live with him thirteen years ago.

One of them was eating on real plates.

When Johnny had been a bachelor and didn't have to share his space with anyone, he'd had no issue with using paper plates (if anything at all). But becoming a guardian had changed his view on some things.

Kids needed stability.

And paper plates were the antithesis of stability—especially the kind Johnny used to buy in bulk. They had basically been glorified napkins.

So he'd bought a set of used Fiestaware at Goodwill. They were orange. And they'd lasted more than a decade. Four dinner plates, four lunch plates, four bowls. Though two of those never left the cupboard. They washed their dishes every night and just took them from the dishwasher as they needed them, returning them at night and running the machine at bedtime.

"I was right, by the way," Shawn said, setting the plates on the small folding table they used as their place to eat.

Johnny had never bothered with tablecloths or anything and the table had been covered in some type of lacquer to make it shiny and hard. The table he'd found in a garage when he'd been helping a friend move. It was going to go to the dump until Johnny decided it could be useful. For a year it had been a desk for his recording tech.

And then Shawn came and Johnny decided they'd be eating dinner as a family every night at a table—not in front of the TV—so they would have to look at each other.

Conversation had been difficult in the beginning. For Johnny. His thoughts had been distracted and he'd had to deliberately focus on conversing with the youngster.

But given enough time and shared meals, they found an easy rhythm. Johnny had always known it was Shawn's sweet disposition that helped them reach that place sooner.

Of all the hands he could have been dealt in his life, ending up with Shawn was the greatest blessing of his life.

"What were you right about?" Johnny asked, wondering which bet he'd lost this time.

"It's her. It's totally her. She looks different but not much. I mean, she's the kind of chick that stands out in a crowd anyway, but—"

"Woman," Johnny corrected. "We don't say chicks."

Shawn muttered under his breath, adding silverware to the table. "Fine. Whatever. *Woman*, then. But it was her." He crossed his arms over his chest and faced Johnny. "Which means you owe me fifty dollars."

"Wait, wait, wait." Johnny waved a hand in the air as he tried to catch up to what Shawn was saying. "Who are we talking about? And I owe you what now?"

Shawn's mouth flattened along with his expression. "Ha ha," he said, not sounding amused in the least. "Don't try to get out of this one. You know how long it took me to learn that damn song."

Johnny studied Shawn's serious expression and debated how to address the current update to their reoccurring argument.

"Did you speak to her?" he asked carefully.

"Yes," Shawn answered smugly. "I played her song and she came right over to me." He dug in his pocket and produced a five-dollar bill. "Gave me this."

Johnny's gaze flicked to the bill and back to the determined glint in Shawn's eyes. "That's hardly conclusive evidence. Did she say it was her song?"

A crack in Shawn's conviction showed for a moment as he swallowed and dropped his eyes to the floor. "Not exactly."

"Hmm," Johnny said and returned his attention to the last pancake on the skillet.

"But it was her. That's a face you can't fake."

Except for the fact that most of her face was actually fake.

But Johnny didn't point that out.

This time.

"Ashton James does not ride the Pink Line on a regular basis," he said instead.

"Yes, she does." Shawn opened the refrigerator and his voice muffled slightly as he ducked his head inside. "Every day at 5:35 she gets off at Washington and Wabash and heads east.

"Slow down, stalker, I don't have bail money this week. I emptied the savings. Or maybe you forgot."

Shawn sighed in exasperation. "I didn't forget. But I don't think it's coincidence that the same day everything becomes final at the studio, I have a conversation with *the* Ashton James. I feel like it's… what's the word? Kismet!"

Johnny set the plate of stacked pancakes on the table and pulled out his customary seat.

"A conversation? What did she say?"

Shawn shrugged and sat down, reaching for the pancake pile immediately.

The appetite on this kid.

It was a miracle Johnny had managed to save enough money at all.

"She said it was a forgettable song on a forgettable album and told me to get some better material."

Johnny paused, holding the syrup aloft as he blinked at Shawn.

Shawn shoved a half of a pancake into his mouth and smiled

boldly at Johnny, as if he could read his thoughts, before snatching the syrup out of his hand.

While Johnny wasn't convinced Shawn had discovered Ashton James' whereabouts, something about those words rang true.

Though Shawn knew the story of the time Johnny had known the famous songstress and he could be lying just to make a point.

Johnny narrowed his eyes at the beaming younger man.

No.

They'd been doing this long enough for Johnny to pick out the telltale signs of deceit.

Still, he wasn't exactly ready to hop on board Shawn's crazy train.

Besides, even if it were Ashton James, all nonsensicalness aside, did Johnny really want Shawn to be influenced by her?

He literally couldn't have a bigger nope.

"Come with me on Monday. You'll see for yourself."

Johnny rolled his eyes. "Not tomorrow?"

"No." Shawn suddenly sounded defeated. He rolled his eyes. "Tomorrow is the first day of my mandatory concession stand service, remember?"

Johnny groaned.

Every year the school somehow managed to not only get an obscene amount of money from him for tuition, but also get them to work for free on their weekend for a quarter.

It was compulsory labor is what it was, and he was fairly certain that they were violating at least a dozen child labor laws, but he didn't have it in him to fight this one.

He'd learned a long time ago how to pick his battles.

Freedom from making popcorn on the weekends wasn't one.

"Right. So we have…that to look forward to."

Shawn grinned, knowing how uncomfortable it made Johnny.

"Maybe you'll finally find a girlfriend," he teased.

"I have no interest in those women," Johnny grumbled. "Besides,

Sarahi would start an actual riot if I dated someone she didn't approve of. Remember when she saw me out to dinner with Grace Limoges?"

Shawn barked a laugh at the memory.

Johnny shook his head and whistled under his breath. "I still can't go back to La Familia."

"Speaking of, let's get La Morena on Sunday. Is Nikki gonna be there?"

Johnny heard the slight inflection in Shawn's voice when he'd said Nikki's name.

"She has the weekend off."

"Cool." Shawn nodded and folded another entire pancake into his mouth.

"But Sunday is a good plan. Bring your stuff and we'll record as much as we can."

The rest of the meal, Shawn chattered on and on about what he wanted to record first and what kind of techniques he wanted to play with. Owning the studio and making their own music had been a shared dream between the two of them for a very long time.

But they'd both refused to celebrate or dream out loud until the final paperwork had been done. Mostly due to them both having experienced heartbreak at the last second.

Sometimes dreams fell through.

After the dishes were done and they'd watched a movie, Shawn went to bed.

Johnny waited until the light under the bedroom door went out, then he waited another thirty minutes.

Making his way to his bedroom, he softly closed the door behind him.

Taking out the laptop, he went straight to Google and searched for Ashton James.

It was a hopeless quest.

Like so many times before, there was no information on her

current whereabouts. Not that she was a missing person, but she had seemingly dropped off the grid.

Her last public outing had been an awards show two years ago where she'd shown up drunk and thrown a drama with her titties out.

That was it.

Everything that came after that was speculation and rumor.

Some said she'd gone to rehab, some claimed she'd died and was being replaced by a look-alike, others said she never existed at all and we were all pawns in a cosmic practical joke.

That was enough of that. No more Tumblr.

Johnny closed the laptop and set it aside.

He didn't care.

He shouldn't care.

All he'd been was a session musician on her first album. He'd done his job and gotten paid. He shouldn't have any lingering thoughts about her at all.

Except that he had.

He lingered.

Every moment with her was burned into his mind.

Knowing her was an experience he'd never gotten over for all the wrong reasons.

He knew one thing, if Ashton James was living and thriving in Chicago, he would do anything in his power to keep her away from Shawn.

CHAPTER TWO

MY PREROGATIVE

HANNAH

"Is that what you're wearing to the game?"

Hannah glanced down at her attire—black skinny jeans and a black and gray flannel.

"What's wrong with this?"

Piper blinked and pressed her lips together pensively. Finally, she sighed and picked up her bag, throwing it over her shoulder. "Nothing, it's fine."

Sure, if by "fine" she meant "definitely not fine."

"We have time, Piper, I can change," Hannah decided to push. Gently. A gentle push. A nudge, if you will.

Piper swallowed and her eyes darted around the room. "It's not a big deal, it's just…"

Hannah waited.

"The other moms and stuff wear school colors to the games."

Ohhhh. Right. Shit.

"But it's not a big deal, let's just go." Piper opened the apartment door and hurried through.

Hannah grabbed her keys off the hook by the door and followed her.

Piper was right. All the moms and dads wore school colors to the games. How had Hannah never considered this fact?

Truthfully, Hannah's priority had been *not* to attract attention. But maybe being the one in the bleachers without school colors on attracted more attention than she had originally thought.

Instead of taking the train, they took Hannah's car to school events. Maybe it was weird to have a car and still ride the train to work every day, but Hannah didn't like to drive places by herself. For personal reasons. Piper never asked. But if she did, Hannah would tell her the truth.

They pulled into the school parking lot and parked. Piper took off for the doors as Hannah did her keys-phone-wallet pat down.

When she entered through the gym doors, the sound rushed over her in a physical way. Squeaking sneakers on the hardwood, a cacophony of voices and movement as friends and family got settled in their seats. It took a second for Hannah's ears to adjust.

Piper shoved her coat into Hannah's arms and took off to warm up with her team. Hannah did her best to fold the coat and tuck it under an arm.

She chewed on her bottom lip as she turned to face her least favorite part of the weekend—deciding where to sit.

Last weekend they had been early, and she'd opted for the top corner of the bleachers.

Not so fortunate today.

She felt rather than saw the eyes of the other families as she weighed her options. There was an open spot right behind Piper's team bench. That seemed a little overbearing, though. Normally the loudest parents sat there. The backseat coaching parents.

And a small opening right exactly in the middle. She'd have to ask people to move.

Asking others for anything was still tricky for her. Apparently, she struggled with correct "tone."

Maybe now would be a good time to check out the concession stand.

The school snack stand, or concession, was in an open window in the wall opposite of the bleachers. When not in use, the window was closed with a metal shade. Currently the shade was open and there were three lines up to the front.

They sold slices of pizza, hot pretzels, nachos, chips, and assorted bottled beverages. They also sold school shirts and merchandise like pompoms and felt pennants.

Hannah got in the line that looked closest to the merchandise. Her eyes scanned the blue and yellow school colors and she tried not to curl her lip.

School spirit was something she had never contracted. Thankfully she'd been born immune.

But Piper meant more to her than her distaste for school emblems and foam fingers.

What was that? A badger?

That couldn't be right.

Could it?

The line to her left moved forward while hers remained in a standstill. Though it wasn't really a line, just one woman in front of her.

Hannah tried to not make it obvious as she craned her neck to look around the woman and see what the holdup was.

Ohhh.

It had to be because of the man working that side of the counter.

And he was definitely *working it.*

Now she understood the reason for the delay. If she had undivided attention from a man who looked like that, she'd be less likely to move along too.

A whisper of melancholy floated through her.

She used to be the pretty one who stopped traffic.

Until she took that pretty thing she had going on and decided to amplify it with anything she could get her hands on.

And it had worked.

It had worked so well, in fact, that she not only stopped traffic but her heart once or twice.

The world will always long for beautiful things.

There will always be a demand for beauty.

Maybe Hannah would be beautiful again one day.

She scanned the man's face, noting his dark eyes, complexion, and hair. The strained smile on his face as he walked the fine line between polite and wanting to scream.

He was dressed in jeans and a burgundy Henley—the top two buttons undone and revealing a strong collarbone with the barest hint of chest hair peeking out. He nodded at whatever the woman in front of him said and crossed his arms over his chest, feigning amusement.

The long sleeves of his shirt had been pushed up to his elbows, and his solid forearms were sprinkled with dark hair as well. Even though his body language communicated his desire for the conversation to be over, it did little to dissuade the woman from talking to him. Probably because it stretched his shirt against his shoulders and biceps, revealing his athletic build.

Hannah felt a little sorry for him.

He was just doing his job, not trying to attract the kind of attention he was getting.

In fact…

She leaned around to look again and confirmed the woman hadn't even purchased anything. She was just chatting him up.

Her movement must have caught his eye because he moved to the left just slightly, lining himself up with Hannah more so than the woman in front of her.

"Are you about done, Krystal?"

Hannah glanced over her shoulder at the same time as the woman in front of her did. She hadn't even noticed the line that had begun to form behind her. She caught the eye of the woman who had spoken and automatically smiled at the woman's open grin.

"He only works the window one quarter out of the year and it brings out all the thirsty bitches." Her speech was slightly accented, but Hannah couldn't place it.

"I can hear you, Sarahi," Krystal said.

Sarahi rolled her eyes and tilted her head to the side. "Good. Now finish up your business so we aren't late to watching our babies play."

Hannah rolled her lips inward as she fought back a laugh. Sarahi noticed and giggled. Which only made it more difficult for Hannah to keep her composure.

Who was this woman?

"Next, please."

Hannah stepped forward, turning her back on Sarahi, still smiling. Her eyes immediately went to the hoodie she'd been eyeing in line.

"How much for the tee with the rabid badger on it?" she asked, reaching into her back pocket for her wallet.

"Johnny, look alive," Sarahi prompted from behind her, snapping her fingers.

Hannah glanced at the man, Johnny, at the counter.

He blinked, seemingly startled, and looked at the pegboard. "Uh, it's twenty dollars." He coughed around a laugh. "And, uh, it's not a badger. It's a supposed to be a wolverine—the school mascot." His palms had been pressed to the counter and he shoved away from it now to move to the clothing choices.

"Right," Hannah replied. "Rabid badger, wolverine, still don't want to meet either one in my kitchen when it's PMSing."

Johnny grinned in a lopsided way, his dark eyes dancing.

Oh, this was what Sarahi had been talking about.

Handsome man was handsome.

His angular jaw was dusted with black whiskers. Straight nose, a little on the large side and wider at the tip. His lips were the perfect cupid's bow and the bottom one stuck out just slightly in a permanent pout.

His eyebrows were black and thick and straight (weirdly similar to Alex Greene's, she noted). The hair on his head was also black but not straight. It was thick and wavy on top but short around the sides.

A thick wave threatened to flop across his forehead, and for a moment, Hannah was certain she had seen him before.

The train? Work? Her building?

No.

None of those rang true.

"Wait. Do I know you?" she blurted with a frown, breaking all of the rules she so carefully followed all of the time and probably sounding just like all his other admirers he had interacted with all day.

He shook his head and glanced at the counter between them. "No," he answered quickly, and then, "What size for the shirt?"

"Uh, large," Hannah answered, not being able to shake the feeling she had *definitely* seen him somewhere. Especially since she had been cataloging everyone in her life in a just-on-this-side-of-obsessive way since she'd moved to Chicago.

For survival reasons.

He placed the hideous blue and gold purchase on the counter and eyed the horrible graphic on the front.

"It does look like a badger," he muttered with a chuckle.

His eyes connected with hers and they shared a moment.

It was just a laugh, a joke, a shared breath.

But it wasn't part of her routine.

Something warm stole through Hannah's insides and startled her.

It had been so long since she'd shared a connection of any kind with a human outside of the twelve-year-old she adored.

Pushing aside the panic that threatened to barge into this moment, she handed over the twenty she'd removed from her billfold.

His hand closed around hers unexpectedly and she froze.

His hand was warm. That was her first and only thought.

Which made her feel like a total moron because obviously a living, breathing person would be warm.

But the sensation rippled across her skin and made her *feel* it.

"Sorry 'bout that," he muttered, slipping the bill free of her hand.

Hannah took a slow breath and swallowed.

Remember that time when you were so numb that you couldn't register being touched at all?

Yeah. Apparently, she had swung the complete other way on the pendulum if a touch of the hand had caused all of her nerve endings to sing at once.

Hannah grabbed the shirt off the counter and hurried out of the line.

Whatever.

Shake it off, girl.

She headed to the bathroom to change.

School bathrooms all had the same smell. Chlorine, rust, and the faintest echo of fruity body spray.

Hannah avoided the mirrors and steered to a stall; she didn't bother locking it. She quickly unbuttoned her flannel, tossed it over the top of the stall door along with Piper's coat that she was still lugging around, and slipped her new shirt on. It hung just at her hips —not too loose and not snug. A general fit as far as shirts went. She tagged the flannel and left the stall.

And paused.

There she was.

In the mirror above the sink.

Seeing her reflection had not gotten any easier. No matter how many therapy sessions she went to, or what kind of meds she was on, seeing her face in a mirror was still difficult.

She'd spent a great deal of her life perfecting that reflection. Every inch of it had been examined, measured, and improved to the point it had become her biggest sense of pride. Even more so than her singing career or musical talent.

The image was all that mattered.

She'd made herself into her own idol.

Just another false god.

She tied the arms of the flannel around her hips and took a deep breath.

Sometimes, if she slowed down for a minute, she'd catch a glimpse of herself. A spark, like the flash of a camera or a striking match. The sudden recognition was startling…and it filled her with a hope she didn't recognize and was unable to hold onto.

And then it would fade and she'd be back to looking at this. This new creature that looked half alive and felt the same.

Cheers from the court echoed into the bathroom and she blinked away her thoughts.

Piper.

She had Piper.

Piper was good and clean, and despite everything Hannah had done, Piper loved her.

That was all that mattered.

Hannah would do whatever it took to deserve that love.

She grabbed Piper's coat and left the bathroom.

Ugh.

That's right.

She hadn't picked a spot to sit yet.

By now the game had started and the bleachers were completely packed. Did public schools have this kind of turnout?

Her attention was drawn to someone waving at her.

Recognizing Sarahi from earlier, she wasn't sure she was the one being waved to. Hannah glanced behind her to check. No, she was the only one nearby. Still, she pointed at herself with a frown. Sarahi exaggerated an eye roll and then nodded emphatically, waving her over again.

Um. Okay.

Hannah made her way that direction. When she was close enough, Sarahi stood up and moved over, leaving exactly enough space for Hannah. Right behind the bench.

Hannah climbed the stairs and stepped around the other spectators, who either glared at her or ignored her.

She finally reached Sarahi and sat down.

"Was this what you wanted? Because I'm not going back," Hannah stated, but she was lying. If Sarahi wanted her to leave, she would do so.

Sarahi giggled wickedly and Hannah couldn't help but smile.

"I wanted to sit by you," Sarahi said. As if that explained anything.

"Mine is number 5, Ana." Sarahi pointed to the girl at the free-throw line.

"I'm with number 3, Piper."

Sarahi eyed her closely. "You two look very much alike. Is she your daughter?"

"No, she's my little sister." Hannah caught Piper's eye and smiled when the girl waved at her.

Saying it out loud filled her with a rush of emotion.

She had a sister.

She'd never forget the day she found out.

It had seemed as if everything in her recent life had prepared her for that moment. If she would've found out about Piper even just a few months sooner, they wouldn't be where they were now.

And what they were now was more than Hannah had ever had.

At that moment, a girl from the other team aggressively bumped into Piper with her shoulder, causing Piper to stumble.

Piper's head whipped around and Hannah stood up, heat filling her face.

Sarahi gripped her arm and tugged her back to her seat.

The girl said something to Piper. Hannah couldn't hear it, but she recognized the lip twist. Hannah's pulse picked up.

Piper took a step toward the other girl. The ref blew a whistle.

But all Hannah could hear was the blood pounding in her ears.

Ana hooked an elbow around Piper's neck and took on a casual posture. She said something in the direction of the opponent and then laughed. Piper smiled and her shoulders relaxed. Ana tugged her teammate back to their bench.

"See?" Sarahi remarked. "Someone has her back."

Hannah swallowed, her anger slowly dissipating.

It helped to know she had a teammate who would be there, but that's not what Hannah was worried about.

The look on the other girl's face, the aggressive way she had behaved. It was all too familiar. Hannah used to be a girl just like that.

JOHNNY

The initial rush slowed down and he finally had a moment to breathe.

But it was a hard breath to take.

Immediately his eyes went to her.

Across the gym floor and just behind the home team, she sat wearing her new shirt that she'd purchased from him.

Sarahi had sat down right beside her.

Of all the school gymnasiums in all the world...

"I told you," Shawn singsonged at his shoulder.

The teenager had been skipping around him in the small gym kitchen area for the better part of an hour. It had taken a lot of strong-arming to keep him sequestered to their zone and not go over there and fanboy all over the place.

But he wasn't wrong.

At least, it didn't appear he'd been wrong.

Johnny had kept one eye on Ashton James all day.

Or the woman who looked like Ashton.

As far as he knew, she didn't have a twin or a look-alike. Not that that would be too far from the realm of possibility. Entertainers often employed look-alikes for various reasons, usually having to do with privacy.

But that electric blue color of her eyes was something he'd never seen in another human being.

"This is the perfect opportunity. I'm gonna do it. I'm gonna give it to her."

Johnny blinked rapidly, trying to catch up with what Shawn was saying as he untied his apron.

"No," he said firmly. "No. Absolutely not."

Shawn's incredulous expression reminded him so much of when he was little that Johnny almost smiled.

"Why not?"

"It's not...*appropriate*," Johnny finished with a tight whisper. He grabbed Shawn by the elbow and steered him toward the back of the kitchen.

Shawn's mouth hung open and his brow furrowed. "You can't be serious."

"I am serious," Johnny reiterated. "First of all, we have no way of knowing if that's her. Not without making everyone very uncomfortable."

Shawn's expression turned that special brand of teenage bored and fed up. "You mean, it'll make *you* uncomfortable." He narrowed his eyes at Johnny. "When are you gonna get over that? It was years ago."

"Second," Johnny continued, ignoring Shawn's question. "This isn't the place for that. You're so close to graduation. Can we please avoid any more trips to the principal's office?"

Johnny glanced back at the Ashton James look-alike.

It was uncanny.

But there was so much about her that didn't add up.

For one, she was laughing.

Admittedly, Sarahi was hilarious and it would take a special kind of demon to not be amused by the woman.

But Ashton James only laughed at people she was stepping on.

And then there was absolutely everything about her.

She was dressed in black jeans, the tee she'd bought earlier, way too large for her frame, a black and gray flannel tied at her hips. Her dark hair was tied in a tight ponytail, she had on her ugly glasses, and she was free of all makeup.

Ashton James didn't go anywhere barefaced and without an entourage.

And she didn't wear glasses because she had perfect vision. One little fact he remembered about her.

But this person, the one sitting on the bleachers and cheering for the girls' basketball team, laughing at his cousin's jokes, smiling, hugging a younger version of herself—this was someone he did not know.

It had to be a trick of the light.

Or of the fates.

Some sort of karmic indulgence designed to mess with his head.

"Fine. But if I see her again outside of the school, I'm doing it," Shawn declared belligerently, yanking his arm forcefully from Johnny's soft grip.

"Fine," Johnny muttered, not really listening.

It couldn't really be her, could it?

It didn't make any sense. Or did it make all the sense?

Why would she be in Chicago? Maybe she was filming a reality show? *Real Homewreckers of the Midwest?*

Yikes, Johnny, that was petty.

He needed some fresh air.

"I'm taking out the trash," he announced loudly, seizing the not-quite-full bag and cinching it closed.

* * *

HANNAH

"Sorry," Piper muttered, averting her gaze and slinging her bag over her shoulder.

"For what?" Hannah snorted. "That was the perfect amount of time for me to finish my book."

She handed Piper her coat.

Piper tried a half smile at Hannah's levity. "Was this one of your sexy books?" she teased.

"It was a romance, yes," Hannah answered. "And it happened to be on the sexy side. I feel no shame in that." She jutted her chin into the air and Piper laughed.

They left the empty building together and crossed the empty parking lot.

Piper didn't like to shower with the other girls, but she also didn't like to get in the car without having showered. Some (okay, a lot) of that was because of Life Before.

Survival instincts that she didn't need anymore but still hung around like psychological poltergeists. Hannah never pushed her to drop them. Her goal was to slowly build a life for them both that did not need those instincts to stick around.

A life of security and love.

All that meant was that they were usually the last to leave the games.

She also hadn't minded waiting because she needed just a few minutes to herself to think about how she wanted to talk to Piper about what had happened during the game. She knew she needed to address it, but she wasn't sure how without losing her absolute shit.

Hannah clicked the unlock button on the key fob.

They got in, buckled their seat belts, and listened as the engine didn't start.

Piper glanced at Hannah. Hannah blinked and turned the key again. The ignition clicked and then nothing.

Well.

That wasn't good.

"What's wrong?" Piper asked.

"I think..." Hannah tried the ignition again. "The battery is dead?"

Her mind raced with all the possibilities. She wasn't a mechanic by any means. But she'd been around vehicles a large portion of her life and picked up a few things here and there.

The battery in her Toyota was original to the vehicle. They'd never had an issue before, but she also didn't drive it that much. She usually took the train when she could.

She pulled the lever for the hood release and unbuckled her seat. Her eye caught on the console under the main display.

"Piper?" she asked slowly. "Were you charging your laptop in here?"

Piper's eyes darted to the car charger still plugged in and followed the cord to the underside of the seat where she pulled out her laptop.

She looked up at Hannah, cheeks pink and eyes sheepish. "Yeah?"

Hannah rolled her lips inward to keep from smiling, and when she succeeded at that, she sighed. "The battery is dead."

Piper shivered as the cold from outside began to permeate their warm coats.

"I can call for a jump," Hannah said, wrestling her phone from her coat pocket. Hopefully they would be able to get there before they got too cold. Hannah didn't care about herself, but thinking of Piper waiting in the subzero temperatures made her uneasy.

Maybe the school was still open. She squinted at the gymnasium doors, getting ready to send Piper running over to check.

The doors swung open and a man emerged, a brown aviation-style coat zipped up to his chin, the collar pulled up around his ears. He plunged his hands in his pockets and strode toward the one vehicle left in the parking lot.

Excelsior!

"Wait here," Hannah instructed as she quickly opened the door. She slammed it behind her before Piper could respond and sprinted across the parking lot.

"Hey!" she called out, hoping she didn't look threatening. Or crazy. And hoping this guy was of the good Midwest variety of helping his neighbors and strangers in distress.

He opened the door to his silver Camaro before he turned her way. His body stiffened and he gripped the top of the door frame with one hand. Probably trying to decide if he should flee or not.

Her sprint brought her to him just as she recognized him as being the handsome man from the concession stand who had sold her the T-shirt.

He recognized her in the same moment and his curiosity was replaced with suspicion.

Crap.

He probably thought she was going to come onto him.

"Hey," she breathed. "Can you jump me? I mean, can you give me a jump? My car died and I can call for a service, but it's cold and Piper is in the car and I don't know how long it'll take. And I know I'm overexplaining, but I don't want you to think I have ulterior motives. I didn't even know it was you until I got all the way over here. I swear, I just need some of that sweet, sweet electricity from your car battery."

He narrowed his eyes at her as she spit out her needless sentences. When she stopped, he leaned to look around her. "The Toyota?" he asked.

She nodded.

He tugged his beanie, which she noted was painfully threadbare, a little further down over his ears. "Just let me get my cables."

"Thank you!" Her exclamation came out a little more forceful than she intended and his dark eyebrows dipped into an equally dark frown. But she didn't care. He was awesome and a hero and now Piper wouldn't be cold for much longer.

She spun around and jogged back to the car.

"Is he going to help us?" Piper asked, watching through the windshield, her words coming out in little white puffs of frost.

"Yes," Hannah declared, rubbing her mittened hands together. "He also sold me my new shirt today. He's a very helpful person."

The Camaro pulled up facing the Toyota and the man got out. Piper inhaled sharply.

"That's Ana's uncle."

Hannah filtered through the events of that morning. Things made more sense with the rest of the information.

"Ana…was I sitting by her mom?"

"Yeah."

It wasn't until that moment that Hannah realized that sitting and talking with Sarahi today had made her feel like she was actually part of a community. Instead of just another outsider.

It was nice.

Piper nodded and her eyes widened when the man approached Hannah's side of the car.

"He's so pretty," Piper whispered.

Hannah snorted and got out of the car. But she wasn't wrong.

"Does your daughter want to sit in my car while we wait for yours to start?" he offered. "It warms up quick and I have heated seats."

Hannah's heart melted just a little bit for two reasons. It was the first time she'd been mistaken for Piper's mom. And it didn't suck. Not at all.

Also, putting Piper's safety and comfort first, even when he was clearly uncomfortable with this strange woman asking for help? Yeah, that was hero stuff too.

"Piper." Hannah ducked her head into the car. "Do you wanna wait in his car?"

Piper scrambled out the door and practically skipped to the Camaro.

Meanwhile, the man had braced open both vehicles' hoods and was already hooking up the jumper cables. Piper stopped at the side of the car and caught Hannah's eye.

"OH MY GOD," Piper mouthed, pointing at Ana's uncle.

Hannah shook her head and flattened her mouth. It caught his attention and he glanced back at Piper, who jumped into the car and closed the door.

"Uh…" Hannah folded her arms across her chest, more to give her hands something to do than to help against the cold. "Should I try starting it?"

Obviously, it was too soon for that. She knew it. But she'd asked anyway and immediately felt like an idiot.

"Let's give it a few minutes," he said, his voice smooth and nonjudgmental. "I'm Johnny, by the way," he introduced, holding out a hand. She glanced at his leather work gloves with stains and tears and ripped seams before grasping it with her pink, fuzzy mitten.

"Hannah," she said. "Piper isn't my daughter," she felt the need to correct. Not because she was embarrassed, but because she didn't feel she qualified for that kind of an honor. But that would be a harder issue to address to a veritable stranger. "She's my half sister. I'm her —" She swallowed hard, her personal information fighting to stay inside. "I'm her guardian," she finished, feeling for the first time how woefully inadequate that word was.

Something flickered in his dark eyes and his frown partially relaxed. "I'm in the same sort of situation with my little brother." He crossed his arms over his chest, mirroring her posture, and then he cracked a smile. "It's actually why I'm here. He's a senior but got himself into *just* enough trouble so he's required to work functions for extra credit." He licked his lips and tilted his head slightly. "Which of course means I have to be here too."

Hannah laughed lightly, getting it completely. "And where is he now?" she asked, even though she was pretty sure she could guess.

He pursed his lips. "He had important plans with his friends. So I offered to finish cleaning the kitchen."

"You offered?" She arched a single eyebrow.

He sniffed a laugh. "If I call it that, it doesn't feel so much like I'm being taken advantage of."

She laughed softly and he smiled at her reaction.

"How long have you been doing the guardian gig?" he asked with a chin lift.

"Oh man, two years almost." Her gaze drifted to the asphalt and she shook her head. "It's weird because it feels longer than that while also feeling like it just happened yesterday."

"I know what you mean."

She glanced back up to see his face had taken on a softer expression. "I've had Shawn since he was five. He turns eighteen next month. But sometimes it's so hard not to see him as that little five-year-old boy."

And for the second time that day, they shared a moment.

Hannah looked over his shoulder at where Piper sat in the warm car. She wondered if it would be the same for her. If, no matter how much of a woman Piper grew into, she'd always see her as a child. Would she have difficulty treating her like the adult she was bound to become?

Would she default to treating her the way she'd been taught?

Shit.

She made a mental note to ask her therapist about that on Friday.

"Go ahead and see if it fires," Johnny instructed.

Hannah nodded and quickly slid into the car, not bothering to close the door or even sit fully in the seat. She inserted the key and sent up a wordless prayer.

It started.

Johnny smiled and nodded with satisfaction. He unhooked the cables and closed her hood. Hannah turned the heater on in the car and started the seat warmers. She climbed back out of the car just as Johnny was closing the hood of the Camaro.

He turned toward her. "Probably drive it around for a little while before parking it again. It may have just been the cold."

Hannah waggled her eyebrows. "Or it was the preteen who plugged her laptop into the car charger for the duration of the basketball game."

He chuckled. "That wouldn't help."

"Thank you, Johnny," she said, stressing the sincerity in her voice. She waved at Piper to return to their car. "You really saved us."

His eyes flashed that confused expression again. "Happy to help." He stopped before using her name and closed his mouth, finishing with a nod. "I'll probably see you around."

"Yeah." Hannah waved, feeling a little sad their interaction was over. But that was replaced with relief when she got into her warm car.

She and Piper buckled their seat belts and silently watched Johnny back away and drive off with a final wave.

"He's so hot," Piper finally said.

"Piper!"

"And his car is clean," she continued, facing her sister. "Like, *so* clean. And it smells like aftershave and leather."

"How do you know what aftershave smells like?" Hannah narrowed her eyes.

"I'm guessing." Piper took a deep breath and melted into her seat. "Please tell me he asked you out."

Hannah put the car in gear. "He did not."

Which she was fine with. Because she would have had to turn him down anyway. Because of all the reasons. This way, she would feel comfortable talking to him again in the future.

And that idea made her feel weirdly hopeful.

Did she want to talk to Johnny again?

Yes.

Absolutely.

For a lot of reasons but mostly because it was nice to chat with someone who knew a little of what she was going through. It had been an unexpected and welcome connection. Something she hadn't experienced with another adult in longer than she could remember.

Piper grunted her dissatisfaction with the statement. "Where are we going?" she asked when she realized Hannah was driving them the opposite way from home.

"Let's listen to Misterwives' new album and get burgers at Flame Trees."

It was in a little suburb just outside Chicago where Piper's favorite burger place happened to be. And they needed to drive the car for a while anyway. Or so she'd been told.

"Yes!" Piper declared excitedly.

Hannah smiled, but a small part of her heart wondered when it would be that Piper no longer got excited about simple things like long car rides and cheeseburgers.

Hopefully it would be a long while.

* * *

JOHNNY

Sunday.

A day of rest.

A holy day to some.

He stood at the heart of his own personal church and felt the peace of a dream realized wash over him.

XY Records was a two-floor brick structure set between a row of townhouses and a row of walk-up apartments in Avondale.

On its outside it was nearly invisible, except for those who knew where to look. No signage, a single door at the front that led to the street. Around back was another entrance used for the other half of the studio and clients who wanted a more private entrance.

It technically had two recording studios.

One large studio with three separate performance spaces and the spacious control room—which had all the bells and whistles, not to mention a customized 48-channel Neotek Elite console with Neve Flying Faders automation.

Studio X was built for larger groups. It was equipped with its own espresso bar, lounge, bathrooms, and private entrance. If a client was into those things.

The second studio, Studio Y, was smaller but still large for what it offered. It had an 800-square-foot live room and a 300-square-foot isolation room. The live room also had thirty-foot ceilings, which made for some unique sound capture.

That's where Johnny was at the moment.

In the small control room of Studio Y, watching Shawn go to town on the drum kit in the live room.

The live room of Studio Y had less of a polished look than Studio X.

In fact, that's how the studios got their nicknames.

While the founder and original owner, Abel Thomas, was building it from the ground up, they left the original brick exposed and untreated in the smaller live room just to see what the sound would be like. And it sounded great, so they kept it. But it had started with the question of "Why not?"

The walls gave off a bright reverb, which was great for acoustic.

The thirty-foot ceilings had large thick windows at the very top, where sunlight streamed into the otherwise dark room, giving a cathedral-like feel.

Which was probably why Johnny thought of it as a holy place for himself.

In a time when professionally recorded music was on its way out, it had taken a huge act of faith for him to follow through on his dream. Everyone in the industry told him it was a dying business. And in most cases, they were right.

But Johnny had worked at XY long enough to see how it kept its momentum. And how it could continue to be relevant in the modern world of music.

The building was almost invisible. Just another unremarkable brick structure in a long row of brick buildings.

An unmarked building in a billboard world.

A secret sanctuary.

And now it was all his.

After years of saving and negotiating and dreaming too much, he owned it.

Well, the bank owned it. But his name was on the loan. And it was his credit that had gotten him that loan.

Credit that he had fought for.

"Kid's got the rhythm," Johnny's head engineer, Justin, said from the doorway of the small control room.

Johnny nodded in agreement. It was true. Shawn had a musical gift he'd never seen in someone so young. It was as if he played with the experience and confidence of a longtime veteran.

"Must run in the blood," Justin joked.

"Maybe," Johnny replied with a half smile.

But he knew, Shawn had passed him in talent years ago.

Not only that, Shawn had the passion and personality of the traveling musician.

Eventually.

Presumably after he graduated from high school.

Johnny sent up a silent prayer that Shawn would make it the last few months without dropping out or getting kicked out. They were almost there.

Shawn cleared his throat and Johnny glanced out the control window to the floor below. The younger man was now positioned on the stool with his guitar on his lap.

"We ready?" Johnny asked, holding down the intercom button so Shawn could hear him in the live room.

Shawn's eyes met his through the glass and he nodded seriously.

Johnny flipped a few switches and Shawn placed the headphones over his ears.

Yeah, his younger brother had a gift.

Even though both of them had been blessed with musical talents, Shawn's artistic prowess showed through in songs he wrote himself. Before a single word was sung, the emotion in him could be heard in how he had weaved his chords together.

Johnny had never subscribed to the idea that young hearts couldn't experience big love. Maybe it felt even bigger to them somehow because their inhibitions were all out of whack.

And Shawn's songs always made him feel things.

Things he remembered feeling once.

CHAPTER THREE

MANNEQUIN

HANNAH

"Did you hear about Hannah and TJ?"

Hannah's eyelids fluttered as she filled her cup of coffee in the break room.

The words had been whispered around the corner from the coffee kiosk. The speaker couldn't see her.

"Yes," came the hushed and eager response. "How have we not talked about this yet?"

Hannah rolled her eyes and took a deep breath.

It was not the first time she'd been talked about behind her back.

Hell, it wasn't even the first time she'd walked in on people talking about her *in this room.* But still, her ears strained for the details of the newest rumor. Maybe it would have some inspiration to it this time. Something she could use to play with, like a cat with the tiny soft bodies of inexperienced mice.

Was that too mean?

"I can't believe she slept with TJ. He's *barely* divorced!"

"I can't believe TJ would even go near her. I wonder how it even happened."

"If I were TJ, I'd be afraid of catching something, you know?"

The last statement was followed by cackles.

Hannah laughed, too, because they weren't wrong. They just didn't know it.

The cackles ceased, followed by mutual shushing.

The mice sensed her presence.

But it was too little too late.

Hannah picked up her mug—Piper had gotten two for her on their adoptiversary so she could leave one at home and bring one to work. It was black and said "I'm a fucking professional." She curved around the corner and leaned a shoulder against the wall.

"Hey, ladies," she said, feeling the old purr of cattiness easily climb back into her voice and eyes. But unlike the old days, Hannah wasn't about to make anyone cry.

But what was wrong with a little play?

Tamara and Amy were both pretty, petty, and cliquey. They laughed behind people's backs and thought that they were the coolest shit around.

But they worked in the same place she did. So they couldn't be that cool.

It was actually kind of sad. When they were apart, they acted like decent human beings. It was like their influence on one other brought out the worst.

Most of it was performance. A show.

And Hannah would know.

She'd been the ringmaster in the bitch circus for most of her life.

These two weren't even sideshow worthy.

They were clowns.

She held her mug so the text was visible to both women. Then she smirked and slowly lifted the mug to her lips for a torturously gradual sip.

"Hey, Hannah."

"Hi, Hannah."

Both of them murmured simultaneously, averting their eyes.

Because it was always obvious when the alpha bitch had entered the room.

"Oh, don't stop on my account." Hannah blinked round eyes. "What happened? Did I seduce TJ? Did he try to stop me? Are we having an affair? Is he pregnant yet?" Her voice took on the characteristics of the ladies' previous conversation as Hannah added her own theories. She leaned toward them eagerly. "Will I have to marry him? You think there'll be a shotgun involved?"

By now, both women's faces were red and their mouths had dropped open like gasping fish.

Hannah chuckled darkly and again sipped her coffee.

At a table near the back sat Courtney.

Hannah only knew her name because she'd heard Tamara hiss at her to get out of her way more than once.

Courtney had a small build and dainty features. She wore soft, romantic colors and floated around like a fairy. Her cubicle was sandwiched between Hannah's and TJ's.

She was also painfully shy.

Hannah noticed Courtney's discomfort when she'd been talking about TJ.

Which was…informative.

Hannah checked her watch and whistled. "I better get going if I'm going to make it to my next illicit affair—oh, I mean, my next call. See you guys later." She wiggled her fingers and strode from the break room.

So dumb.

Had that been mean?

Hannah sat down at her small "desk" in her cubicle and found it hard to care.

"All I can do is all I can do," she muttered to herself.

It had become her personal mantra over the past year and a half.

She couldn't do more than she was capable of; that was where she got overwhelmed, overworked, and oversaturated. Which led to burning out and reaching for a vice. Any one would do. Booze, pills, coke, sex, fast cars, name it. She had a weakness for it.

But if she reminded herself that she was doing all she could do, and nothing more or less, it helped.

It was a comfort and a reminder that she was human.

Some days were going to be harder than others. Not every moment was going to be her next best moment. But maybe the one after that.

JOHNNY

"Just don't call him Lord Business when he's here," Johnny said with a sigh.

Nikki snapped her gum and forced a smile.

That wasn't very reassuring.

"Are you sure you want to do this?" Justin asked for the third time that meeting.

Johnny nodded slowly and emphatically.

"Yes. I know that once Sunshine gets a look at our setup, he'll make his own decision despite whatever his manager says." Johnny pursed his lips. "I know guys like him. He'll want the freedom and professional quality we provide."

As if on cue, a fart ripped loudly from the end of the table. Snickers followed.

"Thank you, Chase. Get it all out now." Johnny shook his head, not as annoyed as he was putting on.

"Any questions?" Johnny asked, looking around at his staff.

They weren't a huge production and they weren't going to win any Grammys, but they were damn fine people and he was excited about their futures together.

Nikki, his building manager, staff engineer, and "front of house" person raised her hand. "Monica Reeves didn't confirm with me for tomorrow."

"That's okay, I'll call her," Johnny replied, making a note on his phone.

"We start in with String Prose tomorrow," Justin said. "Chase and I just have a few things to finish up today, but otherwise it should be a one and done."

"Are they going to mix here?" Johnny asked.

Justin glanced at Chase, who nodded.

"Cool. Sounds good."

The staff meeting dismissed and Johnny headed to Studio Y to make sure it was all ready to go.

It was one thing to record albums for indie bands in town. That was fifty percent of his revenue. The other fifty percent was revenue from video dubs and advertisement agencies.

But this?

Getting to show his setup to an already established artist with a huge following?

This is could put the books into the black for the next year.

"I know that this week is going to be really important, but you've got this. Don't have a stroke over it."

Johnny sank into a squat to look into the far back lower shelving unit where they housed the keyboards.

"Why would you say that?" Johnny asked distractedly.

Nikki sat down cross-legged on the floor beside him. "Because I know how you get when you're afraid something is about go wrong. You get all 'Nikki, you talk too much. Nikki, bring me a ladder so I can jump off the building.'"

"Well…" Johnny reached into the unit and grabbed hold of the top keyboard. He grunted as he lifted it out. "You do talk a lot."

"Right, I know," Nikki agreed. "But it's the way you say it."

"For the record, I don't sound anything like that."

"You sound exactly like that. But don't do that this time. It's not going to blow up in your face."

Johnny dropped the keyboard and sat back on his heels. He frowned at Nikki. "What? Why would you even say that?"

Nikki looked at him like he was supposed to get whatever it was she wasn't saying.

"Nik, spit it out."

"Ugh. It's like you forget we've been together for twelve years and"—she waved her arms around to include the everything that was around them—"all this glorious history. I can tell when something heavy is on your mind."

Hmm. Well, she wasn't far off the mark. Though she had no idea it was Ashton James that was on his mind. Or Hannah or whatever she was going by now.

Johnny took a deep breath and sighed. "I'm not gonna spiral. I'm just a little distracted by outside stuff."

"You wanna talk about it?"

"No, Nikki," he said, his patience slowly draining out of him. "It's personal."

She didn't like that answer. He could tell by the small pout she tried to hide.

He scrubbed a hand over his face. "I know I'm going to regret asking, but why does it matter so much to you?"

Nikki slouched, defeated by his lack of insight into the female psyche.

"Because. You're my friend. I just want you to be happy."

"Okay," he said, softening his tone. "Thank you. I promise, if it comes time for me to talk about it with someone, you'll be the first one I come to."

She smiled, clearly relieved.

"Now can I please finish what I'm doing?"

She hopped up and bounded away like a puppy on an adventure. Which was to say, her usual mode of travel.

As soon as she was gone, though, his thoughts turned right back to Ashton. Or Hannah. Whatever.

He dusted his hands off on his jean-clad thighs and refocused on reorganizing the keyboards.

If he kept busy, he wouldn't have any spare time to think about the ghost of a woman he used to know.

HANNAH

Hannah didn't want to admit that walking in on her coworkers' conversation had…upset her. But she also recognized that something was off inside herself.

Had been since Saturday.

The gossip normally wouldn't be a thing to her, but added on top of all the confusing emotional stuff that the weekend had managed to drudge up?

It was a thing.

A dumb thing.

But it was still there.

She was distracted as she rode the train, choosing to stare at the ground instead of cataloging the other riders and being watchful.

Alex would be so disappointed, she thought with a snort.

She stepped off the train at her stop and hesitated for a nanosecond, waiting for familiar guitar chords to distract her further.

Unfortunately—or fortunately, depending on which side you were on—there wasn't anything that signaled she should dawdle any longer than she had.

She turned to the exit and took a deep breath, trying to inhale something clean to help clear out the smoke of her insides—a dumpster fire that wouldn't quite die.

Dimly, she became aware of a voice calling in her direction. It grew closer, and despite her lack of belief that it had anything to do with her, she glanced over her shoulder.

Immediately she spotted the shaggy-haired troubadour from last week, pushing through the throng of commuters. Startled, she paused, and it was just a long enough second for them to lock eyes. He communicated in his expression that she was the object of his pursual.

What in the name of a motherfucker?

Fighting her instincts to keep marching toward her destination, she moved to the side and allowed the crowd to pass her by.

Almost instantly a flood of anxiety washed over her.

This was off routine.

She needed to get home and get dinner started.

"Hey," the guitar player panted when he'd caught up to her. His guitar case was slung onto his back, the strap wrapped across his chest. His bright pink cheeks indicated that he'd been chasing her for longer than she'd realized. He pushed his floppy hair off his forehead, revealing the sheen of perspiration despite the cold temperatures.

Instead of greeting him in turn, Hannah narrowed her eyes and waited.

He took no issue with her silence.

"Hi. I'm Shawn." He placed an open palm on his chest. "I don't know if you remember me from the other day—" His words came out fast and desperate.

It was familiar in a sinking boat sort of way.

He *knew.*

How had he known? Who else knew? This was all her fault. She should have never deviated from the routine. So stupid. Shit.

"Listen," Shawn kept on talking. "I know I'm a nobody and you're undercover or some shit, but I just had to tell you that you changed my life. I would never forgive myself if I had the opportunity to say it and didn't take it." He took a deep breath and glanced around them furtively before bringing his attention back to her. His dark brown eyes sparkled in a way that reminded her of Piper, and for a moment, Hannah forgot her anxiety. Something else kicked in and she looked at this child in front of her.

Really *looked* at him.

Yes, he was man-sized, with dark facial hair making itself known on his jaw and chin. But there was a softness to his skin, a lack of worry in his earnest frown, a boldness in his carefree smile.

Had she ever been that young?

That hopeful?

"Hi, Shawn."

It wasn't exactly an admission, but the grin that split his face and lit up the underground station even had Hannah fighting a smile.

His blush deepened and he shoved his hands into the front pockets of his jeans.

"Thank you for your kind words. It was nice meeting you." She stuck her hand out to shake his, but he wrapped his long arms around her.

"Oh, we're hugging," she said in surprise.

Before she could be concerned about the physical contact, he released her and stepped back.

A minute before, he couldn't get his words out fast enough and now he seemed speechless. They stood silent for a few seconds. Just staring at one another.

Hannah had questions but was too afraid to ask. Like, how had he known? And for how long? And who else had he told? But at the same time, she didn't really want to know. Especially if it would mean Alex and Quinn's efforts to hide her and Piper were all for naught.

Then it hit her, he'd never actually called her Ashton.

She opened her mouth to ask…

"Okay, see you around," he rushed out before brushing by her.

Hannah turned to watch him and saw him duck onto a train. The doors closed and she lost sight of him.

"Fucking weird ass day," she muttered to herself.

Weird ass weekend, too, if she were being honest.

The train departed and Hannah stood there for a few seconds after, trying to collect her thoughts. Of which she had many. And yet none of them were super coherent.

Between being labeled a whore at work to being thanked for saving lives, Hannah didn't know what to think of herself.

You know, in a pragmatic sort of way.

Neither argument was the truth, but she must fall somewhere along that whore/savior spectrum.

Shit. Was she now bordering on blasphemy?

Probably.

Hannah made her way up the stairs to the street, still pondering the previous interaction.

Shawn, huh? Adorable kid.

* * *

“What’s this?”

Hannah finished hanging her coat on the hook and glanced over her shoulder. Piper was picking up a plain white, legal-sized envelope.

She frowned because she actually didn’t know.

“It fell out of your pocket,” said Piper. She turned it over; there was writing on the back.

“What’s it say?”

“Shawn Torres demo. And there’s an address.”

Hannah took the envelope from Piper to read the words herself. “What the hell?” she asked out loud.

Shawn? Shawn the busker?

She opened the envelope and found a thumb drive. That was it.

“Did someone give you a demo?” Piper asked. Her voice lodged somewhere between curiosity and fear.

Or maybe that was just where Hannah’s heart was at the moment.

“He must’ve slipped it in my pocket at Wabash and Washington,” Hannah thought out loud.

“Wait. Are you saying he knows who you are? Is he stalking you?”

Okay, that wasn’t just Hannah, there was definite fear in Piper’s voice.

“Maybe. I don’t know,” Hannah answered without thinking.

“What?” Piper cried.

Hannah took a deep breath and looked Piper in the eyes. “I will handle this, okay? You do *not* need to be afraid.”

Piper’s eyes bounced in between Hannah’s, wide and worried. “Who is this person?”

“He’s just a kid. A busker I talked to once. He has no idea what he’s doing.” That was obvious. Hannah’s surprise was evolving into annoyance the longer she had to feel Piper's fear race around the room.

Not at Piper. But at Shawn for dropping this little nightmare nugget into her lap.

"What if he's told someone? Will we have to move? Where can we even go?"

Hannah gripped Piper gently by the shoulders. "I will handle this," she promised both of them. "Do you trust me?"

Piper stared at her, and Hannah could see the younger person fight for control of her emotions.

"I trust you," Piper croaked out.

Hannah fiercely pressed her lips to Piper's forehead.

Damn right, she trusted her.

Hannah had not put everything in her life into this girl for it to be called into question over the actions of a misguided teenager.

Hannah picked up her phone and texted Alex.

Hannah: I need you to look someone up for me.

The reply came almost immediately.

Unknown: Meet me in the spot, 2 min.

Hannah slid her phone into her pocket and grabbed her keys.

"Where are you going?" Piper asked, her voice soft.

"To get information. I'll be back in a few minutes," she promised. She held Piper's eyes for a beat and smiled. "I will fix this."

"Okay."

"Okay."

She left the apartment, checking that it locked behind her.

When she arrived at the service elevator, she was only somewhat surprised that Quinn and Alex were both there.

"What's the name?" Alex asked, all business.

Hannah handed over the envelope to Quinn, who dumped out the thumb drive and handed it to Alex.

"He's a busker I interacted with on Friday."

"Interacted with?" Quinn repeated.

Hannah growled under breath. "Yes. He was playing one of my songs. I went over to listen. I didn't think..." She crossed her arms. "I didn't think it was a big deal. But today he stopped me and I found that in my coat pocket when I got home."

"Hmm," Quinn replied noncommittally.

Alex typed furiously.

After a minute or so he sat back, relaxed.

"It doesn't look like anything serious. He's seventeen, eighteen next month, has no criminal record. The thumb drive is just a music file. There's nothing else on it." He removed it from the laptop and put it back in the envelope.

"But he clearly knows who you are," Quinn pointed out.

Hannah chewed on the inside of her cheek.

"The address here is in Avondale. It's mortgaged to a Jonathan Enamorado Torres whose name is also on the title for a recording studio near the address...XY Records. He's been a US citizen for fourteen years. No criminal record."

"The recording studio connection is problematic," Quinn stated Hannah's feelings.

"So they're not dangerous, but they probably want money to keep quiet," she said.

"I would assume so," Quinn agreed. "Would you like me to handle it?"

"No," she denied quickly. Her interaction with Shawn earlier in the day had her feeling sorry for the kid. She didn't want to terrify him by sending Quinn in full force. The guy didn't have a "soft side." "Not yet. I'll go over and see if I can make an offer to keep them quiet."

"And if that doesn't work?"

"Then I guess I'll be moving again."

"You should take an escort," Quinn said, not a hint of a question in his tone.

"I don't think—"

"Just follow my suggestion for once, Ms. James."

Hannah rolled her eyes and scrunched up her nose. She didn't like the idea of having a babysitter bodyguard, that kind of thing attracted attention. Which was the entire situation she was trying to avoid.

"My employee will be discreet," he promised.

Sure.

She went back to her condo to wait for Quinn's muscle and explain to Piper where she was going.

"Now?" Piper squeaked.

"I'd rather talk to them now and get it over with. That way it'll be settled and it won't be on our minds anymore." Hannah spoke with a lot more confidence than she felt. But she didn't want Piper to know how anxious she really was.

Hannah went to her room to change out of her work clothes. What was the point in looking boring and dowdy if they already knew who she was? No, if she was going to feel in control of the situation, she was going to have to wear her own stuff.

She slid on a pair of dark jeans and a thin, white V-neck sweater. She took her hair out of its chignon and shook it out. Last, she put on her favorite black leather jacket.

Piper stood in the doorway of her room, wringing her hands.

"I shouldn't have said anything—"

"No, babe. We don't do that, remember?" Hannah stopped her. "No more hiding how we feel to keep the status quo, remember?"

"Rock the boat, baby," Piper replied softly.

It was their motto they'd adopted during family therapy. Piper had come from a home life where speaking up was punished with emotional distancing. So she'd learned to keep quiet to keep others happy.

Until everything had fallen apart.

Hannah tied the laces of her black combat boots and tugged her jeans down over them just as there was a knock at the door.

She recognized Damon as one of Quinn's security guys who worked in the building.

"Ms. James, I have been instructed to escort you this evening," Damon said by way of greeting.

Ah, hired help, how she missed it.

"I need to go to this address," Hannah said, handing over the envelope with the writing on it. "Piper is staying here."

Damon nodded once and stepped aside for her to enter the hallway. She glanced over her shoulder at Piper. "I'll be right back."

She waited until she heard the bolt latch before following Damon down the hall. She glanced up just as they passed under a domed security camera in the ceiling. Knowing Piper was safe offered a sliver of peace.

Damon escorted her to the underground parking garage and to one of the black Mercedes SUVs parked in a row. He opened the back door and she hesitated because it felt like such a huge step back.

"Do I have to sit in the back?" she asked.

Damon didn't even flinch. "Of course not, Ms. James." He closed the door and moved to the front passenger side.

Hannah slid in and deliberately relaxed her hands onto her knees. They wanted to ball into fists, but she needed to keep a cool head. Losing her absolute shit wasn't going to help the situation.

The drive to the address was silent and Hannah gazed out the window at the passing lights of Chicago.

Her choosing to move here had had many reasons. It was the Midwest. If anyone ever recognized her, they were more likely to dismiss her as a doppelgänger than a real celebrity.

Celebrity, Hannah thought with a snort. She hadn't been that in a long time. Long before Piper and even before her arrest.

She hadn't done anything worth celebrating in many years.

The car stopped in a part of town she'd never been.

One side of the street had tall brick row houses; the other side had brick walk-up apartment buildings.

"Where is this?" she asked, looking around at the charming neighborhood.

"Avondale," Damon replied, parking the car along the curb.

"It's cute."

The black Mercedes seemed to fit right in among the other newer vehicles of the residents surrounding it.

Hmm.

It had her wondering if they weren't as financially dependent as she needed them to be to make this go away.

"Wait here, please," Damon instructed.

Hannah fought rolling her eyes but did as requested because why the hell wouldn't she? The whole point of having Damon be there was for safety. For Piper's sake.

The peace of mind went both ways.

And maybe showing up with a fancy bodyguard would be enough to scare the shit out of the punk who thought he was being cool enough to slip her a demo.

For real, though. A demo? To her? Was he sniffing glue?

She wasn't anyone.

And she especially wasn't anyone to trust your art to.

Damon opened her door and waited for her to exit before closing it again. Then he led the way to a waist-high black gate at the sidewalk and let her pass through first. The narrow walkway up the door of the townhouse was shoveled and ice free. One side had what resembled a small garden, though obviously wasn't in use for the winter. The other side had landscaping that was covered in snow. A security company sign was displayed prominently on a stick at the bottom of the wooden steps.

A cement patio under the front window had a wrought iron table and chairs.

The stairs leading up to the house had a matching wrought iron railing. At the top was a welcome mat. All of it meticulously cleared of any snow and ice.

She took a breath and rolled her shoulders back. Hopefully he had parents and she could put this matter away with some rational words —and maybe a couple thousand dollars.

She knocked on the door.

Good.

It sounded firm and confident. Setting the tone right away.

The door swung open and for a moment Hannah thought she'd made a mistake.

* * *

JOHNNY

After dreaming about her for two nights in a row, he was only half surprised at her appearance at his door. As if his internal conflict had beckoned her for the overdue confrontation.

He was however surprised at the anger that rose inside.

Visceral and defensive, it tightened his chest and quickened his pulse.

Her electric blue eyes widened when they connected with his, and her lips parted in a soft startle.

"Johnny?" she asked cautiously.

He clenched his jaw and his gaze swept over her black leather jacker and tight jeans, then to her bodyguard behind her on the stoop.

His stoop.

The one he owned.

"Ashton," he replied tersely, all previous façades falling away.

She stiffened as if he'd slapped her, eyes narrowing to dangerous slits.

"Or is it Hannah today?" he asked, tilting his head to the side.

She blinked, rolled her eyes, huffed, and leveled him with a glare. A clenched hand lifted, revealing his address written on an envelope.

"We need to talk," she said, all business.

His gaze bounced from the envelope to her face to the bodyguard at her back.

"Where did you get—" He reached for the envelope, but she held it back.

She arched an eyebrow. "Shawn? Is he the one you talked about on Saturday?"

His stomach twisted and his neck got hot. "You stay away from him," he warned roughly.

If she was confused by his change in demeanor since Saturday, she hid it well. In fact, she responded as if she expected him to be angry.

She glanced around the quiet neighborhood. "May I come in... please?" she asked tightly.

Johnny eyed the bodyguard again before nodding and stepping to the side.

The suit followed her in and closed the door behind them. He didn't enter any further, just stood with his back to the door.

Ashton, or Hannah, or whatever she went by, entered his home and paced around the small living area. Her eyes bounced up to the dining table that overlooked the living space. She set the envelope down on the coffee table and crossed her arms over her chest.

"I met Shawn last week on my way home. He introduced himself to me today and must've slipped that into my coat pocket. I found it when I got home." She took a breath and amended, "Piper was actually the one who found it." She put her hands on her hips. "Which is why I came here. I needed to know how far this had gone. And what I needed to do to keep it from going any further."

Johnny shoved a hand through his hair, unable to form words.

Shawn had actually done it. He'd gone behind Johnny's back and talked to the one person Johnny had forbid him from having interactions with.

Okay, maybe "forbid" wasn't accurate. But it had been strongly implied. And the meaning had always been there in the subtext.

"But now," she continued, hostility in her tone. "I'm wondering if you guys had some sort of con planned."

He tore his eyes from the demo and met her gaze. Slowly, he inhaled as he faced her unholy beauty.

"What?" he asked, not sure he was understanding all of her words.

"On Saturday, when I needed help, did you know?" she asked again, her face a mask of cold calculation.

This was the Ashton he remembered. Not the soft, slightly panicked woman he'd met over the weekend. If she had been like this on Saturday, he wouldn't have had any doubts.

His mouth opened to answer but no words came out.

She pressed her lips together, the only outward sign that she was distressed. "How many are involved? Who else knows?"

He shook his head, his mouth still slightly agape.

She dropped her head back and sighed at the ceiling. Taking a deep breath, she righted herself and tried a different approach.

"Let's talk about it," she offered, sitting on one end of the couch. "Johnny?" she asked, eyebrows lifted. "Have a seat."

It was his home, his couch, his life, and here she was—taking ownership all over again.

Except not this time.

"No, I think I'll stand," he said, saltiness evident in his tone. He crossed his arms over his chest.

She narrowed her eyes and he wondered how he'd ever been confused about who this person was. The slight snarl in her lip, the cold detachment in her icy eyes—it was all there. She was a devil woman.

She shoved back to her feet and paced again.

"What do you want? Money?" She arched her eyebrows and shrugged.

"What?" He screwed up his face.

"How much?" she asked flatly.

"I don't want money," he replied in disgust. What the hell was she talking about?

"Everyone wants money," she countered coldly. "Tell me who else you've told first so I'll know how much your silence is worth. And don't lie to me. I have people who'll be able to verify." She cast a look over his shoulder at the bodyguard.

"Are you really that self-involved?" he asked, incredulous. "Why would I want *anything* from you?" The way he said *you* made it pretty obvious what he thought of her. As expected, the remark slid right off her Teflon exterior.

"Really?" she replied in dripping sarcasm. "You just *happened* to be there to rescue me on Saturday? Your little brother just *happened* to be on my route home? You have no motives whatsoever in making sure I ended up with your address? This isn't some messy plan to sue me for stealing whoever's music this is?" she ended by flicking a dramatic hand at the thumb drive on the table. "Too bad for you." She gestured with a hand. "I've already done that one and lost."

He sucked in a breath to argue but found she had a couple points there. "You don't have all the facts."

"You wanna enlighten me, Prince Charming?" She cocked her head to the side.

Johnny snorted. "Don't try so hard to paint yourself as a damsel when we both know that's not true."

"If you knew who I was on Saturday, why didn't you say anything?" she said, her voice rising. "Why the games?" She hinged forward at the waist. "I told you things," she hissed in accusation. "Things that need to stay a secret!"

Johnny rolled his eyes because he wasn't buying it. Maybe the little sister thing was real. Or maybe it was just another gimmick she used to get attention.

She jerked her chin back in realization. "Is this about revenge?"

"Revenge?" Johnny snorted. "No." He shook his head in disgust. "Not everything is about you, princess."

"What did I do?" she asked with a shrug. "It must've been pretty shitty for this amount of conniving. Did I ruin your marriage or something? Not show up for a radio interview? Embarrass you in front of someone famous?" She waved her hands palms up in front of her. "All of the above?"

"You're a real piece of work. You don't even remember me, do you?" Johnny said the words, knowing for years they were true but feeling that hurtful sting having to admit it out loud. He had been a nobody to her then. He needed to make peace with that.

Ashton shook her head. "I don't remember most things," she said, and it had the kind of ring of truth that sounded too real. She rapidly scanned the interior of the townhouse and her gaze paused on his guitar resting in the stand in the living room.

He held his breath for a minute.

The guitar was the one he'd had when they'd first met. Its sound was on her first record.

It wasn't fancy by any means, but it was and always would be his favorite. A black Gibson orchestra model. The years of wear showed the scratches and bruises of the life of a working musician.

He wondered if she remembered the night she'd sat in his bed, naked, holding that guitar and singing to him.

Because he thought about it all the time.

"I don't remember you," she said after a beat, her voice quieter. The admission hurt more than he expected. "But I know that it doesn't matter. Going with the odds and how you're looking at me, it was probably pretty awful."

Johnny wasn't sure why hearing that didn't make him feel any better.

Just then the door opened, or it tried to, but it bumped into the bodyguard, who moved to the side and let Shawn in.

The facilitator of Johnny's current problem.

Shawn frowned in confusion at the bodyguard, and then his gaze drifted to Ashton. All the color drained from his face, and his round eyes darted to Johnny.

"Oh my God," Shawn whispered.

"Oh, He can't save you now," Johnny cautioned.

Shawn dropped his bag on the floor and his hands came up in a placating fashion. Though he couldn't figure out which person to direct them to. He faced Johnny, then Ashton, then the bodyguard in quick succession.

"I-I-I can't believe you're here," he finally spit out, obviously speaking to Ashton. He spun to Johnny. "It's her. I told you it was her."

Johnny ran his tongue over his bottom lip and nodded once.

Shawn shoved both hands through his hair, unable to conceal the sheer joy on his face. "Did-did you listen to it?" he asked Ashton cautiously.

For the first time since Johnny had opened the door, he saw a crack in her exterior as she looked at his younger brother.

"No," she said after a beat. "I haven't listened to it."

Undeterred, and oblivious to the tension in the room, Shawn eagerly grabbed the envelope off the table and removed the thumb drive. "That's fine. You can listen to it here and then I can get your reactions up close."

"Shawn," Johnny tried to get his attention.

"This is better, actually," Shawn continued, a slight tremor in his voice, which was pitching a little higher. "I mean, I would have invited you over earlier today if I'd known you would say yes."

"Shawn," Johnny said louder and sharper.

It got his attention.

"Read the room, bud."

Shawn's hands dropped to his side and his shoulders dropped. "I don't understand. If you're not here about the music, then why are you here?" he asked.

"I think…" Johnny said with a slight grimace. "That she's here to pay us to keep quiet? Did I get that right?"

Ashton glared at Johnny.

"Pay us?" Shawn repeated, confused and devastated all at once.

For a split second, guilt sliced through Johnny. But the sooner Shawn figured out who Ashton James really was, the better for him. In the long run.

Though watching him find out that the artist he looked up to was a lying, selfish, horrible person kind of hurt like hell.

Silence descended like a thick fog as Shawn stared at Ashton, waiting for a response.

Finally, she took in a deep breath and let it out. "Who have you told? I really need to know how far this goes. Please."

Her tone was different than the last time she'd asked that question.

"No one," Shawn replied roughly. "Just Johnny." He waved a hand in that direction. "And he didn't believe me until Saturday when he saw you at the school. Even then, he told me not to do anything about it." He shrugged helplessly. "But I didn't listen."

Her eyes moved to Johnny, looking for honesty and verification.

He hadn't told Shawn about helping jump her car. He didn't want to have to answer any uncomfortable questions that he didn't have the answers to. Like, why was she so different in that moment than the woman he remembered? And was it real? Or did she just get a lot better at faking things?

Shawn took a step toward her, speaking excitedly.

"I was just so happy to finally meet you. I never thought I'd get a chance to, and then one day, I saw you get off the train. I wasn't looking for you. Ashton, you have to believe me. I would nev—"

"Please don't call me Ashton," she stopped him. She regarded both of them carefully. "I haven't been Ashton James in a very long time. And I have no intention of being her again."

"Okay," Shawn replied, confusion clouding his brow. "But I..." Shawn's sentence trailed off as he lost the thought.

She took a deep breath and closed her eyes for a beat.

When she opened them, Johnny could see a crack in her cold exterior.

"Maybe we should talk." She sat down on a chair and waited for Johnny and Shawn to join her.

Shawn took no issue with sitting down, but Johnny still wasn't thrilled about being bossed around in his house. He stood still for longer than necessary to make his point.

To her credit, she didn't challenge him or get huffy.

He took a seat next to his brother on the couch, facing the former pop star.

"My name is Hannah," she said calmly, carefully. Conflict waged a war in her pale blue eyes, and her hands clenched into tight fists in her lap. "Ashton James was a stage name. I left that life behind for a lot of reasons. But the most important one is to keep someone I care about safe."

She locked eyes with Johnny.

The little sister.

He lifted his chin slightly but kept his mouth shut.

"If the media or paparazzi were to find out my name and where I live now, it could create...certain complications."

Shawn fidgeted in his seat.

"Do you understand what I'm saying?" she asked them both, but her eyes remained on Shawn.

"I haven't told anyone," Shawn said, defeat in his voice. "I wasn't planning on telling anyone. I just really wanted you to hear my stuff." He laughed in a self-deprecating way. "You're my idol. I was hoping you could give me some pointers on how to get better."

Her expression softened further even as uncertainty rose in her eyes. She opened her mouth to say something when Shawn cut her off.

"I prayed for you. Specifically you. Seeing you get off that train was like God Himself telling me I was on the right path."

That was news to Johnny. He had no idea the kid had likened this run-in with divine design.

"Oh, Shawn," Hannah replied with a sad chuckle. "The only kind of messenger I've ever been is a harbinger."

Johnny hoped the shock he felt at her words didn't show on his face.

Because...holy crap.

And also, what the hell?

Her eyes darted to his, and for a moment, they were in the same breath again. Just like on Saturday. It was a quick and instant connection that sent lightning down his arms to his fingertips. Her mouth held the hint of a smile, like they were sharing a secret.

And weren't they?

"I have to ask. How much will it take to keep this secret?"

"Nothing," Johnny answered honestly. "We don't need your money to keep a promise."

She studied him for a long moment. "I wish I could believe you. But I think I'd be more comfortable if you took the money."

The truth in that statement made him sad. And feeling sorry for

Ashton James was the last thing he ever expected to feel. He rebelled against the feeling.

"Maybe you'll just have to trust us," he countered with an edge in his voice.

"Hmm," she murmured, unconvinced. "But you really hate me. And from personal experience, that can be tricky to control."

Johnny inhaled sharply at her almost bored-sounding declaration.

"I know that money won't make you feel better about whatever it is I did," she continued, those crystalline eyes narrowing in on his soul. "But it might keep you from trying to get revenge."

Shawn's head swiveled sharply between them.

"I don't want revenge," Johnny said thickly.

"They all want revenge," she replied sadly.

"If you don't give me an amount, I'll just decide what seems fair and bring a check by tomorrow." She rubbed the tops of her thighs with her palms.

"Check?" Johnny frowned, trying to keep up.

"Well, I'm not gonna Venmo it to you." She snorted.

He wanted to repeat that he didn't want her money. That the only thing he wanted was for her never to have moved to this town in the first place. Or maybe that Shawn had never recognized her. Or better yet, if Johnny would have turned down that gig years ago that caused them to cross paths.

He didn't say anything, though. She took his silence as agreement and stood, signaling the end of their conversation.

"Ash—H-Hannah," Shawn said quickly. "Please. Take the demo."

"She can't," Johnny answered for her while holding her eye contact. "It's a liability."

"But I'm not gonna sue," Shawn said. "It's a gift." He looked back and forth between Hannah and Johnny, pleading.

"Shawn," she began, sliding her hands into her pockets. "I'm not a good person. I'm not even an okay person. Whatever your brother told you about me…" She lifted her eyes to the ceiling, and Johnny got the distinct impression she broke eye contact with Shawn so that she could finish her thought. "It's all true. Actually, I'm worse than whatever he said, so please listen to him."

She turned those terrifying eyes on Johnny.

"For whatever it's worth, I'm sorry. I know it hardly matters since I don't even remember what I did." Her eyes flicked over to the guitar again. "But I'm betting it was bad."

Johnny didn't know what to say. He hardly knew what to think.

But he was feeling a lot.

Mostly confusion. And regret.

"We won't tell anyone," he said as Hannah reached the door.

She turned just her head to glance over her shoulder. "Thank you, Johnny."

CHAPTER FOUR

CIRCUS

HANNAH

It wasn't what she expected.

XY Records didn't look like it should be taken seriously.

Honestly, it looked like a dump.

Hannah hesitated outside the unmarked steel door, the bribery check burning a hole through her purse.

It was weird, she'd never struggled with the bulky weight of her over the shoulder bag until after she'd put the check in it. Then it seemed to weigh an enormous amount. As if the one hundred thousand dollars were in small, unmarked bills and stacked in tidy rows. Maybe this was why payoffs were done in back alleys with gym bags full of twenties. Because the weight was there anyway, even if it was only a check.

Except she needed it to be a check. So that when he cashed it, there would be a record.

According to the financial pull Alex had done, and under the advice of Quinn, the money Hannah was offering would be too good to pass up.

Even for someone without any ethical fading like Johnny Enamorado.

She pulled the door open and stepped inside. It took a moment for her eyes to adjust to the darker interior.

It was just a small entry area with hooks for coats, a snow shovel propped in the corner next to a bucket of ice melt.

"Can I help you?"

Hannah's eyes landed on a blonde standing in the entryway to a long, narrow hallway. Young, perky, fashionable.

"I'm here to see Johnny Enamorado," Hannah said, hoping she pronounced his last name correctly.

"He's in the back." She pointed to a doorway on Hannah's left with one hand while the other scrolled the screen on her smartphone. "Do you have a preference in fish, chicken, or steak?"

Hannah blinked at the question. "Uh, no."

The blonde smiled brightly and went back to her phone.

Weird.

Hannah went through the door and down a hall that emptied into a live room with a drum kit set up at the center. The ceilings were high, and light filtered in from windows up above.

She did a small circle in the room and spotted another doorway to a smaller room. She entered and it was as she'd guessed, a dead room. A variety of guitars lined the edges, and various cords and plugs hung on organized rows.

Hanging up one of those nicely coiled cords was Johnny.

The strong lines of his back, the way the thermal hugged his shoulders and tapered to his tight waist. Her eyes skated over his backside, but she didn't linger.

She cleared her throat.

He turned around and his polite expression dissolved when he realized it was her.

"What are you doing here?" he asked tersely.

She narrowed her eyes and ran her tongue over her teeth.

What was it about this man's hard exterior that made her old instincts of protectiveness kick in? None of the good ones, of course, just the bitchy ones.

She took an extra breath before she answered.

Lord, help me not fuck this up too.

"I'm here to make you a deal."

Johnny pushed past her, not even bothering to pretend to listen to what she had to say.

"I have a lot going on today, princess. I don't need you around to ruin it."

Fair point.

She followed him through the live room and back down the hall. He kept going, bypassing the front door and going down the hall on the right. This hall had four closed doors, three on the left and one at the end.

He entered the first one and closed it behind him.

Mother. Fucker.

Hannah stuffed her shit back down and prepared to play nice.

She rolled her eyes to herself because she really fucking hated playing nice.

"Piper. You can do this for Piper," she whispered to herself.

Okay. Better.

She opened the door and was relieved that it wasn't a bathroom. Not that that would have stopped her, but this would be less awkward.

It was a large, bright (and frankly glorious) control room. Bright lights, oak floors, a large window looking into a heavenly live room with matching oak floors. Truly, she could salivate over the setup.

Johnny stood at the board with headphones but turned around when she slammed the door behind her.

Ignoring his sputtering, she crossed the small room and set her heavy purse on one of the three leather couches. Reaching inside, she found the business check easily and slid it out.

Johnny took it her from her without breaking angry eye contact. "What's this?"

"If it's not enough, I can get more," she said, watching him open it.

Contempt and disbelief twisted his handsome face and he tried to hand it back to her. "I told you I didn't want your money."

"If you don't take the money, then I have no guarantee that you'll keep quiet," she persisted.

"You don't have the guarantee anyway, babe."

She flinched at his declaration, knowing that was true.

"You just want legal recourse in case I call a magazine or something." He folded the check in half and held it up between two fingers. "You'll just have to take me at my word."

Hannah ran a hand through her hair and sighed with defeat.

Something passed through Johnny's eyes as he watched the movement. She didn't know him well enough to know what it was, though.

"Please," she said, throat thick. "Wouldn't you do anything to protect Shawn?"

His eyes flashed with anger and his jaw tightened.

"You want me to believe that *you*"—he gestured with his eyebrows at her—"have altruistic intentions?" He snorted.

Again, fair.

Especially if he knew her outside of what the press revealed.

In most cases, the media made up things to add drama and intrigue. Ashton James had been the exception to that fact. They only ever had to post the truth. And even then, they didn't know the half of it. She'd always had enough money to hide the bulk of her misdeeds.

"So what you're saying is my money won't save me now?" she replied grimly.

He watched her carefully, suspicion heavy in his eyes.

"You, of course, have no reason to believe me." Her eyes wandered to the control board, little lights and switches. Oh, how much easier would it be if she could adjust a fader and change the entire direction of this current track in her life.

"This is my nightmare," she murmured.

"What do you mean?" he questioned.

Her gaze darted back to him, realizing he'd heard her.

She bit her bottom lip while debating internally how much she could reveal.

Nothing.

Everything.

How much *should* she reveal. Maybe that was a better question.

Or maybe all of it was irrelevant and she should give up on successfully keeping Piper in her life.

The very thought, as fleeting as it was, caused sudden emotion to sting her eyes.

Piper.

She could do anything for Piper.

Go to the mat, fight to the last breath, start over until she died kind of devotion.

"It's my biggest fear—that what I have coming to me, what I deserve, will ruin one more person's life."

Johnny's frown deepened, but he remained silent.

"I have no way of preventing it. All I have is the hope of delay." She nodded at the check. "Piper is…good, and right, and pure. She doesn't deserve me as her caretaker. She deserves a real mom, and a real home, and an actual life. Not me. I'm…." She snorted. "Well, I'm sure you know."

Johnny put his hands on his hips and looked to the floor. He still held the check in his fingers.

And her future in his hands.

"Sorry this took so long." They were interrupted by the perky blonde from the front. She pushed right in between them and set a couple of bags on the table in the middle of the room.

"Nikki, it's not a great—" Johnny stopped midway into his sentence and shot a look at the clock on the wall. "What time is it?" he asked, checking his watch and glancing back at the clock on the wall.

"It's two fifteen," Nikki replied, unpacking what smelled an awful lot like tacos. "La Morena's was so busy. I had to wait for them to finish making the order. Anyway, they threw in some extra avocado salsa. You know, the spicy one that ruins my makeup." She cast a knowing look at Hannah, which caught her off guard. "I guess if my eye makeup is going to run, I'd rather it be Mexican food than a shitty man. Am I right?"

Hannah bit back a smile, surprised at the other woman's friendly demeanor.

It wasn't something Hannah experienced often.

Hell, it wasn't something she experienced, period.

"I got you your usual, Johnny." She nodded at Hannah. "And I got you a trio. So all three: chicken, fish, steak. Have you ever had La Morena's tacos?"

Hannah dumbly shook her head.

"They are the *best* tacos in town. You will not be disappointed." She finished setting out the food and grabbed a smaller bag for herself. "I'm going to eat at my desk. Lord Business called. They're going to be early, so eat fast, babes."

Then she was gone.

Johnny rubbed his fingers over his forehead. "Of course they'll be early," he muttered to himself.

Hannah took a second to catch her breath at the small (but refreshing) tornado named Nikki.

Johnny tossed the check on the table with the food while pulling his phone out of his pocket, muttering to himself.

"Nikki?" he bellowed toward the doorway.

She appeared, clearly having sprinted down the hall.

"Did Monica Reeves call?" he asked.

Nikki frowned and pointed a finger at Hannah.

Hannah shook her head, some of the past few minutes beginning to make sense. She placed a palm on her upper chest. "Hannah."

"Not Monica?" Nikki asked, as if Hannah might be messing with her.

"Cool. Cool, cool, cool, cool, cool, cool, cool." Johnny paced to the far wall and back again, one hand going through his hair and the other selecting something on his phone and then pressing it to his ear.

Nikki's eyes widened and she screwed up her mouth to bare her teeth and smile awkwardly. Hannah snorted involuntarily. Johnny's attention darted their direction.

"Hey, Monica," he said, sounding strained. "Did I misunderstand the time you said you'd be here? It's after two now and we need to get started soon. Uh…call me back, I guess."

"Monica Reeves is supposed to play piano for a track that Johnny is supposed to produce for—" Nikki whispered conspiratorially to Hannah.

"Nikki!" Johnny barked. "This is a great example of oversharing."

Nikki pursed her lips. "Sorry, boss." She blew air from her mouth and bugged her eyes at Hannah.

Two things happened in Hannah's mind at that moment. One, she decided she liked Nikki a lot. Which was a very new feeling for her. Liking anyone, let alone another woman, right away was strange and foreign. And two, she saw the opportunity for what it was.

"I play piano," she offered.

Nikki's eyebrows went up in interest and she looked to Johnny for his reaction.

"Absolutely not," he said firmly.

But Hannah recognized that look. It was the look of a man beginning to unravel.

"I can play the piano very well, actually," she said, taking a seat on the couch. She found her three tacos easily and began to unwrap them. The avocado salsa sounded promising and she dug around in the bag for that. After a moment of silence, she glanced at Johnny.

He silently shook his head at her. "You have no idea what you're suggesting," he said, his face slack, eyes wide as his mind raced with all the terrible things he was imagining.

But she did know what she was suggesting. For the first time since leaving his adorable townhouse the other night, she finally felt like she had the upper hand.

He didn't want money? Fine. But he *needed* a musician.

She'd never met or heard of Monica Reeves, but at the moment, she wanted to thank her for flaking on her agreement.

Nikki cleared her throat and took a small step toward Johnny. She laced her fingers together in front of her. "I'm not sure you have much of a choice," she whispered.

Again, Hannah had to stop herself from laughing.

Nikki was both adorable and hilarious. She reminded her of Anna Faris in basically every movie she'd ever been in.

A bell rang at the front of the building and Nikki spun around and hurried toward it.

Hannah took a bite of her taco, holding eye contact with Johnny.

"This isn't happening," he growled to himself. He turned around to face the soundboard, and by the rise of his shoulders, he took a deep breath.

Voices up front came closer as they headed down the hall. And then they were there.

A large man in a large suit entered directly behind Nikki, who had a plastic smile on. Which was odd because she'd been more than affable with Hannah. Behind the big man was a young man, probably in his early twenties, tight skinny jeans and a football jersey. A long gold chain around his neck and an unkempt ponytail at the nape of his neck.

Tattoos covered his pale arms and went all the way up his neck. He had a few words scrawled across his face as well.

Hannah recognized him immediately.

He was the newest big sensation. Blasting into fame a year ago and sending himself into the stratosphere with his clever lyrics and hip-hop sound.

Not to mention his look was its own attention-getter.

He *looked* like he needed a shower.

Hannah unconsciously braced for when the smell that accompanied the look made it to her.

He spotted her and took a seat next to her with a chin lift.

"Hey."

"Hey," she replied, trying not to frown when she was enveloped by the scent of laundry detergent and fresh shampoo.

Ohhh, it's a real *gimmick.*

Hmm, interesting. And surprisingly pleasant.

"I'm Dave," he introduced himself.

"Hannah Lee," she returned around a mouthful of chicken taco.

He nodded once and continued messing around on his phone.

Dave. Right.

The rest of the world knew him as Sunshine Capone.

But "Dave" probably wouldn't have gotten as much attention as a tattooed white boy named after a legendary gangster.

Hannah just nodded her head and kept eating. She had one ear trained on the suit and Johnny's conversation.

Drawing from her experience, she guessed the suit was a manager.

And judging from the bits and pieces of conversation she could hear, Johnny was being given a chance to produce one track for Sunshine Capone's sophomore album.

Ah, the dreaded second album slump.

She didn't miss those days.

Trying to get people to listen to your shit enough that you became a household name, but not so much that they were sick of you. Then trying to produce a follow-up album that was fresh (because, again, people tired of the same thing quickly) but also similar enough to your first release so it didn't alienate the small fan base you'd managed to acquire.

It was exhausting.

And the only way Hannah had gotten through was with the help of a lot of alcohol.

And sometimes hard drugs.

Usually both at the same time.

Yeah, she didn't miss those days.

Even if her mouth sometimes watered when she thought about the taste of chilled Chardonnay on a summer evening.

Nikki hadn't been kidding about the hot sauce. Hannah's eyes watered, and her mouth sucked in air to try and cool off the interior. She glanced around, looking for a beverage of some kind. She remembered seeing a small refrigerator in the main lobby and she shot to her feet, headed that direction.

"You have something to drink?" Hannah labored through the question, fanning her face and neck with a hand.

Nikki laughed and opened the mini fridge door to reveal an assortment. "We have plain water, bubbly water, Coke, and beer."

Hannah leaned in and snatched a bottle of plain water. She cracked the lid off and took a long, refreshing drink.

"Whew, you weren't kidding about that avocado salsa." Hannah wiped under her eyelids. If she'd been wearing any eye makeup, it would definitely have been ruined after that.

Nikki smiled and shifted closer to Hannah, dropping her voice. "Johnny won't say because he's like that, but he can't lose this client. And he's shit on piano. So, for all our sakes, I hope you have the razzle-dazzle required."

Hannah knew she was smirking, but she couldn't help it.

"Oh, I'm amazing on piano," she answered honestly. "I can pretty much play anything."

Nikki breathed an obvious sigh of relief. "Then do what you do, mama. I'll cover you from here."

Hannah returned back the way she'd come, feeling a new type of warmth spread through her chest. This time it wasn't from the hot sauce.

She liked Nikki.

It was a strange and sudden emotion…this *like.* Was it safe? Was it okay to like Nikki? Was it okay to think she might actually be liked in return?

No.

Nothing was safe.

Especially not relationships with others.

Often vulnerability was just a setup for betrayal.

And Hannah was often doing the betraying.

That little factoid soured her stomach and she swallowed hard.

It didn't have to be that way. She could choose differently this time.

She could…be kind.

Ugh.

Okay, maybe being kind was easier said than done. It often entailed more than just rewinding a VHS tape before returning it. Which Hannah actually couldn't remember ever doing. Though VHS had gone the way of the dodo years ago. Maybe her memory was just bad.

And hopefully kindness wasn't as boring as it seemed. Maybe she could punk rock the shit out of kindness.

"Are you the musician?" the suit asked when she'd made it two steps back into the control room.

The musician. Hannah liked the sound of that.

Why yes, I am the *musician. By which all other musicians are measured.*

"No, she's—"

"Hannah Lee, nice to meet you," she interrupted Johnny's sputters of protest. The suit shook her hand and she held it a second longer than necessary, adding a flirty smile.

"Ah, talent and beauty, a lethal combination."

"Excuse me," Johnny interrupted them, touching Hannah lightly on the elbow. "I need to speak to my…person." He put just enough pressure on her elbow to steer her away from Lord Business and into a small equipment room off the main room.

"Your person?" Hannah asked with a smirk.

Johnny's pleasant expression evaporated and he narrowed his eyes at her. "The lies just pour out of you, don't they?"

Hannah mirrored his eye narrowing but without the venom behind it.

They were less than six inches away from one another, and the smell of electrical equipment mixed with leather and cinnamon was a heady combination.

"The secret to lying is to tell the truth ninety-nine percent of the time." Her eyes dropped to his mouth, to his collar where the top button on his Henley was open, exposing the barest hint of dark hair. Her eyes came back up to meet his angry ones. "Would you like me to leave?"

His eyes flashed and his breathing got heavier. His gaze dropped to her mouth and then bounced back to her eyes, angrier than before. "I can't afford to be a game you play," he growled.

She frowned, wondering if he was hinting at their past that she still couldn't recall.

He closed his eyes and sighed. "My livelihood," he amended. "This is all I have," he confessed.

She softened her expression and blinked slowly. "I know. I won't fuck it up."

She slipped around him and rejoined the others. Johnny took another moment before he returned.

"Time is money, my friends, and I'd like to stay rich," Dave said, standing up. He nodded at Hannah. "I'll show you what I'm thinking and we'll see what you can do."

* * *

JOHNNY

"No, I get it." Hannah nodded at the tattooed face of Dave Hansen AKA Sunshine Capone. "But what if you added this…?" She played something infinitely delicate on the ivory keys of the baby grand piano set up in the live room of Studio X.

Sunshine's grin was immediate. "Fuck yeah!" He jumped off the piano bench and made a rapid lap around the room.

"Please, oh, please, oh, please, oh, please," Johnny found himself muttering. Or perhaps praying was more like it.

Today had not gone as planned. Not even remotely.

The moment *she* had shown up, it had gone significantly downhill.

Except it hadn't.

Which was more frustrating than he could articulate.

All he knew was that he didn't want her there, and yet he didn't want her to leave.

Because she was saving his ass.

What were the chances?

Never mind, he didn't want to know the odds.

He didn't need it explained to him in math and numbers that nothing could have predicted this moment.

That would make it feel like it was destiny or some other such bullshit and those things did not exist.

Life was chaos. There was no divine plan.

They were all just random bits of matter, colliding into each other until they disintegrated.

All he had to do was survive the collision.

Dave began rapping softly over the melody that Hannah was playing. Johnny flipped the record switch because magic was currently happening.

"Okay, okay, okay." Sunshine sat down beside Hannah and pounded out a bridge. She nodded and took over.

"What if you put it here," she said, humming the melody of what Sunshine had just made up on the spot and working the bridge in.

"Then walk it back down." Sunshine nodded along to the beat, grinning.

I keep my words light
And my thoughts at the ready
And I keep my mouth tight
Or it's audio spaghetti
I know a thing or two
'Cuz I'm well-read
You may doubt it's true
But like I've said

You come to my shop
You will wind up fed

They both dissolved into giggles. Hannah scribbled the changes on the paper in front of her.

Hannah wasn't being a session musician.

She was being a writing partner and producer.

It was…unsettling.

It was as if she could read Sunshine's mind, knew what he was trying to create, and met him there, music in hand.

Johnny had seen it once before. The first time he'd ever stepped foot in a recording studio with Ashton James.

"Man, I thought this idea was crazy when I had it, but you make me feel like a genius," Sunshine remarked.

Hannah took a drink of water and nodded. "It's clever. It's a song about clout while poking fun of yourself. It makes total sense."

No, it didn't.

It didn't make any sense until Hannah Lee had sat down at the piano and played like her heart was weeping.

Before Johnny had fully processed what was happening, it was over.

It had happened.

The track was done and mixed and ready for public consumption.

He was sweating.

"I've never laid down a track that fast and that solid." Sunshine lifted his chin at Hannah. "I'm supposed to be down in Texas at the end of the week to record the rest of the album. Are you available to join me?"

Johnny wanted to punch a wall and laugh out loud.

In one session she'd hornswoggled an artist into thinking he actually needed her to do what he could probably do in his sleep. That was supposed to be Johnny's job. He was supposed to be the producer who everyone trusted to make them sound their best.

"Sorry, I only work here." Hannah pointed a thumb over her shoulder at Johnny. Johnny fought the urge to look behind him to see who she was talking about. "Johnny's the best and I don't work without him."

Sunshine eyed the two of them appraisingly. "You got a good thing going here, man." He clapped hands with Johnny. "I'll be in touch."

And then they were gone.

"You didn't have to do that," Johnny murmured in the now quiet studio.

Hannah slowly turned around to face him, her expression sober. "Yeah, I did." She checked her watch. "Shit. I'll have to grab pizza on the way home. Piper will be wondering where dinner is."

She picked her purse up off the couch and slung it over her shoulder.

"Thank you." The words came out halting and tense, causing Johnny's neck to heat.

She scrunched her nose. "Oof. That wasn't easy for you, was it?"

He snorted and shook his head. "No. It wasn't. But it needed to be said."

He held her eyes, wishing like hell he could read her thoughts and wondering where on earth they went from there. Because it didn't feel like an end.

He'd resisted taking her money for just this reason.

He didn't want to be tied to her in any sense of the word.

And yet, there they stood, on the threshold of what could only be a beginning.

Beginning of what? Probably his utter and total ruin.

"See ya around, Johnny E." She backed to the door.

"Wait." He grabbed a Sharpie off the console. "Gimme your number in case we need to make any adjustments."

Valid excuse, ol' boy. And not desperate sounding at all.

She smirked and rolled her eyes but approached him nonetheless, holding out her hand while simultaneously holding eye contact.

He dropped the marker in the other hand and flinched when she grabbed his arm. She shook her head, still with that half smile, like she was amused by him. She turned into his body just slightly and he held his breath as she scrawled a phone number on his forearm. Not his hand, his arm. Then she blew on it to dry it.

And Johnny could feel his heartbeat in his fingertips.

He took a deep breath before opening his eyes. She was gone.

He glanced down at his arm.

315-555-0197 xx

He tugged his sleeve down so he wouldn't have to look at it. Especially the double *x*'s at the end. Those weren't kisses. Because no.

He would not entertain the idea of kissing her. Or her kissing him. No way was he going to picture what it would be like to slide his thumb across her bottom lip, those icy eyes fluttering closed, her face tilting up toward him—

"That was so amazing!"

Nikki's exuberant interruption caused Johnny to jump and knock over the wastebasket, spilling empty food wrappers on the floor.

"Whoa, you okay?" Nikki asked with a concerned frown.

Heck to the no.

"Yeah, you just startled me." He ran a shaky hand through his hair.

Nikki began to clean up the wrappers and garbage. "Hannah is great. I hope we get to work with her again. She really saved our asses today."

"Yeah." Johnny sat down at the console and flipped the switches and saved the work one more time.

"I'm surprised her name didn't come up when I was searching for a session musician for you. Have you known her a long time?"

"Uh…" Johnny swallowed, trying to figure out how to answer such a straightforward question. "We used to run in the same circles. Haven't…uh, seen each other in a few years."

Nikki hmmed at his answer and took the trash out.

Leaving Johnny alone with his untrustworthy thoughts.

It wasn't until he had made it home that night that he realized he hadn't thought of her as Ashton all day.

Hmm. Something to think about later.

CHAPTER FIVE

ALIEN

HANNAH

"So, pizza?" Piper asked, biting into her second slice and eyeing Hannah from across the couch. "On a school night."

Hannah nodded grimly. "I ran out of time today."

"You ran out of time," Piper repeated flatly.

How much should she tell her? All of it? Parts of it? None of it?

Honesty was their keystone. Everything relied on both of them being truthful with the other.

"Not that I'm complaining," Piper added quickly. "It's my favorite. The best part about moving to Chicago was the deep-dish." She shrugged nonchalantly. "But you usually stick to the routine."

The routine.

Hannah hadn't stopped feeling the twisting guilt and underlying terror that accompanied it since she called into work that morning. Even the distraction of being at the studio and her very convincing arguments to herself that justified *why* she was doing what she was doing didn't make those queasy emotions fade entirely.

She wondered if guilt would always accompany any decision that let her feel even a smidgen of happiness.

Not general happiness. Not the kind she got from knowing Piper was safe and healthy. Happiness like that was borne of fulfilling responsibility and "doing the right thing."

The personal, selfish kind she had felt today was different. It was happiness that only benefited her.

The guilt roiled in her stomach again and she set her plate down in her lap.

"I didn't go to work today. I called in so I could take the check over to Johnny Enamorado's recording studio. And I stayed all day."

She peeked sideways at Piper, who was sitting perfectly still, mouth hanging open.

"Please say something," Hannah pleaded softly.

The younger girl shook her head to snap herself out of whatever daze she'd been in.

"Did he take the money?"

Hannah began to answer no when she stopped and thought. "Actually," she snickered, "he said no, but he still has the check." He'd tossed it aside when his day had gone (more) awry. "Anyway, an opportunity presented itself and I took advantage. Now he's indebted to me." She picked her plate back up and held it to her chin as she balanced the sloppy deep-dish slice with her other hand. "Which should buy us a lot more time than the money by itself."

"I knew it," Piper declared smugly.

"You knew what?" Hannah asked around a laugh.

"You were singing when you came in the door. You were happy. You're only happy when you're writing music."

"That's not—" she protested.

"Not like that," Piper said. "You're happy with me a lot. But you're never happy by yourself."

Hannah wanted to object but found it too difficult to form any words that didn't feel like a straight out lie.

And also, what right did she have to be happy on her own? It was one thing to be happy *for* someone else. Because it was *their* happiness. *They* owned it. She was just a witness to it. That seemed to be okay in the grand scheme.

But happiness for her?

That seemed like a slippery slope.

"It was just a song stuck in my head," Hannah disregarded the observation. "Because I happened to be present during a recording session."

"Are you going to tell me who? Was it you? Was it Johnny?" Her eyes widened. "Please tell me Johnny has a super deep voice."

Hannah's laughter almost made her choke. She waved Piper away. "It wasn't Johnny. And if I tell you, you have to keep it a secret. You know that, right?"

Piper nodded eagerly.

Of course she would keep the secret.

Besides, what was one more secret between them anyway?

"It was Sunshine Capone—"

She didn't even finish the guy's name before the room erupted in excited twelve-year-old girl squeals. Piper bounded around the room, barely caged energy vibrating through her preteen body.

"*Ohmygodohmygodohmygod*," she said rapidly. Then, turning to Hannah, she grabbed her by the shoulders and said seriously, "Oh. My. God."

Hannah was laughing uncontrollably at that point.

Oh to be that young and excited. What a terribly wonderful thing.

"Is he cool? Was he nice? Did you talk to him? Did you mention me? Of course you didn't mention me." She leveled those bright eyes at her. "Did you mention me?"

"No," Hannah laughed.

Piper dropped to the floor in what could only be a preteen swoon.

"I love him. I actually love him."

Hannah eyed her little sister. "Yeah, well, over my dead body and all that."

Piper giggled manically and propped herself up on an elbow.

"Are you going to go down there again?"

"That's the million-dollar question, isn't it?" Hannah stood and picked up the pizza leftovers. "I left Johnny my number." She shrugged as if that was all there was to say.

And for Piper, that really was all there was to say. She didn't need to know the flirty way that Hannah had decided to leave her number with Johnny. Or how exciting she found it to push his buttons. Especially when she wasn't actually doing anything wrong.

She tucked the leftovers away in containers and folded the box into a manageable bundle, which she tucked under her arm. "I'm taking out the trash," she called, grabbing the full bag and tying it shut.

The trip down the hall to the garbage chute was always a nice walk.

Maybe that seemed weird to some, but Hannah found she often looked forward to it.

The halls of the apartment building were clean and quiet. The carpeted floors under her bare feet were cleaned regularly. She hardly ever saw neighbors since Quinn had put her on a nearly vacant floor. So the trip to the trash chute felt like it was an extension of her home. She didn't have to worry about hiding her face or being alert to who was around.

It felt safe.

She found herself humming the song she'd recorded with Sunshine that day, and a wide smile stretched across her face.

She pulled the garbage chute open and dumped the bag inside. The cardboard pizza box went into the recycle chute.

Then she spun around and did a small forward bend with a twist. She sung the words to the song out loud and stepped gracefully down the hall. A shimmy here, a spin there.

She swung her arms over her head and spun four times.

Not that she'd ever have described herself as a dancer per se. But her job often entailed lots of dancing. Her manager, Terrence, had gotten her some real lessons early on so it didn't look so scattered when she performed. Because the music…the music always moved her. After a while they had added a choreographer and backup dancers. And then she wasn't playing instruments as often, and the music…became something different.

She had forgotten this part.

The part about discovering your soul inside a melody and the effect being weightlessness.

She made it back to her apartment door and took a deep breath. Wiping the inexplicable moisture from her eyes, she went back inside.

JOHNNY

The track ended and Johnny sat perfectly still. Listening to the clicks and silence of the studio surrounding him. Eyes closed, he leaned a little further back in his chair and wondered again how this had happened.

Because the stupid track was perfect.

He'd gone over it too many times to count and didn't find any places where it could use just a little extra or a little less of anything.

Hannah's voice blended solidly with Sunshine's, and her piano skills were enough to make a grown man cry.

The bell up front rang as someone entered. He listened to Nikki send them back his way.

He expected it to be a package delivery—he was expecting a box of used pedals that may or may not have been a waste of money.

But it was Sunshine Capone, without Lord Business this time.

Johnny stood and they greeted each other with hand clasps and back slaps.

"How's it sound?" Sunshine asked, nodding at the board.

"Let's hear it." Johnny queued up the song that he'd listened to more than a hundred times already and let it play.

Sunshine's head began to bob along with the beat.

"Oh, that's nice," he said with a grin.

Hannah's vocals joined in and Johnny braced for a reaction. He'd turned her up just a fraction, because in his opinion, it sounded better that way.

"Ooh," Dave crooned, grooving to it. "Nice."

The vocals were crisp, the piano bright, the mixing perfect.

It was hard for Johnny to admit that about his own work.

Except he didn't really feel like he had *done* anything.

"I gotta say, Johnny E, it's better than I expected."

Same, Johnny thought, but didn't say so.

Sunshine pulled on the weirdly thin beard, deep in thought. "How's your schedule look for next week?"

Johnny held his face impassive, determined not to look too eager.

"I'll have to ask Nikki what we have booked—"

"We're totally free next week!" Nikki hollered down the hall.

Johnny pressed his lips together and nodded once. "It seems we're available."

Dave thought some more.

"What about Hannah Lee? Would she be around?"

The skin on Johnny's forearm grew hot at the mention. "I'll have to call her and check."

"I wanna do the whole album here. I like the energy. And your people. But only if Hannah can do more backing vocals. Plus her whole vibe stokes my creativity. I need it."

"Yeah, sounds good." Johnny couldn't believe he was agreeing without making sure. Actually, he couldn't believe that Hannah had turned herself into someone important in his business in such a short amount of time. With a plot twist he hadn't seen coming, she'd flipped the power into her hands. And now she basically owned his life, his dream, his future.

It hadn't been an accident.

That much was obvious.

But neither was he willing to call it fate.

Sunshine left with Johnny promising to be in touch as soon as he knew if Hannah was available.

He sat in silence for a solid ten minutes, staring at the empty piano bench where he'd witnessed actual magic just the day before.

Johnny tilted his neck from side to side, cracking it.

"Ugh, I hate that sound."

He glowered at Nikki. She was the reason he was this tense in the first place.

"You wanna call Hannah for me? See if she's able to come in next week?"

"Why me?" Nikki asked suspiciously. "You never let me call people."

That was true. It was because Nikki tended to gab and reveal way too much about all the things.

On second thought, maybe having her call Hannah wasn't a good idea anyway.

Johnny sighed loudly and tugged the sleeve up on his arm, revealing the feminine scrawl along his skin.

Nikki cackled. "Did she write her number on your arm?" She sank back into the couch cushions and laughed harder. "That's such a cool move." She waved a hand at Johnny's arm. "I mean, look at it. She even writes cool."

"Maybe she should have left her number with you," Johnny quipped.

"Oh, I wish. What are those? Little *x*'s?" Nikki squealed. "So hot."

Johnny shook his head, unamused. "Get out of here."

She jumped up and smacked her gum. "Remember to be nice," she called over her shoulder.

Freaking Nikki.

Johnny pulled out his phone and dialed the numbers.

He hated this.

He hated how he felt like he was over a barrel with this.

He never wanted anything to do with Ashton James ever again.

And Shawn couldn't leave well enough alone. One more of those irritating instances that reminded him they shared parents.

His thumb hovered over the "send" button.

What was he supposed to tell Shawn?

It would be impossible to keep him out of the studio if she agreed to do this.

But maybe she wouldn't.

She hadn't been in the scene in years. Said she wanted to leave it behind…but then the magic that happened yesterday sort of belied her protestations.

He really needed to stop thinking of it as magic.

He didn't believe in magic.

He believed that if things could go badly, they would.

So why had yesterday turned out so…great?

The only way to know if what happened yesterday was real or a fluke was to try it again.

* * *

HANNAH

The freight elevator was empty when she reached it.

That was a first.

She entered and frowned at her reflection in the stainless steel doors as they closed. Should she just wait? Was she supposed to hit a floor? Maybe she was supposed to pick them up?

She didn't even know what floor Alex and Quinn lived on.

Probably not the same floor.

Right?

Her stomach lurched in conjunction with the elevator as it began to move.

Ah, decision made for her.

The lift stopped and the doors opened to reveal…

Nothing.

Well, not nothing. It wasn't empty space.

It was a hallway. Like the one she'd come from.

But no one was there. Just an empty hallway.

Hannah pursed her lips and took a tentative step out of the safety of the freight elevator.

She thought she heard muffled noises. Almost…was that kissing?

Oh, God! Was that what kissing sounded like to other people?

Wait. Was the kissing consensual?

She picked up speed as she turned the corner and stopped short.

"Ah, geez." She grimaced. "Sorry. I'll-I-" Garbled noises of no distinction.

She'd caught Quinn in a clinch.

And never had she ever had such instant regret.

The worst part (yes, there were differing horrible parts) was how *close* she was to them.

It wasn't as if she'd come around the corner and Quinn was in a clinch twelve to fifteen feet away. That would have been a safe distance. Still uncomfortable. But *not like this.*

Quinn unlocked his lips from the porcelain neck of a redhead and narrowed angry eyes at Hannah.

Inches.

That was all that separated them.

Hannah never frightened easily.

But if she were being honest, she almost peed her pants.

And not in a fun way.

And then, against her very minimal better judgement, she didn't immediately get back into the elevator. Instead, she took a second look at Quinn's paramour.

"Jem?" she asked, the name coming to mind at the same time as the unlikelihood of it actually *being* Jem.

Quinn and the redhead both stiffened.

"Not Jem," Hannah corrected quickly.

The redhead emerged from around Quinn's protective stance and gave Hannah an apologetic smile.

"No, not Jem. Janie."

"My wife," Quinn growled.

"Mazel tov."

Was this one of those moments normal people felt shame? Embarrassment? Regret?

Because Hannah didn't have that reaction.

Yes, she regretted walking face-first into a clinch.

But that was only because she'd never been much of a voyeur. Her regret was for herself and having that image now in her mind. It could surface at any time. Unbidden and unwelcome.

She didn't feel apologetic.

They were the ones clinching in a hallway.

That he owned.

Okay, so not exactly public property.

But still.

Hannah ran her tongue over her teeth and jerked a thumb over her shoulder.

"I'll just go."

She hit the button and the lift doors opened immediately. When they closed with her inside, she let out a loud groan.

"Well, that sucked. How else can you make relationships with people a little bit more uncomfortable, James? Because you are nailing it."

The doors opened again, and this time Alex and Quinn entered together.

Alex's eyes met Hannah's and he smirked.

"You call his wife the wrong name?" he asked.

Hannah pinched the bridge of her nose.

Quinn let the lift begin to move, and then he hit the emergency stop.

"How do you know Jem Morris?" he asked coldly.

"Unfortunate life choices."

He narrowed his eyes at her, weighing her words.

"You know I was a party girl. She was often a supplier of certain party favors. I'm sure you can guess." Hannah tucked her hands into her pockets and shrugged. "We weren't friends. Our circles occasionally overlapped."

"That seems to be a trend with you."

"Pretty sure that if you tried to map my life, it would be a Venn diagram from hell. You know that game Six Degrees of Kevin Bacon? Yeah, with me—er, Ashton—it was more like two and a half. And the half is almost always a criminal of some kind."

Quinn measured her reply with his usual stoic judgment.

Whether he believed her or not didn't matter. She was telling the truth. Whatever issues he had with Jem were his. She didn't have anything to do with that life anymore.

Speaking of Life Before…

"I decided I'll do the backing vocals for DBS. I found a…studio here in town where I think I can do it without anyone finding out."

"Do you mind if Sandra makes the call? She really likes to role play." Alex blushed and averted his eyes. "I mean—"

"I didn't ask, my dude," Hannah stopped him. Quinn looked relieved she had.

"How are things with the Enamorado family?" Quinn asked. "The check hasn't been cashed."

Not exactly a surprise.

"He refused the money, but he still has the check. I think I've made a deal that should keep him quiet for a while, though."

She explained to them what had happened with Sunshine. And even though it was only the second time telling the story, it still felt strange. Maybe it was because being in the studio and working and creating had come back to her so naturally.

Which had the undercurrent of terror running through it.

The last thing she wanted was to get trapped in another habitual pattern of self-destruction. But one song was hardly a pattern.

Besides, Johnny had been very clear about not wanting her around.

"What about the kid?"

"The kid doesn't know, I don't think." She pinched her lower lip, remembering Johnny's protectiveness. "I got the feeling that Johnny doesn't want me around his little brother. So I imagine he'll keep my recent and temporary return to music from him too."

"Good. The fewer people who know, the easier it is to contain."

"So far, there's no buzz. Not even a hint that you're here or even alive." Alex smiled lopsidedly. "I started a Tumblr account making up conspiracy theories about you. Right now, people think you may have been an alien and you've been called home."

"Sounds good to me," Hannah agreed.

As long as no one came looking for her, Piper would be safe.

And the longer Piper was safe, the better.

"What about your time in the studio?" Quinn asked.

"What about it?"

"Will you be needing access to it, or anything similar in the future? Outside of the DBS backing vocals, that is. Or is it a one-off?"

She tapped her chin with her finger. Her feelings on the matter were somewhat foggy. She needed to sort through them. But she also needed guidance in doing so. "I'm seeing my therapist tomorrow. I'm going to ask her what she thinks."

* * *

When her phone rang at six o'clock that night, she was making dinner.

Chicken alfredo. Homemade.

Because cooking had proved itself to be a healthy distraction. She wasn't ever going to be someone who liked to cook as a hobby. But that was because she abhorred doing dishes. And the more cooking/baking/sautéing you did, the more dishes got dirtied.

And washing dishes was not a happy hobby for her.

Not to say she wouldn't wash her own dishes. But why do more than necessary?

The phone rang as she was stirring the cream sauce.

A glance at the caller ID told her nothing. It was a local number with the same number prefix as the school. Which was why she answered it. The school loved to send out automated calls at dinner time.

"Hello?"

She hit the speaker button and set the phone on the counter, ready to listen to whatever message they had for her this week. Flower fundraiser? Early out next week for a staff meeting?

"H-Hannah?"

What was this? A real person?

"Yeah…?"

"It's…it's Johnny…Enamorado Torres."

"Oh, shit," she said without thinking.

He chuckled and the pleasant sound caused her heart to pound.

Just the one.

One extra heavy pound.

Not even enough to be noticed, except that she noticed.

"I'm kind of surprised you gave me your real number. Considering how much your privacy means to you."

You're not the only one, buddy, she thought with an eye roll.

"Did everything turn out okay?" she asked. "With the song? Do you need me to come down and redo anything?" she asked, quickly getting to the point. The sooner she got off the phone, the better.

Right?

He cleared his throat and she could picture his tightly knit black eyebrows and the crease between his forehead.

"No, the song is actually, uh, perfect."

Perfect?

Warmth hit her chest and she smiled widely into the cream sauce, happy no one else was around to see her happy expression.

"Oh," she said, proud of how indifferent it came out.

"Yeah. Sunshine likes it so much he wants to do the whole record here. With me."

"That's great!" she declared, knowing what a big deal that was for him.

He laughed softly. "Yeah. It is really great."

"Is that why you called?" she asked, her chest getting tight. Was this a thank-you call? He'd already thanked her once at the studio and she'd almost frozen up. Another thank-you? That was bordering on excessive.

How should she respond? With nonchalance and cool girl grace? Smug self-assurance?

Maybe she could just hang up.

She had no idea what the *right reaction would be.*

"Yes and no," he said begrudgingly.

Oh. So, no thank-you.

That was fine.

Cool.

No, really, it was better that way. She didn't know how to respond to gratitude anyway. For crying out loud, she'd almost just panic-ended the call.

"There's a caveat," Johnny continued cautiously. "Sunshine will only record if you're available to be on the record as well. Apparently," he said sardonically, "he seems to think you have some talent. And would like to work with you more."

Hannah grinned.

He was asking her for a favor!

This was great!

Then he'd really, *really* owe her.

He'd owe her for so many things!

But she stayed silent. She was *not* going to offer.

If he wanted this, he was going to have to ask.

After a minute of silence, he cleared his throat.

"You're really going to make me do this, aren't you?" He sounded truly indignant.

And it delighted her.

Hey, change took time.

Being a good person came in ebbs and flows.

This was obviously an ebb.

A leopard can't change its spots overnight.

And to tell the truth, Hannah wasn't sure her spots would ever go away.

"Hannah Lee, would you please join me in making an album for Sunshine Capone? Nothing would make me happier," he said through clenched teeth.

"Ha ha," she mocked. "You need me."

Johnny sniffed a humorless laugh.

"Somehow I knew you'd love this," he said darkly.

"You hate me so much," she declared happily. Which might seem weird to someone else, but Hannah was loving it. "How much did it hurt to have to call me?"

"A lot, actually," he responded flatly, sounding just as disgruntled as she was picturing him.

And color her even more surprised, she was all about it.

Something about his open and honest dislike for her, but knowing he also wouldn't be able to sell her out to the media, created a new and fun dynamic.

It was the most authentic form of trust she'd ever had outside of her and Piper.

"Listen, I know this is great fun for you," he said around her cackles, "but I need to know if you'll do this."

"Oh, yeah. For sure," she agreed wholeheartedly. She dipped a spoon in the cream sauce and tasted it. Perfect.

"Really?"

"Fuck yeah," she replied smugly. "When do you want me there?"

"I hope I don't regret this," he muttered. "Can you come in tomorrow, say, eleven? And we'll go over ideas and the studio space."

"Sure. I have an appointment in the morning, and then I'll just take my PTO at work. I've been saving it. Might as well use it now."

"You have a job?"

She screwed up her face and glared at the phone. "Yes, I have a job. I happen to be a productive member of society."

"Uh, okay."

Did she feel bad for snapping? Not even a little.

Know why?

Because he already disliked her! Besides, he was the one being rude about his assumptions.

"See you at eleven, Johnny E." She didn't wait for his reply and hit "end" with her pinky.

Fuck.

Yes.

This had gone from being a potentially terrible situation to being beneficial.

All she had to do now was check with her therapist.

Because she had questions.

Hannah finished her info dump to her doctor and then stared at the floor.

There was always this moment after sharing information where she felt completely transparent.

As if Brenda was going to look at her and think she was full of shit and tell her to get out.

Not because she was full of shit, but because she had become so accustomed to no one believing her.

Which was what had made the transition to lying full-time that much easier.

Because truth was subjective.

People believed what they wanted.

And it was usually based on their personal feelings on the matter and not on anything else. Like, say, facts.

"How did being in the studio make you feel?" Brenda asked (*not* throwing her out, Hannah noted).

Hannah's lips twitched with the memory.

"Happy," she confessed.

Brenda caught her eye. "And being happy isn't what you expected?"

"It wasn't unexpected..." Hannah swallowed, trying to put into words what she was afraid of without saying it in a way that might get Brenda to raise her eyebrows. "In the moment, it felt amazing. I was a little dizzy. Like I was buzzed."

"Like with alcohol."

"Yeah." She winced.

"But you weren't drinking."

"But it felt like it. I was...cocky, and smug, and..." She closed her eyes, remembering the feeling. "And I loved it."

"That sounds good, Hannah," Brenda said gently.

Hannah opened her eyes. "But it's not. It can't be. Also," she added quickly, before Brenda said something too nice that shouldn't be directed at her, "isn't this entire thing *wrong*? I mean, from start to finish, this whole scheme feels...tenuous."

Brenda took in a slow breath. Something Hannah had picked up on pretty early in their sessions. It usually meant that Brenda had a lot of thoughts about what Hannah had just said.

"Let's start with the part where you called it wrong. Where's the wrong?"

Hannah's gaze bounced around the room, wondering why it wasn't obvious to Brenda.

"Hannah," Brenda called her back.

"It's too good to be true," Hannah replied, matter-of-fact. "The fact that it's good at all is…problematic." She leveled her gaze at Brenda. "C'mon, Doc. You know. You know all the things. You're a smart person. Nature corrects itself. I had a shot at happy and I fucking blew it. Now there's a correction."

"Life isn't so black and white. Everyone deserves to be happy. Look at what you've done for Piper. When you began sessions with me eighteen months ago, you weren't sure you'd be able to make dinner. And now?"

"But life with Piper is a different happy." Hannah felt the sting of tears in the back of her eyes and she took a deep breath to silence it. "That doesn't feel selfish."

Brenda nodded as if understanding just hit. "And enjoying music again feels selfish." She added that to her notes.

"Music is the epicenter of Earthquake Ashton."

"Was."

"What?"

"It *was* the epicenter," Brenda repeated gently. "What if this is a fresh start? New name, new city. A second chance, maybe."

"How do I trust myself to not wreck it? How do I—I mean, the fucking audacity, right?" Hannah swallowed hard and felt her jaw tighten. "How is it okay?"

Brenda gave her a soft smile. "You have to give yourself permission to be happy, Hannah. I can't do that part for you."

* * *

JOHNNY

He would not look at the time again. He'd already checked it forty-five times in the past three minutes.

The clock on the wall taunted him with an extra loud "tick."

He glanced up.

Forty-six.

He shoved to his feet and stalked down the hall to where Nikki was putting together an amp in Studio X's dead room.

She didn't look up from her work.

"What's up, boss?"

"Has anyone…" He scratched the side of his neck. "Called?"

"Nope." She smacked her gum.

"Hey, Nik?" he asked, pretending to be distracted by a twisted cord on the wall. "You have anyone you could set me up with?"

Another gum smack.

"Nope."

"Nope?" he repeated. "What about that one friend of yours…Amy or Des?"

"Babe, that was two years ago. Des is married now. Besides, I'm not getting in the way of true love. I'm not that stupid."

"True love?"

She lifted just her eyes, annoyed.

The front door opened and he looked at his watch.

Why did she have to be on time?

She wasn't a different person and he refused to entertain that idea.

He told himself that the jump he felt in his chest was anxiety, not excitement.

Which, okay, maybe that was the opposite of healthy.

But he was not going to be excited about working with her.

She couldn't be trusted.

And he would do well to remind himself of that as often as possible.

Hannah came around the corner in slow motion, her hair blowing back out of her face like a Charlie's Angel.

Spotted him and stopped, a perfectly bored expression on her face.

"Waiting for me?" she asked, that smoky voice with a slight edge to it.

Maybe her life circumstances had changed.

But little else had.

She could still make him stop breathing for a second.

How he hated her.

But all he had to do was get through a week of recording. And then he could hopefully put all of this behind him.

He turned on his heel and headed back to the control room without a word.

This was his turf. His home. His sanctuary.

She would not corrupt it by getting under his skin.

"I thought it might be helpful if I made a list of all instruments and equipment I'm proficient in. Though I may have to practice on a few of them to shake the dust off." Hannah handed him a printed off piece of paper. She took off her coat and hung it on the hook along with her purse. Then she sat down on the biggest leather couch.

Johnny chose to sit at the round stool near the soundboard.

"Did you tell Dave, er, Sunshine, who I am?" she asked casually. But there was nothing casual about the sharpness in her gaze.

If this was a test, she was going to be disappointed.

"Nope. Didn't even occur to me." He laced his fingers together behind his head and leaned back. "In fact, I tried very much to discourage him from you at all."

"Good."

The relief evident in her expression caught him off guard.

"That's great," she said, sounding bored again.

He tried to shake off the glimpse of humanity he saw in her. Again.

"Okay, a few things. I can be here as early as eight, but I need to be home in time to make Piper dinner. That's a must-have."

"Fine. That should be easy. What's your going rate?"

Her lips twitched. "Just your silence."

He was uncomfortable with that but didn't expect anything different. For a brief moment he thought about digging the check out of the file where he'd tossed it, giving it back to her again.

"Also, no drugs or alcohol in the studio if I'm here. That's a nonstarter."

"It's a studio rule, so that won't be an issue."

She grimaced. "Just the same. I want it to be stated."

"Fine." He sighed heavily and rolled his neck to crack it. "I don't like this."

"I know," she replied, a hint of smugness in her tone. She turned thoughtful, and then, "I won't do anything to wreck this for you. I…" She tipped her head back and closed her eyes. "I remember what it was like. To have a shot. I won't mess this up for you."

"You mean again?" he said before he could stop himself.

She sat up a little straighter and studied him carefully.

"Again?" she repeated, her eyes searching his face.

"I shouldn't have said that," he grumbled.

"But it was said, so let's talk about it," she offered reasonably.

Nope. He didn't like that.

He propped his ankle on a knee and held on to his calf. "I don't trust you at all," he stated firmly.

If he thought she'd flinch, he shouldn't have held his breath.

She nodded, waiting for more. As if not being trusted were the same as liking the color blue.

"Do you want to tell me what I did?" she asked calmly.

"Why? You don't even remember me." Old hurt burned inside his gut and he pushed it aside with familiar anger.

She pushed her glasses to the top of her head and rubbed her eyes with her thumb and forefinger. She took a deep breath and clasped her hands in front of her with a nod.

"You're right. But it's not your fault that I don't remember. There's a lot." She rolled her eyes at herself. "I have an entire life of ghosts just waiting to jump out and ruin my week."

She bit down on her bottom lip and gazed soberly at the floor.

"If you'd rather not say, that's within your right. But maybe it would be cathartic, for you, if you tell me why you're mad." She raised her eyes to his and he could see how difficult this was for her. "You won't find an argument from me."

Johnny wasn't sure what to think of that. On its face, it seemed too easy. She was so matter-of-fact about it. But there was a genuine remorse laced through her tone that he was mad at himself for noticing.

"I played on your first album."

Her expression turned inward as she tried to access what he was referencing. Testing its truth.

"We hooked up that week." That was the part he hadn't told Shawn. Or anyone. "And you told me I would get to come with you on tour."

Her eyes moved rapidly over his face as she tried to find a thread of memory. It hurt that she didn't remember. It felt like another rejection. He hadn't even made an impression that could be triggered with reminders.

"And then"—he raised his eyebrows—"you got me fired."

Her face went slack and she stared at him.

"I got you fired?" she repeated in a whisper.

"Yep. I had one more day of recording, and when I got to the studio, your manger was waiting for me. He told me that you said I was harassing you and asking for money, and he fired me."

Her head jerked to the side, her expression deeply troubled.

"It took a while for me to get work on another project."

The rest of the story didn't involve her, so he stopped talking. He'd done all right for himself and he knew it. He'd worked hard, fought for it, and now he had something better anyway.

Didn't mean he forgave her, though.

And it sure as hell didn't mean he trusted her.

She took a deep breath, her eyes tracking to the floor.

They sat together in silence for several minutes.

In that time, Johnny realized that saying it out loud had done something. It alleviated a pressure he had been carrying around.

For so long he'd been carrying around this massive secret that he couldn't share because it would be wrong to do so.

But saying it to the person who had caused the wound in the first place?

It felt weird.

Good weird.

She'd been his first real heartbreak. Not because he was in love—he hadn't been. But he'd loved the idea of being with someone so fascinating and creative. And the future she'd promised was more than he'd ever dreamed in his life at the time.

Getting fired shattered more than one dream at a time.

And he never saw her again. Never got to ask her why she said those things or what he had done to deserve it.

Until now.

"No wonder you hate me," she said calmly.

He didn't argue.

She sucked in a breath. "I hate me too."

"Maybe you can understand why I'm less than comfortable with my life being in your hands once again."

She offered a sad smile. “I also get why you want me to stay away from Shawn.”

Again, he didn’t respond because it wasn’t needed.

She might not remember what she’d done, but she understood the consequences of it.

Something about that actually helped him heal a little bit.

“You’d have every reason to throw me to the wolves,” she pointed out quietly.

“I’m not that person, though,” he said. He thought that would be obvious. He’d had every opportunity to sell his story over the years and he never even considered it.

“I’ve always had good taste in men.”

Her casual response raised his eyebrows.

She noticed and rolled her eyes. “Like that’s surprising. Look, Johnny, I know my word is less than nothing. I have no delusions that this will grow to be a buddy cop comedy by the end. But I would very much like to make up for ruining that shot for you years ago. I will do my best. You can have all of my remaining talent at your disposal. Wring me dry. And when it’s done, I promise to bow out.”

“You don’t have to do this. I won’t tell anyone you’re here.”

“Clearly we have trust issues. Interestingly enough, I’m the source of that for both of us. So let’s call this mutual insurance.”

He bit down on his bottom lip. It made sense. Except that he would always feel like she had the upper hand simply because he hadn’t been lying—he wasn’t that person. Airing someone else’s dirty laundry wasn’t in his arsenal and he had no desire to add it.

So her secret would always be safe with him.

And he would never feel safe with her.

* * *

HANNAH

It wasn't often she craved the foggy release of a bottle of wine and a long drive.

One time, years ago, she'd stolen her manager's car and tried to drive it to Seattle.

The boredom of the interstate and a couple bottles of wine caused her to fall asleep whilst driving.

She'd woken up in an empty field, still behind the wheel. Thankfully, she hadn't hurt anyone.

Some would say at least she hadn't hurt anyone *else*. But she never counted herself. She wasn't a victim. She was a scared little bitch without any self-control.

Her revealing conversation with Johnny had triggered an emotional free fall.

She had two choices as she saw it.

She could fall right back into the bottle and lose everything she had fought so fucking hard for. Or she could call her sponsor.

"Hey, Josh," she said when he answered. "You gotta minute?"

"For the record, knitting was your idea."

Josh ran his heavily tattooed hands lovingly over another bundle of yarn, and Hannah eyed him suspiciously.

"Yes, but you were the one who got excited when I mentioned it."

"Knitting is cool. Don't hate."

Hannah held up her hands in surrender.

She was glad she'd called Josh. She wondered if she'd ever reach a point in recovery where she wouldn't need that touchstone. Would uncomfortable and painful conversations ever not make her want to run away and hide?

The yarn store he had told her to meet him at was actually in the main entrance of the building where she lived: Mad About Ewe.

Josh had met her at the entrance. With his studded leather jacket, ripped jeans, shaved head and visible neck tattoos, he seemed a man out of place. But he greeted the owner of Mad About Ewe with familiarity and then showed her through the store.

He helped her pick out all the beginner supplies she would need. They checked out with their purchases and walked down the street to get coffee at a café.

As they sat in public and drank their coffee, Hannah finally began to relax.

"I wish I had a better hold on myself," she confessed among their benign conversation.

Josh nodded in understanding. "You have more than you give yourself credit for."

For some reason, hearing Josh say that had more of an impact than when Brenda said it. Maybe it was because he'd been there. He understood the shitty reality of addiction and recovery and the fucking awful blackness that wanted to swallow her whole.

"And to think, it all started because I wanted to have fun."

"Too much of a good time," he added with a knowing smile. He scrolled through his phone for a moment and then set it down. "I sent you a few tutorials to get you started. Knitting can be your go-to when the mood hits. And if you need to talk to someone while you're knitting, just call."

"All I can do is all I can do," she reminded herself.

"You got this," he reassured with conviction.

"Thanks, Josh."

"So, what do you think you're going to make first?" he asked.

"I don't know. Maybe a hat?"

CHAPTER SIX

TROUBLE FOR ME

JOHNNY

"What's going on?"

Johnny jumped at the sound of Shawn's voice behind him. He slammed the top of his laptop closed and winced.

"Dude. Were you watching porn in the living room?" Shawn asked with disgust. "This is the family space, remember? It was your rule."

Johnny glared at his younger brother. "No, I wasn't watching porn."

"What are you doing home anyway? I thought you'd be down at the studio." Shawn wandered into the kitchen and opened the fridge.

"Yeah." Johnny scrubbed a hand over his face. "About that."

He hadn't told Shawn about…well, anything yet. In his defense, it had all kind of happened really fast. It wasn't one thing after another so much as it was everything at once.

Shawn cracked open a bottle of BODYARMOR and stood in the middle of the living room.

"You gonna tell me or should I start guessing?"

"Sunshine Capone wants to do his whole album with us."

To his credit, Shawn didn't freak out. His eyebrows lifted and he nodded in cool appreciation.

"And…" Johnny rolled his head from side to side, cracking his neck. He folded his arms over his chest. "Ashton—" He dipped his head to signal correction. "Hannah is going to help me produce it."

He watched Shawn for any signs of fainting. Shawn frowned, looked around the room, came back to Johnny.

"You're not joking with me, are you?" he asked, voice tight.

"No." Johnny wished he was, but he couldn't get that lucky. "Not joking."

Shawn's eyes got bright and he shoved a hand through his hair. "This is incredible!" He paced rapidly around the living room. "This is amazing!" He waved a hand at Johnny as he paused in front of him. "I mean, this could be everything!"

"Slow down, kid. This doesn't mean what you think it means."

This was why Johnny hadn't wanted to tell him. Because the kid's dreams were always sky-high and he hated having to be the one to bring him back to earth.

It fucking sucked.

"No, I know!" Shawn was already trying to emotionally backpedal. Probably having recognized the familiar tone coming from Johnny. "It's cool. I won't get carried away. I'm just excited for *you*, you know. I won't do anything to mess it up."

Johnny clenched his jaw, trying to decide whether or not he should call the kid on his crap or just wait.

"It's a temporary job. She's gonna come in and do some work during the day next week. And then that's it." He tried to catch

Shawn's dancing eyes. "She's not sticking around. This is a favor she's doing for me."

The words had barely left his mouth before he realized what he'd said.

It wasn't a favor. It was extortion.

"A favor?" Shawn repeated in disbelief.

"In a manner of speaking." Johnny needed to get off this train. "But the fact remains, we can't tell anyone she's here. You know that, right?"

"Of course." Shawn shrugged like it was obvious. "But when she announces her return, it'll be epic."

"No, Shawn," Johnny stopped him. "She's not returning. She's done. Which is why the secret is so important to keep."

Shawn's expression faded from exuberance to thoughtful until he was totally sober. He sank down on the edge of the coffee table. "Really?"

"Yeah, man. She's out and doesn't want to go back. We need to respect that, okay?"

Shawn couldn't understand because he'd never been there. He'd only ever dreamt of the lights and the smoke and the thousands of fans singing his words back to him. He had no idea how ugly it got for some.

Especially for those who rode that fame train all the way to hell and back.

Johnny had met all kinds.

Some musicians were built for the life. They lived for the travel and the people and the shows. But some just weren't a good fit. Maybe they started bad with bad people. Maybe they started out too trusting and were worn down along the way. Some got lost and never found their way back.

He didn't know what kind Hannah was.

Honestly, he hoped he never found out.

He already knew more than made him comfortable.

"Do you have homework?" Johnny asked, changing the subject.

Shawn groaned. "Vice Principal Shatface assigned a paper to the senior class today about 'why we are the way we are.'"

"Seriously?" Johnny frowned.

"She called it something else, but it was basically that. She hates everything about Generation Z."

"I've got news for you, bud. That woman hates everything, period."

Shawn grimaced and Johnny saw something else there, something he wasn't saying. He waited for Shawn to bring it up, but it cleared. Maybe he should have said something about Shawn calling Vice Principal Shatford "Shatface" again. But it was hard to chastise him for something Johnny agreed with.

That woman hadn't made Shawn's enrollment there easy. She was always on his case about something. Johnny was looking forward to the day they didn't have to deal with her anymore.

"I'll be in my room," Shawn announced, heading up the stairs. "Let me know when there's food."

"You got it."

He waited for Shawn to leave and then opened his laptop again.

This whole process was a headache.

Sunshine had emailed him several sound files and Word docs that he wanted to use for the record. Now, Johnny had to decide whether to forward that to Hannah or just let her come into the session on Monday blind.

Waiting meant the recording might take longer, thereby delaying her exit from his life.

But emailing her now meant increasing communication.

And there was that pesky detail that he didn't have her email.

He opened his phone and dialed, his other hand clenched in a fist.

"Hello?"

The moment her voice hit his eardrums, his fist relaxed and so did his shoulders.

"Sunshine sent over those sound file samples and Word docs. Would you like me to forward those to you?"

There was a pause, and screw him, but he could picture her slow blink.

What was it about her slow blinking those inky black lashes over those icy blue eyes? It was quite possibly the hottest and most irritating thing he'd ever seen.

She rattled off her email and he immediately typed it into the address bar.

"Okay, it's been sent." His thumb reached for the "end" button.

"Don't you dare hang up on me, Johnny." She chuckled softly. "Let me make sure I got it so I don't have to call you back." She shuffled some things around in the background. "I'm going to put you on speaker."

"All right," he said tightly.

There was an intimacy in a phone call. People reduced to sound waves in which to connect. Forced to focus on tone and verbiage. It was an authentic connection that had always made Johnny more than uncomfortable.

Soft puffs of breath, murmured words not meant for public consumption.

It was like two people whispering to each other in a dark canyon while life existed outside and all around them.

"What are you doing?" he asked and immediately regretted it. "I didn't interrupt something, did I?"

"Oh," she sounded distracted. "No. I was doing the dishes, but I am more than happy for the interruption."

"Not," she began to correct quickly. "Not that I was waiting for your call. Or that I was anticipating it. I just hate doing the dishes."

Something about the awkward way she was trying to put him at ease was actually working. With anyone else, no, but with Hannah, it felt genuine.

Both of them were uncomfortable with their current situation.

That realization was probably why Johnny did what he did next.

"Yeah, that was my main motivation for getting a place with a dishwasher. I don't know anyone who loves doing the dishes."

She laughed softly. "We have a dishwasher, but I make a lot of food from scratch, so there's always pots, pans, and things that are marked 'hand wash only.'" She groaned, sounding annoyed. "That sounded pretentious." She pitched her voice deeper and mocked herself, "'*I make a lot of food from scratch.*' I didn't mean it like that. I *have* to make all the food. Eating out is too…precarious. I can't have delivery because no one can ever know where I live. And going to restaurants is too dicey. If someone recognizes me, it's all over."

Johnny hadn't thought about any of the details involved in trying to live secretly when you'd previously been an It Girl.

"Have you ever thought about surgery? To change your appearance?"

Hannah sighed. "Yes. And I would do it in a heartbeat. But rule number one is to keep Piper safe. And we look way too similar. I'm afraid that if I altered my appearance, she might internalize that about her own features. Even if she said she understood and blah, blah, blah. There'd be no way of knowing how she'd react until after the fact. And her mental health isn't something I'm willing to risk."

A moment of silence passed as Johnny tried to figure out how to respond.

Feelings whispered inside him and he physically pushed against his chest to keep them from getting any louder.

"Anyway," she kept going.

Like she hadn't just opened a window into herself, revealing a soul he didn't think actually existed.

"I learned to cook." She chuckled. "Poor Piper had to eat a lot of experiments before I finally figured things out. Okay, I'm ready." Her tone switched from casual conversation to all business. "Are we going to incorporate all of his ideas? Is that the plan? Do you have any samples you wanna play with? What would you like to see from me?"

He opened his mouth and closed it again.

"Johnny?" she asked. "Did I lose you?"

"Uh..." He swallowed. "Yeah, I have a few things I think sound like him. I haven't shown him yet, but I'll send them to you." He selected the files and sent another email.

"As far as expectations, just be on time and ready to work. You can park in the back. There's a door that will be unlocked. No one will see you from the street that way."

"Cool."

He heard one of his samples start playing on her end.

"Oh, I like this." Her tone soft and excited. "I like this a lot."

"So I'll see you Monday?" He cleared his throat. He needed to get off the phone now. For his own sanity.

"Oh." She sounded confused. "Yeah."

"Great."

He hung up the phone and threaded both his hands through his hair, holding his head in his hands.

This was such a bad idea.

CHAPTER SEVEN

OUT FROM UNDER

HANNAH

"Are you serious right now?"

Hannah looked down at her appearance. "What do you mean?"

Piper reared back with wide eyes. "People will see you like that."

Hannah couldn't, nor did she want to, hide her smirk. "That's the point, pipsqueak."

"You look hideous," Piper rejoined flatly.

Hannah barked a laugh that went all the way to her gut. She loved this kid. Everything about Piper was amazing, but Hannah took special joy in the moments when Piper felt free to say exactly what she was thinking.

They felt like little victorious fireworks in her heart. Boom, boom, boom.

Also, Piper was correct. She *did* look hideous.

She had decided to go the face paint route this week. She bought a pair of yellow skinny jeans, of course the shirt she'd purchased last week. But the best part was the realistic badger face paint she'd done on herself.

Wolverine, whatever.

She found a face paint tutorial online last night and thought she'd done a pretty damn good job making it work.

"Why?" Piper asked with a wave at Hannah. "What's the purpose of this?"

"To support you." Hannah grabbed her keys. "We should go."

"What—" Piper pinched the bridge of her nose and huffed. "What are you supposed to even be?"

"A wolverine." Hannah gestured at the shirt to help with the visual. "Your mascot."

Piper dipped her head to her shoulder and scrunched up her nose. "Remember that abomination you made me watch with you? *Cats?*" She nodded. "*That's* what you look like."

Hannah grinned. "I love you."

"You show it weird," Piper said, trying to stifle a giggle.

They drove to the school, grooving to 311. When they parked, Piper didn't wait for Hannah. She just grabbed her gear and ran for the gym doors.

Hannah smiled to herself.

Last week she had waited for Hannah to lead the way, hanging back. Either she was feeling more comfortable with her role on a team, or Hannah had underestimated how terrible she looked as a rabid badger.

She checked to be sure nothing was plugged into the car and charging before she locked the doors. She didn't need a repeat of the week before.

Geez, had that really only been a week ago?

Casually, her gaze drifted around the parking lot. No silver Camaro.

She expected to feel relieved. But was startled by the heavy disappointment that settled in her chest.

They weren't friends.

Far from it.

Not even frenemies.

They were…

Lessons.

That's it.

Just more lessons to be learned.

* * *

It was the line of middle-aged women lining up at the concession stand that tipped her off.

Now that it had been pointed out to her by Sarahi, she couldn't not see.

They were ten deep by the time the shutters opened and the bustling kitchen was revealed.

Johnny stood at the counter, wearing a light blue Henley this time. Sleeves shoved up to his elbows.

"Vultures."

Hannah glanced up to see Sarahi standing over her.

She took out a napkin from her designer handbag and wiped off the wood of the bleacher seat. Then she carefully turned around and took a seat. She was wearing a pale blue bodycon dress with four-inch stilettos that looked like blue snakeskin.

Sarahi eyed Hannah's attire up and down, and her lips twitched.

"I like this look. Very wild kingdom."

Hannah just shook her head. How else could she respond?

Also, why was Sarahi sitting beside her again?

Was it possible?

Did she have a bleacher friend? Someone to sit with at the games?

The idea was so sudden and fun that Hannah found herself grinning at Sarahi.

"Cut it out. You look like a lunatic."

Hannah's grin shrank to a smile and she turned her attention back to the kids warming up on the hardwood. Which just happened to be right between her and the concession stand.

"Every year the school asks him to participate in the bachelor auction," Sarahi supplied without prompting. "And every year he says no. It makes me wonder if he just said yes and let the women tear each other to pieces, it would be finished."

Hannah chuckled. "He's your cousin?" She tried to remember what Sarahi had told her last week. Cousin sounded right.

"Our mothers are sisters." Sarahi took a breath. "It's a long story."

Hannah's gaze flicked up and down Sarahi again. She still couldn't get a read on this woman who had apparently decided to adopt her as a bench-mate. To Hannah, Sarahi looked like she'd fit in better with the wealthy side of the spectators. Her shoes, bag, and dress were all designer.

But there were little things that didn't seem to fit that persona.

Sarahi wasn't wearing makeup. At first glance, no one would notice. Her dark eyes and thick black lashes provided a perfect frame. Her hair wasn't professionally styled. It hung in black, curly ringlets around her shoulders—healthy, clean, no styling products.

Her nails were bare. Well-manicured and strong. But no polish.

And she held her head with her chin parallel to the ground. Shoulders back, spine straight. And she drew attention.

Men and women alike stared openly at her when she entered a room. But she didn't seem to notice. Or maybe she was really that indifferent to public opinion.

The idea was foreign to Hannah as she had spent so many years being *very* aware of public opinion. The public and how they viewed her was how she had stayed relevant and made most of her money.

Also, it should be mentioned that Sarahi didn't seem to mind being seen with Hannah and the face paint.

Interesting.

This week's game was against a different school. Hannah didn't see the girl from last week who had given Piper a hard time.

And boy, was she proud of that little firecracker. Piper never seemed to tire. She ran up and down the court with ease. Probably because of the extra practice she'd been doing in the condo building. She'd been running sprints in the stairwell and underground garage.

Hannah joined her occasionally for the extra exercise, but Piper was like a machine.

By halftime she had barely broken a sweat.

"I'm so thirsty." Sarahi pointed her toes on one foot, showing off her eye-catching heels. "I'm afraid if I push my luck on these stairs, I'll break my neck. Would you get me a bottle of water?"

Hannah stood. "Sure. Anything else? Chili dog? Nachos? Something sloppy with red food coloring?" she teased.

Sarahi narrowed her eyes threateningly and Hannah laughed before hopping down the bleacher stairs.

This could work.

It wasn't a conventional friendship by any means.

But it was weirdly genuine.

The line for Johnny hadn't dwindled by halftime. Hannah was beginning to think that maybe Shawn getting roped into these weekends was just a way for the school to make more money selling overpriced bottled water and popcorn.

She slid into the line that seemed to be moving a hell of a lot faster.

Johnny's laugh caught her attention and their eyes met briefly. He squinted, probably trying to figure out if it was really her.

Then it was her turn.

"Two waters, please," she said to Shawn, who to his credit only gaped for a second.

Shawn set the waters on the counter and took the bill she'd set down. She picked up the bottles and sent one more smirk to Johnny.

"I see it now," Johnny said. "The rabid badger. It's terrifying." His lips twitched.

The woman at the front of Johnny's line turned to frown at Hannah.

Hannah bowed slightly. "I'm here to enlighten."

She returned to her seat, handing Sarahi her water.

At the third quarter buzzer, Johnny joined them on their bleacher bench. The crowd parted when he made his way from the floor up to the third row. Sarahi slid closer to Hannah to make room for her cousin.

Hannah sent him a cross between a smile and a grimace. It was weird. They were more than strangers, but not friends. And he was obviously close to his family, and one of the members of that family just happened to be sitting right beside her.

All the details collided in her head and tried to sort themselves into a linear order of sense.

They failed.

Or she failed.

He didn't say anything and so she proceeded to ignore his presence. After a few minutes she had blocked him out entirely. Maybe that was a gift she had. Maybe it was borderline cognitive dissonance. Maybe she just wanted to go back to sitting alone in the corner and not caring about anyone else around her.

In the fourth quarter, Sarahi stood, excusing herself to the restroom. There was seven minutes left of the game.

Johnny stood to let her out. Hannah couldn't help but notice that he took Sarahi's hand and helped her navigate the steps down from the bleachers.

No wonder the women flocked to him.

He was attractive, polite, single, and attentive.

That was an enormously rare combination.

When he returned to his seat, he sat right beside Hannah instead of leaving space between them.

"Which one is Piper?" he asked.

"Number 3," Hannah replied without thought. She stood when Piper drove down the lane to the basket. "Yeah! That's my girl!" she shouted loudly. She put her fingers in her mouth and whistled loudly.

Hannah sat back down, clapping. Piper shook her head like she was embarrassed by her sister's antics.

"She's lucky to have you."

Hannah frowned in surprise at Johnny. She even did a double take.

"What?" he asked.

"She's lucky to have me?" Hannah repeated, arching an eyebrow. His eyes tracked its movement and he shrugged.

"You're right. I misspoke."

"Yeah, you did," she readily agreed. "You know better than most that she lost the sibling lottery with me."

He inhaled and narrowed his eyes at the action on the gym floor.

"All I can do is all I can do," she muttered to herself.

Piper sat down on the bench and waved subtly at Hannah.

"Aren't you supposed to be working right now?" Hannah asked, noticing that the shutters of the concession were closed.

"We ran out of everything," Johnny explained. "That happens sometimes. So I just come out and visit with Sara."

She noticed he called her Sara and not Sarahi and it made her smile. Just a soft renaming of someone in his family.

She'd never had that.

She had that with Piper when she called her Pip or Pipsqueak. But she'd never had anyone give her a nickname. Well, not a nice one anyway. Plenty of people had called her lots of mean names.

"Where's Shawn?" she asked.

Johnny rubbed his palms on the tops of his thighs as he craned his neck, looking around the gymnasium. "He should be around here somewhere. He wanted to wash the popcorn smell off his hands before he came over to see you. Still trying to impress you, I think."

Hannah waved at her face. "Yeah, 'cause that makes sense."

Johnny rubbed his jaw with a hand, trying to hide a smile.

"I have to admit, I'm a little surprised to see you like this."

"Really?" She tilted her head. "Why's that?"

He slowly shook his head and shrugged one shoulder as he observed her painted face. "It's…" He made a noise in his throat and didn't finish the sentence.

"It's gross?" she guessed.

"Yeah?" He nodded. "But it's also not…you know. It's not cool?"

"Mm-hmm." She pursed her lips and tapped her chin with her forefinger. "Or is it so cool that it's intimidating?"

He frowned thoughtfully. "No, I don't think that's it."

She ran her tongue over her teeth and pretended to act worried about his observation. He cracked a smile.

"I'll tell you a secret. Ugly is a different form of invisible. People's eyes look away from things that make them uncomfortable. It keeps them from looking too hard." She shrugged. "And I get away with it for one more day."

"Hmm," he grunted thoughtfully.

The constant tension that Hannah carried in her belly every day eased.

Something about being able to be honest and open with someone who knew who she was. It was weird and wonderful.

She absolutely couldn't get attached to it.

They were only colleagues (and him under duress). In a few weeks, they would have drifted back into their regular life. No more crossing paths.

But she was okay with her stress being lifted for a minute. Temporary or not, any little bit helped.

The bench cleared and was replaced again. Sending Piper back out on the court.

Hannah stood, cheering loudly.

The game ended and the Wolverines won by two. The winning basket coming from Ana, Johnny's little cousin. But it was with an assist from Piper.

The two girls hugged and jumped on the court as their teammates swarmed them. Hannah wolf-whistled, so proud of the little athlete Piper was becoming.

Who would have thought?

Not Hannah.

Athletics had never been something she was into.

The closest she got to sports was running away from her problems. Hey-Oh! That was a joke.

She bounded down the bleachers and wrapped Piper in a hug from behind.

"That was amazing!"

"Did you see me do the thing with the thing?"

"I saw it!" Hannah confirmed, weirdly knowing exactly what Piper meant. So very proud of this little tiger. She'd come so far in a such a short amount of time.

Sarahi reappeared and was giving her own congratulations to her daughter, Ana. Abruptly she turned and grabbed Johnny by the arm.

"Jonathan," she said sternly. "We are having a lunch at Mama's. Will you come?"

Johnny's gaze bounced to Hannah's and she looked away so as

not to eavesdrop. Their family dynamic was fascinating to her, but it wasn't her business.

"C'mon, kiddo, let's celebrate."

Piper shoved away from her. "Not until you wash that atrocity off your face."

* * *

JOHNNY

"How's the studio?" Dr. Ignacio asked, passing Johnny a basket of bread.

"It's going well," Johnny answered honestly. "We have an important client lined up for next week."

"How about you?" Mia asked, nudging Shawn with an elbow. They were the cousins closest in age. Mia was Sarahi's youngest sister and only a year older than Shawn. "Have you picked a college yet?"

Shawn darted a look to Johnny before answering. "I haven't."

"Come to Northwestern with me!" she said excitedly. "You'll love it! It has all the things you love there."

"Maybe," Shawn said noncommittedly.

What he didn't say was what Johnny already knew.

Shawn was putting off accepting any offers. He wouldn't admit why, but Johnny guessed it was because he was hoping he'd make it big in music sooner rather than later. Which would make college a nonissue.

Johnny was trying not to push it. He was hoping Shawn would make the right decision on his own.

Even if that didn't match what everyone else thought was the "right" decision.

"Don't do what your brother did. He put all his eggs in one basket," his aunt Carmen warned from the end of the table.

"We don't actually have to go over this again," Johnny reminded her with a pointed look.

"And what happened?" she went on like he hadn't said anything. "He had nothing to fall back on when his dreams didn't come true."

"It all worked out, *Tia*," he said soberly. "I have my own home, my own business. I'm happy."

"No wife, no babies, and don't lie to me about being happy. I know you better than that."

Johnny grit his teeth together and stared down at his plate. This was why his visits with the family were few and far between.

Being lectured was his least favorite part of being the oldest male child.

Especially since he wasn't a child in the least. He was thirty-six and still getting scolded like he was eight.

Not that it was really anyone's fault.

They only knew the story he had told them.

Which was mostly the truth.

With a few key details left out.

Like how he'd fallen in love dick-first.

He had failed to mention that.

There was no way of knowing if things would have gone any different had he never fallen for Ashton James. No one had ever mentioned to him anything about going on tour. That had solely come from her. And that was just pillow talk. He could see that now, obviously. Now that he was an adult and had a few more years of experience with life.

Rational people didn't open themselves to empty promises made with wine-stained kisses.

* * *

After dinner was finished and the dishes were done.

After cold beers had been passed around and imbibed.

Aunt Carmen cornered him in the sunroom.

Ambush.

Johnny should have seen it coming.

Carmen had always been a stealthy hunter. She was patient and gentle. And just when her prey thought they were in the clear, she pounced. Like a jungle cat.

"It's been sixty-three days since I have seen you, *mijo*."

"It's weird that you count."

"I made promises."

That was true. And he really couldn't fault her for that. It was the only connection she had left to someone they had both lost for all the wrong reasons.

He finished his beer and set it aside. One of the middle children ran by and picked it up. Adding it to their take, no doubt.

The kids spent the day playing and secretly gathering all the empty bottles and cans to take to the recycler the next day. On a good weekend they could make enough money to buy movie passes for most of them.

"Have you heard from her?" he asked, the words sticking in his throat.

Instead of answering, Carmen ran her fingers through his hair, tugging at the longer strands and tsking under her breath. "Such long hair."

He stared into her dark eyes, so much like his mom's. Her fingers touched his chin softly and their eyes met. Hers turned sad.

No, then.

Johnny looked away, the old sting of loss and grief hitting him in the chest.

It had been two years since he'd last spoken to his mother.

It had been fifteen years since he'd last seen her.

He wished she knew about what was happening in their lives. He wished he could call her and tell her about Shawn and the list of colleges he could choose from. He wanted to brag that even though she'd abandoned them, they were okay.

Maybe they were better for it.

"I wish she would've stayed," he said, voice rough with emotion.

"So do I. But at least she got you boys out of that life first. She had enough clarity for that."

Maybe it should've made him feel better.

But it didn't.

It hadn't helped fifteen years ago, and it didn't help now.

It still felt like loss.

How was he supposed to qualify it?

Shawn didn't even have any memories of her anymore. She'd faded from his mind and Johnny had allowed it.

He didn't want to make him remember the shell of the woman who had given birth to him. That wasn't the mom Johnny knew.

Johnny's mom had been alive and vivacious. She'd been bright and warm and loving.

So he held those memories to himself. Always hoping maybe…

Maybe that person would come back. Even though he knew she wouldn't.

That person was gone.

"It might be time to let her go," Carmen said.

"How?" Johnny asked, because he really couldn't figure it out.

"I don't know," Carmen confessed, wiping at tears on her cheeks.

Johnny put an arm around his aunt, his mother's only sister, and they cried quietly together.

The only two people who really knew what the world had lost.

CHAPTER EIGHT

I'M A SLAVE 4 U

JOHNNY

It was only the first day and Johnny was already in trouble.

"What if we add a little of this? You know? Like a little Bowie vibe happening?"

Sunshine barked a laugh when Hannah slightly wiggled while playing a riff on the piano.

This was bad.

He knew it was going to be bad, but he had no idea how bad it would get so quickly.

She'd been on time. A fact that Johnny was unhappy he'd noticed.

And not just on time but prepared.

And on a morning when they'd woken up to freezing rain. It would have been the most excusable reason to be late or not show up at all.

But there she was.

In baggy jeans and an oversized sweater.

Her hair was braided on both sides and she was wearing those ridiculously oversized black-framed glasses.

And she'd brought coffee for everyone.

"I like her," Nikki said dreamily at his shoulder.

He grimaced her direction.

"She's cool."

"She's not a nice person," Johnny muttered, more to remind himself than anything else.

"I didn't say she was nice." Nikki bounced on her toes, sucking on the straw of her frozen coffee. "I said she was cool and I like her." She looked up at Johnny with mischievous eyes. "Can we keep her, dad?"

"You're a pain in my ass," he growled in reply.

Nikki snickered and bounced toward the door without an argument.

He ground his teeth together and flipped the intercom switch. "That sounds really good. Let's try it."

Hannah glanced up, her blue eyes startled.

And wild.

This was exactly why he didn't want her in his studio.

She was like a drug.

Intoxicating, fun, addictive. And she'd drag everyone down with her if he wasn't careful.

HANNAH

Well, fuck.

She had forgotten Johnny was there.

This was the problem.

Music made her drunk.

Not literally…but it was close enough.

It had gone straight to her head.

She was giggly, buzzed, hyper, happy, fucking *enamored.*

But there was Johnny. The cold bucket of water to her overactive endorphins.

Good thing she'd brought her knitting along.

Yes, she was now someone who carried knitting in her purse. She'd always thought she'd be a lot older and have grandkids before something like that happened. But that was probably just a stereotype taught to her by the entertainment industry.

When she'd been in Mad About Ewe with Josh last week, no one in there appeared old enough to have grandkids.

Perhaps knitting was what the cool kids had been doing all along.

Right now, she needed to focus.

As much fun as she was having with Sunshine, she couldn't let it get out from under her. Promises would be kept this time.

Johnny wouldn't miss his shot because of her.

One of the fun and exciting parts about working with Sunshine was his immense talent. His voice alone belonged on Broadway.

His mind for rhyme was like nothing she'd experienced. It was as if his mind moved faster than others.

"How do you do it?" she asked, scribbling down the last few lines he'd spit at her.

"Do what?" he asked, tugging on his thin beard.

"Think that fast. Writing takes me a lot longer."

He laughed deeply. "The blessings of ADHD."

"No shit?"

"The way it was explained to me is this." He sat down at the drum kit on the other side of the live room, picked up the sticks, and tapped on the snare. "Your brain can process information one thing at a time, filter it into a list of priorities, and you deal with each thought in order." He rattled the high hat. "Mine doesn't do that." He tapped out a beat as he spoke. "Everything enters my brain at full speed and all at once. All of it comes across as a priority."

"That sounds…" She stopped before she said something insulting.

"Frustrating?" He stopped drumming and set the sticks back down. "It really is. But I've been managing my symptoms for years. I can use it to my advantage now."

She studied his face. "Is that why you have tattoos on your face?"

He barked a laugh. "No. Those are just because I'm an ugly dude and I know it."

She raised her eyebrows and laughed despite herself. "What?"

He gave her a look. "C'mon. I am *not* good-looking. But I'm really fucking rich. So chicks want to fuck me all the time. There's literally no way to know if they like me at all. I figure if I beef up my ugly factor, I can weed out the shallowest of the bunch."

She frowned. "That's kind of brilliant. And also incredibly sad."

He lifted his chin at her. "But you get it. You're the hot chick."

She jerked her chin back, uncomfortable with the statement.

"How many times have you questioned whether someone was into you for who you are and not your body?"

She snorted. "Dude, I wonder that about *myself* all the time."

JOHNNY

These little heart-to-hearts that Hannah and Sunshine were having in between recordings was driving Johnny mad.

But he also recognized the bright moments of beauty in them. Which was why he recorded all of it.

Maybe Sunshine would want to add them in between tracks or on a bonus release.

Either way, Johnny felt in his gut that both of those people had gems to share and had no idea.

Taking a small break, Johnny went to the supply closet to get a couple fresh mics. He wasn't happy with the way the one they'd been using sounded on playback.

When he came back to the control room, Hannah was sitting on one of the couches, knitting.

He nearly stumbled.

Sunshine entered right behind him, coming back from the bathroom.

"Knitting?" Sunshine asked.

"Maybe," Hannah replied with a snort. She held up her needles and the yarn. It didn't look like anything.

"Whatcha makin'?"

"A hat?"

Sunshine barked a laugh. "You don't sound so confident."

She sighed and dropped the knitting in her lap. "I'm having difficulties."

"Then why do it?"

Hannah's eyes bounced to Johnny's, and he looked away but kept his ears tuned to her answer.

"Two-fisting Cabernet and a long drive in a Cadillac isn't an option. My sponsor suggested knitting. Music happens to be a fairly huge emotional trigger for me still." She rolled her eyes. "Go figure. Music? Trigger emotions? What?" She tried to laugh it off.

But no one else laughed.

Sunshine studied her silently for a beat. "Can I have the hat when it's done?"

She glanced up with a frown. "Seriously?"

He nodded with a smirk. "Oh, hell yeah."

Did Sunshine know who she was? Johnny was tempted to ask. But if Sunshine didn't know, that would at least alert him to the fact that she was *someone*.

"We're ready," Johnny announced.

Sunshine stood and headed into the isolation room.

It was time for his vocals.

Which Johnny was thankful for, because if he had to hear any more about Hannah being a different and better person, he was going to scream.

Except that deep in his chest was a craving to know more. His mind was flooded with questions. His desire to know more needed to be squelched.

"I like his face tattoos," she said.

Johnny closed his eyes, not realizing she had brought a chair over and was sitting by his side, close enough to touch. His ears flamed hot, but he reminded himself that she hadn't heard his previous thoughts. Those were still private.

"I've never understood face tattoos," he mumbled, switching the intercom switch. "Whenever you're ready."

He flipped the track and the beat started.

I miss you,
I wish you the best, though,
Despite good advice, I have tried to come home,
Suffice to say it didn't work, though,
I'm not good with solo
With me and control
You're better off alone

For real, I am reeling,

I'm feeling I'm broken
My soul is contorted
I can't be restored, though
I hope this recording
Finds you emotionally supported
It seems I have witnessed
The disappearance of my best friend but
I hope that your halo on your head
Is forever protected

'Cuz I would have wrecked it.

"Perfect," Johnny declared.

"What if you add this," Hannah murmured at his shoulder. She clicked and flipped and switched the board like she'd done it a hundred times.

A piano riff she had been playing with earlier came through the speaker, added to the beat.

Johnny heard what she was doing and made a few changes, morphing the sound.

Sunshine grooved in the booth, and on instinct, Johnny flipped the record switch.

Sunshine sang/rapped once more, this time with more emotion in his voice.

"Damn, he's glorious," Hannah whispered.

Johnny cast a glance her way. She sat with one leg crossed over the other, leaning forward with her elbow on her knee and her chin on her fist. Completely absorbed in the magic happening in the booth.

"How was that?" Sunshine asked after.

"Even better," Johnny replied, like he didn't believe it himself.

"That's fuckin' tight," Sunshine agreed. "Let's do the next verse."

Johnny made the changes quickly and nodded in Hannah's direction. "You wanna?"

"Yeah, I got it," she said, already moving.

She had to lean into his space just slightly, and her side pressed against his arm for the briefest of seconds.

Johnny flinched.

"Sorry, my dude," she apologized, sounding sincere but also amused. "Okay, ready."

Johnny ran everything together and hit play.

Sunshine grinned and bopped along in the booth.

Johnny hit record.

HANNAH

"Are you okay?"

Hannah glanced up from the grocery list she was making and smiled at Piper. "Yeah. What's up?"

"Are you sure?" Piper asked, frowning slowly. "You've been staring at the wall for ten minutes."

That wasn't surprising to hear.

She'd been thinking about the day's events and how fun it had been.

And now she was just enjoying the peaceful feeling of her creativity having been stroked.

Hannah lifted a shoulder. "Just thoughtful is all."

"About today?"

Hannah narrowed her eyes at Piper. She was too insightful for a twelve-year-old.

"Yes, about today."

Piper pulled a chair out and sat down. She folded her hands together on the tabletop, like the tiny adult she was.

Little alarm bells went off in Hannah's mind as she observed the strong tilt to Piper's jaw, the determined glint in her eye, and the vague flicker of fear.

It was still too easy for Piper to assume the role of counselor or adult in any given situation. It was too heavy a burden to bear for one so young.

Hannah wondered if Piper would ever lean out of that role. A pang slid through her heart at the thought of Piper never being liberated from that.

The best way to silence Piper's fears were to address them honestly.

Hannah sat back in her chair.

"It's been interesting being back in the studio. It's given me a lot to think about."

Piper licked her lips and squared her shoulders.

"Do you miss it?"

And that right there told Hannah that no matter how messed up they had started, or how many times she still got things wrong, they were on the right path together. Because Piper could ask the real question. The one that was at the heart of her. Without fear of reprimand.

"No." Hannah shook her head. "I don't miss it."

Piper's determination wavered with the unexpected response. "Are—isn't it fun?"

"Yeah, it's fun." Hannah smiled sadly. "I will always love writing and creating music. But that doesn't translate to missing what I had. The fame, the schedule, the heartbreak? No, I don't miss that."

Piper's eyes shined with held back emotion and she looked away. "Are you sure?" she asked roughly.

She leaned forward and placed a hand over the top of Piper's folded ones. "Look at me, Piper." Piper looked, biting on the inside of her cheek to keep herself from crying. "I didn't leave all that for you. I left for me. I left before I even knew about you."

"But I worry," Piper whispered, her throat thick with tears. Large drops formed in her eyes and slipped down her cheeks. "I worry that I'm keeping you from what you love."

"You're not," Hannah answered simply. "I've never been one to be pushed around. I have made every one of my choices. Good and bad. Getting sober and jumping ship, that was one of the good ones. Finding out about you came at just the right time."

"What if you regret taking me on?"

"Nope," Hannah said solidly. "I know regret. I'm comfortable with regret. Regret is my soul sister."

Piper snickered and wiped away the tears.

"But…"

Hannah held up a finger, silencing the girl. "Butts are for pooping."

Piper giggled despite herself and then sighed. "You're so weird."

"Yeah. Don't tell anyone else, okay? I have a reputation to maintain."

She touched Piper's dark bangs and brushed them out of her red-rimmed eyes. "You feel any better?"

"A little." Piper nodded and tried a watery smile.

"C'mere, pipsqueak." Hannah slid away from the table and opened her arms. Piper dove in headfirst, burying her face in Hannah's chest. Hannah smoothed her hair back and kissed the top of her head. "I love you. I will always love you. I promise, I have no regrets when it comes to you."

Hannah didn't make promises anymore. Not unless she was certain it was one she could keep.

That one?

Easiest promise she'd ever made.

* * *

JOHNNY

"That sounds amazing."

Johnny turned the song off and spun in his chair.

"Hey, you made it." Johnny stood and embraced Shawn. He was hoping he'd make it down to the studio before he'd left for the night. He was excited to show him what they'd accomplished that day.

Shawn looked around the studio.

"Is she still here?"

"Nah, she had to get going. But you should hear what she helped put down today."

Shawn's face fell a little and Johnny felt for the kid.

Ashton James had been his musical idol for years. To have her this close and not be able to do anything with that had to be one of the hardest things the teenager had ever experienced.

"She has to be out of here by five so she can get home," Johnny explained softly.

"Right, no, that makes sense." Shawn flopped onto the couch and forced a smile. "Show me what you made today."

"You're gonna love this," Johnny promised. He flipped the switches to get back to where he needed to be.

Sunshine entered the control room at that moment. He'd been playing with a guitar in the dead room.

"Hey, you must be Johnny's brother," Sunshine greeted, sticking out a hand.

Shawn stood up and greeted the rock rapper with a coolness that Johnny didn't have at that age.

"Cool to meet you, man," Sunshine went on. "Johnny tells me you're a musician too."

Shawn smiled shyly and ran a hand through his hair. "I dabble. Nothing interesting, though."

Hmm.

"Fire it up. Let's see what the kid thinks," Sunshine instructed, taking a seat on the arm of the couch.

The track began to play and Johnny heard Hannah's touch through the entire thing.

One word: golden.

He remembered her having that gift way back when she had little to no experience and flirted her way into making sure her tracks came out to her preference.

"Damn, it does sound like Bowie," Sunshine chuckled.

"But not overtly," Johnny pointed out. He turned it up and glanced at Shawn, who was grinning.

He could hear it too. The unmistakable fingerprint of Hannah Lee. No matter what her name was now, her heart still beat in perfect, musical rhythm.

It was actually kind of sad that she had left the entire industry behind. They were less without her.

Well, not Sunshine, obviously.

And now Johnny would benefit from her gift as well.

Potentially.

He didn't want to get ahead of himself. They had two tracks down and four more days of work ahead of them.

But the rest of the week would probably go fast if it was anything like that day had been. They'd spent a portion of the day getting a feel for each other's vibe and learning how best to work together.

It had all clicked pretty quickly.

All Johnny had to do was not get sucked into her undertow and everything would be fine.

He just had to keep reminding himself that she was a devil woman. Beautiful, talented, and smart.

But also mean, selfish, and cruel.

He couldn't forget that.

CHAPTER NINE

EVERY TIME

HANNAH

She'd been early on purpose.

For whatever reason, walking into the studio and having Johnny stand there with his arms crossed was more intimidating than she had expected.

She needed to feel more grounded before she lost her cool and found her bad attitude.

Good thing Nikki had already been there to let her in. Though she wouldn't have minded waiting in the cold if only to feel superior in a weird way when Johnny showed up.

"When did you get here?" came the expected growl behind her. And damn but if it didn't turn her insides to Jell-O.

Strong men were always a weakness.

She had a serious problem with guys who enjoyed calling the

shots. If only to drive them crazy and show them who was *actually* in charge.

She didn't look up from her knitting when he entered.

"About a half hour ago."

He stalked into the room, his energy taking up the entire space.

He smelled like leather and cheap soap.

"I brought you a coffee."

"You don't have to do that."

Again with the growl.

She raised just her eyes to him and he scowled at her.

"Does it bother you? That I brought coffee?"

This was dangerous territory. Deliberately baiting him.

Her heart pounded with excitement.

"Kinda," he snapped. He turned around and hung his coat up on the hook by the door. Hannah pressed her lips together to keep from smiling.

"You sound like you need coffee." She hid her smile behind her cup.

He huffed, putting his hands on his narrow hips.

It probably was a little like torture for him to have her in his space. Considering all the history he still carried around. She didn't have quite the same burden. While she most definitely did what he remembered her doing, she had very little memory of it. Which meant it was easier for her to push it aside.

"How old were you?" she asked, tilting her head to the side.

"What?" he asked, thrown off by her question.

"When we met the first time. How old were you?"

He looked around the room, agitated. "Old enough to know better."

"That's not a thing."

His eyes sharpened on her. "Yeah, it is."

"No," she disagreed. "It's not. No one is old enough to know something they haven't learned. Age isn't a stipulation for knowledge. And it certainly doesn't replace experience."

"So why does it matter how old I was?" he countered.

She studied his face, the life she saw there. His eyes were so *lived in.*

"Because I wonder if it would make a difference in triggering my memory. If I could see you at that age." She shrugged because she really had no idea. "Maybe if I could remember what you do, I'd feel just as uncomfortable about this as you do."

He stared at her.

"I'm not uncomfortable."

She raised her eyebrows, challenging his declaration.

He sighed. "I'm working on it."

She didn't push it and instead focused on her knitting. Which actually took a lot more focus than she was proud of.

"How's the hat coming along?" he asked.

She was thankful for his soft subject change. It felt like he was trying something new and she didn't want to discourage it.

"It's a very expensive disaster."

He chuckled. "Having trouble?"

"You know, I don't usually have this kind of problem learning new things. Not to brag too much, but I happen to have many undiscovered talents. Things that are difficult for others have always come easy for me. Music, for example. But this." She shook the ugly mess of yarn and needles in her hands. "This is not easy."

After a beat of silence, she glanced up and caught his small smile. Their eyes met for a breath and he looked away. He sat down at the board and started flipping switches.

Maybe seeing her struggle with something was amusing to him.

It *was* kind of amusing.

And if she could do her part in helping him not feel so threatened by her presence, she would.

There was no way for him to know this, but she wasn't going to bail. She was done ruining lives. It was too exhausting of a reputation to maintain and she didn't need that kind of burden hanging around for Piper to inherit.

"What is wrong with you people?" Sunshine grumbled as he shuffled in and collapsed on the far sofa. He twisted his head so his face was facing outward instead of in the cushions. "The whole reason I became a rock star was so that I didn't have to be awake before noon."

Hannah couldn't help but smile.

Yeah, she had told Piper she didn't miss the life, which was still true. But if everyone she had worked with had been like Sunshine and Johnny, her answer may have been different.

* * *

"I found this funk guitar in the dead room last night," Sunshine announced and then left the live room.

Hannah looked up at Johnny in the control room. "Well, that's an exit."

Johnny shook his head, confused as usual by Sunshine's moves. It made more sense to Hannah now, since their small talk yesterday about his ADHD.

It was a small break in between tracks. They were making good progress that day. Johnny was very focused, and Hannah had successfully been able to keep Sunshine on task even when he'd found anything and everything to distract himself.

But they all needed to take a breather before the next one.

The next one was going to be a tad bit complicated, and they would need to multitrack it very carefully and in a certain order.

Hannah could tell Sunshine was getting a little bored, so she called for a breather despite Johnny's very handsome glare through the control window.

But if she didn't, it was possible Johnny was going to strangle Sunshine.

She couldn't imagine what it must be like to work with him full-time. The job had to come with a specialized butterfly net. The guy was all over the place.

But she had noticed that if she kept him filled up on caffeine, keeping him focused was a slight bit easier.

Just when she was considering following him, Sunshine came back into the live room with said guitar in hand. He plugged it in and gave a couple test strums.

The song he began to play was more than a little familiar and Hannah started to nod along with it.

She wasn't sure if she'd ever heard Cat Stevens' "Wild World" played as funk. But damn it sounded good.

Though Hannah had always been a sucker for some funk.

She began to slightly bounce on the piano bench and do a little beatbox with her mouth.

Johnny stood up in the control room and stared down at them with wide eyes.

Out of the corner of her eye she saw Nikki and Shawn rush in, grinning.

Hannah stood up and bopped closer to Sunshine, who was clearly born to play funk.

Sunshine began to sing the song, but he didn't know the words. Though he tried. Laughing, Hannah began to sing with him to help him out. He faded out just as Shawn took a seat at the drum kit and came in with a beat. Nikki produced a tambourine.

Something happened in that moment, both familiar and intoxicating. A particular anomaly she only experienced with other creatives.

All three of them sang along with the chorus. Nikki harmonized with Hannah for the next stanza, and then it was just an all-out jam session.

By the end, all of them were singing the chorus at the top of their lungs.

But Cat Stevens had always had the power to bring people together.

Hannah threw her head back and laughed deeply.

These people.

What a riot.

Sunshine put the guitar down and went over to greet Shawn.

"That kicked ass," the artist told the younger man, causing him to blush.

Shawn shot a shy look to Nikki, but the blonde wasn't paying attention.

But Hannah saw it.

And it did something to her heart. A little stumble of awe and understanding.

He glanced up to her and smiled more fully. "Hey, Hannah," he said, careful to use the name she preferred. He picked up a guitar case he had put down when he'd gotten there. It wasn't the one she was used to seeing him with.

"Hey, Shawn." She smiled at the younger version of Johnny and that weird feeling of familiarity hit her again.

Was her memory trying to connect him to the Johnny of the past or of the present? It was all so foggy and disconnected. Like a smoke tendril quickly dissipating even as she grasped for it.

"Guitar, drums, singing, is there anything you can't do?" Sunshine showered the young musician with praise, grasping him by the shoulder and steering him to the stairs that led up to the control room.

Nikki bumped Hannah's knuckles with a fist and ducked out, headed back to what she'd been working on before.

Hannah took a deep breath, the electricity from the previous moment still coursing through her body, making her feel tipsy.

She sprinted up the metal staircase and joined the guys in the control room.

"Why aren't you at school?" Johnny asked Shawn sternly.

Hannah exchanged an "Oh, shit" face with Sunshine.

"It was a half day." Shawn shrugged, unconcerned with Johnny's inquiry.

Johnny's eyes narrowed suspiciously, and Hannah almost laughed.

"Besides, you left this at home." Shawn set a beat-up guitar case down.

"It was a choice," Johnny responded darkly.

Shawn shrugged, the picture of teenage nonchalance.

"You were playing it last night and I thought you might need it today." He gestured to Sunshine and Hannah. "Looks like it's a jam session right now anyway."

Johnny's jaw ticked and Hannah could tell Shawn had overstepped. Whether it was deliberate or not, it was harder to discern.

"Ooh, Johnny's guitar," Sunshine said eagerly, not reading the room correctly.

Shawn knelt and flipped the locks. He lifted the lid and pulled aside the blanket that covered the instrument.

Hannah recognized it from the night she had stormed into their home. It had been sitting in a stand, off to the side…

The slither of familiarity crept further up her insides.

Shawn lifted the guitar from its case and handed it over to Sunshine for his assessment.

Sunshine sat down on the sofa and laid the Gibson across his lap. He tested a few strings, checking for tune.

"I forget sometimes, you know." He chuckled. "How it all starts with the simplest thing. With wanting to be a part of something that connects us. As people. Music and emotion are so huge." He sniffed a soft laugh. "And I get to make it."

Hannah swallowed and her eyes darted to Johnny, who was already looking at her. Johnny crossed his arms over his chest and swiveled his chair away.

Hannah was missing something.

She could feel it.

"She's a beauty," Sunshine admired, delicately plucking the strings in a vaguely familiar tune.

"Johnny's had it since high school," Shawn supplied, taking a seat on the arm of the sofa. "You should hear him play. Most talented guy in the world."

"You wanna play us a lick, Johnny E?" Sunshine asked.

"I don't think anyone wants to hear that." Johnny laughed it off.

"C'mon, Johnny, show them what you were playing last night."

Johnny glared over his shoulder at Shawn. "That wasn't anything. Just messing around."

"He must've been inspired or something because it's not often I can get him to play Bowie."

"Bowie?" Hannah blurted, despite herself. Thinking about the slight Bowie-esque feel they had incorporated into yesterday's work.

Johnny glanced her way. "You don't want to hear me play it."

It sounded like a warning.

A personal one.

For her.

That familiar slither climbed higher and wrapped around her throat.

"C'mon, I need it. A little break. You guys have been working me harder than I'm accustomed." Sunshine handed the guitar over to Johnny. "We all played something to let off some steam. It's time for the team leader to do the same."

Hannah felt trapped in a swirl of memory and dread. And instead of agreeing with Johnny and trying to hide from the moment, her curiosity took over.

"Go ahead," she encouraged.

Johnny took the guitar…the way his fingers wrapped around the neck.

He licked his lips and settled it on his lap.

His black eyelashes fluttered in slow motion and he gazed at her for a beat that stretched on forever.

The guitar strings reverberated through the quiet of the small studio setting, and something broke loose in her mind.

It all came together, like a cloudy night suddenly full of stars.

Johnny's deep voice, blending with the guitar, the chipped paint on the base of the instrument, the lyrics…

Maybe it had been there the whole time, like a perfectly ripe pear on a limb. It just needed a little shake to break it free.

And Hannah was there to catch it with both hands, saving it from a bruised landing.

She turned the memory over in her heart, unable to look away. Unable to respond.

Johnny's focus remained on the instrument, and his voice both soothed and burned her soul as he sang her favorite song of all time: David Bowie's "Heroes."

A song she hadn't sung since…

She remembered.

All of it.

The day she'd walked into the studio and had seen his beautiful face.

The week of singing and writing and loving.

The intensity and immaturity.

The passion and insanity.

Oh, God.

No wonder he hated her.

Silent tears traveled from her eyes down her cheeks as the words wrapped around her heart and mind, unlocking emotions and memories that seemed too beautiful to be hers.

* * *

"I've never known anyone like you," he whispered against the soft skin of her belly before placing a tender kiss there.

His hands, strong and careful, traveled slowly from her hips to her ribs. He rested his cheek on the space between her breasts and she could feel his breath on her skin as it came back to normal.

She threaded her fingers through his hair, soothing strokes, calming, comforting, intimate. His body cradled between her thighs, the heat they'd created cooling in the night air that came in from the open window. She wondered if anyone had heard her soft cries of pleasure as he'd found her again and again.

Sex was something she enjoyed as frequently as she was able. With or without a partner, as long as she got hers.

But it was rare to have a partner who craved her enjoyment as much as his own.

Her heart pounded through her body and she pretended like it wasn't fear. She shoved the terror to the side and focused on the warmth of his skin, the feel of his heartbeat against her belly, his breath cascading over her breast.

She'd never known anyone like him either.

But she couldn't tell him that.

Sometimes the truth was hard to say. She wished she knew why.

A tear leaked from the corner of her eye and traveled slowly toward her temple and into her hairline.

"Do you think good people know if they're good?" she asked the dark.

Johnny raised himself up onto his elbows and gazed at her. She glanced down, smiling at his tousled hair and beautiful eyes. He held eye contact and pressed a kiss to her chest, right between the valley of her breasts.

Her heart did circles around them, chasing itself into exhaustion.

He didn't answer, but that was because she'd asked a question that didn't have an answer.

She hadn't ever felt like a good person.

But these moments in the dark with Johnny felt like she might be touching something good.

Which meant it wasn't for her.

She rolled out from under him and went to the bathroom to clean up.

When she returned, he had fixed the blankets on the bed and held them open for her.

She paused, taking in the quiet stillness of the moment.

And she allowed herself to feel safe.

Just for this one day.

She found his guitar in its case and crawled onto the bed, her back against the headboard. He shifted to sit beside her and she settled the guitar across her naked legs. The chill of the guitar against her breasts was a refreshing escape from the heat of her heart.

His guitar hummed with the song she played, another singer between them. David Bowie's words became a tether between their hearts, and as she sang to him, she felt him become threaded through her insides.

"That was awesome. I always forget about that song. I wonder if I could get permission to cover it for a B-side feature or some—"

"No!" Johnny and Hannah both yelled at the same time.

Sunshine jumped in his seat.

Johnny shot a look to Hannah, who ducked her head. Because everything was different now.

Now she understood more of why he didn't want her around, how uncomfortable he felt, why he tried to get out of playing the song.

It was weighty.

Like trying to push a mountain off herself.

But Hannah had never been one to be overwhelmed by an emotion.

If anything, she was more in control of her emotions than any other part of herself.

Apparently, there was a downside to therapy.

She inhaled slowly through her nose, held it for a count of four, and then slowly released it between her lips.

Sunshine said something; Johnny replied. Shawn had a rejoinder; they laughed.

She fixated on a spot on the floor and took another deep breath.

And repeated it three more times.

The discussion around her progressed, though she didn't participate.

Which was fine.

First, she had to set aside the shame and regret and grief that the memory had brought with it. The breathing technique worked.

It didn't make the feelings go away. But it no longer felt like they were getting on top of her.

She stood and rubbed her hands on her thighs. "I'm going to get something to drink. Anyone want anything?"

"No, we're good," Johnny replied.

Three sets of eyes watched her go.

When she got to the lounge, she stood in the open fridge door, feeling the cold air against her face.

Nikki was at the desk behind her, talking on the phone.

Hannah blocked all of that out and just felt the air cool her cheeks and breathed carefully, getting her heart rate back under control.

This was part of the deal.

Healing, growing, changing.

It required moments of reflection and awareness.

Sometimes she didn't get to choose when that took place.

But she knew she would have space tonight after Piper went to bed.

That's when she would unpack this and let herself cry about it.

Feeling much more in control, she turned away from the door and went to the cooler. She chose a bottle of water and returned to the studio.

Johnny's eyes came to her instantly. She sent him a soft smile, but that felt too intimate and so she averted her gaze and sat down by Shawn.

"What do you think of that?" Sunshine asked her.

"Which part?" She cracked the lid of the bottle and took a drink.

Sunshine went into a rap that she hadn't heard yet.

While shining a light, I got fries on the side,
I'm finding a lot to get by, I don't mind,
Exciting and trying, but these are the times
Holy diving and thriving, man, you are my guy,
Kind of like when you find out you're the spy.

She laughed, thankful for the lighthearted break in her thoughts.

"I like it."

"We can put it right here," Johnny said, having already made the adjustments on the board. The beat played back, and then Sunshine repeated the words again.

And just like that, they were back to work.

* * *

She stared at the call screen on her phone, straight up conflict happening at the forefront of her mind. Which wasn't like her. Hannah found it easy to be decisive. Even if she made a wrong call, she felt good knowing it was something she had chosen and could therefore handle.

But Johnny's name on the screen of her phone had her frozen.

She'd just finished yoga and was planning on meditating before going to bed.

It was late.

Too late for a work phone call.

Maybe it was an accident. A pocket-dial perhaps.

It stopped ringing, and while she'd expected to feel relieved, it felt more like disappointment.

Before she had a chance to analyze that, her phone rang again. This time it was the doorman, Charles.

"Hello?"

"Sorry to bother you so late, Ms. James, but there is a gentleman here who is asking for you."

"We work together." She heard Johnny's voice in the background, and he sounded so disgruntled, she smiled.

"Tell him I'll meet him downstairs in the lobby."

"Very good, Ms. James."

Instead of feeling worried that Johnny had determined where she lived, a thrill ripped through her.

Followed by a warning bell.

Thrills weren't great, considering her history.

Boring, bland, predictable.

That was her sweet spot these days.

She grabbed a large cardigan sweater—navy blue—and wrapped it around her, covering her gray sports bra. She slipped on her sneakers and grabbed her keys and phone.

Piper slept hard. But if she woke up and Hannah wasn't there, she'd call first.

And it wasn't like Hannah was leaving the building.

They lived in a secure building with overlapping security features.

One conversation downstairs wouldn't put Piper in any risk.

When she got to the main floor, she spotted Johnny almost immediately.

He was gazing up at the architecture in the middle of the area. His hands on his hips.

He was wearing gray joggers and a black hoodie.

"Johnny," she greeted, wrapping her arms tighter around her middle.

He turned his attention to her, mouth open to say something, but then stopped when he saw her. His gaze moved up and down her person, his brow furrowing.

"Every time I see you, you look different," he grumbled.

Self-consciously she touched her face and remembered she wasn't wearing her glasses. After yoga, she'd let her hair out of its braid to let it dry before going to bed.

She rolled her eyes and jerked her head toward a seating area where chairs and couches had been arranged into conversation circles.

Choosing a large club chair, she sat down with her legs crisscross-applesauce style.

Johnny chose the chair directly across from her.

This hour of the day, the lobby wasn't empty, but it also wasn't bustling with activity.

"What are you doing here?" she asked. "And also, how did you know I lived here?"

Johnny blinked up at the ceiling and made a noise that sounded like yet another growl.

"As a suggestion," she added, "if being near me makes you this unhappy, then don't do it if you don't have to."

He finally met her eyes and his jaw pulsed as he ground his teeth together.

"I didn't know you lived here. I took a guess."

"That's a pretty lucky guess," she remarked warily.

"Yeah, no. This is the fourth set of secure condos I've been to tonight. Pretty sure I'm on whatever amounts to the doorman watch-list of Chicago."

Her lips started to smile without her permission. The idea of grumpy Johnny going from doorman to doorman, trying to be granted access, was amusing.

He noticed the half smile and flattened his lips. "Yeah, it was hilarious."

"Why didn't you just ask me?"

"Would you have told me?"

He had a point.

"And I tried to." He sighed. "You wouldn't answer your phone."

"It's midnight," she pointed out.

He shrugged, like maybe she was right and he was being unreasonable.

"Why are you here, Johnny?" she asked again.

He tilted his head back and forth, cracking his neck. Then he leaned forward, putting his elbows on his knees, and folded his hands together.

She should have braced.

His dark eyes, usually so guarded and suspicious, gentled. His expression relaxed and he took a deep breath.

"I wanted to see if you were okay."

She slowly sat back in her chair, a strange feeling stealing through her body.

"Of course I'm okay," she said with a shrug. "Why wouldn't I be?"

He swallowed and bit his bottom lip.

"Because of today. Because I saw you."

I saw you.

Never had such a small sentence had such a significant impact on her.

She'd never been *seen*. And that was by design.

Instead of playing it off, she made a choice. A significant one.

"You weren't wrong," she admitted. "I remember..." She took a steadying breath. "All of it."

"All of it?"

"Oh yeah." She laced her fingers together in her lap and looked at her hands. "I remember you and me. I remember that whole week. I remember what I did." She brought her eyes back to his and was startled to feel tears welling in her eyes. "I know it doesn't make a difference now, but I am sorry. I hate myself too."

He didn't reply. Just watched her in that gentle way. A way that somehow gave her comfort and also made her feel worse.

She didn't deserve comfort or understanding.

And that's when she realized she was much more comfortable with him hating her.

That felt right.

"I..." He sighed. "I don't think I hate you."

She raised her eyebrows.

He nodded, like he agreed with her incredulity. "I thought I did. But now I just...I don't think that's it."

"What is it, then?" she asked, not wanting the answer. Somehow hate felt better. It was cold and easy and definitive. Anything else was uncharted territory.

Guess we're just gonna keep growing, huh?

He sat back and scrubbed a hand over his face, fatigue deepening the lines around his eyes.

And she remembered his youth. The bright, innocent hope he'd had when they'd met.

And she'd sucked it out of him like a vampire bat with a songbird.

She had seen his hope and had wanted it for her own.

Hannah closed her eyes, trying to block out the hot shame that came with unfiltered truth.

Her stomach rolled, and for a moment, she thought she might get sick.

Quickly, she pressed her fingers against her eyelids and fiercely wiped at whatever tears may be present.

"I'm so sorry," she whispered, unable to look him in the eye. She swallowed several times and took several deep breaths, trying to stop the overwhelming build of emotion.

This was why she had wanted to be alone.

The yoga had helped to focus her thoughts and calm her mind. She had planned on unpacking all of this alone.

Alone.

Alone.

Alone.

In that moment, she was exposed and cracked open. A piñata broken open with the well-placed strike of a memory. And the devastating realization that there wasn't any candy inside. No heart, or soul, or humanity.

Just more broken pieces.

A piñata filled with piñata parts.

"Hannah, Hannah, Hannah."

Somewhere, through the rush of blood in her ears, she heard her name being called. Soft and slow.

The desire to run, to hide, to get away was growing. A pressing need that rose higher in her chest, making her heart race and her breath quicken.

Oh shit.

She was going to have an anxiety attack.

No, she wasn't going to, she was having one right now.

Mother*fucker.*

"I need to go," she whispered, her voice sounding strained and rough in her ears.

"Okay." Johnny stood with her.

She could just make out the elevator doors and she headed that direction, ignoring all the demands her unreasonable body was making.

Alone.

Alone.

Alone.

"What floor?"

She licked her lips and focused on the keypad, pressing the correct ones. All she had to do was get back to her home.

Anxiety was such a tricky bitch. One minute she had complete control of her faculties, and the next she was in a losing battle with intense emotion and waves of shame.

Getting to a space where she could be alone and let it run its course had been the only lasting method.

Brenda, her well-meaning therapist, had told her that having a compassionate relationship with her anxiety would be key to not having it take over and rule her life.

Okay, Brenda.

Hannah made it to the door of her condo, opened it, and took a deep breath of comfort.

This was her space.

Her home.

The safest home she had ever lived. Piper was sleeping down that hall, her bed was just next door to that. The living room she had decorated herself with colors that made her think happy thoughts.

"What can I do?" Johnny asked.

Vaguely, Hannah knew Johnny shouldn't be there. He should go. This wasn't meant for anyone to see. But her speech was limited to only one word and she refused to utter it out loud.

Alone.

Alone.

Alone.

She took a breath and patted his shoulder. Hoping he could read from that that it was fine if he left.

She kicked off her shoes and dug her toes into the thick carpet, feeling the sensation against her skin.

Gently she sank to the floor and stretched out on her back.

The soft light from above the sink filtered into the living space. She closed her eyes and felt more tears flee the sides of her eyes and run down her temples to her hair spread out under her.

"I'm so sorry," she whispered to no one. "I wish… I wish I were different. I wish I wasn't this way. I wish I was a good person."

She rolled onto her side and her body shook with sobs. The echoes of past choices colliding with present accountability. Tremors of distaste and self-loathing.

She wanted to be a good person.

But that wasn't for her.

She knew it, but she couldn't stop wishing it.

It was the same secret wish every year on her birthday, every shooting star, every eyelash.

Wishes were as close as she'd ever get.

A hesitant hand landed on her shoulder and warmth seeped through her cardigan to her skin.

Johnny ran his hand up and down her arm. He adjusted his body to cradle hers from behind but was careful to only touch her with his hand.

On instinct, Hannah rolled back the way she'd come and faced his body. She buried her head against his chest and the warmth she found there.

All of this was wrong.

But the part of her that sensed the wrongness wasn't in control at the moment.

Right now, the anxiety was having its moment and she just needed to let it have its day.

Pushing it off only lasted for so long.

He could have left at any time. He could leave right then and she would be fine with it.

This wasn't his responsibility.

Every single part of what was happening landed squarely on her shoulders.

He wrapped his arm around her and held her close.

And Hannah Lee cried until she fell asleep, touching something good.

CHAPTER TEN

MAN ON THE MOON

JOHNNY

"Is this early call time going to be the usual or is it just for this week?" Nikki yawned and tapped her pen on the desk in the lounge.

"I think it's just for this week," he said with a tired smile.

"You look like hell, by the way," she decided to point out.

He already knew that.

He hadn't slept.

Not even a little.

Hannah had cried until she'd fallen asleep. And then it just felt weird for him to stay. What if Piper had woken up and found them together on the floor? How would that have looked?

So he'd left her there, covering her body with a blanket he'd found along the back of the sofa. And then he'd hightailed it out of there.

By the time he'd made it home it was three in the morning and he was too wound up to sleep.

He still wasn't sure why he'd sought her out last night.

What he'd told her was true, he'd wanted to check on her.

But what he didn't know was why he even cared. He'd spent fifteen years not caring how she was.

At around four he decided to go to the gym. Then he came back and showered. It was while he was picking up coffee for everyone that he realized he still didn't care if Ashton James was okay.

But it wasn't Ashton James who had fallen asleep in his arms last night.

That had been Hannah Lee.

And he barely knew her.

He handed a coffee to Nikki.

"A double dose kind of day," she remarked.

His eyes flicked to the cup already on her desk.

"She's here already?" he asked, glancing toward the hallway.

"About an hour now." Nikki yawned again. "She texted me at six and bribed me with breakfast to let her in."

Johnny let that information take a seat next to the spot he had been keeping his confusion and headed to the studio.

She was at the piano in the live room.

Her dark hair was styled in loose waves and hung down her back all the way to her waist. That's all he could see of her, but he could smell her flowery shampoo and it reminded him of last night. She'd buried her face so deep against his chest, and in turn, he had spent a good deal of time inhaling her scent.

Light came in from the windows up high and settled on her like a halo.

Dammit.

This was only the beginning of day three and he was already

letting her get away with too much of his time. And it wasn't even her fault. His mind sought her out whenever he let it relax.

Even going so far as to seek her out in the physical sense last night.

He was lucky the doorman hadn't called the cops. He hadn't realized until he'd gotten home that he'd gone out without his identification.

She was playing the piano, her voice ringing loud and bright against the unfinished walls. It was a song he didn't recognize. But the soulful sound hit him in the gut and shook his good sense.

Previously, it had hurt that she hadn't remembered him, them, or any of it.

Now?

He wasn't sure how to feel.

But he knew he didn't feel better.

She must've heard or sensed him come in because she looked over her shoulder.

The smile on her face was immediate and he had to look away or risk smiling back.

"Coffee?" he asked, heading for the stairs that led up to the control room.

He was not going to tell her how long he'd been standing there listening. It was best to act like he'd just arrived.

"I was just thinking I needed more coffee." She left the piano and followed him up the stairs.

When she reached the control room, she tossed her empty coffee cup in the nearby garbage can.

And then she approached him.

He braced.

"I, um…" She cleared her throat and slid her hands into the back pockets of her jeans. "I'm not sure how much you saw last night."

He met her gaze and recognized the red tint to her cheeks as embarrassment.

She swallowed and closed her eyes. "Sometimes when the anxiety shows up, I have to just let it happen."

"Is that what it was? An anxiety attack?"

"Not as tough as I used to be." She tried to laugh it off.

"Is it…" He wasn't sure how to ask the next question. Or if he even had a right to ask anything. "Does that happen a lot?"

A wariness entered her eyes. "Not often. I keep it managed pretty well. But sometimes, like yesterday, something can feel too big. And it overwhelms me for a minute." She blew air out and rolled her eyes at herself. "Sorry you had to see that. I know I've been saying that word a lot. It's starting to lose its meaning," she muttered. "But I am sorry. I'm sorry for a whole helluva lot."

He nodded, knowing it was true. Feeling the sincerity in her response but not knowing how he was supposed to react.

His confusion compounded.

"As scary as it was to feel all that last night, I feel better today."

He scanned her face and noticed she didn't look like how he felt. She didn't look like she'd missed any sleep at all. If anything, she looked the most refreshed she had all week. No dark circles, a healthy glow to her skin.

"A good cry does that, though." She stretched her arms over her head and arched her back into a full body stretch. "Anyway, I came in early because I wanted to work out something on the piano. And I also thought"—she scrunched up her nose as she watched his reaction—"I should probably listen to Shawn's demo."

"Why?" Johnny didn't try to hide his bewilderment.

She shrugged. "Maybe I just need a way to make it up to you. If you'd rather I stayed out of it, I will." She took a breath and he saw her brace herself. "I can't make things right. I know that. But I need to do something to prove to myself that I can make better choices now."

"And what would that entail?" he asked cautiously.

"I don't know. I thought I'd start by fulfilling a young troubadour's request."

He started to smile despite himself and cleared his throat instead. "Knock yourself out."

"Johnny—"

Out of the corner of his eye he saw her reach for him and then withdraw.

He turned to face her.

"I lied." The troubled look was back on her face.

"Lied about what?" he asked slowly.

"I lied to Terrence about you. That's why you got fired. I'd turned my phone off so he couldn't find me. And I blamed it on you." She fidgeted with her fingers and powered through her confession. "I needed to get rid of you anyway, and I took the opportunity to do it then."

Wow. That hurt. Maybe it shouldn't have, but it did. *Had* to get rid of him? As if he were some kind of hanger-on?

Nope.

No.

She didn't get to see it hurt him now.

He swallowed away the bitter taste in his mouth.

Obviously, she'd lied about him. That wasn't the issue. But he didn't realize until that moment what the issue really was for him.

It was the lies she'd told when they were alone.

Those were the ones that killed in the aftermath.

He shrugged. "Yeah, I figured."

Her brow furrowed with his response. She sucked in a breath and nodded once. "Okay."

"Okay," he repeated, and turned away.

If she was suddenly looking to be friends, that wasn't going to happen.

He sat down at the board and started switching things on to get warmed up.

"All I can do is all I can do," she muttered behind him.

He knew it wasn't meant for him to hear. She'd said it a couple of times to herself that week. But this was the first time it gave him pause.

* * *

HANNAH

Of course, there would be more.

It hadn't even occurred to Hannah that Johnny wasn't only upset about being fired. That was just a tangible focal point. Something he could point at and say, "There. That sucked."

But she was just now recognizing that she couldn't begin to know how he felt about any of it. She was only guessing.

Leaving the control room, she headed to the upstairs lounge that was normally empty.

Yahtzee.

She sat down at the work desk and pulled out her phone. Never had she needed to call her therapist between appointments. She'd been proud of herself for that fact.

Logically she knew that was a stupid reason to feel pride. Brenda was a doctor and her business was to help people. Hannah wouldn't be "bothering" by calling during business hours to ask business-related questions.

But it still felt weird to think of her emotional baggage as someone else's business.

She left a message and then made sure her ringer and vibration were on so she didn't miss the callback.

When she went back to the control room, she entered quietly, not wanting to disturb Johnny any more than she already had.

Life was a difficult motherfucker.

She wanted too many things. She wanted to be better and to do better and choose better, but she also wanted to be comfortable and at peace. Those things hardly ever coexisted.

Sometimes she would remember something she had said or done in the past and it didn't match what she would do now. It felt like someone else's memories.

Except she remembered being her.

She wasn't new, she was the same.

Just…different.

"Here's Shawn's demo," Johnny said, flicking a thumb drive her direction.

She caught it with both hands. "Thanks."

"Don't…" Johnny stopped and took a deep breath. "Don't get his hopes up, okay?"

"Okay," she managed to say around the tightness in her chest.

He nodded once and spun back to his work.

Hannah chewed on the inside of her cheek as she studied the small thumb drive in her hand.

"I have to get set up for the list today. You can use this space if you want to." Johnny nodded at her hands and then quickly left the room.

She listened to him jog down the metal staircase, and the sound rattled through her mind.

Taking a seat on Johnny's customary stool, she had a perfect view of the live room below. He was down there, moving the drum kit out of the way and getting the pedals and cords arranged.

She plugged in the thumb drive and put the headphones on.

Her ears were filled with Shawn's delicate guitar playing.

There were echoes of Johnny in there, but mostly he had his own style and sound.

Four tracks later and she had a page full of notes.

The music ended and she tapped her pencil on the end of her nose as she watched Johnny work in the live room.

Could she even do anything beneficial for Shawn? And could she do it without getting his hopes up?

He had so much talent, he just needed a few tips to really punch it up.

Her phone vibrated in her pocket, making her jump. She took the headphones off and moved to sit comfortably on the leather couch.

"Hey, Brenda." Hannah didn't waste time. She info-dumped everything that had happened that week.

"I get it better now, though I don't fully, and I know that." Hannah paused, trying to make sure she got all of her thoughts out and didn't waste Brenda's time. "But I get that there is more there than I can make up for. I did some damage to him. And he's a good person. Like, take what you think a good person should be, and then add some Captain America to it. That's Johnny. And I remember using his goodness…" She stopped, blinking back tears. "The worst part," she whispered because her voice was suddenly gone. "The worst part is I know I would do it again. I'd take his goodness and use it for myself for as long as it lasted."

"So far, during this journey you haven't had to face people who knew you from before. This is a new challenge and it's okay that it feels so out of proportion."

"But how do I fix it?"

"You can't fix it," Brenda reaffirmed what she already knew, but it fucking hurt to hear anyway. "But you can be careful with how you treat him now. Be more sensitive to his feelings. Don't push him to act like he's okay with you being there. He might not ever be. And that's okay."

"That sucks, Brenda," Hannah said forcefully, and Brenda laughed.

"I know it feels that way. But you're doing fine."

Hannah hung up the phone and stared at the floor, her emotions doing a bad impression of a limbo in her chest.

"Hey."

She glanced up to find Johnny leaning into the doorway.

"Can you come help me with something?" he asked, sounding just a little off. Had he heard her conversation with Brenda?

"Yeah, for sure," she replied quickly.

She followed him down the stairs into the live room, where he handed her an electric bass. "You can play this, right?"

She nodded. It might take her a minute to remember, but instruments were way easier than people to handle.

Johnny looped a guitar strap over his head and pushed a pedal with his foot. He strummed a few practice chords and turned to face her.

"What if we did something like…" And he started to play the melody of Sunshine's last track.

And she heard it.

Exactly what he was going for. She contributed with the bass, and after a few false starts, they found their rhythm.

A smile spread across Johnny's face as they played together, in perfect syncopation.

If only relationships were like music.

A few false starts, but if they both kept at it, they'd find a brilliant and beautiful new sound.

Hannah swallowed her remorse and focused on what Brenda had advised.

She would be sensitive of his feelings and not force him to talk about anything he didn't want to.

JOHNNY

The rest of the day was strictly professional.

Well, as professional as a recording studio could be.

Everyone did their jobs.

What more could he ask for?

He played the track back again. The one where he and Hannah had added their own energy to it.

How she'd picked up his idea so quickly still sort of blew his mind.

But there it was, evidence in the finished track.

He hated to admit that they worked really well together. Better even than the clowns he called colleagues, who ran the studio with him.

"This is your best work," Nikki said quietly, sliding into the control room and onto the couch.

"What are you still doing here?" he asked, turning off the music and shutting things down.

"What are *you* still doing here?" she countered.

"Working."

"Working or thinking?"

His lips twitched. "A little of both. Are you checking up on me?"

"Shawn asked me to see if you'd be home for dinner."

He frowned and spun around to face her. "You talk to Shawn a lot."

She picked at her nails and pursed her lips. "Not a lot. He texts me memes sometimes. Why?"

"He has a crush on you, you know."

Nikki's expression turned severe. "Jonathan Enamorado Torres, that is a serious brotherly betrayal! I can't believe you'd violate his trust like that!"

Johnny held up his hands. "You're right. I shouldn't have said anything."

"Damn right you shouldn't have said anything." Nikki sounded like she was genuinely disappointed in him.

He thought it would be some harmless ribbing. He didn't realize she'd react so strongly.

"Let's just pretend like it didn't happen," he suggested. "What do you think about what you heard a minute ago?" he asked, changing the subject.

She glowered for a few more seconds before sitting down again. "I already told you, it's your best work."

He wagged his head back and forth. "Okay, but really. What do you think?"

Nikki had a critical ear. She heard things that no one else did. He never felt finished with a project until she'd given him notes.

"I know what you're looking for and I just don't have it. No notes."

"What?" He jerked his head back, rejecting her words. "No notes?" he scoffed. "Don't be crazy."

She shrugged. "I mean, I'll listen to it again when it's finished. But so far, no notes."

She rubbed the space between her eyebrows with her fingertips and leaned forward. "Johnny, you've always been way too talented to be stuck here with us. And that becomes clearer every time you and Hannah have a moment."

He rolled his eyes and crossed his arms over his chest.

"Did you know that we call it the magic? Me and Justin and Chase. We sneak around here, listening to you two make shit up, and it's giving us life. We're here for it."

Johnny barked a laugh at her description. He shook his head because what she was saying was comical and absurd. Of course it seemed like that to them—they had no idea who she was and all she could do.

"Laugh all you want, but you know it's true." Nikki stood up to leave. "Whatever she's doing to get you to be your best, hold on to that. For all our sakes."

She left, and with her went the rest of his anger.

An idea had been trying to form in the back of his mind since that morning, but he'd refused to give it space to coalesce. So far, it was a shapeless image of impressions and feelings.

But what if…

What if they could move away from their ugly history and make something new? This record they were making together was a hint at what they could accomplish when they worked together.

What if instead of going back to work wherever she worked, she came to work with him?

Would she ever consider making music full-time again?

That was a huge question, filled with so many nuanced emotions and implications.

He'd have to think about it before he brought it up with her.

But what if, right?

CHAPTER ELEVEN

KILL THE LIGHTS

HANNAH

"He keeps reminding me you're not a nice person."

Hannah watched Johnny from her seat on the piano bench of the live room. He was up in control, checking and double-checking all the things. His brow furrowed, his jaw tense with concentration.

"He's not wrong. I'm not a nice person."

Nikki sniffed in disbelief. "Nice people are just covering the fact that they're assholes. I'd rather be around honest assholes than fake ones."

Hannah smiled, but it was a sad smile.

Nikki might think that, but she didn't know how mean Hannah had been. The potential she still carried to be that person. As much as she tried to change and be someone new, she would always be connected to Ashton James.

And no one knew that more than those who had already had a run-in with Ashton.

That included Johnny.

Sunshine shuffled into the room and yawned. She played an intro for him on the piano.

"How are you this chipper so early in the morning?" Sunshine rubbed his eyes and gave her a sleepy smile.

"It's ten, babe," she replied, waggling her eyebrows, and added a *dun dun dunnn* with the piano.

"I haven't been to bed yet, *babe*," he countered with a goofy grin.

"And whose fault is that?"

"Probably mine," he conceded. "You know they don't tell you how much hard work it takes to be this kind of popular."

You ain't kidding about that, she thought but didn't share.

"How come you haven't done anything more with this? I looked you up and asked around. No one knows you."

All at once, the world seemed to stop.

Hannah kept her gaze fixed on the piano keys, like she hadn't heard him.

It had always been a risk making music and spending time with anyone in the industry. But she also knew that the industry changed drastically all the time. Her life's Venn diagram didn't intersect with Sunshine or any of his people. Alex had checked.

But all it would take was one candid photo and a phone call, and everything could come crashing down.

"Hannah? Hannah Lee," Sunshine called.

She looked up and raised her eyebrows. "What's up?"

He squinted at her suspiciously. "How long have you been doing this?"

"Not long," she lied.

Liar, liar, pants on fire, her inner bitch mocked.

Which was fine. She could handle being mocked internally. Just as long as that bitch stayed locked inside and didn't come out to play, they were all safe.

Sunshine looked at her with heavy skepticism.

"Hannah," Johnny called through the intercom. "Can you play something? I need to check some readings up here. Piano and vocals, please."

"You got it, boss."

Sunshine and Nikki made their way up the metal staircase to the control room.

Thankfully, Hannah already had a song in her head from that morning. She and Piper had been listening to MisterWives' "Superbloom" and dancing around the condo. The song was still stuck in her head.

And it was such a fun song to sing and play on the piano.

What Hannah wouldn't give to be a part of a band like them.

If she were still in the game, that is.

By the end of the song, she was half standing on the piano bench as she sang and danced. It was just one of those songs that filled you up, and you had to let it out for fear you might die if you didn't.

* * *

JOHNNY

Maybe that had been a bad idea.

Johnny had overheard Sunshine's question and he'd offered a distraction.

But if he thought asking Hannah Lee to play and sing on her own would hide her immense talent, he had woken up stupider than usual that morning.

Her crystal voice rang through the live room, picked up by the mics he'd set up that morning and piping that sound into the control room.

He didn't recognize the song, but he was going to be asking about it later because holy crap! The way her fingers flew on the keys while also sounding powerful sent chills down his spine.

All of it was a visceral reminder of who he was dealing with.

She wasn't just the alluring young woman of his past who broke his heart and shattered his dreams.

She had been the reigning queen of pop music. She may have abdicated her royal crown, but that didn't change the fact that this woman, this inexplicable powerhouse of artistic energy, still had all the skill to return to the throne at any time if she chose.

When Hannah began dancing on the piano bench (without missing a single key stroke), he was reminded of Sir Elton John and Lady Gaga and all the greats who had come before.

The music was inside her.

And every once in a while, she graced them with her talent.

"What the fuck?" Sunshine mumbled from his side.

"Pure magic," Nikki agreed, elbowing Johnny in the ribs on his other side.

He didn't respond, choosing to keep a stoic expression.

But both the current number one artist in the nation and his long-time sound engineer were correct.

She was fucking magic.

And if Johnny could figure out how to get past just a couple of things, he was going to tell her.

* * *

PIPER

"Your mom packs your lunch every day, huh?"

Piper glanced up, unsure if she was the one being spoken to.

Ana was looking directly at her and lifted an eyebrow in encouragement. Piper shifted in her seat, her gaze drifting through the other students at the lunch table. They weren't exactly staring at her, but they were listening.

"Um, no. But yes," she quickly corrected. "She's not my mom."

"What happened to your mom?" a boy sitting beside Ana asked. Ana elbowed him.

"She died in a car accident." Piper shrugged and took another bite of her sandwich.

"Whoa," said the boy.

Sure. Whoa. Maybe to others.

To Piper it still felt weird.

Not good. Not bad. But definitely not good.

Her mom dying in a car accident had seemed almost…expected.

"So you live with your sister?" Ana asked. She batted her round brown eyes, trying to keep her talking.

Piper nodded.

On one hand, it was nice not having to sit alone at lunch. But on the other, she still felt out of place.

She finished her sandwich and reached for her water bottle.

At first, transitioning to a private school had really sucked.

Carlton Baxter Christian Academy was exactly how she'd pictured it when Hannah had told her. Stuffy, boring, and terrifying.

Piper had only ever gone to public school before. Except for that year and a half she basically didn't go to school at all.

"Where did you go to school last year?" Ana asked.

"Oh, I was homeschooled," Piper said. It wasn't totally the truth, but it's what she'd decided to say instead of trying to explain it.

Besides, she'd have to lie through most of the explanation anyway since she couldn't exactly tell people she'd been privately tutored in the Hollywood Hills until her sister got everything in order and moved them to the middle of the country.

At first, she'd tried to get Hannah to let her go back to public school.

But she quickly realized that was a losing battle.

Though it was kind of a new sensation being able to battle for herself at all.

"Homeschooled? That sounds awesome," Ana commented. She gathered her tray and stood up. "What class do you have next?"

"Study hall."

"In the auditorium or the library?"

"Auditorium."

"I'll walk with you. I have science."

Piper stood off to the side, trying not to feel conspicuous as she waited for Ana to return her lunch tray. It was probably just her imagination, but it always felt like everyone was constantly looking at her. Wondering why she was there.

Ana returned and pulled a package of wet wipes out of her backpack. "Here." She handed one to Piper. "They don't give us enough time between classes to wash our hands."

"Thanks." Piper smiled at her teammate. Maybe they were becoming friends? She would like that. Ana was a really great ballplayer, but she was also funny without being mean.

Piper had decided that a good sense of humor was going to be important for a solid friendship of any kind.

Well, that and not being an asshole.

They tossed their used wipes into the trash and Ana squeezed her hand at the doorway to the auditorium.

Piper was startled by the unexpected contact and failed to squeeze back. But Ana didn't seem to notice. She just grinned at Piper and kept going.

"See you at practice," Ana called over her shoulder.

Piper tried to reply with an affirmative, but it was stuck in her throat. And then someone pushed her from behind and she was shuffled through the bottleneck of the doorway into the large auditorium.

"Fucking hallways clots," an angry upperclassman muttered as he shoved by her.

It was strange to be in a school with grades six through twelve. At first she thought they'd be more separated. But the size of the campus didn't seem to be up to the task. She was twelve and was very often being batted through the halls and classrooms like a pinball.

Half pint knocked into the garbage bin, fifty points.

She shuffled to her preferred seat in her study hall section and waved at the teacher who was supposed to supervise them. Usually he read.

He nodded and marked her down on the attendance sheet.

There were signs all over stating how it was "study" hall, not "talking" hall. But none of the teachers really enforced that unless someone got unusually rowdy.

They didn't have assigned seats and so Piper usually went high. She was the youngest one in the class because of her late admission. So she didn't have any peers with whom to study or converse.

She set her backpack in the chair next to her and took out her journal.

No, the Carlton Baxter Christian Academy wasn't what she'd call ideal. But she was getting used to it. She wondered if kids of famous people had to keep their lineage a secret too, or if it was just her.

Not that she wanted people to know.

Actually, if Hannah had stayed in the public eye, Piper might have pushed harder to be homeschooled.

The short time she'd spent in LA after the accident had been like jumping into a spinning fan with razor fins.

A noise behind and to her right caused her to glance over her shoulder.

In the top row of the theater seats, half hidden in darkness, was a group of teenage boys. Four of them. She recognized them from her study hall, but they usually weren't in the back like they were now.

She darted a nervous look to the teacher. He was absorbed in his book. She looked back to the boys.

They were giggling and whispering and grunting.

Squinting, she made out the shape of a long folding table that had been propped against the wall.

The boys had maneuvered it to the top of the (very steep) auditorium stairs, flat side down.

One of the boys saw her watching and he held his finger to his lips in a shushing gesture. Piper blinked at him.

Because what in the world were they thinking?

The auditorium was an enormous room, with theater-style seats from top to bottom. It sat a thousand people. The stairs were narrow, steep, and carpeted.

If they let that table fly down the stairs, they could seriously injure someone.

No. Wait.

Piper inhaled sharply, and her hand flew up to cover her mouth.

The boys filed onto the table, cradled back to front with each other. The legs of the table created flimsy bookends. They rocked back and forth.

The table paused, tilting just slightly to the front, holding them in suspended animation, their faces frozen in excited expectation.

And with a sudden *whoosh* that startled Piper, the table flew down the stairs—the boys riding it bobsled style all the way to the bottom.

CRASH!

Piper slowly stood, staring at the wreckage at the bottom of the stairs.

The boys' bodies were dispersed around the table like bowling pins. The table was in multiple pieces, the front legs embedded in the front of the stage.

Mr. Davidson jogged down the stairs just as the boys started moving about.

"Oh, they're not dead," Piper said on an exhale.

For a solid minute there, she had been terrified she'd just witnessed a prank gone tragically wrong and she was not okay.

Shakely, she sat back down.

Mr. Davidson scolded the boys and escorted them out of the auditorium.

"Oof, I bet they have to see Shatface now. I think I'd prefer death by stage collision than having to go to her office."

Piper jumped. Sitting to her left was a familiar face.

He must've joined her during the commotion.

She narrowed her eyes at him, trying to remember his name, if she had ever known it.

"Shawn," he introduced, tilting his head at her unspoken question. "You're Piper, right?"

She narrowed her eyes further.

"My brother is Johnny."

Oh, right.

"You're the stalker." Piper put it all together.

He flattened his expression. "Fan."

"That's what all stalkers say," she muttered, shaking her jittery hands at her sides.

Shawn eyed her movement and licked his bottom lip. "You okay? You look a little pale."

"Yeah." Piper nodded. "I'm fine…ish."

"Did they really freak you out that bad?" he asked, kicking his long legs up onto the seat in front of him and bouncing a Superball on the floor between his legs.

"I startle easy." Her therapist called it a "trauma response." Hannah called it anxiety. Piper called it annoying.

"Gotchya," Shawn replied, but didn't ask for further explanation.

"Why are you over here?" she asked, just now putting together that he was not in her study hall class normally.

He rubbed a hand along his chin and grimaced toward the doors. "Avoiding responsibility."

Piper snorted at his unexpected answer.

He didn't say anything and resumed bouncing the Superball on the floor-seatback area. She decided to put away her journal.

"So, if Johnny is your brother, then that would make Ana your cousin?" she guessed.

"Yeah, you know Ana?" he asked with a smile.

"We're on the basketball team together."

"Right." He nodded like things were clicking. "That's why Hannah's here on Saturdays. Makes sense."

She tucked her hands under her thighs, not knowing what to talk about now. Shawn was an upperclassman. Probably a senior. And he was hiding out by a seventh grader? Yeah, that had nothing to do with who her sister was.

"I can't tell you anything," Piper finally blurted. "If you're wanting to know things about her, I can't say." She hurriedly shook her head. "I don't know anything anyway."

Shawn stopped tossing the Superball and glanced her direction. He dropped his feet to the floor and faced her more directly.

"You know she came to my house, right?" he asked.

She swallowed.

"She's terrifying," he finished seriously.

Piper chuckled despite herself.

"I can see why you'd think that's why I'm over here, but nah." He shook his head, lips downturned. "I have no intention of ever getting on her bad side again."

Piper smiled softly, her gaze drifting away. "She's not so scary."

Shawn snorted in disbelief.

"Why are you here, then?" she asked curiously.

He shrugged. "It's an open hour for me, and Shatface gets on my case." He growled low in his throat. "That woman hates me, I swear." He shook it off. "I recognized you. Thought I'd sit by you. Do you want me to go?" he offered.

"No," she answered quickly, surprising herself. "You can stay, I guess."

He grinned and resumed bouncing the Superball.

It was nice to have someone who acknowledged her existence as a human being. She understood the need for privacy for her and Hannah, she did. But it was incredibly isolating.

Isolating in a completely different way than the first ten years of her life had been.

Life Before had consisted of being alone at home. And when she wasn't alone at home, she wished she was. But she always looked forward to school because she could see her friends. *That* had been her life. Not the mockery of a life she lived with the woman who claimed to have birthed her.

If she hadn't looked exactly like the woman, Piper wouldn't have believed it.

Weren't moms supposed to love and care for their children just automatically?

Maybe that was naïve.

But then Hannah had just done it. Without being a mom ever.

So maybe maternal instincts weren't instincts for humans. Maybe they were choices.

If that was the case, she was really happy that Hannah was such a hard-ass who made deliberate choices.

CHAPTER TWELVE

UNUSUAL YOU

HANNAH

It was the final day of recording, and for the most part, things were better than usual. Everyone was on time and in a good mood.

Even Johnny, surprisingly.

Or maybe not so much.

Since that day when Hannah's memory had been jogged and she'd had a good cry about it, he'd been much more relaxed. Or perhaps that was just his response to her being a little more sensitive to him and what she'd caused.

She hated it.

Knowing what happened.

Not knowing was so much easier.

Knowing was better but more painful.

"Is this my hat?" Sunshine asked, holding her first (and hopefully her worst) attempt at making a hat.

"That's a hat?" Johnny asked around a robust laugh.

"It is a hat," she confirmed proudly. "The Flash Cache hat." She named it after the album they'd made that week.

Sunshine put it on and some of the loose strings of yarn dangled down into his eyes. "Do I look like a thug?" he asked with a chin lift.

"If thugs wore mangled stray cat regurgitation," Johnny replied thoughtfully.

"Har har." Hannah grimaced because she knew they were right. The hat was hideous. It was frustrating because she didn't usually have this kind of trouble with most things. Usually her worst handling was reserved for her human relationships. Maybe that was why. Maybe because the knitting had become a way for her to process and deal with uncomfortable emotions, it came out like that.

Or maybe knitting was really hard and she needed to stop overanalyzing it.

"Will you make me a hat?"

Johnny's question caught her off guard.

Today was the last day of recording. After today, they probably wouldn't be seeing each other again.

Except there was a teasing glint in his eye that made her want to see him again.

"You want one of those things?" she asked.

"I do," he replied with a lopsided smile.

Sunshine took out his phone and took a selfie, getting Johnny and most of the control room in the screen. Hannah ducked her head and slipped out the door.

"Team Flash Cache," he said, throwing up the peace sign.

She couldn't risk being in the background.

"Hannah Lee," Johnny's voice called down the hall. "Will you bring me a water, please?"

"Yeah," she called over her shoulder.

Did he see her duck out of frame and was he just giving her a valid excuse to be gone? Because that would be really cool if it were true.

She got a water for each of them and came back into the room. When she handed one to Sunshine, he gave her a very familiar up and down.

It wasn't one she got too often anymore and she was a little taken off guard.

Was he checking her out?

What?

But she was like ten years older than him.

Though to be fair, she had felt safe that morning and had worn clothes she liked. Black skinny jeans and an off the shoulder, sheer white sweater with a black lace bralette underneath. Black high-heeled ankle boots and a matching leather jacket. Which was just her favorite jacket of all time. It still sometimes smelled like cigarette smoke from years gone by. Something about the aged smell gave her good memories. Like getting to have a stiff drink without *actually* drinking.

Maybe that wasn't right.

Maybe it was.

Maybe she should have just left it in a donation bin long ago.

When was her next therapy appointment again?

"Do you have a man, Hannah Lee?" Sunshine asked, casually stepping into her space.

"Oh, Sunshine," she replied. "No human man could handle all that I bring to the table."

Johnny barked a laugh and Sunshine raised his eyebrows.

"So I take it my flirting is wasted?"

"You were flirting?" she questioned with a head tilt. "Are you sure?"

Sunshine laughed then too, and Johnny's had grown into a robust belly laugh.

"So this wasn't a love beanie?" Sunshine asked, rolling with her insult easily.

"Does it look like it was made with love?" she countered.

"It looks like it was made with hook hands," he quipped.

"I think if that had been the case, it would have turned out better."

"All right, all right, all right," Johnny cut them off, waving both hands. "Cut it out. We're not done, and if you keep this up, I'm not going to be able to finish."

"That's what she said," Sunshine mumbled quickly.

"I thought keeping it up was the best way to finish." Hannah tilted her head and smiled sweetly.

Johnny closed his eyes and sighed heavily.

Hannah bit her bottom lip and gave Sunshine the high-five he offered.

It had taken five days to get to this level of comfort in the studio with Johnny. But it had been worth it.

Too bad this was the end.

Unless she finally asked him if he'd record her Double Blind Study backing vocals.

She'd been considering asking Nikki to do it.

But that would tip Nikki off that maybe she and Johnny hadn't gotten along as well as they'd put on for everyone else.

She knew she needed to ask Johnny.

And she would.

Eventually.

* * *

SHAWN

"Does that make sense to you?"

Edgar nodded, his brow furrowed in concentration as he finished scribbling out his notes.

Shawn noticed his notes were in English this time.

He glanced at the clock on the wall. Nearly lunch time. Perfect.

"You're picking this up really fast," Shawn encouraged, closing his textbook and sliding it into his bag. Edgar followed suit. "You should be able to change your grade easily before the quarter ends."

"Gracias, Shawn," Edgar mumbled.

"De nada."

They made their way to the door of the science lab and Shawn held his hand up for them to pause.

Technically, they weren't supposed to be in there. But Mr. Mitchell had left the door unlocked for Shawn so he could work with Edgar in private. They used to study together in the library, but Shatford had shut that down almost immediately.

The period ended and the bell rang.

They waited in the darkened room behind the closed door for the silence of the hallway to give way to students pouring out of classes and filling the hall.

Shawn cracked the door open and followed Edgar into the steady sea of teenagers.

He collided with a small body, nearly knocking them down.

"Oof!" Piper exclaimed, ricocheting off two upperclassmen who didn't even notice. On her way back in Shawn's direction, he grabbed her elbow and steadied her.

"You straight?" he asked, keeping their momentum going with the crowd.

"Sure," she replied, not sounding sure at all.

Edgar leaned around Shawn and waved at Piper. He tipped his head back to grin at Shawn. "She's a Marty."

Shawn nodded in understanding.

He checked his watch like it mattered and followed the clot that deviated to the cafeteria. Might as well check in with the Martys.

Carlton Baxter was a weird school. It was too small for the amount of students they had, but the board couldn't agree on whether or not to expand. So lunch had to be divided into three separate periods—A, B, and C. Seniors ate first in Lunch A, grades six through eight had Lunch B, grades nine through eleven ate last. But they also had open campus, so a lot of the students just left for lunch, which helped prevent overcrowding in the cafeteria.

Since Shawn's friends usually went out and also had Lunch A, and he'd started using his lunch to tutor Edgar, he normally grabbed a snack from the à la carte line.

He swerved into the line, his gaze sweeping through the younger kids as they found their spots.

The Martys sat at the furthest table from any of the popular kids. He smiled when he spotted them.

Piper was already there, unpacking her paper bag lunch and looking like she still felt out of place.

Which was the entire reason for the existence of the Martys.

Shawn bought a bottle of lemonade and a soft pretzel and headed over.

He sat down across from Piper and Ana and right beside Edgar.

"What are you doing here?" Ana asked with suspicion.

"Eating lunch," he answered, gesturing at his soft pretzel.

"You know you're too cool to sit with us anymore," Ana pointed out.

"I'll never outgrow the Martys," he reassured, and enjoyed the snickers around him.

"He's my cousin," Ana explained to Piper.

"We've met," Piper said. Her smile was so hesitant that it made Shawn hurt a little.

"Which Marty are you?" he asked.

Piper lifted a shoulder, her expression just as lost as he expected.

He grimaced at Ana. "You didn't explain the Martys to her?"

Edgar cleared his throat and waved his hand to take over.

"She's Marty Seven."

"Yeah, that doesn't help," Piper stately flatly.

Shawn barked a laugh.

"Okay, okay." Ana waved her hands at everyone to calm down even though no one was being loud. She swiveled to face Piper.

"We are the Martys. It's something that started with Shawn and his friend Javier. It's kind of a long story, but the general idea is simple. Everyone who sits at this table doesn't fit in anywhere else. Mostly because they're ESL kids. One of the movies that we've *all* seen to help us with our English is *Back to the Future.* So we just call everyone who sits here Marty."

"I'm not an ESL kid," Piper said slowly.

"But you were sitting all alone," Edgar pointed out.

Piper blushed. "I don't know anyone."

"Now you have the Martys." Ana held her hands out like she was offering a gift. Satisfied with her brief explanation, she went back to her lunch.

Piper considered this information, and a small smile crept onto her face as she ate quietly.

Lunch was almost over when Edgar bumped him with his shoulder.

Shawn's head shot up to scan the room and he locked eyes with Shatford just as she found him.

"Fuck," he hissed under his breath.

Shatford made her way across the room and stood at the end of the table.

"Mr. Torres, I don't believe this is your lunch," she said in that uppity, stick up her ass way.

"It's an open period. I was just eating with my cousin." He waved at Ana.

Ana lifted her chin.

The conversation at the table had died and tension filled the silence.

Shatford's mouth twitched and her nostrils flared. "See me in my office after this to discuss your paper," she said coldly.

Shawn didn't reply, he just stared at the table in front of him.

After a few more uncomfortable seconds, Shatford left and conversation resumed. But Shawn didn't have anything to contribute.

If that witch thought he was going to spend one more second in her office this year, she was out of her mind.

He had more than enough credits to graduate. He was just fulfilling the attendance requirements until he turned eighteen. His volunteer services on the weekends should have been more than enough to satisfy whatever elements Shatford thought he was missing as a human.

The bell rang, and instead of going to the administration wing, he followed Piper into the auditorium for study hall.

She eyed him quizzically but didn't object when he took a seat beside her.

The bell rang, signaling the start of the next class, and he slid way down in the theater seat in case Shatford came looking for him.

"Why didn't you go to her office?" Piper asked softly.

"Because she's evil and I hate her and she can't make me," he answered blandly.

Piper nodded. "Fair enough."

Shawn sighed. "It's just been this year. I don't know what happened in her personal life, but she's been an asshole to all the students."

Piper frowned. "That's not okay."

"I miss Dr. Mendez," Shawn declared wistfully. "She had a baby in the fall and so she's gone for a little while, and Shatface is on a power trip. It fucking sucks." He glanced her direction. "Sorry for swearing."

Piper chuckled. "Oh, no worries there. I live with Hannah Lee 'Motherfucking' James."

Shawn joined in her laughter and then grew thoughtful.

"What was it like? Before she left everything behind? Can I ask that?" He ran a hand through his hair nervously. "I don't mean it in a creepy stalker way. Just…I want that life. I want the fame and the success. So, I guess I'm wondering why she left it."

Piper scrunched up her nose. "I think you'd have to ask her."

That made sense.

"But just the short time I saw it firsthand, it was actually really scary," Piper went on.

"What do you mean?"

Piper chewed on the inside of her cheek. "Like…there were helicopters hovering over her house every single day. And photographers would literally camp out at the end of her driveway like a narcissist's tailgate party. One day, she left to go to her lawyer's office and wrap up some things. She came home with all these scratches on her arms that bruised eventually because they were so aggressive with getting close to her." Piper shuddered and rubbed her arms up and down like she was remembering it vividly.

"Huh." Shawn had a lot to think about.

That didn't sound like the kind of fame he wanted.

The door to the auditorium swung open and he spotted Shatford's orange hair before she'd fully entered. He slid out of the chair like a snake and onto the narrow floor space.

Piper casually set her book bag on top of him and focused on the book that had magically appeared in her hand.

After about five minutes, Piper nudged him with her toe.

"She's gone."

But Shawn stayed for another minute.

He hoped Dr. Mendez came back soon.

* * *

HANNAH

Her phone rang and she smiled when she saw Johnny's name.

Answering it and putting it on speaker, she continued slicing the green onions.

"You left early today," he accused.

"We were finished," she countered. "And besides, it's Stir-Friday. I needed to stop at the grocer and get a couple things."

"Stir-Friday?" She could hear the smile in his voice.

"Tonight is beef udon."

"That sounds delicious. One of these days, I'm going to have to make you cook for me."

"Just say when," she replied before thinking. Immediately she closed her eyes, disappointed in herself as usual.

Johnny cleared his throat.

"I just wanted to say thanks again for all the work you put in this week. I think this record is something special and it wouldn't have happened without you."

Hannah glanced at the phone, wishing she could see his face to gauge where they were as people now.

Did this week's work help to fill in the crater she'd created years ago?

A huge part of her didn't want to be finished yet. It's the main reason she ducked out early that day.

She sucked at goodbyes. It was easier to act like things weren't really finished.

"It was really fun," she said, hoping the tightness in her throat wasn't obvious. "Thank you for letting me be a part of it."

He chuckled deeply. "Pretty sure I didn't have much of a choice."

This would be a really good time to ask him if she could record those vocals now.

"Hey, Johnny?" she asked, trying to sound like it was an afterthought and not something she'd been putting off. "I need to record some vocals for a DBS song I did a while back. Do you think you would be able to help me with that?"

The silence on the other end of the phone had her checking to see if the call was still connected.

"Would tomorrow night work for you?" he asked, sounding different.

"Tomorrow night?" she repeated, trying to remember the days of the week.

"I know Piper probably has a game in the morning," Johnny said. "But if we wait until after eight, there won't be anyone in the studio. We can go in and get it done and no one will even know."

She accidentally let an "oh" slip out. It was the same noise her heart made when it realized he was thinking about all the ways to protect her identity. He would even hide her from his colleagues.

"Does that work for you?"

"Uh, yes." She tried to regain her sensibilities after the somersault her soul had done. "Can I bring Piper?"

"Of course," he said, and again, she could hear his smile. "In full disclosure, Shawn will be with me as well."

"Then it sounds like a plan."

They hung up and Hannah did her best to concentrate on the food she was making. But she couldn't ignore the excitement of knowing she'd be seeing him again very soon.

CHAPTER THIRTEEN

RADAR

JOHNNY

"Why are you so excited to get to the school today?" Shawn asked, barely getting his seat belt on before Johnny put the car in reverse.

"Not excited," Johnny denied.

Shawn turned slightly in his seat to face him. "Yes, you are. And you've left the top three buttons open on your shirt." He gasped. "You like her!"

"I'm sure I have no idea what you're talking about." Johnny glanced at himself in the review mirror and buttoned two of the buttons. "Thanks for pointing that out."

"Like you didn't know." Shawn snorted. "The only time you show the chest hair is when you want attention. So, either you like Hannah Lee and you're excited to see her, or you're trying to hook up with one of the other women at the game, and sorry, but gross."

"Not looking for a hookup," Johnny said, realizing a half a breath too late that Shawn would infer he was admitting to the first part of his ridiculous accusation.

But it wasn't true.

He hadn't left his shirt unbuttoned on purpose. He'd simply been in a rush.

And he wasn't excited to see Hannah.

They had reached a comfortable existence. He didn't hate her, and she no longer held any power over his livelihood.

They had worked together for a week and had finished successfully.

As far as he was concerned, she had made up for everything in the past and he felt fine moving on. She didn't owe him anything, and he didn't have any feelings for her, positive or negative.

He was indifferent.

But that seemed like an empty word for what he was actually feeling.

It wasn't indifference.

It was something else.

Something new.

But not like and not hate and not indifferent.

He pulled into their regular parking space and put the car in park.

"Well, look at that. She got here early too. Hmm. Interesting." Shawn unsnapped his seat belt and opened the door to the cold before Johnny could respond.

Not that he had anything to say.

He just stared at her for a minute. She was tugging Piper's hat down over her ears and Piper was trying to wave her off.

Both of the younger people took off at a sprint for the gym door, anxious to get away from their older siblings.

Hannah shook her head and shoved her mittened hands into her coat pockets.

He could stay in the car and pretend to mess with his glove box. Or he could get out of the car and walk with her to the door.

Like they knew each other.

Like being in each other's space was okay.

Was it okay?

He jogged to catch up to her.

She smiled when she saw him.

He smiled back.

* * *

HANNAH

The toilets in the ladies' restroom were broken.

At least that's what the harassed janitor had told her when she'd tried to use the facilities. She wanted to ask if there was another restroom nearby, but he was busy setting up orange cones and cursing in a language she couldn't identify. Polish, maybe?

No matter, it was a school; there were toilets somewhere.

Besides, it was halftime, so Piper wouldn't be playing for a few minutes anyway.

Hannah made her way through the darkened halls of the school and finally found what she was looking for.

The stalls were very clean for a high school, she thought. Minimal graffiti, nothing lewd scrawled on the doors.

Maybe private schools were just better at keeping it cleaned up.

She washed her hands and caught her expression in the mirror.

Huh.

There she was.

The customary avoidance of her image stayed suspiciously silent.

She took a moment to just look at herself.

And for the first time in a long time, the primary feeling she had wasn't hate.

Voices carried to her through the door.

She frowned, the tone unsettled her immediately, and without thinking she opened the door and went into the hallway.

"You're on thin ice, Mr. Torres."

A woman Hannah thought she recognized as the vice principal had a student cornered on the stairs, a finger pointed in their face.

Not just any student, but Shawn Torres.

The bathroom door made a clunk noise as it closed behind her, alerting them to her presence.

Vice Principal Shatford turned around to see who was interrupting her dark hallway lecture.

"Hey, Shawn," Hannah called, unease sliding into her chest. "What's going on?"

Shawn slipped past the VP and headed to Hannah, his face pale, eyes downturned.

"Nothin'," Shawn muttered.

Vice Principal Shatford waved and smiled bigly, showing her teeth, then turned and walked up the remaining stairs that led to the administration wing.

Hannah didn't wave back because, well, she wasn't familiar with the woman, and also, she wanted to tell her to fuck off. Just because.

Shawn bumped her with his shoulder and she kept her eyes on the vice principal as she turned her body to follow him.

When they reached the entrance to the gymnasium, Hannah touched his elbow and drew him to a halt.

"It's obviously none of my business, but what was happening back there?" she asked.

Shawn rolled his eyes and shrugged. "She just likes giving me a hard time. Don't tell Johnny, 'kay? He overreacts."

He sidestepped her and returned to his post at the concession.

Hmm.

Hannah knew two things. She had a bad feeling about Shatford. And she was definitely going to say something to Johnny.

* * *

JOHNNY

Oh, his middle name should be regret.

He should give seminar lectures on all the ways a man jumps into things he can't handle.

The day before, when he'd realized that Hannah had left the studio without even saying goodbye, he'd felt bereft.

Which he'd ignored.

Instead, he'd called her and jumped at the opportunity to get her back into his creative space as soon as possible. Literally the next day.

"This is a dream come true," Shawn said at his shoulder.

Johnny shifted his eyes to look at his brother, and then he refocused again on the dark-haired harbinger in the live room.

He leaned forward, flipping the mic switch. "Whenever you're ready."

Hannah appeared a little nervous. Maybe even shaky. She nodded and shook her hands out at the sides.

They'd discussed running through a few practice vocals before committing.

"She's not gonna do it."

Both men turned around to see Piper on the couch. She was slouched back with one foot propped on the table and the other draped over her knee as she flipped through a guitar magazine.

"What do you mean?"

"She's totally freaking out," Piper stated, flipping another page.

Johnny glanced back down into the live room. Hannah was pacing back and forth with her hands on her hips.

"Why is she freaking out?" Shawn asked.

"Ugh." Piper dropped her feet to the floor and tossed the magazine aside, a powerhouse of preteen attitude. "Because she hasn't recorded her own stuff in years?" She stuck her chin out and waved a hand. "Because this is a song she wrote with the last great love of her life, Luke *'oh, my God'* Casey?"

When she said the "oh my God," it was high-pitched and overly exaggerated Valley Girl voice.

Johnny cracked up but recovered faster than Shawn.

"All right, let me try something," he said, heading for the door. He turned around and narrowed his eyes at Shawn. "No shenanigans."

Shawn waved him off with both hands.

Johnny jogged down the metal steps and right up to Hannah.

Yeah, she was definitely freaking out.

But like all things Hannah Lee, it wasn't like anyone else's freak-out.

She was mad.

"This is bullshit," she said when he got to her.

"Do you want to try the isolation room first?" he offered, since that's where they'd probably end up anyway.

"No." She shook her head. "I like it better in here. It feels... better." She sighed, looking around at the high ceilings.

Most of the lights were off, so it was dark and subdued. The sun had set hours ago, so the windows were in shadow.

"I don't know what's wrong with me," she confessed, keeping her eyes on the dark windows.

Johnny glanced up at the control room window. Shawn was showing Piper the soundboard.

"C'mon," he said to Hannah. "Let's go for a walk."

Having an artist get butterflies during recording wasn't unusual, though it didn't happen too often. Usually Nikki was the one who took them out and gave them what amounted to her version of "You can do this! Rah! Rah!" speech.

But this wasn't just anyone.

He led her down the hall to Studio X's lounge.

It was a quiet space when there was no one else around. Several comfortable places to relax: an espresso maker, small kitchen.

He didn't bother with the bright overhead lights, opting instead to turn on the lights above the sink. He grabbed two sparkling waters from the fridge and motioned for her to join him on a long couch.

After they had both sat down and had opened their waters, Johnny put an arm along the back of the couch as he faced her.

"Tell me what's happening in your head. What are you thinking about?"

She pursed her lips and hummed in the back of her throat. "I'm thinking about all the reasons I shouldn't be doing this."

"Such as?"

"That part of my life is over. It's not like I can just put the Ashton James mask back on and go to work." She grimaced, like the very idea was gross.

"What if you don't think of it as being Ashton James? What if you're Hannah Lee and you do what I saw you do all week long," he suggested.

She nodded, soberly considering his words. But she didn't say anything, and after a beat, she started to chew on the inside of her cheek.

"Piper mentioned that you wrote it with Luke Casey. Is that another reason for your hesitation?" he asked haltingly, because he didn't need to know. He was fine. He could have this conversation.

She frowned as she thought about it. The fact that she didn't protest immediately meant she was actually considering that as a possibility.

Johnny didn't really want to know either way if she was pining for her most famous ex. She hadn't even remembered Johnny, yet Luke Casey got unrequited feelings when he wasn't even in the room. But yeah, Johnny was fine with it.

"No. I mean, yes. But no." She growled under breath and it sounded sort of like a crackle purr. Not that he was noticing her adorable quirks. He wasn't.

She straightened her shoulders and looked at him seriously. "Maybe you don't know this, but I've been kind of a shit."

He smirked but kept himself from smiling outright.

"But sometimes, when I tried really hard, I could be an asshole of the grandest kind." She took a breath and remained thoughtful. "I think…I think Luke was just one more good guy that I tried to use to my advantage. And that song, our time together, that part of my life, it just reminds me of how much I always wanted to be better." She shook her head sadly. "But I just couldn't commit to doing it myself. I wanted someone else to do the hard work for me. And it was so obvious."

She sighed heavily and looked around the lounge like she was seeing it for the first time.

"You've got a good thing going here, Johnny," she said softly.

"Hey," he got her attention. She looked at him and he smiled gently. "You do too."

"Yeah," she replied, and sounded like she agreed. "I do, don't I?" She stood and stretched her arms over her head and gulped down the last of the sparkling water. "Okay. I'm done being a baby. Let's do this."

Together they went back to Studio Y and Johnny headed up to the control room.

"She ready?" Shawn asked, getting out of Johnny's chair.

"I think so." Johnny flipped switches and checked the settings again.

Hannah leaned into the mic and let out a huge belch, followed by a giggle.

Piper laughed darkly. "She's ready."

"Roll tape?" Johnny asked.

Hannah gave him two thumbs-up from the live room floor.

He flipped the right switches, and the track began to play.

Tell me are you beautiful on the inside,
or do you just pretend?
Do you understand the ending,
or is it all cloudy again?

Does it make you happy
when I don't talk to you?
There is no ever-after,
and you don't have a clue.

What's the point in all the yelling
when there is no one to blame?
My silent lips are shouting,
your eyes spell out my name.
And we're both standing tall,
there's questions in my eyes.
You shudder at the thought
that I could read your mind.
And we're both only somewhat alive
Alive
Alive
Alive

You don't know the reasons,
so you stall for time.
You don't want to surrender,
but we've switched sides in the fight.

And you just want to win
for the first time in your life.
I'm sick of all the yelling
and your silent tears in the night.

All you have are questions
that won't get answered again.

A race with no beginning,
an empty letter to send.

What's the point in all the yelling,
there is no one to blame.
My silent lips are shouting,
your eyes spell out my name.
And we're both standing tall,
there's questions in my eyes.
You shudder at the thought
that I could read your mind.
And we're both only somewhat alive
Alive
Alive
Alive

Johnny remembered the song. But having her sing her parts live in front of him?

That was a whole new twist to his gut.

How did a woman like this, with so much raw talent and power, end up in his tiny nowhere studio?

She brought so much energy to the song, so much emotion and pain…

He was such an idiot for thinking she could be in his life in any kind of a small way.

* * *

HANNAH

She watched Johnny prep and prepare her recording to send to Luke.

It had been so long since she'd recorded something of *hers*, she was still sort of out of her head.

"That was incredible," Shawn said for the third time.

She cracked a half smile and studied her nails.

"We need to work on your stuff next."

The control room grew so quiet she glanced up, expecting to be alone.

"What?" she asked.

"Whose stuff?" Johnny asked for clarification.

"Shawn's." Hannah snorted. "Duh."

"I have to lay down," Shawn declared, and proceeded to sprawl onto the couch, putting his feet on Piper's lap.

"Dude, no." Piper shoved his feet off her lap and onto the floor in disgust.

Johnny rubbed a hand along his jaw, fighting a smile.

"Are you sure?" he asked, his eyebrows lifted and his expression soft.

She loved to look at him.

The way he spoke, especially when he was being tender because of Shawn. Or when he'd give her an extra moment to adjust to something. His face and voice and eyes were comforting and safe and exciting all at once.

Was she sure she wanted to spend more time with this little family she had stumbled into? Was she sure she wanted to make music just a little bit longer?

Was she sure she wasn't risking too much?

"I'm sure," she said.

"Then let's make a plan," Johnny said, gentle challenge in his gaze.

All she could do was grin.

But her heart was dancing.

CHAPTER FOURTEEN

JUST LUV ME

HANNAH

The snow had started to fall that morning.

Big, fluffy, white snowflakes that floated slowly to the ground and collected in slushy piles.

By afternoon, the city had mostly shut down. School was canceled the next day.

Hannah lit candles and decided to watch movies with Piper. They didn't have much of a wintertime tradition except for one. If school was called off for weather, they marathoned *The Office*.

Her phone rang and she paused the show with one hand while holding up her phone with the other.

Her heart thumped once seeing Johnny's name.

This was becoming a pattern.

She hit the speaker button. "Hey, you're on with Hannah and Piper."

Johnny chuckled on the other end and she smiled at the sound. He did that more often and she had noticed.

"I'm here with Shawn. I was wondering if we could come up."

"Wait, you're here, here? Like, in the building?"

Johnny sighed. "Yeah, I was finishing the mix at the studio, and I was going to call you and ask if you'd come down tomorrow and listen to it. But the weatherman said I shouldn't be asking anyone to drive around town tomorrow."

"So you're driving around town instead?" she asked with a snicker.

"Yes. And if Jarvis would let me, I would have already dropped this off and been home by now."

"You're not on the list of approved visitors, sir."

"I do like how he calls me sir, though. I don't usually get called that. It's nice."

Hannah laughed, picturing the doorman's polite disgust at Johnny's sour attitude.

"I'll call down and add you to the list," she offered.

"To the list, even? Woo, that's some privileged access," he teased.

"Shut up, dummy." She hung up the phone and kept laughing as she dialed down to the desk.

"Yes, you can send him up. And the young man with him. They can come over anytime, Charles."

She hung up the phone and shook her head.

"Anytime?" Piper repeated.

Her arched eyebrows felt like looking in a mirror.

Hannah shrugged. "Why not? Alex and Quinn checked them out. They seem safe enough."

Piper nodded, and then said, "You should ask them to stay for dinner. It would be nice to have someone else to eat with besides you."

Hannah's mouth dropped open like she was offended.

"Maybe we can get them to do the dishes," Piper added, tapping her chin thoughtfully with a finger.

"Hmm, devious. But I like it." A knock sounded exactly as the timer went off. "Let them in and mind your manners," she instructed, putting on the hot mitts.

She set the pan down on the stove top while the voices came closer.

"That smells amazing," Shawn exclaimed.

"It's lasagna," Piper said proudly. "It's an old family recipe."

Hannah rolled her eyes and looked at Johnny.

"That's what we say when we've made it up. We don't have any old family recipes."

"Except for the hooch in the bathtub one," Piper spoke up.

Hannah rolled her lips inward. "Except for that one."

Johnny rubbed his fingers over his forehead. "I'm not sure I should laugh at that."

"Why not? It's hilarious." She took off the oven mitts. "You wanna stay for dinner?" she asked.

"Yes," Shawn answered for both of them.

But Hannah was focused on Johnny.

His lips twitched and he nodded. "I'd like that."

She smirked, liking his response more than she should. "Make yourself useful. Dishes are in the cupboard."

He moved past her into the kitchen and her heart did that weird thump thing.

Twice in the same night. That was a new record.

What was she doing inviting Johnny for dinner?

Not just Johnny, but Shawn, who had already proven to be too innocent for his own good. That's probably what happened when someone was raised by a legitimate superhero.

She had no business messing with what they had going for themselves. Yeah, it would probably do Piper some good to hang out with positive masculine energy, but was that enough of a reason to put two other people at risk?

Johnny's chuckle brought her around to look at him.

He took her "I'm a fucking professional" coffee mug out of the open cupboard and held it up with a smirk.

She lifted one shoulder. "It was a gift from Piper. I have one at work too."

"I bet that helps you make a lot of friends."

Her smile died and she went back to what she was doing.

He put it away and got plates out, setting them on the counter.

"Where do you work?"

"Superior Electronics. I work in the call center."

"That seems…"

"What?"

"It just seems a little beneath you, I guess."

She barked a laugh. "As compared to what?"

He sidled up to her and crossed his arms over his chest, back to the counter. "Compared to what you're capable of."

Wasn't that the truth. Of course, Johnny probably meant it in a complimentary way, not the way she was thinking.

"I am capable of a great many things," she agreed soberly.

He inhaled to say something. Probably something nice and undeserved.

She didn't want to hear it.

They would be wasted words.

"It's on the table!" she hollered, taking the salad bowl and spinning around.

* * *

After dinner, Shawn provoked Piper into helping him with the dishes. It started as a weird competition of who washed more hard-to-clean pans more often. Which also included a comparison of Hannah's and Johnny's baking skills.

Hannah thought it sounded like she won on that.

But Piper was offended that Shawn would even suggest she didn't have the upper body strength to get the lasagna pan truly clean.

"I think you're just afraid I'm going to embarrass you on your home court," he said slyly, rising from his chair and taking his dish with him.

Piper shot to her feet. "Whatever, rookie. I can scrub circles around you."

"I feel like I should be worried about the slight sexism at play in my kitchen," Hannah muttered to Johnny. "Except I also know Piper can hold her own."

"It would do Shawn some good to get shown a thing or two." He regarded her thoughtfully and took a deep breath. "What a week, am I right?"

She nodded in agreement.

They were both in the same headspace it seemed.

So much to say and yet they were having difficulty finding both the right words and the courage to say them.

She wanted to thank him for the week of being in the studio. For the chance to write and produce again without all the toxic baggage that used to come with it.

For the opportunity to show him she had other qualities besides "insufferable asshole."

And for being someone she could exist honestly around.

But saying the words also felt like saying goodbye.

And that didn't sit too well in her chest.

"You wanna hear this thing or what?" he asked.

"Has Sunshine heard it yet?" she asked.

"Most of it. I wanted to get your perspective on it first. Just in case you hear something I can fix in post."

Hannah's heart warmed with his words.

"You realize it was only a week ago that you tried to throw me out of your studio," she said smugly.

He tried to hide his smile by twisting his lips to the side. "Biggest mistake of my life."

Hannah sat down cross-legged on the floor and grabbed a throw pillow off the couch. She hugged it to her chest with both arms and rested her chin on the top. "*That's* the biggest mistake of your life? Wooow, you're such a good person," she said sardonically.

He shook his head, that smile growing by the second. "Shut up."

She chuckled darkly. Teasing Johnny was one of her most recent favorite pastimes. It was very easy, for one. For another, the tops of his ears turned bright red when he was flabbergasted.

It was adorable.

He fiddled with her CD player for a few minutes and finally got it running.

He started the first track and she closed her eyes.

Music she'd made always sounded different when listening to it postproduction. This was Sunshine's record, but she could hear her touches in it.

Unexpected emotion crept under her eyelids and burned. She took a deep breath, breathing in the sound and the feelings it evoked.

Sunshine's lyrics hit those carefully crafted notes just right and goose bumps broke out over her arms. She drew the throw pillow closer.

"We make a good team." Johnny sat down across from her, also choosing the floor.

"I've never been on a team before," she considered out loud.

"Well, you have one now," Johnny said. She opened her eyes to find him gazing at her earnestly. "If you want it."

She didn't reply.

Mostly because the size of her heart had gotten too big for her to form words and she would have to wait for it to shrink back to its normal size.

The album was only ten tracks.

But they sounded incredible.

Johnny had included some of the studio banter between her and Sunshine.

"I can take that out if it's too weird."

"No," she stopped him. "It's perfect."

Shawn and Piper joined them when the dishes were finished and filled all the pockets of silence with questions. Which Johnny answered patiently.

When the album was over, Hannah started it over again.

"Let me get this straight," Shawn said. "Your sister is one of the most proficient musicians of our time and you don't know how to play…anything?"

"I've wanted her to teach me guitar forever." Piper sent a glare toward Hannah. "But she won't."

"Uh, I don't have a guitar, pipsqueak."

"Right. Like you couldn't just order one on Amazon." Piper crossed her arms over her chest.

"Shots fired," Johnny murmured, and Hannah scowled at him.

"I can teach you the basics." Shawn stood up and went to Johnny. "Can I have the keys?"

"You gonna give her yours?"

Shawn snorted. "No. I'm gonna get the spare you drive around with. She can borrow that one, right?"

Hannah opened her mouth to protest, but Johnny was already tossing the keys to Shawn.

"Can I go with him?" Piper asked. "Charles might not let him back in without someone he recognizes."

"Because I'm brown?" Shawn said with a knowing nod.

"What? No." Piper shook her head, her nose scrunched.

Shawn rolled his eyes but lifted his chin at Johnny. "We'll be right back."

The door closed behind them, and Hannah could hear Piper chattering all the way down the hall.

"Thanks for having us over," Johnny said. "The food was very good."

"Surprised?" she asked.

He held her gaze for a beat and it felt like the floor dropped out from beneath her. "No. You have many undiscovered talents."

Those were words she said about herself a few days ago.

Something about him remembering it made her stomach swirl with confusing emotions.

"I'm glad you guys stopped by," she said, deciding to hand that disarming honesty right back to him. "It's good for Piper to be around other people." She chewed on her bottom lip. "My life choices have had the adverse effect of keeping her fairly isolated."

"Can't you just vet them through whatever agency you used for me?"

She stared at him for a minute, trying to figure out what he was referring to. "Agency?"

He shrugged like it was all the same. "You didn't walk into the studio a week ago without having all the information you needed to get me over a barrel."

She laughed. "Is that how you saw it?"

"Tell me I'm lying."

"I can't. I did my due diligence." She narrowed her eyes at him. "But I didn't use an agency. Too risky."

"Oh yeah?" He reached for his beverage.

"I went the less conventional route." She waited for him to take a sip of his drink. "I used my landlord."

He lurched forward, trying to prevent the beverage from shooting out of his mouth. He wrestled the liquid back under control and laughed out loud at her. "You're kidding."

"Sort of. Not really. Someday I'll tell you all about it."

"I hope so. It sounds like a heck of a story."

"You don't swear, do you?" she asked, noticing it again and deciding to just ask about it.

"Not really." He shook his head. "Maybe if the situation called for it I would. It's not like I don't know how." He waggled his eyebrows. "I can swear in *two* languages."

"Oh, fancy."

He smiled and his eyes lost focus as he got lost in thought. She liked watching him when he was like this. Quiet, still, like a Renaissance painting. So much happening behind those dark eyes. She was tempted to push his hair back and feel the strands between her fingers. She'd bet it was as healthy as it looked, and probably twice as thick.

Whatever was on his mind came to the surface and he pinned her with his gaze.

"Can I ask you a question?" he asked softly.

"Oh boy." Hannah made a face. "I know that tone. It's about something from before, isn't it?"

Johnny nodded, watching her carefully.

"You can ask. Doesn't mean you'll like the answer," she warned.

This was cautious territory.

They were getting along, friendly even. But she wasn't going to lie about the past to keep him content in her presence. She'd learned from experience that ambiguity or glossing over uncomfortable aspects of a person only led to a more damaging outcome.

Clarity was kinder.

"Was it Piper who changed everything? I mean, was finding out about her what made you change everything?"

She'd not anticipated that direction. And found she was delighted by it, scarily enough.

Hannah frowned as she thought back to that foggy time in her life, wanting to be as precise as possible. "Yes and no. But mostly no."

Johnny's confused expression mirrored the one Piper had given her when she'd tried to explain the same thing to her. Except Johnny was an adult, so maybe he'd be able to understand the nuances of what she was about to tell him.

If he really wanted to know it.

"I can give you the long version if you really want to know," she offered. "But it's a lot. And it won't make you like me."

The silence between them was filled with thoughts. Both his and hers. Did he realize what she was saying? That by offering to tell him these private moments of her past and the catalyst for her change, she was giving him more ammo to use against her if he chose? Did she really want to do that? Was she willing to risk her safety and privacy for this man?

She already knew the answer to that question before she had finished asking it.

Yes.

She trusted him.

And that was both an exhilarating and terrifying realization.

He rubbed his hand along his jaw. The slow motion thoughtful and sexy all at once.

"I would really like to know," he said finally.

The pause in between her question and his reply let her know the honesty in his response. He had weighed the risks and was willing to hear it.

What did that mean for their burgeoning camaraderie? She couldn't say.

But it felt like faith and sounded like friendship.

"The details of what I'm about to tell you have to stay between us. Piper isn't old enough to hear them. Not yet. I will tell her someday. When I feel she's ready."

"Okay." He sat up and draped his forearms over his knees.

She liked the way he leaned in toward her, preparing to listen. To learn something new.

Something new about her.

"Things began to really shift for me after my ex got married. It was..." She took a stabilizing breath and shook her head. "Weird. There was a lot behind our situation, but the truth of it was I knew Luke Casey was too good for me. I thought if I could hitch myself to him, he could...I don't know, save me, I guess? Which sounds ridiculous now, but I was in a chemically induced delusion for a lot of our relationship. After that, seeing him grow and find love and be happy, I spiraled.

"I think I was trying to prove that I could still get what I wanted without changing anything. I slept with anyone I thought could get me something. I drank constantly. I don't remember even half the people I..." She rolled her eyes and didn't finish that sentence. Because it was obvious.

"I don't know if you remember a couple of years ago, a producer was accused of drugging and raping a young female artist." Hannah clenched her jaw as the young woman's face floated through her memory. "Everyone came out of the woodwork, declaring his professionalism and innocence." She pursed her lips. "But I knew better."

He sat up a little straighter and she knew he was aware of what she was referring to.

"It was the weekend of the NMAs. I had gotten into an argument with my manager because I wanted to get involved in the case. I wanted to stand by her side. Let her know she wasn't alone. And he told me it wasn't financially responsible. Said that doing that would end my career. The record company could punish me. That my word could actually hurt her case because of my reputation."

She chewed on her bottom lip and smiled bitterly.

"He wasn't wrong. The producer accused of sexual assault? I'd slept with him willingly. It was part of my brand at that point. But I *chose* to do that. I wasn't tricked or drugged—" She tilted her head and corrected herself sardonically. "I mean, I wasn't drugged *by him.* But I knew him. A man with a need to control and own the people around him."

Her stomach twisted with the memory. She hated that was part of her past. That it existed.

"I was so disgusted by it all. By him, by myself, by the life I had created for myself. I had painted myself into a corner that they were more than happy to keep me in. I'd weakened my word and my name. I confronted Riley backstage. Decided that if the courts weren't going to do anything about it, I would."

"The news said you were drunk and incoherent. That you stripped naked and attacked someone unprovoked."

Her lips twitched.

"It was the first time in a long time I was actually proud of the fact that I'm pretty fucking fearless."

Johnny chuckled.

"I was drunk, that part was true. But I knew what I was doing. Somewhere there's a video of me breaking his nose." She closed her eyes and smiled wistfully, reliving it. "I'll never forget the crunch it made when I crushed it with my fist. My tiny woman hands, tits out, no fear." She opened her eyes. "I have a lot of regrets. But that isn't one of them."

He shook his head, incredulous. "I had no idea. None of that was in the news."

Her lips twitched. "You were checking up on me?"

"I may have hate-Googled you a few times." He rubbed his jaw again, a slight smile on his full lips.

She really liked it when he smiled.

"Anyway, I knew in that moment everything had to change. I had to get sober. I had to be better. I had to get out of a life that let pieces of shit like him get away with that kind of evil."

She wasn't apologetic with her next words.

"I'm not nice. I'm selfish and cruel and a liar. But I'm better than him. And some days, that's all the consolation I need."

She licked her lips. This was the part of the story where things got tricky.

"I was in rehab and I started to make this plan. I was going to use all the power I had, and whatever power I could steal, to create something new in the industry. I wanted to start my own label, sign real talent. A new generation of artists free from having to fuck someone ugly just to get featured on a B-side.

"Fucking should only be done for the fun of it," she said seriously. Because it was true. And it deserved to be said. Life was too short and the fuck should be worth it.

His ears turned bright red and she almost pointed it out but decided to keep it to herself for now.

So adorable.

And good.

"But then I found out about Piper and my priorities changed."

"You're half sisters?"

"Same mom. I never met my dad. I don't think my mom actually knew who he was. I hadn't spoken to her in fifteen years. I didn't even know Piper existed until my lawyer called."

"But you were already sober by then?"

Hmm. The timing and motivation of all this seemed very important to him.

"I was two months sober when I met Piper." On a hunch, she leaned toward him, catching his eye. "I got sober for me. I stay sober for me. Piper isn't the reason or motivation. That's too heavy a burden for a kid. She's my gift."

Johnny stared at her, and his eyes, dark storms of conflict, started to gloss over.

"What's going on, babe?" she asked gently.

The door opened, causing both of them to jump slightly.

"I told you I would beat you," Piper gasped, red-faced, her ponytail askew. "You owe me ten bucks."

"I let you win." Shawn bent over, putting his hands on his knees.

Piper humphed and marched into the living room. "He tried to tell me that because his legs are longer, he's faster." She crossed her arms over her chest. "So we raced up the stairs."

"The stairs," Hannah repeated. "From the car park"—she pointed to the floor—"to here?"

Piper nodded smugly.

"Are you trying to kill him?" Hannah got up and headed Shawn's way. "You need some water, kid? Paper bag? A defibrillator?"

"Nah, I'm good." He waved her away, but his face was taking on a purple hue. His thick hair was matted to his scalp with sweat, which also poured down his face and soaked the collar of his shirt.

"She hustled you." Hannah placed a comforting hand on Shawn's bent back. "She runs those stairs every day." She shook her head in disbelief. "My crazy little athlete."

Shawn straightened and pointed a finger at Piper. "You," he gasped. "Are mean."

Oh.

Well.

Maybe it ran in their blood.

"I was carrying this and everything!" Shawn removed the strap to the guitar case and set the instrument down.

"I offered," Piper said, annoyed.

Hannah's mouth drew up on one side in a half smile, half smirk.

She hadn't been witness to this side of Piper before.

Ballsy, bright-eyed little troublemaker.

Her eyes met Johnny's and they shared a secret smile.

Yeah, she really liked it when he smiled.

* * *

JOHNNY

Unexpected complications.

That's the only thing he could think as he watched Shawn try to show Piper how to hold down guitar strings.

They were laughing.

And he was full and happy.

He couldn't remember being this comfortable in a long time.

How had this gotten so far from what he'd thought it would be?

He'd been so intent and focused on getting her out of his world. Never letting her near Shawn. Ignoring the magnetic pull of her.

And now…

Now all he wanted was to have enough excuses to see her every single day.

He liked talking to her.

She answered his questions with thoughtfulness and honesty. Even the hard stuff that anyone else would shy away from. She was bold and deliberate in her pursuit of *better*.

"What do you think? Am I corrupting her? Or have we both been cursed with bad in our blood?" Hannah asked, also watching the younger kids.

Piper was giving Shawn a hard time and loving it.

Johnny faced Hannah and regarded her carefully. Taking time to think about his words before voicing them.

"I think that she sees you being brave and that gives her the courage to be brave."

Hannah's lips parted slightly and she swallowed hard. "I'm not." Her voice cracked and she cleared her throat. "I'm not all that."

"You are, though. And it's okay to admit that."

She held his gaze for a beat and then stood up quickly.

"Who wants ice cream?"

CHAPTER FIFTEEN

NOW THAT I FOUND YOU

HANNAH

"Anything else I can help you with today?"

They didn't respond, just hung up.

Which was a response all on its own.

Hannah signed out to take her lunch break. She leaned back in her chair and stretched her hands over her head.

Back to the daily grind. Her day job. The most unremarkable job that never had anything exciting or unpredictable happen ever. Never.

She sighed.

That was the way she'd wanted it, right?

She rolled her neck, trying to stretch out the tightness that had been building since she'd put her headset on that morning.

She couldn't remember the last time she had been this tired. Which was saying something.

But it was a different kind of a fatigue.

It was the kind that came with dissatisfaction. And that was a dangerous notion.

She grabbed her coffee cup and headed to the break room. In the fridge, there should be the lunch she'd made for herself this morning. She'd been in a rush, since she'd been up late last night and had accidentally slept in that morning. Good thing Piper didn't have school because the kid was sawing logs when Hannah ran out the door.

She sat down at an empty table in the corner of the break room and unpacked her sandwich. The real crime was that it wasn't tacos from La Morena.

She wondered what Nikki and Johnny were having for lunch.

Last night had been…

Maybe there wasn't a word to describe last night. Maybe it was a just one of those magical moments that happened, and if you blinked, you missed it.

She hadn't blinked.

In a rare show of presence, she had spent the evening with both eyes open. Cataloging small details she wanted to remember.

Piper's laugh. Shawn's frustration with how small Piper's hands were. Johnny's calm presence. The snow and the music. The warmth. The peace.

Johnny calling her brave.

She pulled out her phone and went to her last text thread. It was from Johnny, telling her they had made it home safe.

It was an odd feeling she'd had when she'd asked him to be careful on the icy streets. Genuine worry had gripped her and she'd nearly offered to let Johnny and Shawn stay in the living room.

But she'd resisted and he'd texted when they'd gotten home.

Her response had lacked any kind of warmth. It was just the thumbs-up emoji.

If he knew her true relief that they were safe, he'd probably call her therapist himself.

Was this…?

She chewed thoughtfully, not sure if she wanted to pull that layer back and ask the question.

Was this what it felt like to have friends?

Did people think about them throughout the day with smiles and concern? Did people just wander around with thoughts full of people they cared about?

Or was she behaving obsessively? Perhaps she needed to curb these thoughts and notions.

It was tricky business being an addict. One minute you think you have a handle on your vices, and the next you've discovered a brand new one.

Relationships of any kind were too dicey for her. She had Piper and she knew that her feelings for Piper were healthy and right. Anything outside of that had the potential to be just another escape tactic.

She deleted her text thread with Johnny.

No reason to tempt herself.

* * *

"Did you finish your homework?"

Piper sighed loudly, like a disgruntled old man. She shut the TV off and slouched further into the couch.

"I'm tired."

"From all the nothing you did all day?" Hannah snickered.

"Yes."

Hannah leaned against the doorway and crossed her arms over her chest. "I'll let you in on a secret. Snow days are mostly hype."

Piper rolled her eyes. "Or maybe it's only fun for people who are allowed to have friends," she retorted with enough sass to take the varnish off the coffee table.

"You're allowed to have friends," Hannah argued with a frown.

"Yeah, right."

Piper stood up and stalked to her room, slamming the door behind her.

Well.

That was new.

Hannah went to the kitchen to make dinner.

What had gotten into Piper?

"Was it something I said?" she muttered to herself as she dug vegetables and chicken out of the refrigerator.

She set her ingredients on the counter and paused. From down the hall came the sound of loud music.

Piper usually went the headphones route.

Everything had seemed fine when she'd gone to bed last night. Happy, even. Piper had seemed to really enjoy the guitar lesson from Shawn. Even though she had given the poor kid a harder time than was necessary.

Her phone on the counter rang and she glanced over to see Johnny's name.

Her heart didn't pound, but it did pause.

"Hello?"

He chuckled and the sound soothed her worried nerves. "You always answer like you're confused that I'm calling you."

"That would be an accurate assumption. I am confused. Why are you calling me again?"

"Sunshine loves the record. We are go for launch."

"Johnny, that's great!" she exclaimed.

"Yeah," he agreed, and she could picture his grin. "It's really great. And I couldn't have done it without you."

"Oh my, Johnny Torres, are you…*thanking me?*" She exaggerated a gasp and then slipped into a southern lilt. "Why, I do declare, I am positively overwhelmed by your kind words."

"Shut up."

His soft laugh. That's what got the thump.

She liked making him laugh.

"What are you doing?" she asked, trying to change the subject so she didn't do something stupid like, oh, tell him how much she liked his laugh.

"Making dinner."

"Ooh, what's for dinner tonight in the Enamorado Torres house?"

"Hey, you pronounced that really well."

"Thanks, I've been practicing."

"You have?"

"No. I—Never mind." She shook her head and squeezed her eyes closed. "I was trying to be funny."

"I am making chili."

"Do you make your chili with cornbread or cinnamon rolls?" she asked.

"Cinnamon rolls," he said with a scoff. "Who makes cornbread?"

She smiled. "Some people."

"That doesn't make any sense. Cinnamon rolls with chili. That's how you eat chili," he said, getting intense. "Why would anyone ever make cornbread with chili?" He paused. "Wait. Do you…eat cornbread with chili?" he asked.

"No. But I know people who do."

He was quiet for a minute.

"Nope. I don't believe it. That's not a thing."

"Oh my God, you're ridiculous." She tipped her head back and laughed deeply.

God, that felt good.

So very good.

Laughing was a luxury she hadn't been able to afford for…well, forever it seemed. Being able to laugh regularly hadn't been part of her life before.

Maybe she could make space for it now.

Especially if she was able to have good people in her life who made laughing feel so normal.

A thought struck her, and like usual, she went with it.

"Hey, since I have you on the phone, can I ask you a question?"

"You can ask, but I can't promise you'll like the answer," he quoted her from the night before.

"Har har." Hannah leaned her head around the corner to make sure Piper's door was still closed. She turned off the speaker and put the phone up to her ear.

"So, Piper did something…different tonight."

"Different how?" Johnny asked, the frown evident in his tone.

"She complained about not being allowed to have friends and went to her room to listen to music really loud."

Silence.

"Like, really loud," she reiterated.

"What kind of music?"

"I don't know. Her usual stuff. Big vocals, big emotion, same producer."

Johnny barked a laugh. "It's gotta be weird to have you for an older sister."

"Because I'm a slow-motion train wreck with a great ass?"

A loud burst of laughter hit her through the phone, followed by the clatter of his phone dropping onto something hard.

He picked the phone back up and was still laughing.

"You have to stop doing that," he chastised around his chuckles.

"Stop doing what, exactly? Being honest?" She grabbed her biggest knife and chopped through the romaine hearts with a satisfying crunch. "It's not my fault that the truth is hilarious," she flatly reminded him. "Back to my question, though."

"You didn't ask a question," he replied. "You made an observation."

"You know what I mean, though."

He hmmed softly. "It doesn't sound too unusual. I mean, she's in seventh grade, right?"

"Yeah."

"A little attitude here and there, some loud music, bouts of rebellion, it's all par for the course."

"This is puberty?" she asked, not liking the sound of that.

"Probably. In seventh grade, Shawn got really into punk rock. I just let it happen. I didn't make a thing out of it until I caught him with weed."

"Weed's not the worst thing," she remarked.

"Maybe not for a white girl. But he's brown with an unpronounceable last name. Getting caught with any amount of marijuana could have ruined any chance he had for certain things in the future."

Something in his voice had her waiting for more of an explanation. But he just sighed and let it end there.

Hmm.

Interesting.

"I think my best advice is something I got from my auntie. She said that teenagers are basically clinically insane. Their brains are on a constant up and down of hormones and chemicals and they can't keep up. So try not to take anything they say or do personally and just keep them alive. And try to get a vegetable in them every once in a while."

"That's...actually really helpful," Hannah commented.

"Right?" Johnny sniffed a laugh. "Some days it was really hard not to take it personal. But if I ended the day knowing he was alive and safe, I called it good. We went through a particularly rebellious phase where I secretly crushed up kids' vitamins and put them in his cereal in the morning."

Now it was Hannah's turn to belly laugh.

"I had to make sure!"

"He's a good kid," Hannah said softly.

"Yeah. He really is. A little forceful when it comes to tracking down his idols, but overall, really great."

She chuckled. "Overall."

Neither one of them spoke for a minute and it was obvious the conversation had come to a natural close. But she didn't want to say goodbye.

Which was both a new and melancholy feeling.

"I'll talk to you later, Hannah Lee," he said gently, his voice deep and rough.

"Okay," she replied. "Hey, Johnny?"

"Hmm?"

"Thanks."

* * *

He didn't call her again that week.

And she'd set her phone up in the kitchen in just the right spot while she'd made dinner so that if he did call her, she wouldn't miss it.

He didn't call.

Which was…fine.

She also hadn't called him.

Because they didn't have a friendship that she understood, so how could she know the rules?

Was it a friendship?

Maybe not yet.

But she was pretty sure it was in the very delicate beginning stages of one. All she had to do was not ruin it.

Saturday came, and with it, more snow.

"Make sure you bring that hat you made for Shawn," Piper said as she tied the laces of her winter boots by the door.

"Are you sure?" Hannah asked, eyeing the blue and gold ugly pile of yarn that she had had the audacity to call a hat. It was an insult to hats and yarn everywhere.

"Yeah, you worked really hard on it!" Piper proclaimed. She pulled out her own hat that Hannah had finished a few days prior and stuck it on her head. "See? Perfect fit."

Hannah's mouth turned down as she observed the terrible thing her sister was so willing to wear in public.

"Ughhh." Piper stomped through the apartment with her boots on (which was a violation of the "house rules") and shoved Shawn's hat into her coat pocket. "Let's goooo."

Don't take it personal.

"'Kay." Hannah grabbed her keys off the hook and followed Piper out the door.

It was strange. Piper could be both very sweet and very salty in the same minute.

Hannah didn't remember puberty. It was mostly just flashes of memories that didn't make any sense, followed by a general queasiness.

But with the cocktail of hormones coursing through her body, as Johnny had pointed out, maybe that was normal.

They made it to the school parking lot without incident despite the roads being totally fucked.

Piper didn't run off right when she parked the car, but lingered. And walked with Hannah to the door.

Strange days indeed.

The gymnasium was warm in comparison to the outdoors and Hannah was thankful. She removed her coat and was almost immediately hit in the face with Piper's coat.

"Yeah, I'll just take your stuff," Hannah said flatly to no one. Because Piper had already kicked off her winter boots and was running to the locker room, her sock feet slipping on the wood floor, the gym bag bouncing against the back of her legs.

They were earlier than normal.

Piper's coach had emailed them all the night before, asking everyone to show up a half hour early for some practice since Friday night's had gotten canceled.

Hannah didn't mind. That meant she had her choice of bleacher. And she didn't have to wrestle Piper's winter coat and wet boots in front the grand assembly.

"I hate winter."

Hannah finished tucking Piper's coat into the space between the wall and bleacher and looked up to see the familiar face of Sarahi.

She had grown accustomed to Sarahi's presence (and commentary) during the basketball games and secretly hoped Piper and Ana would become friends so that Hannah had an excuse to see Sarahi more often.

Sarahi looked her usual polished, designer self. She was in faux leather leggings that looked like liquid on her legs, and an oversized Chanel sweater. Black diamonds at her throat and wrist.

Sky. High. Heels.

"How do you walk in those when there's so much snow on the ground?" Hannah had to ask. It didn't make sense to her.

Sarahi smirked. "Very carefully." She tapped her dainty feet on the wood bleachers. "If it's very deep, my husband carries me."

"He carries you?" Hannah repeated in disbelief. She couldn't remember having ever met Sarahi's husband, but now she really wanted to.

The gleam in Sarahi's eye turned sneaky. "I have to ask very nicely."

Hannah threw a hand in the air. "I don't want to know."

Sarahi cackled and gripped Hannah's arm tightly.

"You two look like you're up to no good."

Hannah just stopped herself from smiling like an idiot at Johnny's handsome face. But she may have smiled a little.

"You know what they say," Sarahi answered him. "Birds of a feather plan bank heists together."

Hannah snorted. "That's not the saying."

Sarahi feigned shock. "It's not?"

"It's not," Johnny confirmed sternly. He pointed his finger at Sarahi. "Don't corrupt her."

Sarahi cackled wickedly.

Hannah was taken aback.

She was in danger of being corrupted? Wasn't she the one who usually did the corrupting?

"Uh, sir," Hannah said to Johnny. "I think you have me mistaken for someone else."

His eyes made a slow perusal of her person, up and down and back again. Her cheeks began to heat. His lips twitched and he shook his head. "No, I don't."

He stepped down from the bleachers and walked to the concession on the other side of the court.

Hannah watched him go.

* * *

Vice Principal Shatford made an uncharacteristic appearance during halftime.

She came out onto the court and gave a weird pandering speech about good sportsmanlike conduct. Then she reminded the girls that modesty was rewarded.

It wasn't a speech directed at Piper. But it was one that Hannah had had to endure a time or two herself.

Modesty.

Yep. Definitely made an impact.

Hannah rolled her eyes and Sarahi caught her. She leaned over and said in a low voice, "She makes my life a living a hell."

Hannah frowned severely. "How?"

"She makes it difficult to get things done. Loses paperwork, can't manage to keep an appointment, refuses to speak to me on the phone."

Hannah hadn't had that experience. She didn't like the VP, but that was just a gut feeling, not because of any tangible reason.

She decided not to say any of that to Sarahi, though, because what good would it do?

Oh, I get all those things! Why not you?

Yeah, no.

Besides, it couldn't be easy being the Vice Principal at a private school that was both junior high and high school. Though if she was overworked, the school could just hire another one with the tuition that Hannah paid for Piper alone.

"I'm thirsty, you want anything?" Hannah asked, standing.

"Water, please," Sarahi responded with a warm smile.

Okay, yeah, Sarahi could be a little intimidating at times with her direct approach and flawless appearance. But that wasn't a reason to disregard the woman.

It didn't sit right with Hannah and she was very deep in thought about it when she made it to the window.

"Hey," Johnny greeted, putting both his hands on the counter in a wide placement. Something in his tone had her dropping her previous thoughts and searching his face for an explanation.

He leaned a little over the counter and dropped his voice.

"Shawn's been gone for a minute." Johnny glanced around to see if anyone nearby was listening. "Would you do me a favor and see if he's somewhere in the building?"

Johnny was asking her for a favor? Yeah, he was agitated.

"Sure. Any place I should start?"

Johnny drummed his fingers nervously on the counter. "The east wing. Sometimes he helps this kid Edgar with his science." He shook his head tightly. "He's been warned not to, but..."

"I'll find him," Hannah promised.

She left the loud gymnasium and headed into the darkened part of the school building

Carlton Baxter Christian Academy was like most rich kid schools she had gone to. And she'd gone to a few. Well, until her grandpa died and her mom got custody.

It was laid out in a pretty generic floorplan and getting to the east wing was easy.

She heard voices as she walked down the hall and slowed down.

That did *not* sound like Shawn. She'd gotten to know his voice pretty well rather recently.

It sounded like...

When it clicked, she picked up her pace.

The door was open and she entered the science room unseen.

In the back stood Shawn and a young Hispanic kid about Piper's age, their heads hung low as Vice Principal Shatford scolded them with her words.

"If Edgar here can't understand the language enough to pass his classes on his own, then he should learn it. This is America. He's been here long enough." She bent at the waist and raised her voice. "Do you comprende?"

Edgar shrank back from the woman but didn't lift his eyes.

Shatford rolled her eyes. "See? It's a waste of time."

"You, Mr. Torres, are not a qualified student aid."

"But I applied. I have all the requirements—"

She held up a finger and interrupted him with a tsk. "It's like you forget how little you matter to me. How little you matter to anyone. You were an anchor baby. Just a tool to use. You know what I *don't* need? I don't need you running around behind my back and helping all the ESL kids. If they can't learn the language, then they can't learn here."

And then, despite all her months of meditation and yoga and deep breathing, Hannah lost her absolute shit.

"What's going on in here?" she asked, mock sweetly.

She could feel it, the caged cat breaking free inside.

Lord have mercy, but her bad bitch was bloodthirsty.

Shatford turned around and plastered a fake smile on her face. "Oh, Ms. James. What are you doing here? The game is down in the gymnasium. Here, I'll show you." She moved closer, a hand held out to usher the way.

"I know where it is. Did you, as an educator, just dismiss the needs of one of your students? And then minimize the viability of the other? And then close with some light racist ideological trauma? I want to make sure I heard it correctly before I take action." Hannah titled her head and pursed her lips.

Shatford glared at her and dropped the niceties. "I think you heard what you wanted to hear."

Hannah narrowed her eyes. A smarter person would have recognized the power shift in the room. Shawn and Edgar did. They scurried around the perimeter and hustled out the door.

Shatford jutted her chin up and moved to her right. She walked down the righthand aisle of desks toward the exit. Hannah followed her.

It was more a stalking than a chase.

"Oh, I don't think I heard enough. How about you give me the long version?" Hannah clicked her nails along the desktops as she slowly gained ground on Shatford.

Shatford spun around, eyes flashing. "You have no idea how hard this job is. Everyone is always trying to take advantage. Those kinds of people are toxic to our children. I refuse to let our future be ruined because no one was willing to make the hard calls."

Hannah had stopped moving. Her stomach twisted and soured.

"Hard calls? Are you delusional?"

"You can try to report me, but I have a stellar reputation. The parents love me," Shatford hissed, her orangey hair bouncing around her ears like a fluffy helmet. "They're more likely to throw you and your orphan out than risk losing me."

Hannah decided she'd heard enough. And if they kicked Piper out, then so be it. But this was going to be something she enjoyed.

"Fuck you," Hannah said, voice deep and powerful. She drew out the words, enjoying the feel of them as they crossed her lips.

Shatford's eyes widened and her head jerked back. Clearly no one had ever told her off before.

That was all right, Hannah would make this one count.

"You prissy, middle-aged, white trash, cunt-faced fuck," Hannah continued, her tone bored and deliberate. "You think I'm afraid of you? I've never been afraid of anyone."

Shatford's mouth opened and gaped like a fish realizing it had taken its last clean breath.

"You enjoy reducing children to labels and racist opinions? I wonder how you would fair with that kind of analysis held up to you?" Hannah tilted her head to the side. "Let's find out."

"You can't talk to me that way," Shatford sputtered.

"Oh, I think I can." Hannah chuckled darkly. "Let's talk about your cheap shoes and bad teeth. Or is that too shallow? Shall I go deeper? Let's talk about your lack of compassion and how bad you are at your job."

Shatford's whole body trembled with anger and probably fear. She inhaled through her nose and held her shoulders back. And for a moment, Hannah thought the woman might actually try to fight back. But then Shatford cut and run. Right out the door of the classroom and into the hallway.

"Ugh," Hannah groaned loudly as she followed. "Don't make me chase you. Fight me like a woman."

"You're crazy and I'm going to report you to child services," Shatford declared, walking backward down the darkened hall so she could keep an eye on Hannah.

"Oooh," Hannah mocked. "Scary."

Shatford quickened her pace.

"You're just mad because I caught you. And I will tell every person I can find what I heard you say. And then we can all talk about your ugly, cunty soul together, you self-righteous motherfucker." Hannah remained calm in her delivery, making sure to enunciate every word so Shatford heard her clearly.

Who knew how long this woman's reign of terror had gone on? The idea of a school administrator not only believing the horrible things she'd said but actually acting on them filled Hannah with a fiery vengeance she didn't know she had.

She was in charge of *children.*

Hannah was so focused on her quarry that she didn't register Johnny had entered the hallway with them until he grabbed her by her biceps and looked her directly in the eye.

She scowled at him and leaned over so she could see Shatford, who was nearly running away from her at this point.

"Hey, hey, hey," Johnny tried to get her attention. "What's…" He shook his head, trying not to smile. "What's your plan here?"

"To make her regret all of the choices she's made that brought her to this moment," Hannah replied seriously.

Was it mean?

Yes.

But maybe someone needed to be the mean one every once in a while.

"She's crazy. She just started attacking me out of nowhere," Shatford cried, turning on the waterworks now that she had an audience.

"Oh, fuck you." Hannah shook her head in disbelief. Was she for real?

Johnny still held her arms in a gentle grip. But he also looked like he was holding back laughter,

"Is this funny for you?" Hannah asked. "Really?"

"Keep her away from me or I will call the police." Shatford had made it to the exit and threw out her threat with about as much believability as a snowball in a tire fire.

"C'mon, Shatford," Hannah called, taunting her. "Why are you running away? I thought you wanted to use your words. Why are you so scared?"

Shatford sputtered as she found the door handle, and then she left the building.

Hannah glowered at the empty space where the vice principal used to be standing. "Maybe we'll get lucky and she'll freeze to death."

"That's dark, James," Johnny commented.

"Finding it hard to care, Torres," she countered.

He put his hands on his hips, a lopsided smile on his handsome face, and shook his head at her.

She shrugged. "I'm not even sorry."

His lips quirked up and he hooked an arm around her neck—much the same way that Ana did to Piper—and led her back to the gym.

"Don't want to draw too much attention, huh?" he said.

They reached the door to the concession and he removed his arm but turned to look her in the eye. His dark eyebrows tipping up.

"What were you thinking?" he asked, sounding amused.

Which was good. Because if he'd been upset about it, she would have had a few things to say to him as well.

"You know the saying," she replied lazily. "Stick and stones may break my bones, but verbal abuse is trauma that lasts forever."

He arched an eyebrow. "That's not how it goes."

"Yes, it is," she replied seriously.

He looked around, the corner of his mouth once again showing his amusement. He returned his gaze to her and sobered slightly. "What did she say that set you off?"

"She called your brother an anchor baby." Just saying it made her get hot again. Shawn's defeated posture, the disconnect in his eyes. It obviously wasn't the first time he'd heard that.

Johnny took a deep breath and nodded. He pressed his lips together into a hard line, keeping his composure.

"Thank you," he said to her. "For saying something."

"I said all kinds of things. And I'll say them again if given the chance."

Johnny glanced over her shoulder and lifted his chin. "Get back to Sarahi. She saved your seat and she'll want to know what happened."

"Do I tell her the whole truth?"

"And nothing but."

Hannah smirked and backed away from Johnny. She turned around and made it back to her seat. Unfortunately, she felt dozens of pairs of eyes on her. That probably wasn't great. She didn't need anyone looking too closely.

But she still wouldn't go back and do it differently.

Maybe that made her a terrible person.

Maybe that was all she was ever going to be.

She sat down by Sarahi and gave her the details. To which Sarahi had a lot to say. Most of it in Spanish. After a few minutes, Shawn came to sit by them.

He sat very close to Hannah, his leg pressed against hers, but didn't say anything.

For some reason, she understood anyway. It was a thanks, an acknowledgement, and a comfort. She wished she could do more. Make it so that he'd never had to hear those ugly words.

But Hannah knew how wounding words could be. That's why it was her weapon of choice.

She reached over and dug through Piper's coat pockets until she found the ugly hat she'd made for Shawn.

She spread it out gently on her knee. He glanced down at it. She handed it to him.

"Here. I made you this."

He sniffed a laugh and immediately put the blue and yellow mottled mess on his head.

"How do I look?" he asked, grinning at her.

"Like I tried my best," Hannah said honestly, with a disappointed grimace.

He bumped her with his shoulder and chuckled.

By the time the game ended, it seemed no one remembered the drama during halftime. The spectators swarmed their players on the court and made their getaways.

Hannah waited on the bleachers since she knew Piper would want to shower first.

Shawn waited with her.

"Shouldn't you be helping clean the kitchen?" she teased.

Shawn just shrugged and remained pensive.

Sarahi followed Ana back to the locker rooms and then returned to Hannah and Shawn. About that time, Johnny joined them as well.

"Do you like my hat?" Shawn asked Johnny.

Johnny narrowed his eyes at Hannah. "Where's mine?"

Her mouth dropped open. "I thought you were kidding."

"That doesn't sound like me." He shook his head.

"Okay, well, it's gonna be a few days. And also, it's going to suck. So you've been warned."

He cracked a sideways smile.

"Hannah," Sarahi said gently. "We were wondering if you and Piper would like to join our family for lunch today."

Hannah's mouth opened in soft surprise. Her eyes darted from Sarahi to Shawn to Johnny, looking for confirmation.

Johnny nodded, as if reading her mind.

"I'll have to check with Piper, but…" She lifted a shoulder. "That sounds really fun."

And she wasn't kidding.

How had that happened?

Had…had she made friends?

"I'll text you the address?" Johnny asked.

"Yeah." She nodded. "That would be great. Thanks."

He held her eyes for a beat and then smiled, like he couldn't quite believe this was happening either.

She was deep in thought when Piper emerged from the locker room.

"Hey," Hannah said, approaching her little sister. "How do you feel about going over to have lunch with Ana's family?"

Piper jumped up and down. "Yes! Please tell me you said yes." She tilted her head, worried Hannah had said no. Which made sense. Hannah said no a lot.

"I said yes."

Piper breathed a sigh of relief and skipped to the door of the school.

Hannah wasn't sure what she'd expected.

Family dinner sounded intimate.

And this was.

To an extent.

But it was also very large.

She couldn't be sure, but she guessed there was probably close to twenty people in the house.

It was a large two-story older home with a brick structure. When they'd pulled up outside, Hannah thought they had it wrong.

For one, it was in Rogers Park on the far north side of the city. She double- and triple-checked the address. She and Piper stared out the car windows, wondering together if they should go up to the door before Shawn opened the front door and waved them inside.

After that, it was a lot to take in.

The house's interior had obviously been completely refurbished. Glossy wood floors, granite countertops, trendy light fixtures.

And it smelled amazing.

Like all of her favorite foods that she never knew she loved.

Very quickly she was ushered into the kitchen and put to work slicing peppers.

Shawn actually showed her the ropes on that. She had no idea where Piper had ended up.

Through the kitchen window she could see the snow-covered backyard. It had a high fence and was large enough to host this entire party out there comfortably. She pictured them there during warmer months.

It was a surreal experience.

The last time she'd been around her family in a large group setting, it had been the Fourth of July and her fifteenth birthday.

Her mother's then-boyfriend, Blaze (no, really, that was his name), had started a fight with her uncles about whether or not the Indianapolis Colts were the greatest football team in the NFL. And long live Peyton Manning.

The cops came and arrested damn near everyone on outstanding warrants.

Yep. That was life back then.

But this family? They actually seemed to like each other.

And while some of the adults were drinking alcoholic beverages, no one was drunk.

The music they had on in the background was a variety of old-school hip-hop, modern pop, country, and some blues. It was eccentric and unpredictable and *fun.*

"What church do you go to?" Carmen asked Hannah when she went to hand her the bowl of sliced peppers.

Hannah's eyes darted to Shawn's, but he made an "O" with his mouth and ducked out of the room.

"Uh..."

"She doesn't go to church, Mama," Sarahi interrupted, handing Hannah a bowl of apples. "Peel and slice these."

"Yes." Hannah took the bowl and turned back to her previous station.

"Who doesn't go to church?" Carmen asked, sounding offended.

If this was a test, Hannah was going to fail.

"Sometimes people don't go to church," said one of Sarahi's sisters. Hannah wanted to say her name was Daniela?

"Did you hear about the church the Diegos were going to?" the other sister, Mia, asked. "They had to leave. It got too wild for them."

"Ah, I thought they really liked it there," Carmen replied.

"I guess they are really strict." Daniela leaned against the counter at Hannah's side and stole a slice of apple, popping it in her mouth with a wink.

"What's so bad about being strict?" Carmen asked with accusation.

"No, Mama," Daniella continued. "They spank their wives and stuff."

Hannah's back straightened and she turned wide eyes to Daniela.

"So? What's so bad about a good spanking?" Sarahi asked.

The kitchen went stone silent.

Sarahi, oblivious to what she'd just said, took the rice and peppers to the dining room.

Hannah's gaze darted back to Daniela, whose eyes were just as big and round as Hannah's. They both cracked up.

"No," Carmen scolded them with a finger wag. "We will never speak of this again." Then she too left the kitchen.

Hannah, Daniela, and Mia burst out laughing.

* * *

JOHNNY

"You look a little overwhelmed." Johnny took a seat on the stairs beside Hannah.

She cracked a smile. "You're not wrong. But it's not a bad feeling."

He handed her a sparkling water, hoping for another soft smile. He was rewarded.

"I guess I had no idea Piper was such an extrovert. No wonder she's been so pissy lately." Hannah cracked open the can and took a drink.

"What about you? Introvert or extrovert?" he asked.

She took a deep breath and hummed lightly. "I think I'm one of those ambiverts. I'm comfortable with crowds and people and attention, but I also really enjoy my alone time."

"My family didn't scare you too much, did they?" he asked, knowing it would take a lot more than that to scare Hannah.

She chuckled and then scrunched up her nose. "Not scare, no. But I know more about your cousin's sex life than I ever wanted."

"Ah, yeah. Sometimes that happens." He scratched his chin and leaned his elbows back against the stairs.

"Sarahi's husband is…"

Johnny nodded, rolling his lips inward. "Yep."

Hannah turned her head to address him directly. "He's very white."

"So white," Johnny agreed, trying not to laugh.

"I don't know why that surprised me," Hannah said.

"Truthfully, it surprised us all at first. But he treats her like a queen, so…" He ended it with a shrug.

"They've been together a while?"

"Since high school." Johnny thought back to that time. "We grew up in the same village. It wasn't an easy life. I think that's one of the reasons why her husband dotes on her and spoils her. He's trying to make up for the shit hand she was born with."

Hannah sat quiet, thoughtful, before she swiveled on the stairs to face him. She rested her back against the wooden banister, her bent knee resting against the stair.

"But this house doesn't reflect a bad upbringing," she pointed out curiously.

He nodded and cleared his throat. "You'll understand this better than anyone." He adjusted his can in his hands and rested his fore-arms on his bent knees. "For some people, there's a hard line between Life Before and Life After. We grew up poor. Our parents were poor. We came here when we were kids, and they seized an opportunity. Carmen is a doctor now. She married a doctor. They have this nice house and live in the best neighborhood in the city."

He turned to her and smiled sadly. "But there's always going to be the memories of life before."

"That's what I call it too," she said, voice rough.

Sometimes when he looked at her, he could swear she was being born right in front of him. Never had he met a person so dedicated to their own growth that he could witness it in real time.

But that was Hannah Lee, wasn't it?

A surprise, blooming with every sunrise.

When Shawn had come to get him during the hallway showdown with Shatford, he'd been worried. Worried for Hannah. Worried she'd get in over her head with that black-hearted self-appointed headmistress.

But seeing her declaring profanities with such gusto, such passion…

It was enough to make a grown man cry.

Which he almost did.

And then finding out what it was that had sent her over the edge? That had done it.

He'd forgiven her a while ago. But today he decided he might actually adore her.

Which was scary and confusing all at once.

"Would you tell me about your Life Before?" she asked cautiously.

It wasn't a demand, just an inquiry. One he was certain she would drop if he resisted. But he actually did want to tell her. For no other reason than letting her know more about him. For whatever that was worth.

"I was born in Honduras."

"Wait. You're not from Mexico?"

"Ah, no. And try not to say that too loudly around here," he warned with a soft laugh.

Her eyes darted around them. "I'm sorry. I don't know…things."

He nodded in understanding. "Honduras is a little further south of Mexico. It's in Central America. Yeah, we speak Spanish, but we're our own people.

"Our village was small. We didn't have a lot. My father was an enforcer in a local drug cartel. Sometimes I think back to some of the things we saw and lived with and it's a miracle we didn't die there."

He swallowed hard, images of Life Before springing to mind.

"One time we saw a woman get shot in the street to make an

example. Her body stayed there for three days because everyone was afraid to move her. We had to walk past her to get to school."

Hannah went completely still.

If she thought his stories would be easy to hear, she was mistaken.

"Another time, Sarahi fell into an old cistern. She was five, I think. I went to get help, but it took a long time. Her mama, Auntie Carmen, used a long tree branch to get her out. Sarahi was covered in cuts from broken glass. People used the cistern as a dump of sorts. She was down there with floating pig heads and garbage."

"Oh my God," Hannah breathed.

"Yeah, so if her husband wants to buy her fancy shoes and spoil her for the rest of her life, none of us are going to stand in his way." Johnny cleared his throat. "But that was so long ago now, it feels almost like it didn't happen."

"When did you move here?" Hannah asked softly, shifting toward him.

He liked that. That she wanted to know more and to be closer when he told her.

"I was a teenager. Carmen convinced my mom to leave with her. They secretly applied for their visas at the same time, but my mom's came through first. She packed us up and we left in the middle of the night. I didn't know it at the time, but she was pregnant with Shawn."

"Do you guys have the same father?"

"Yeah."

"Where's your mom?" Hannah asked, looking around. "Is she here?"

"No." Johnny dropped his gaze to the floor. "She went back. To be with my father. She never could quite let the life go."

Hannah put a hand on his knee.

He laughed humorlessly. "She said she'd come back, but she never did."

"How old were you?"

"Twenty-ish. Shawn was five. And I found myself his sole provider and guardian. It was…an intense time."

"That was around the time I met you," she murmured.

He licked his bottom lip and nodded.

A lot of things had started to unlock and click into place for him over the past couple of weeks. Talking about when his mom left and his subsequent meeting of Ashton James, who was also on a similar self-destructive path, caused discomfort to twist his stomach.

"So she's still back there?"

"I have no idea. I haven't spoken to her in two years. She went back to my father, who's running the whole operation now and…" His words failed and he swallowed the anger and helplessness that wanted to come out shouting.

"Shawn was born a citizen. I couldn't apply until I was twenty-one to become a citizen and that made everything crazy.

"It was hard to keep custody of him. The State tried to step in so many times. First, with the citizenship stuff, then with having to prove I could provide for him. I had to work ridiculous jobs and hours to make sure we had enough money for things that we never would have had in Honduras. For example, did you know that if a child doesn't have a proper dresser and their own bed, CPS calls that neglect and it's enough to remove the child from a home?"

"I see now why him getting caught with weed would be so scary."

"It was a chance I wasn't willing to take. And Carmen helped me as much as she could. But she was raising three kids and putting herself through school."

He tried to exhale the tension that had built in his chest as he'd talked. "It was just me and Shawn. Fighting for our lives."

"Johnny," she said with a soft frown. "You're so *good.*"

He snorted.

"No, really. You're the kind of man who they design superheroes around."

"I'm nowhere near perfect."

She chortled. "Of course not. You have terrible taste in women, for one."

He rolled his eyes.

"Just saying." Hannah shrugged. "And you also hold a mean grudge."

His smile was immediate.

"But I've never met anyone in my life who tries so hard to do the *right* thing so consistently. It's actually really annoying, if I'm being honest."

Johnny stared at her, wondering where in the world his choices were leading him.

Every time he was alone with Hannah, he only wanted more.

She seemed to reach a part of him that he thought no one else knew existed. But she saw it, zeroed in on it, and held it in her grasp.

He dropped his eyes to her mouth and wondered what she would do if he tried to kiss her.

Would she push him away?

Or would she kiss him back?

She tilted her head to the side, listening to music coming from the other room. He heard it too, and he almost pretended like he didn't. Mostly because he was enjoying their private conversation. But the way her eyes lit up when she recognized the song that was playing made him happy to move into this new moment with her.

"Is that the Cupid Shuffle?" she asked, gripping his forearm.

He nodded. "We really like hip-hop around here. It's sort of a tradition."

She stood and grabbed him by the hand. "Piper!" she called.

But Piper was already headed in the direction of the music.

Johnny followed them into the large room that was normally the dining room, but it doubled as a dance floor in the winter since it was the largest room in the house with wood floors. Carmen's husband,

Dr. Ignacio, had moved the table and chairs to one of the bedrooms, and his cousins were already doing the dance.

Hannah and Piper joined a line and found the beat.

Johnny rubbed his arms with both hands, trying to get rid of the uninvited goose bumps.

Her first time in his auntie's home and she was dancing with the cousins. And doing a damn fine job at it.

And she was laughing with a freedom he hadn't seen yet.

Shawn bolted through the door and got in-line between Piper and Hannah.

And Johnny thought he might have just caught a glimpse of a future he never dreamed possible.

CHAPTER SIXTEEN

TRIP TO YOUR HEART

HANNAH

"What are you doing?"

Hannah glanced over her shoulder.

It was TJ.

"The Cupid Shuffle," she replied, not missing a beat. Sure, the song was only in her head, but that didn't mean she had to stop. "And making coffee."

Her cup finished filling and she bopped over to the counter to add half-and-half.

"You seem different," TJ said, pushing his glasses up the bridge of his nose.

She felt different. But that wasn't any of TJ's business. She peeked around the corner into the rest of the break room to see if Courtney was around. She wasn't.

"TJ," she addressed, leveling him with a serious look. He sucked in a nervous breath. "I overheard Courtney saying she wanted to try Wylde Pub, but she didn't want to go alone."

TJ's Adam's apple bobbed as he swallowed.

"Oh."

Hannah shrugged and shuffled out of the break room.

She hadn't woken up that morning expecting to take an interest in her coworkers, but what the hell, right?

* * *

Three things happened all at once.

The spaghetti sauce boiled over on the stove, she answered her phone, and Piper whipped into the kitchen with wild eyes.

"I have to go to the library *right now!*" Piper panicked.

"Shit!" Hannah said, forgetting to use a glove to grab the handle of the saucepan, thereby burning herself. "What?" she asked, not sure she heard Piper correctly.

"The *library*," Piper repeated much too loudly.

Hannah almost touched the pan handle again before remembering and grabbing the hot mitt. She turned the burner off while moving the pan to the back burner. "We're about to have dinner—"

"No, you don't understand. I completely forgot about this report I have to do tonight and I have to go the library to get what I need."

"Can't you just use the internet? Isn't that why the internet was invented?" She felt kind of like an asshole for having to point that out.

"No! My English teacher said we had to use an actual library and I have to use the Dewey Decimal to prove my sources. I have to know the page number and paragraph, Hannah!"

Okay.

Hannah stared at the overdramatic almost-teen and tried not to point out how hysterical she sounded.

Because match meet gasoline.

"Do you know what time the library closes?" Hannah asked, proud of herself for not losing her absolute shit.

"It closes at ten."

Both of them looked down at the phone on the counter.

Right.

Because Johnny had called and she'd hit the button right when everything had boiled over—the sauce, Piper's sanity, Hannah's routine.

"Well, the one closest to you closes at ten," Johnny amended.

"I'll get my stuff!" Piper dashed down the hall.

Hannah groaned out loud. "How does her lack of preparation translate to an emergency for me?"

Johnny chuckled. "What was for dinner?"

Was was right.

"Spaghetti."

"Mmm, I bet you make good spaghetti."

"I do," she agreed. "Thank you for saying that."

It would probably save just fine. She stuck a lid on the saucepan, and instead of putting it into her fridge (which would just create another mess), she carried it out onto the snow-covered balcony.

"I hadn't made the noodles yet, so all is not lost. I guess we'll just have it later."

Her stomach growled in protest. But it was fine. Everything was fine.

"You happened to know the library's hours pretty quick there," she said, going back to the kitchen to wash her hands.

"Shawn had Mrs. Pritchett in seventh grade too. We've done this dance."

"Oh fabulous. So it's not just me who gets informed last minute about these things."

"Nope." Johnny chuckled.

Piper opened the door of the condo while tugging on her coat. "We have to go now."

Oh, the sass.

Hannah took a deep breath, because again, she was not going to lose her shit. It wasn't worth it and it wasn't warranted.

"I'm being summoned," she said, picking up her phone.

"I'll talk to you later."

He hung up and she slid the phone into the back pocket of her jeans.

* * *

JOHNNY

"Mrs. Pritchett's impossible task?" Shawn asked from his seat on the couch. He was slightly reclined, guitar across his lap, as he casually practiced a new riff he'd made up.

Johnny was constantly impressed by the music his little brother created. And he never stopped. Every spare minute, he sat down with an instrument and worked on it.

He was better than Johnny.

He was better than most artists Johnny had worked with.

And he was still so young.

"Sounds like it."

Shawn snorted and rolled his eyes. "That old bat is never satisfied. That assignment is a joke. She has hidden expectations that no one can hit. It's seventh grade, not a doctorate program."

"You say that like you know anything about doctorate programs."

Shawn rolled his eyes and made a fart noise with his mouth, making Johnny's point.

"Too bad you can't tell Piper about that ahead of time. She sounds pretty stressed about it."

Shawn strummed the guitar in thought. He put his hand over the strings and sat up straight.

"Why can't I?"

"What's that now?"

Shawn stood and put the guitar in the stand. "We're not doing anything. We should go to the library. I'll help Piper with the impossible paper." His grin turned devious. "Show Mrs. Pritchett something new."

Johnny started to protest out of habit. Shawn had a lot of half-cocked ideas. Most of them should never see the light of day. But this one?

"Have a late supper?" Johnny asked, already planning ahead.

Shawn nodded eagerly. "Let's do it."

* * *

It wasn't until he spotted her at a table on the top floor, her hair a tangled mess, eyes crossed as she stared at the pages of a reference book, that he thought he may be pushing this too hard.

He had literally followed her to the library. That was as close to stalking as he had ever gotten, and it made him a little queasy. The one thing she had made clear to him repeatedly was her need for anonymity.

Shawn had no such hesitations.

He pushed past Johnny and slid into a chair across from Piper and Hannah.

Hannah smiled at Shawn and immediately searched behind him, finding Johnny. Her smile changed to something new and small and soft, and Johnny felt it hit him right in the chest.

"Shawn thought he could be of help," Johnny explained when he reached the table.

"We can use all the help we can get," Hannah replied, sounding relieved.

She stood up and he took a moment to look her over.

"Work clothes?" he asked.

She glanced down at her wide leg, high-waisted dress pants, cream colored V-neck blouse, high-heeled boots, and shrugged.

"I didn't have time to change before the crisis hit. I got my bra off at least. So there's that."

"Oh my God, Hannah," Piper hissed in horror.

Johnny dropped his gaze to her chest, as if to verify what she'd just casually mentioned, but he looked away swiftly, hoping no one noticed.

"What?" Hannah asked Piper. "It's a bra. A lot of women wear them. It's hardly a scandal."

Piper dropped her head into her hands. "Please go away. Please. Just stop speaking to me in public."

Hannah rolled her eyes and shook her head. But she left the table and wandered closer to Johnny.

"Hannah Lee James, causing trauma among the innocent since she was conceived."

Johnny cracked a smile and arched an eyebrow. "But it's almost like you enjoy it."

She waggled her eyebrows and he barked a laugh.

Shawn and Piper shushed him.

Hannah gestured for him to follow her and he was more than happy to oblige.

They wandered into the stacks, walking slow and speaking soft.

"Should I be embarrassed about what I said?" she asked, genuinely curious.

"About not wearing a bra?" he guessed. "I guess that depends; did you lie?"

She snorted and faced him, catching him glancing over her top half less than stealthily. He decided not to lie about it.

"I can't tell," he admitted.

She giggled, her happiness a warm welcome from the winter outside.

"You shouldn't be able to. They were constructed to stand on their own, so to speak."

His ears got hot. This conversation was going to test him, he could tell.

But what about Hannah wasn't a test?

"So why wear a bra at all?" he asked.

"I wear one for society's comfort, not my own." She sighed and slid a book out of the shelf, opening it.

He glanced at the title, *Honduras in Pictures.*

"It's such a beautiful country," she remarked, paging through photos of jungle, beach, mountains, acres and acres of green.

"It is," he agreed, feeling unsteady.

She tucked the book back into its place on the shelf and searched through the ones nearby.

"What are you doing?" he asked.

"Learning."

It was such a casual response for what he saw as a very complicated question.

"Learning about what?" he decided to be more direct.

She frowned at him, like the question was confusing. "Learning about you and where you came from."

Finding another, larger book, she slid it out. "I mean, not you, you. But your people and culture. I didn't know anything before."

"And now?" he asked, his throat tight.

"I want to know more." She opened the book and carefully paged through it, hesitated. "And I want to know more about you." She looked up at him, unguarded curiosity in her brilliant blue eyes.

* * *

HANNAH

This was strange territory for her.

Being this honest while simultaneously feeling safe to do so.

All other times she was ready to be misunderstood or disregarded.

But these moments with Johnny had started to happen more frequently.

And she found herself diving into them without thinking.

"What do you want to know about me?" he asked, his deep voice rough and quiet.

"Tell me something no one else knows," she said, feeling both bold and afraid.

He licked his lips and she found herself distracted by the motion.

"My name, Enamorado, was my mother's maiden name. It means 'in love.'" He rubbed his chin with a hand, making his lower lip move around.

She couldn't take her eyes off it.

It wasn't the first time she had noticed Johnny's perfect mouth.

But it was the first time she'd noticed it while he spoke to her in hushed tones in the darkened stacks of a library.

Pulling herself back to reality, she hefted the book between them. She turned a few pages, not really seeing the images.

"I've been reading e-books for so long, I forgot what it felt like to hold a hardcover in my hand." She ran her fingers over the spine, feeling the texture, grounding herself.

"What kind of books do you read?" Johnny asked, standing just a little closer than he normally would. His nearness sent shivers down her spine.

"Anything I can get my hands on. Romance, mystery, fantasy." She tilted her head to the side. "All the books on how to not screw up a kid and the ones on how to be a better human."

She closed the book, giving up on being able to focus, and slid it back into its place on the shelf.

She turned to face him, her back to the stacks, and found him even closer than she expected. His eyes scanned her face, something new in them she couldn't identify. But it made her heart thump.

Just the once.

Like a stone falling to the bottom of an empty well.

Did that sound melodramatic?

"Hi," she said, not caring that it sounded stupid.

"Hi," he whispered, taking a small step closer to her.

She responded by taking a step back and losing her balance.

Not in a dramatic fashion, just a little slip, a teetering on the edge of being solid and falling. Her hands went back to catch her and gripped the shelf.

Simultaneously, Johnny caught her around the waist, stabilizing her.

She smiled hugely because of the silliness, and his eyes dropped to her mouth.

"I like your smile," he said.

"I like yours too."

He smiled in response.

He moved one of his hands slowly from her waist to cup her jaw, a slow, tender slide of fingers on skin.

The sensations it created were completely foreign.

And exciting.

She licked her lips and tried to inhale, but breathing had become too complicated.

His mouth drifted over hers, the barest of touches. He applied gentle pressure to her neck, tilting her head. She closed her eyes and surrendered to his request for her offering.

Every nerve ending in her body was aware of every small touch. His fingertips on her waist, the light stroke of his thumb along her jaw.

He slowly, almost lazily, kissed the corner of her mouth. His lips repeated the motion on the center of her upper lip, then again on her lower lip. Her mouth tried to follow his retreat, but he held her just out of reach. Then he came in again for the tenderest of salvos. Warm, lingering touches on her mouth, melting her reserves, stirring emotions in her head and heart that she didn't understand.

It was all so deliberate.

And delicate.

"Please," she whimpered as he again drew a breath away.

"Please what?" he had the audacity to ask.

But she didn't care. She was soft clay in his hands, needing to be formed into something more.

"Please kiss me." She heard the desperation in her voice. It was a poor echo of the need knotting inside her. She gripped his biceps, and his muscles tensed beneath her hands.

His mouth hovered over hers again and she pushed onto her toes, needing to fuse their connection.

Finally, he relented and allowed her access.

Lips parted, tongues tasted, twisted, hands searched.

Her hands slid up his biceps to his shoulders and into his thick hair, pulling him closer to her.

His hand at her waist crossed her back at a slant, pressing their torsos together. The hand on her jaw went down to her hip and then to her backside in a grip so powerful and primal that she let out a startled gasp.

Her blood, her skin, her thoughts sang in harmony. All she wanted was to kiss this man forever. His taste, his heat, his strength—they met her in her need and she chased it. Wanting to give him the same sensations he was giving to her.

He groaned into her mouth and it sent shivers through her body.

This…

This was nothing she had known.

Beauty and profanity all at once.

"Oh, geez. Seriously?"

Hannah's smile drew her lips away from Johnny's. He rested his forehead against hers, breathing heavily.

I did that, she thought with delight.

"Shawn," Johnny warned, deadly serious.

"Sorry. I just didn't think it would freak me out that much." Shawn shifted on his feet but didn't leave.

"You can go now," Johnny reminded him tersely.

Hannah's body began to shake with silent laughter. His grip on her had relaxed significantly and she planted her face in his chest.

"The library is closing…so…"

"Thank you, Shawn," Hannah said, twisting her face out of Johnny's shirt.

"Yeah, whatever," Shawn grumbled, and walked away.

Hannah gripped his shirt at his waist and tried to hold on for one more second before the moment was well and truly over.

He kept one hand on her waist and put the other on a shelf behind her head.

He drew back and those beautiful dark eyes scanned her features. She could only imagine what he saw. She hoped he saw the satisfaction he'd created.

The muscles in his jaw flexed under the skin and she instinctively touched it with her fingertips. He froze, his eyes darting to hers.

She didn't know what to say. For once, words had failed her.

She didn't want to come across as snarky, and yet she was too afraid to say something sincere. So she remained silent.

So did Johnny.

After a minute, their breathing had returned to mostly normal and Hannah realized it was over.

She forced a smile and then ducked under his arm to leave.

"Hannah," he called when she'd reached the end of the stack.

She turned.

But he just stood there, hands at his sides, conflict in his eyes.

She nodded.

He didn't need to explain to her about temptation and regret.

She knew all too well.

CHAPTER SEVENTEEN

MOOD RING

HANNAH

Work was hard to focus on.

Hannah kept staring off into space, her fingers lightly touching her lips, the memory so intense she wanted to live there.

Johnny Enamorado Torres was a helluva kisser.

She couldn't remember ever having such a lingering sensation.

His hair in her hands, the feel of his body pressing against hers, the scent of cinnamon and leather and soap.

She exhaled heavily and tried to come back to the present.

But the present was not nearly as fun.

"We've had an increase in escalations and I'd like to see those numbers drop."

"You know what else had increased? Shitty product," she muttered under her breath. Someone nearby snickered.

She glanced at her supervisor, Collin, and realized he was looking at her.

She rolled her eyes and went back to scribbling lines and hearts on her notepad.

The point of the staff meetings was to get everyone on the same page, get them fired up to give the "best customer service available."

Easier said than done.

It was hard to give good service when you'd been given a faulty product to coerce your caller into thinking they had mismanaged. Also, being called a "sonofabitch" twenty-five times a day didn't help either.

When had this happened?

When had she gone from not really caring about her boring little job to being so sick of it, she wanted to drive a spear through her headset?

Her phone buzzed in her pocket, answering her question.

Right.

It happened around the time she'd met a young busker with an agenda.

And damn her if she hadn't gotten suckered into his adorable pleas for help.

Not to mention he had a seriously hot older brother who could kiss like a Greek god.

But that was beside the point.

The "when" for disliking her job was established. But the "why" was a little less clear.

Or she was just really clever at avoiding having to directly answer her own question.

The meeting dismissed and Hannah went to the restroom to check her messages.

Shawn: Johnny says we can use the studio on Saturday since there's no game

Right. There was no game on Saturday. She'd forgotten. It would be nice to have a break from all the prying eyes.

It had started to feel a little invasive the past few weeks. Her friendship with Johnny and Sarahi had drawn attention.

When her entire life goal was to avoid attention.

She sent a reply to Shawn that she would be there and then headed to the break room for a much-needed caffeine jolt.

* * *

Her phone rang on the counter and she froze.

She had not spoken to Johnny since he'd kissed the motherfucking hell out of her the other night. In fact, this was the first time he had called her since.

Perhaps they were just going to pretend like it hadn't happened.

If only that were possible on her end.

Unfortunately, she couldn't stop reliving it.

"Hello?" she answered.

"What are you making for dinner?" he asked, like all was normal.

"Meatloaf."

"Mmm," he said into the phone, the sound sending tingles throughout her body.

"What's up with you?" she asked, trying to sound as casual as possible.

"Shawn told me that you're coming down to the studio on Saturday to work on stuff with him."

"You heard right," she verified.

Okay, so far so good. Maybe she could do this. It wasn't too different from how relationships were with guys before. Just instead of pretending she liked them so they'd have sex with her, now she had to pretend that she *didn't* like him so that she never tried to have sex with him.

She rested her forehead on the counter and whimpered internally.

This was really all his fault.

He shouldn't have kissed her.

"Is there anything I can get ready for you ahead of time? Any equipment that you want to use?"

This was regular, normal conversation with Johnny. It was about work and was also a great display of his helpfulness.

Fucking bastard.

"Um, I'm not sure. Nothing comes to mind." She straightened and put both hands on top of her head.

"You okay? You sound weird."

Piper came around the corner, eyes narrowed suspiciously. Hannah held her gaze.

"Everything is great! Can I call you later? My meatloaf is on fire."

She hit the "End" button.

Both she and Piper stared at each other in silence for thirty seconds.

"So..." Piper raised her eyebrows. "You're a liar."

Hannah exhaled and let her hands drop to her sides. "I know."

"Why are you lying to Johnny? I thought you two were cool as cucumbers."

Hannah opened her mouth to reply but stopped, confused by Piper's verbiage. "What decade are you from?"

Piper crossed her arms over her chest, unimpressed.

Hannah sputtered, groaned, and growled as she put on her hot mitts and retrieved the meatloaf from the oven.

She set the pan down and tried to think.

But nothing happened.

All she could hear was her lies, and all she could see was his smile.

"Hannah," Piper snapped.

Hannah glanced up.

"Was he mean to you?" Piper sounded worried.

"No." Hannah shook her head immediately. "He wasn't mean. He just…kissed me."

Piper nodded slowly. "Yeah…"

"You knew about that?"

"Shawn told me days ago."

Oh, shit. Right.

"Was it…bad?" Piper tried to guess.

"I wish."

"Huh?"

Hannah closed her eyes and groaned again. This was not something she wanted to talk about with her little sister. It was grown-up things for grown-up minds. Besides, she saw the way Piper looked at Johnny—like he was a hero in a fairytale come to life.

She didn't want to create any more complications for her preteen brain.

"I don't want to talk about it right now, okay, pipsqueak?" Hannah said gently.

Piper scowled, but she dropped it.

Besides, she wouldn't even have the first clue how to talk about it. He had kissed her like a sailor coming home but then called her and asked about dinner like it was all the same?

Either she was missing something or that kiss had been much better for her than for him.

But that didn't seem likely. She had been an expert kisser.

Hadn't she?

Had everyone been faking?

Oh, shit.

Was this how guys felt when then found out they were bad in bed?

Nah, she was overthinking it.

Had to be.

Right?

* * *

The next day, work was even more boring than usual.

Hannah had not yet successfully been able to stop thinking about Johnny.

She also hadn't called him back last night. Which made her feel guilty. Like she was avoiding a major responsibility.

You know what always helps stress and overthinking? More coffee.

When she entered the small kitchenette, TJ and Courtney were speaking with heads bent and voices hushed. Courtney giggled.

"Hey, you guys," Hannah said coyly.

They jumped apart, flustered.

Hannah filled her cup and turned toward them.

"So, that restaurant must be pretty great."

Courtney blushed and averted her eyes. TJ smirked, a cockiness in his posture that usually wasn't apparent.

Who would have thought? Hannah Lee James, former train wreck turned matchmaker.

Tamara and Amy entered the break room and Tamara deliberately bumped into Courtney, causing her to spill her coffee.

Courtney suffered silently and shrank away from the two mean girls as they took over the coffee counter.

Or tried to.

Hannah decided to take up more space than she needed and hopped her ass onto the counter.

"So, Courtney," Hannah said, spreading her legs and setting her cup down on the counter in between them. "Did TJ pick you up in his fancy car?"

If she listened carefully, she could hear the sound of tires screeching in Tamara and Amy's collective brain.

Courtney blushed and tucked her hair behind her ears.

"Yeah. And then he took me dancing. I didn't even know he knew I liked dancing."

"TJ!" Hannah exclaimed with admiration. "What a great date you must be!" She struck him on the shoulder with a fist.

TJ rubbed the spot she'd hit and shrugged, his face reddening.

"Well, Courtney's really cool. And I wanted to make an effort to show her that." He looped an arm around her waist and kissed her cheek.

It was actually Hallmark movie schmaltzy and Hannah was into it.

Tamara made a noise that sounded like a gag and a cough.

"You okay over there, Tamara?" Hannah asked, taking a sip of coffee.

Tamara ignored her. Which was too bad because Hannah was just itching for a reason to make her hate her day. She knew she was pushing it, but she honestly didn't care.

"I just threw up in my mouth a little," Tamara said, turning around to face the happy couple.

Amy cackled.

Hannah stifled her unbridled glee.

"Why?" she asked bluntly. "Did you remember what you looked like?"

Tamara's eyes flashed as she whipped her head around to point daggers at Hannah.

"What did you say?" she hissed.

Hannah licked her lips and leaned forward and spoke slowly. "I asked if you threw up in your mouth because you remembered that you were a disgusting person."

Faster than she thought possible, Tamara slapped her across the face. The smack echoed through Hannah's head.

Everyone grew very still and held their breath.

Hannah shook her head, trying to snap out of the shock of being hit across the face.

"Damn, Tamara!" Hannah touched her red-hot cheek. "You hit me in the face." And then she started laughing.

Not a small laugh either. But a deep, hearty chuckle that grew into raucous belly laughter. Tamara and Amy hurried from the break room.

Hannah wiped the tears from under her eyes.

"Are you okay?" Courtney asked, placing a baggy of ice gently on Hannah's cheek.

"I'm going to get Collin," TJ said, and hurried off.

Hannah took the ice gift and nodded at beautiful Courtney.

"I'm fine. It's been a while since a bitch slapped me, but I'll recover."

"I can't believe she did that." Courtney's gray eyes were round and worried.

"Oh, I can. I've always known how to push the wrong buttons." Hannah grabbed Courtney by the hand. "Hey, don't let people like that get under your skin. Mean bitches are all the same. They hate themselves so much that it spills over onto other people. You're a good person."

Courtney looked uncomfortable with the compliment, but she stuck out her chin bravely anyway. "You didn't have to do that, you know."

"I know. But I wanted to."

Courtney laughed despite herself.

Then Collin came in and the fun was over.

* * *

JOHNNY

He hated being called to the school.

But it felt different today for some reason. Maybe it was because he'd been waiting for the hammer to drop since the moment he'd caught Hannah telling off Shatford.

When he'd tried to talk to Shawn about it, he couldn't get much out except what he already knew.

But since he hadn't been directly involved in the incident, he didn't know if he could go to the higher-ups himself.

Or maybe he should call Aunt Carmen.

After all, she had connections.

He rounded the corner, and the bench outside Principal Mendez's office came into view.

On more than one occasion, it had been Shawn waiting for him.

This time it was Hannah.

His steps faltered for a moment, and then he picked up speed, excited to see her.

She heard him approach and turned to face him.

All of his previous thoughts fled when he saw the red hand-shaped welt on her face.

"What happened?" he asked, sliding onto the bench and gently taking her face into his hands. He hovered his thumb just over the angry skin, afraid to touch it.

Her hands caught his and she sniffed a laugh.

"Oh, a woman at work slapped me."

"What? Why?!" he exclaimed, anger gripping his heart.

"Because I'm mouthy, babe," she answered sincerely, giving his hands a squeeze.

His eyes bounced between hers as he struggled for what to say. The anger he'd felt didn't fade and he took a deep breath to help it along. But he still didn't understand.

Hannah, still grasping his hands at her face, gently removed and lowered them.

"I'm fine. It's not like I've never been slapped before. And, as usual, I totally had it coming."

He wasn't sure which part made him more angry, that she thought she deserved it or that it wasn't a new sensation.

She patted his hands, an attempt to soothe what she didn't understand.

"It looks worse than it is. My body always overreacts to the most minor of injuries. It'll fade in an hour or so and it'll be like it never happened."

When he didn't respond, she cleared her throat and looked up and down the hall.

"Do you know why we've been summoned, by the way?" she asked, addressing their location.

He shook his head and ran a hand over his jaw. "They didn't say. Just that it was urgent."

"Same here."

"I imagine it has something to do with Shatford," he muttered. No one was nearby, but he didn't want to be heard by anyone anyway. As far as he knew, no one else knew about Hannah's interaction with the vice principal over the weekend. But he'd been wrong before.

The door opened and Dr. Mendez waved them both in.

Johnny settled into his customary chair in front of the principal's desk, Hannah taking the seat next to him.

"I imagine you're wondering why I've asked both of you to come in at the same time," Dr. Mendez got right to the point.

The principal was a small Latina woman, dressed in a smart pantsuit, her black hair styled in a close-cut pixie. She quickly returned to her side of the desk and took a seat.

"The CBCA Board has received a number of complaints this year and they are going to proceed with an investigation. As such, they have asked me to interview a few of the people mentioned as witnesses in the complaints. Both of you came up a number of times as being present during a few instances. If you would rather we do the interviews separately, we can schedule that."

Dr. Mendez shifted some papers around on her desk, like she was sorting them.

Hannah turned wide eyes to Johnny, who shrugged in return.

"Uh, complaints?" Hannah asked the administrator.

Dr. Mendez glanced up and folded her hands on top of her desk. "Yes. A number of complaints about Vice Principal Shatford."

Hannah made a small, satisfied sound in the back of her throat and eased back in her seat.

"Who made these complaints?" Johnny asked curiously, trying to hide a smug smile by rubbing his hand over his chin thoughtfully.

"At this time they wish to remain anonymous." Dr. Mendez forced a smile. "If it's all right with you, I only have a few questions for you, and then you can be on your way."

Hannah relaxed in the chair, her arms hanging loosely on the armrests. "I am happy to help in any way I can."

* * *

Thirty minutes later, Johnny and Hannah were standing at the front door of the school, zipping up their coats to go back into the cold.

"That was way smoother than I thought it would be," he remarked, still shifting nervously out of habit.

"Right? Maybe evil gets what's coming to it after all," Hannah said thoughtfully.

All they'd had to do was tell the truth, Dr. Mendez wrote everything down, and they were free to leave. It didn't look good for Shatford.

"Do you have to go back to work?" he asked.

"Nope," she replied, her lips popping with the word. "I got fired today."

She tugged her mittens on and pushed the door open, leaving him standing there with his mouth open. He hurried after her. The wind whipped through the parking lot and she ducked her head, hurrying to her car.

"Hannah!" he called after her.

She opened her car door and turned to face him.

"It's cold." She tossed her bag into the car. "Just call me later. I'll tell you all about it."

She got into the car and started it in one motion. Johnny stepped back to get out of her way.

Why did it feel like she was running away from him?

He watched her drive away before he got into his car and started it. He checked the time and decided he'd just wait for Shawn to get out instead of making him take the train. It was incredibly cold.

He sent a text to Shawn, letting him know he was there.

Then he turned on the radio, trying to distract him from thoughts of Hannah.

He didn't want to think about her unless he could be with her. Because then he could talk to her, hear what she had to say, try not to kiss her…

Everything about that moment came rushing back to him and he inhaled deeply, trying to push it aside.

But he couldn't.

He'd crossed a line that could never be uncrossed, and now things were different.

The look on her face when she'd walked away from him in the library.

She *knew*. She knew he had acted on impulse and wasn't going to hold it against him.

But that was the thing—he wasn't sure he wanted to be free of it.

For as good as she was always declaring he was, he didn't feel good about that decision.

Not even a little.

It had been selfish and stupid.

He knew exactly where the blame fell, and there was no going back.

He'd made a choice, and now they both had to live with it.

The question that kept harassing him in the back of his mind was whether or not he wanted to kiss her again.

His body screamed yes in all the languages he knew.

His heart seemed to be on board with that notion as well.

It was his mind he was having trouble making sense of.

Which was why he wanted to talk to her.

Her view, the way she said things, her bold manner, they encouraged him to think for himself. To let go of what he was "supposed" to do and just do what he wanted.

But how could he have an open dialogue with her if she was avoiding him?

And how could he get her to stop avoiding him without him bringing up the very topic he wasn't ready to talk about with her?

How had this woman become so vitally important to him, and how did she not know it?

* * *

HANNAH

She stared at the phone as it rang. Deep remorse filled her chest when it finally stopped ringing.

She didn't feel good about the lie she'd told him. But she couldn't look him in the eye for one more minute without saying something stupid.

Cravings were a normal and natural part of an addict's life.

She just had to ride the wave, and eventually, she'd come out the other side.

It wasn't his fault. He had no idea that by kissing her it would spark a dangerous hunger. Healthy people were allowed to kiss and love and fuck and satisfy their urges. She'd corrupted those urges a long time ago.

It would take some time, space, and mindfulness.

Johnny would see it eventually.

She'd be more responsible in the future.

But that started here with staying away until she felt strong enough to say no to something she really, really wanted.

Her phone rang again and she tipped her head back, groaning out loud.

Then she put her phone in the silverware drawer where she couldn't hear it anymore.

CHAPTER EIGHTEEN

TOXIC

HANNAH

She just had to say it out loud. It wasn't like Brenda didn't already know. But saying it, the actual words, made it all the more real.

"Just say it," Brenda prompted gently.

"The herpes…" Hannah said, hearing the sorrow in her voice and being even more confused than before. Why should she be sad? This wasn't new information! She'd been living with HSV-2 for three years!

"Are you having an outbreak?" Brenda asked gently, her pen hovering over the yellow legal pad.

"No." Hannah shook her head.

"Have you…had a sexual encounter recently?"

Hannah's eyes darted up to Brenda's, but she found no judgment there. Only compassion.

"Johnny kissed me."

She didn't miss the ripple of surprised delight that hit Brenda's face before it smoothed over.

"Was it unwelcome?" Brenda asked.

Hannah's gaze tracked to the design of the rug on the floor beneath their feet.

Had it been unwelcome?

The kiss that had shaken all of her convictions?

No.

"Shouldn't it have been?" she whispered. She inhaled slowly and raised her eyes. "I don't know what to do now."

That was the most honest statement she'd been able to utter since Johnny had kissed her in the library. In the moment, while it had been happening, she had seemed to know exactly what to do. Where to put her hands, how to move her mouth.

How to walk away.

"Have you spoken to him?" Brenda prodded gently.

"No." Hannah frowned. "I haven't answered his calls."

"Why not?"

"Because I don't know what to say."

"How about the truth?"

"I don't want to hurt him."

"And the truth would hurt him?"

Hannah didn't respond.

But her thoughts were swirling.

How could a conversation with Johnny *not* hurt?

She had obviously led him to believe that something could happen between them when that wasn't possible. She had even *asked* him to kiss her. Shame flushed fresh through her system as she remembered her begging him to kiss her.

It wasn't his fault.

He didn't know what she was capable of.

It was her responsibility to protect others from herself.

"Hannah, can I interrupt your shame spiral for just a moment?"

Brenda recapped her pen and folded her hands on top of her legal pad, leaning forward.

"We've been doing this for a while. For more than a year, we've been meeting once a week. You have always been very candid with me, so I think you will appreciate it if I am candid with you."

Hannah nodded once.

"You can have a healthy romantic relationship that includes sex."

Well, that was candid.

"It's important to tell him. I would recommend having that conversation before you're in an amorous condition. Do you understand what I'm saying?"

"I should have told him before I kissed him."

"No." Brenda's frustration was obvious. "It was a kiss—"

"It wasn't just a kiss," Hannah interrupted.

Brenda tilted her head to the side. "It was more than a kiss?"

Hannah huffed a sigh. "Yes. But no." She ran her hands through her hair and held the crown of her head in both hands. "If it was just a kiss, this wouldn't be an issue. But it was…more."

She dropped her hands in her lap helplessly.

"Because you have feelings for him," Brenda guessed.

"Sure." Hannah shrugged. "But what good is that?"

Brenda tried to withhold a smile but couldn't.

"What?" Hannah asked accusingly. "Tell me what I'm not getting."

"Hannah," Brenda said seriously. "You're very lovable."

Hannah's face screwed up and she sat back in her chair.

"If Johnny has feelings for you, and you have feelings for him, I don't see a reason why you can't discuss that with him."

Hannah flattened her lips, because the reasons seemed obvious. She could take that legal pad and make a list if Brenda needed reminders. But, as had become the norm, Brenda was already anticipating Hannah's religious need to sass and she cut right through it.

"I'm going to repeat something I've said to you many times. I can't give you permission to be happy." Brenda spoke with such authority that Hannah wanted to shrink back.

Tears burned the back of Hannah's throat and she swallowed.

"But love is dangerous," she said, her voice rough and raspy.

"Love is a risk," Brenda agreed. "But you already know who you are. You have agency and self-awareness. You're not looking to Johnny to complete you or to save you. You've been saving yourself for a long time now."

Hannah stared at her therapist as her words sank in.

"What if I tell him about having herpes and he doesn't want me?"

It was a stupid excuse, but it was the only one she could articulate.

"Then he's not the right partner for you," Brenda answered simply.

JOHNNY

He checked his phone. Again.

No missed calls. No texts. No messages.

He scrolled through social media and typed her name into Google.

But nothing came up.

Irritated with his repetitive actions, he tossed his phone over the railing of the kitchen and onto the sofa in the lower living area. It bounced and landed on the floor.

He stretched and flexed his fingers anxiously, shaking his hands out by his sides before stirring the macaroni.

Yep. He was making comfort foods in the middle of the night because he couldn't sleep. Baked macaroni. It was one of Shawn's favorites when he'd been little, one of the only dishes Johnny had been able to make early on.

This was stupid.

The entire situation was absolute bull.

Hannah had been avoiding his calls all week and it was driving him crazy.

He'd left messages, he'd sent texts. All of them had been ignored.

If she hadn't made solid plans with Shawn to be at the studio on Saturday, he would have driven over to her place and confronted her.

At least that's what he told himself.

But truthfully, he had no idea.

He didn't want to force her to talk to him if she didn't want to.

The very idea of her not wanting to talk to him stung in ways he'd never experienced.

It was strange and beautiful how a person's thoughts and words could have such a grounding effect on another.

How she could have an effect on him.

But if she didn't want to talk to him, he couldn't make her.

But he could make macaroni.

And then he'd eat it like a bear and go back to bed, hopefully to sleep off the lost feeling he had and couldn't explain.

Distantly, he heard little bells tinkling and froze.

Recognizing his ringtone, he dropped the spoon and dove over the railing to the couch below. He landed with more force than he expected but snatched his phone off the floor, hitting the answer button.

He glanced at the call screen and frowned at Nikki's name.

"Hello?" he asked with a wheeze, pushing himself back onto the couch and sitting up.

"Did I wake you?" Nikki asked, her voice hushed.

"Nope." Johnny ran a hand through his hair and stood. "I'm up."

He couldn't breathe because he'd knocked the wind out of himself, but he was definitely not sleeping.

"I'm, uh, I'm still at the studio," Nikki said.

"Why? Is everything okay?" Johnny glanced the direction of the studio as if he could see it through the walls.

"Yeah," Nikki said, sounding unsure. "I just, I feel like you should know that Hannah is here?"

Johnny took a second to process what Nikki said, and then he sprinted back to the kitchen and shut off the oven and stove top.

"She texted me a few hours ago and asked if she could use the live room to work through some ideas, and I thought it would be okay since you guys seemed to be pretty cool with each other."

Johnny tugged his shoes on by the front door and grabbed his keys off the hook.

"But she hasn't really said anything. She's just sitting at the piano."

"I'm on my way," Johnny said, slipping his coat on. "You can take off. Thank you, Nikki."

"Are you sure?" Nikki asked.

"Yeah. Already have my coat on."

He hung up and sent a text to Shawn, who was sleeping, just in case he woke up.

The air outside had that cold kind of bite where it stung the inside of his nostrils as he tried to breathe normally. He left, hurrying down the walkway and out the gate, devouring the thirty feet to the front door of his second home.

Nikki opened the door as he approached. She had her coat on and their eyes met.

"Do you want me to stay?" she asked.

"No," he replied with a smile that he hoped she bought. "We were supposed to get some work done and I just forgot. See you Monday."

"Okay," she said, not sounding like she believed him, but also not willing to argue about it.

He waved goodbye and made sure the door was locked behind him before seeking out Hannah.

Why would she be here?

And why would she call Nikki instead of him to let her in?

He was afraid he knew the answer, but he didn't want to think about it.

She was in the live room of Studio Y.

The one they had spent the most time in so far. None of the lights were on, but the full moon shone through the high windows, bathing the room in a silver glow.

She sat with her back to him at the piano.

On top of the piano was a bottle of wine.

His heart squeezed and he paused, taking in the shape of her.

She turned her head slightly.

"Nikki must've called you," she said.

Johnny swallowed. He took off his coat and tossed it in the corner. Then he made his way to the piano bench.

He got closer and saw that the wine was still corked.

And the lack of surprise he felt surprised him.

He broke his attention from the bottle and looked to Hannah, who was watching him carefully.

"Are we rolling tape on this?" he asked with a half smile, trying to gauge her mood.

She smiled, but it was a sad smile. And something else.

"I had a lot of thoughts and I needed to work them out." She danced the fingers of one hand along the keys and then returned it to her lap.

His worry and building frustration from earlier disappeared, and all he cared about was her.

Her mind, and her heart, and her pulse.

"You want to talk about it?" he asked.

She chewed on her lower lip, hesitating. She let out a soft huff that was almost a laugh but not quite.

"It's funny, all I've wanted this week is to talk to my friend." She lifted her eyes to him, making her point. "But it was you I wanted to talk about, so…"

He took a deep breath, catching her meaning. An unexpected warmth spread through his chest.

They were friends.

And she had missed talking to him too.

As far as declarations went, it was small.

But significant.

At least for him.

"You can talk to me about me," he prompted.

"Right," she replied with an eye roll.

"I'll get you started." He squinted one eye like he was thinking. "I have a tendency to be too awesome and completely outshine you. Which, obviously, makes you self-conscious." Her smile lit him up from the inside.

"You nailed it." She laughed softly and trailed her fingers over the keys again.

Soft music filled the live room as she played almost absentmindedly. With no direction or end—just gentle notes flowing from her delicate fingers, like her thoughts were on a musical journey of their own.

"I came here because it was the closest I could get to you without actually having to see you," she said, keeping her hands moving slowly.

"And then I showed up anyway."

She sent him a soft look. "I'm not complaining."

The song at her fingertips took off and the music swirled around the room.

She was unfairly beautiful in the moonlight.

Her dark hair was loose, in the soft waves she'd been wearing recently, reaching to her waist. It was longer than he ever remembered it being.

The soft gray sweater she was wearing was too big and the neckline dropped off one shoulder.

He wanted to hold her and kiss her and soothe her and he couldn't explain why.

Just that he wanted it in a way that seemed too nuanced to be impulsive.

And maybe that was what he'd been struggling with all week since he'd kissed her.

Not that he regretted it, but that he hadn't treated it with the importance it deserved.

He hadn't treated *her* with the importance she deserved.

Is that why she was here, playing ballads to an old vice in the dark?

He glanced at the wine, untouched, on the top of the piano. She caught him.

"Saw that, did ya?" she asked. She pounded dramatically on the piano. "Dun dun dunn."

He chuckled, not feeling the worry or fear that perhaps someone else might. But he did have questions.

"Is there a reason you're treating this Cabernet to an exclusive performance?"

She looked at the bottle, her hands paused lightly on the keys.

"Therapy is hard," she stated after a minute.

She glanced up at him and the doors were wide open. No pretense, no walls, no conflict. Just raw honesty.

"Did you have therapy today?" he asked.

She nodded, took a breath, and started playing the piano again. "Talked about you."

Her eyes flicked back up to him and he met her gaze without asking for more. Whatever she wanted to share with him, he'd take.

"Talked about me," she went on. "Talked about happiness and consequences. And then I drove around for a while." She smirked his direction. "Because no matter how smart and gifted your therapist is, you still have to do the work yourself. And I am…so tired."

The piano seemed to sing along with her words. Goose bumps scattered along his arms and retreated, only to return again.

"I stopped at a store and bought this beautiful bottle of wine. An old favorite. And then I came here because I missed you."

She closed her eyes and smiled a sad sort of smile. When she opened them, they were glossy with unshed tears.

"All the people I've betrayed in my life—and there's been a lot—I betrayed myself the most. And I don't want to do that anymore."

A tear slipped down her cheek and he didn't stop himself from being right there.

He cupped her cheek in his hand and caught the tear with his thumb, wiping it away. The music stopped. She turned her face into his hand and closed her eyes.

What could he have ever done to end up with a woman like this in his life?

At first, he thought she was a temptation or a distraction. Or worse, someone to ruin him all over again.

Those thoughts felt like a lifetime ago.

She wasn't any of those things he'd feared.

She was a solar flare. An explosion of light and heat, changing the world around her with every burst of her heart.

And she had no idea.

She opened her eyes, and again, he saw right to the soul of her.

"I wasn't going to drink it," she whispered.

"I know." And he did know. He knew it the way he knew he was going to take his next breath. It wasn't even something he had to entertain with a thought.

He moved to join her on the piano bench, taking his hand from her face and sliding it along her lower back. She made room for him and rested her head on his shoulder.

And together they shared the same space.

They probably needed to talk through a few things, clear the air, clarify some details.

But in that moment, he just wanted to hold space for her. Show her she didn't have to shoulder her burdens alone if she didn't want to.

"Play me a song, Johnny," she requested in the stillness.

"Hmm, you know I'm not great at the piano," he reminded her.

She sat up, removing her head from his shoulder and gave him a look he couldn't remember ever seeing before.

"Please."

Yep.

He would do anything for her.

Weirdly, he knew exactly what he wanted to play for her the moment she brought it up.

He brushed her hair out her eyes and tracked the movement of his fingers as he tucked the strands behind her ear.

"Okay."

It was too big for them. Too honest, too soon, too much.

But it was the only song he wanted to sing to her in that moment.

He tested the keys, finding his chords, and took a deep breath.

"I assume you've heard of Paul McCartney?" he asked, trying to add levity to what he was about to do to both of them.

"Are you going to make me cry, Johnny?"

He licked his lips and shrugged.

Then he played "Maybe I'm Amazed."

And he played it with gusto.

Hoping that his enthusiasm would overshadow his lack of skill.

But the words…those he meant.

He just had no idea how much until he'd already sung them out to her.

He finished the song and waited for her reaction, but she just leaned against his side. Her warmth seeped through their layers of clothes, and the rest of the studio felt cold by comparison.

After a moment, she sat up and placed her hands on the keys.

But instead of playing anything, she turned to face him, concern lining her eyes for the first time since he'd walked in.

"You kissed me," she said, but it came out like it was almost a question.

"Yes," he replied, his chest tightening.

So now they were going to talk about it.

Okay.

"Why?" she asked, the crease between her eyebrows deepening.

Why?

"Because you're beautiful and I wanted to."

A shadow passed through her eyes and he knew he'd said the wrong thing somehow.

"Is that why you were avoiding me this week?" he asked, trying to be careful. But his heart was hammering so hard in his chest, he thought it might crack a rib.

"Yes," she said, eyes downcast.

Johnny ran his tongue over his lower lip as he tried to understand what they were both saying. Or not saying.

All the words that came to mind seemed grossly inadequate for what he wanted to convey.

So, he just sat there silently.

After a moment, she straightened and her fingers danced along the keys. It was a song he didn't recognize, but it was beautiful.

He watched her hands move effortlessly and glanced at her face.

Her eyes were closed and her lips were silently mouthing the words to the song.

He wished he knew what it was.

But he also didn't want to stop her.

Maybe they were having trouble finding that easy communication between them, but the music had never left.

They'd always been able to say more to each other with that than anything else.

One song turned into three.

After the third song, she stopped and rested against his side again.

"I really missed my friend," she said.

He put his arm around her, hugging her closer.

"I missed you too."

Wasn't that the truth?

A few days without Hannah had him making mac and cheese in the middle of the night.

Speaking of…

"Are you hungry?" he asked.

She sat up and looked at him with interest.

"Did you hear my stomach or something?" she asked with a crooked smile.

Something about that eased the tension building inside him.

Maybe things weren't "better" yet between them, but they weren't bad. They were still friends.

And that was more important to him than he had realized.

"I was making mac and cheese before I came over here."

Her eyes lit up and he knew he had her.

"Homemade mac and cheese?" she asked.

He scoffed. "What do you take me for?"

They both stood and he went to retrieve his coat.

Hannah ran a hand lovingly over the top of the piano.

"I love this thing," she said by way of explanation when she caught him watching her.

He stopped himself before he blurted out that it could be hers. It basically was anyway.

No matter what happened in the coming days, he would always see that piano as Hannah Lee's. Because it had never truly been played until she arrived.

Something occurred to him.

"Why don't you have one?" he asked. He'd been to her condo; it was big enough. If she wanted to get a piano, she could have gotten a piano.

She picked up her coat from the floor nearby and he took it from her. She hesitated as he held the coat open.

"Well." She slid her arms inside and he settled the coat around her shoulders. "Waaaay back in the day, when I was someone else, I would require all my hotel suites to have a piano in them."

He whistled.

"Yeah, I was a brat." She pursed her lips. "I guess I thought I'd already had more than my fair share of things like that." She frowned, considering. "But I don't know. Maybe I could get myself one now."

She shoved her hands in her coat pocket and froze, giving him a look.

Before he could ask what it was about, she pulled a bundle of yarn from her pocket.

"Is that my hat?" He reached out, delicately taking the messy creation.

"My best one yet," she declared proudly.

He held it up, in awe that she had really made him something. Made it. With her hands.

"Oh my God." She laughed. "You don't have to do that to make me feel better."

He hugged it to his chest, not joking at all. "I love it. Thank you."

"You do not." She rolled her eyes and strolled out of the live room.

"I do too," he argued with a huff. He pulled the door closed behind him and followed her to the back exit.

He met her at the door and made a point of pulling the hat on over his head.

She shook her head at him like she thought he was ridiculous.

"See? Now my ears won't be cold anymore." He turned his head right and left so she could get a good look at how the hat covered him.

She touched the lock of hair that poked out from a hole in the front.

"What about that, huh?"

"Adds character," he replied smugly. "I have a one-of-a-kind Hannah Lee James. It's priceless."

She huffed a soft laugh and he realized how close they were in the darkened doorway. His eyes dropped to her mouth and the way her lips were curved in that smile he had grown to adore.

She glanced up, eyes glinting in the light of the exit sign.

Her dark hair framed her face, turning her into a portrait of music and melancholy, wrapped in one.

Exquisitely intoxicating.

All at once he was reminded of how he'd missed her over the last few days and how he didn't want to do anything to jeopardize her place in his life.

In a deliberate move, he opened the door, letting in the cold and extinguishing whatever it was that was trying to fight for a voice.

She shivered against the cold and buried her nose in the neck of her coat as she stepped outside.

Johnny set the alarm and locked the door.

She looped an arm through his, and he told himself that it was because there was fresh frost on the pavement and she was in high-heeled boots.

But when she leaned her head against his bicep and matched the timing of his steps, he didn't have anything else to say.

* * *

HANNAH

For some reason, Hannah didn't think Johnny's place would look exactly as it had the night she'd stormed in, offering him a bribe for his silence.

She tried to hide her embarrassment, because obviously it was the same place.

It was the same small living area where she'd realized he hated her, but she didn't know why. The guitar in the corner that had almost triggered the right memory on its own, but then got the job done when combined with the magic words.

And Shawn walking in, and the hope falling from his face as he realized why she'd really been there.

"Where's Shawn?" she asked, letting Johnny take her coat. A small thing that he probably had no idea she noticed.

But she noticed.

"Sleeping, hopefully." Johnny cast a look toward the upstairs and the dark rooms at the top. "What about Miss Piper?"

"Same. Hopefully." Hannah thought about the conversation she'd had with her sister earlier in the evening. She'd been worried. Not about Hannah, but about Johnny.

Hannah couldn't tell her that she was worried about Johnny too, but for different reasons.

Reasons that seemed so clear earlier and were now…murky.

"They must have stellar security at that place," Johnny remarked.

"They do. I wouldn't live there without it." Let alone leave the twelve-year-old there in the middle of the night.

"I just have to pop this in the oven for a few minutes to heat it up," Johnny said from the second level. "Come up here. Talk to me."

She wanted nothing more.

How she had gone a few days without his particular brand of nonsense, she had no idea. How had she lived her entire life without it?

Because living was living. And blooming was something else.

She slipped off her ankle boots and left them by the door.

"Is it okay that I'm barefoot?" she asked, scrunching up her nose.

He stood at the top of the steps and tossed his head back with a scoff, like she was being stupid.

She laughed at his response.

"I had to ask. Some people don't like feet," she pointed out.

"Those people need to get over themselves," he grumbled, not moving as she ascended the four steps to the kitchen.

They came face-to-face and he finally stepped back and held out his arms. "So, here's the kitchen. Nice, right?" He ran a hand over the granite countertops. "I added these myself. Put in all new appliances one at a time as they failed. Did all the floors myself too."

Johnny crossed his arms over his chest and leaned a hip against the counter.

She studied flooring, the countertops, the cabinets. "I didn't realize you were a carpenter."

"Started working for a contractor right when we moved here. He paid me cash to do the ugly jobs no one else wanted. Over time he showed me how to do pretty much everything. I could probably build a house from the bottom up by myself."

"Johnny, that's really fucking impressive," she said, meaning it.

"Thank you." He ducked his head, the tops of his ears turning pink. "It's not the East Randolph Residence, but it's okay."

She shook her head because she knew he was teasing, but she wasn't falling for it.

He grinned and ran a hand under the cabinet to his left. "And I added this."

Lights lit up under the top cabinets, bathing the counters below them in a soft glow. And music began to play from under-the-counter speakers.

She tilted her head, listening.

"Reggaeton?" she asked.

It wasn't a genre she was overly familiar with, but she had heard quite a bit of it when she'd been to his aunt's house.

He shrugged. "I like to dance while I cook?"

She snickered. "Now *that* I wouldn't mind seeing."

"It's hooked up to my phone, so it's usually a random assortment that plays."

"Sure, sure, sure. Or you could stop lying and show me what really happens in this kitchen."

He narrowed his eyes at her suspiciously, but the lopsided slant to his lips told her he wasn't serious.

She pumped her eyebrows once, challenging him.

His hips began to wiggle from side to side, seemingly of their own volition.

That's when Hannah realized she'd made an error.

She had not anticipated how Johnny Enamorado Torres would turn into liquid fire when he started dancing.

Her heart did that thud thing, but she felt it in various pleasure points around her body.

"C'mon, you have to do it too," Johnny said, dancing closer to her.

"I don't know how." It sounded like a lie, because she obviously knew how to dance. He'd seen her do it. But she was telling the truth.

She didn't know how she was supposed to move from where she was planted in awe.

Their eyes met and he held out his hand.

She took it with a small groan because she had no idea how she was going to manage this without turning into molten lava.

"It's the *punta*," he explained. He put his hands on her shoulders and held firm. "You don't move the upper body. Hold your shoulders level. All you move is your hips. Keep your feet as flat on the floor as you can and take small steps. Watch."

Oh, she was watching.

His hips wiggled to the beat. The light blue Henley he wore stretched and moved around his chest and trim waist.

She did her best to match the rhythm while following his instruction.

"Yeah, like that," he encouraged, sounding proud and happy.

A laugh bubbled out of her—half excited, half nervous.

This man had a way of making every moment important. Whether it was because he was being thoughtful and still, or silly and fun.

She loved it…being with him.

"Were you ever gonna tell me what happened at work?" he asked, keeping his eyes on her. But she knew what he was doing. He was using the distraction of dancing to disarm her.

And it worked.

"I called a woman ugly and she slapped me."

Johnny's smiled slipped and the expression in his eyes grew concerned.

"And then we were both called into HR for conflict resolution, where I refused to apologize." She smirked as she remembered the flustered HR rep. "In fact, I doubled down and got slapped again. Same cheek." She shrugged. "They fired both of us."

He stared at her, eyes round, and she waited for him to react in some way.

When he still didn't say anything, she huffed and stomped a foot on the floor, stopping their dancing.

"What? She was really mean!"

Johnny dropped his head back and laughed, placing the palm of one hand on the center of his chest. His voice rumbled and echoed through the kitchen, and Hannah nervously looked toward the upper rooms. Hopefully he wouldn't wake Shawn, because she really didn't want him to think less of her on the eve of her trying to mentor him.

Johnny righted himself and wiped moisture from under his eyes.

"Please," he begged, still trying to stop laughing. "Please promise me that you will *always* stay who you are."

She stared at him. Maybe he was crazy.

That would clear up a few things.

He rubbed a hand over his face, still smiling broadly. "Hannah Lee, the woman who never backed down," he murmured, looking her right in the eye like…

Like he was very pleased with what he saw.

"I'm not a nice person," she reminded him.

"True," he agreed. "But you're a real person."

For some reason that small compliment hit her in the center of her heart and fanned a flame that had no business being there.

The song switched, and he must've been telling the truth about it being on random because this time it was Paul McCartney. The same song Johnny had played for her in the studio.

Their eyes met and held.

After a beat he held out his hand to her. Without thinking about it, she took it.

He gently pulled her into his arms and slowly began stepping them around the kitchen, humming. He folded their hands together and held them to his chest, his other hand pressed softly on her lower back. He bent his neck to hold his cheek right at her temple. Which brought his mouth to her ear, where he began to softly sing to her.

Her feet lined up with his, and her body followed his lead to a point where she didn't know she could dance so effortlessly.

Soft, graceful, tender.

And his deep voice murmuring words written by a legend in her ear.

The timer went off and they stopped dancing, but they didn't jump apart.

It felt too perfect.

Too safe.

She didn't want to move.

He pressed a kiss to the top of her head and slowly backed away. His eyes let go last.

As he got the mac and cheese out of the oven, she found plates and forks. He dished up their middle of the night meal and they moved to the couch in the lower living room.

Neither one said anything about the dancing, and maybe it was okay to just let those small moments be small moments shared with one another.

He treated her with such kindness and beauty that she dared to feel lovely.

Hannah knew that she had begun to treasure those experiences with Johnny. She kept them locked away in a secret part of her heart. And if she didn't have him in her life someday, she would be able to look back and know those things had happened. And she'd been there.

For a moment, she had been cherished.

They sat in opposite corners of the couch to eat.

"So he can cook too," she murmured between bites.

He grinned, like he knew he was good at it, and she held on to that too.

Looking around the living space, she spotted a large canvas with a wordy quote on it, hanging on the opposite wall. She read it out loud.

"*Friendship is unnecessary, like philosophy, like art... It has no survival value; rather it is one of those things which give value to survival.* C. S. Lewis."

She read it again to herself.

"Nikki got that for me for a housewarming gift when we first moved in," he explained.

"Have you and Nikki been friends a long time?" she asked.

"A while. Decade or so."

"I like Nikki," Hannah revealed. A tremor shook her stomach at her admission. Liking people, being friendly, it wasn't exactly her "normal."

"She's likable," he agreed. "Really good at her job."

She wondered what it would be like to have a friendship last that long. To work with someone she respected and trusted.

Fear rushed through her body and she sat up a little straighter, placing her fork on the plate. She took in a deep breath and held it, then let it out.

As unwelcome as the fear was, that never stopped it from barging through the door without notice.

She took in another deep breath and reminded herself where she was.

She was in Chicago. Terrence didn't know where she was and he didn't care anyway. She was safe. Piper was safe.

"Having thoughts?" Johnny asked when she hadn't said anything else for a minute.

"Yeah," she confirmed, staring at the quote on the wall, just realizing how true it was.

She faced him, needing to tell him...something.

She just didn't know what. Or how.

It was as if what she needed to say was a huge ball of emotion tangled up in her thoughts, and she couldn't unravel enough of it to make sense.

She cared for him, that much was clear.

But she cared for him in a way that was new and scary.

In a way she was afraid of losing.

Hannah had lost people before, many times over.

But she could pick up and move on and know they were better off without her anyway.

"Did you know you're my best friend?" she asked all of a sudden.

His eyebrows tilted up just slightly and his face softened.

"Your friendship gives value to my survival."

He didn't leave her out there all alone with her big reveal.

"Yours is the most important friendship I have ever had," he said roughly. "I've never valued anyone's opinion or ideas or…life the way I have yours." He swallowed.

She bit down on her bottom lip and nodded, peace spreading through her from the center out. A laugh bubbled out of her and she covered her mouth.

"What?" he asked.

"I just…it's stupid," she said. "But I've never had that."

"Never had what?"

"This." She waved a hand between them. "A best friend. Someone who cared about me just for the sake of caring about me." She shrugged one shoulder, attempting to shrug off the sadness of the truth. It kind of worked.

He blinked at her before he scrubbed a hand over his face. Then he hit her with his trademark Johnny earnestness.

"It's not difficult, babe."

Warmth hit her square in the chest and turned her insides to melted rubber.

"You're great," she blurted, smiling crooked.

He chuckled and bit down on his bottom lip.

She liked that too.

She liked everything about him.

"So, tomorrow we're recording a new demo for Shawn?" he easily segued.

"Yeah." She nodded. Shop talk. Yes! She loved shop talk.

No one ever wanted to talk about work with her *outside* of work. What kind of artist stopped thinking about art just because they weren't in the studio?

Lazy ones, that's who.

She brought up some ideas she'd bounced off Shawn, and Johnny nodded along, putting in little tidbits about his brother he thought would be helpful.

"I definitely want to get him to open up in the live room. I still feel like he's holding back in places."

Johnny's lips twitched. "Hold his feet to the fire, babe."

He would let her too. She just knew it. He trusted her to do right by Shawn, and what a wild difference that was from where they'd started a few weeks ago.

They continued chatting about what they planned on doing tomorrow and it was easy conversation.

But in the back of Hannah's mind was the herpes.

Or at least the knowledge that she needed to tell him.

Or maybe she didn't.

Really, she only needed to tell someone who was a potential sexual partner. It's not like she had to tell someone who was "just a friend."

Also, there was the fact that once Johnny knew, he wouldn't be interested in sex with her anymore.

If he even was.

Gah!

This was so crazy stupid and difficult.

This was why she'd bought the bottle of wine and driven it around town.

Because she needed to prove to herself that temptation wasn't stronger than choice. She could be around Johnny and not have sex with him.

But the memory of that kiss had her confused.

She wanted him. In all the ways.

But sex for her wasn't so much a hello as it was a goodbye. It was the final thing before she or they moved on.

And she didn't want to say goodbye to Johnny.

Maybe she could tell him in a joke form.

That was a friend thing, right?

Ooh, she'd come across a vintage sex-ed video on one of her streaming services. Maybe she could send him that.

"Herpes: The Scourge of the Earth! This video will teach you how to avoid getting herpes. Also known as the Worst People's Disease."

That was probably not an actual quote from the movie, but she wouldn't be surprised if it was.

"What are you thinking about?" Johnny interrupted her self-deprecating thoughts.

"Hmm?"

"You got quiet," he commented, not pushing.

She glanced down at her empty plate and then set it on the nearby table. Folding her hands in her lap, she held her shoulders back.

Just do it, James. Be an adult.

"I have to tell you something," she started. His eyes grew wary, but he didn't say anything. "There is literally no good time to tell someone this. I've been trying to come up with the perfect scenario, but it doesn't exist."

Her heart pounded hard in her chest and she squeezed her hands together to keep them from shaking.

"Are you moving?" Johnny accused, his voice hard.

"What?" She frowned and jerked her chin back. "No, of course not."

He heaved a sigh of relief that surprised her. "Thank God."

"Why would I be moving?"

"I don't know. You sounded like you had really bad news. I panicked."

Oh, buddy, don't relax just yet.

"I'm not moving," Hannah clarified, trying to get back to her original point. "I have herpes."

Bleck.

There.

She'd said it.

She stared down at her hands and waited.

He didn't reply for a long time and she finally looked up.

His expression was uncharacteristically blank.

She swallowed and decided to continue. Though when she'd practiced this in the car, he'd had more of a reaction.

"It's HSV-2. The STD kind. I'm on medication for it and it's being managed by a doctor." She licked her lips and looked around the room.

"Do…do you have any questions?" she asked.

He shook his head slowly. "No."

No?

"Okay." She rolled her lips inward and tried to not freak out.

It was out there now, and he had the information. She'd done the hard part and told him. Which fucking sucked. But part of her was just relieved to have it done.

She picked up her phone and checked the time.

"I should get home and sleep a little before we have to meet tomorrow."

They both stood and he took her plate up to the kitchen. She put on her boots. He met her back at the door and helped her into her coat.

It was all very sweet and sad at the same time.

"Are you parked in the back lot or in the street?" he asked, putting on his own coat.

"The lot."

They left his townhouse and he helped her down the steps.

In silence, they walked to her car. He waited until she started it and drove off before he went back to his home.

She drove home in silence, wondering if everything would be different now.

Why hadn't he asked any questions?

He hadn't said *anything.*

And she'd been worried he'd have questions that might make her uncomfortable.

She should have known better. Johnny was often on the side of unexpected.

Fuck.

Well, now he knew and he couldn't unknow it.

She got home, washed her face, took off her clothes, and crawled into her big, empty bed.

He knew now.

His lack of communication on the matter felt so final.

Like closing a door on something that hadn't been revealed yet.

She rolled onto her side and hugged her pillow to her chest.

And cried.

CHAPTER NINETEEN

PASSENGER

JOHNNY

He heard the front door open and stepped out of Studio Y's live room into the hallway.

Piper came around the bend first, bright smile on her face.

"Hey, Johnny!" Piper greeted.

"Hey, kid," he returned, holding up a hand for a high-five.

She smacked his hand and bolted past him into the live room, already hollering at Shawn about what kind of socks she was wearing.

Hannah came around the bend next, and like usual, it happened in slow motion.

He inhaled deeply, his stomach tightening, his shoulders relaxing, his fingers tingling.

When he'd sent her off in the dark last night, it had felt unfinished.

Most of him was worried she wouldn't show up this morning, though he couldn't articulate why. Paranoia, maybe.

She greeted him with an arched eyebrow and a small smirk.

"Coffee?" she asked, holding out a to-go cup.

She was absolutely gorgeous.

And not just because she was handing him coffee.

Black distressed skinny jeans, high-heeled boots, a white and pale blue flannel with a pale blue silky tank underneath. It was just a small change from her black and gray wardrobe, which she also rocked. Her hair was in loose waves again and she looked fresh and awake.

Unlike himself.

He ran a hand over the stubble on his face as he remembered that he hadn't shaved that morning.

At least he'd showered.

"Mmm," she said, breezing past him. "You smell nice."

He'd been in a hurry because he'd lost track of time and had accidently used Shawn's body wash. He would now be going out to purchase a case.

Johnny followed her into the live room, where she was already holding court like the queen she was.

She stripped out of the flannel and tied the sleeves around her waist.

"Get up to the crow's nest, pipsqueak." Hannah nodded at Piper, who skipped up the steps.

Hannah turned her attention to Shawn.

"I'm going to tell you something you don't want to hear."

Shawn's eyes bounced from Johnny to Hannah, and Johnny thought he actually heard the kid gulp.

"I want to multitrack it," Hannah said. Multitracking was a common method of recording, where each instrument, including vocals, are recorded separately and then put together. That way, each sound can be engineered separately to sound their best.

Some artists preferred live recordings of the entire band in the same room at once. This was usually done to capture the energy of the live sound they wanted on their album.

Shawn only ever used one instrument and he preferred to play and sing at the same time.

Johnny raised his eyebrows. He hadn't expected Hannah's suggestion.

Obviously neither had Shawn, because the teenager's mouth was already open to argue.

"I like playing live. It's more of an authentic sound."

Hannah was nodding, her hands on her hips.

"Okay, maybe. For some people." She tilted an eyebrow toward him. "I have an idea and I want you to trust me enough to try it."

"I..." Shawn was already rethinking this entire thing.

"I've really thought about this, Shawn. You're too comfortable when you hide behind that guitar."

Johnny came to stand beside her, but he didn't have anything to say. He just wanted to watch whatever happened next. Shawn looked to him for help, but Johnny only shrugged.

Hannah also glanced at Johnny, her blue eyes flashing in the morning light streaming through the upper windows.

This live room had always been his favorite, but the added images of Hannah in this room had cemented it.

"I lose track when I don't have my guitar," Shawn said.

She shook her head once. "No, you don't. You feel safe with the guitar."

Shawn's chin dipped, like he'd been caught in something.

"Guess what, kiddo," Hannah said, her tone flat and edged with dark amusement. "It's about to get really fucking unsafe in here."

Shawn held her gaze for a beat and finally acquiesced.

"Great. Let's get you in the isolation room." Hannah looked to Johnny, who nodded. He knew what she needed.

Energy raced around the room, touching every person in it.

This wasn't going to be just a favor or a placating appearance to make a young musician feel almost important. Hannah was ready for work.

He'd worked with musicians for half of his life. Only the truly great artists could make work feel like it was just as necessary as having fun.

And only the really great ones shared their magic with everyone else.

Hannah and Johnny worked to make sure everything on the tech end was ready as Shawn tried not to hyperventilate in the isolation room.

Hannah had seen something even Johnny had missed.

Never would he have guessed that focusing on vocals would leave Shawn shaking.

"Let's roll," Hannah gave the go-ahead, putting on the second set of headphones.

Johnny hit play and he heard Shawn inhale loudly.

The track played and Shawn remained silent. Frozen in place.

Johnny waited for a second and then glanced at Hannah, who was watching diligently by his side.

Her lips twitched and she leaned over him to flip the intercom switch.

"Shawn?"

"I know, I know." Shawn pinched the bridge of his nose. "Can we start again?"

Johnny reset the track.

"Shawn?" Hannah spoke with authority. "It's okay to be scared. I live terrified every day. Be scared. Then do the fucking thing."

Shawn nodded and Johnny hit play.

This time, Shawn opened his mouth and out came a voice more in control than Johnny thought the sweating teenager in the booth would be able to have.

Hannah smacked Johnny on the shoulder and he caught her grin.

"He's better than he knows," she said. "You're going to have to have a serious talk with him about it."

"What do you mean?" Johnny asked.

"I mean, he's on the edge of everything."

Johnny studied her face as she watched his little brother, and he saw something there, but it was hard to identify. Excitement? Wistfulness? Sorrow?

Shawn's vocals increased in volume and energy as he belted out a chorus he'd sung a hundred times.

And Johnny realized Shawn had been phoning it in.

How had he not seen that?

How had he let the little stinker get away with it?

The song ended and Shawn came bursting out of the isolation room.

"Oh my God!" he yelled. "What a rush!"

Hannah was laughing when Shawn picked her up and spun her around the room. He put her down and then tackle-hugged Johnny.

"If you touch me, you die," Piper warned, holding up a finger.

Shawn grabbed her finger and shook it anyway. The twelve-year-old remained mostly unimpressed. But Johnny caught her phantom of a smile.

"What do we do next?" Shawn asked.

"Now we make the music match those stellar vocals."

All the time Johnny had spent working with Shawn and teaching him as much as he could didn't compare to what Hannah had brought out of him.

But that was her real gift, wasn't it?

She could see to the soul of a person and draw it from them effortlessly. She demanded the truth out of a person's heart, and they found themselves giving it happily.

Just like she had done with Johnny.

* * *

HANNAH

What a long and wonderful day.

Ten hours and way too much pizza later, they had several songs for Shawn to choose from if he wanted to release an EP.

Which was what Hannah was lightly pushing him to do.

As long as it was something he and Johnny discussed—*really* discussed.

But she was positive he could release an EP without needing a big label, and the rest of the industry would start making calls.

This kid had talent like she hadn't ever seen.

And she'd seen a lot.

All he needed was to get out of his own way. And that's where she had come in—to be the bad guy and tell him what he didn't want to hear.

And honestly, the huge day made for a decent distraction from her melancholy thoughts. It wasn't like she was ignoring the truth anymore.

She'd said it. It was out there.

No takebacks and no second chances.

That last thought hit her directly in the solar plexus, nearly winding her.

Most of her life had been that way. Second chances were for

suckers and idiots. People made their choices. If they couldn't live with the consequences of those choices, they were shit out of luck.

She knew that.

She believed it.

If she had a creed, it would be that.

Consequences were part of living. Even if they were hard to accept.

She'd torpedoed her musical career by choice. She'd fucked or fucked over all the people she'd wanted to. The outcome of those choices was just stark reality.

Ashton James would never have a comeback.

And Hannah Lee would never have a happily ever after.

"All I can do is all I can do," she repeated to herself as she put the mics away.

Sure, maybe she wouldn't get the hero in the story. But she could be his friend. And that was more than she'd ever had before.

So, she'd take it.

And eventually, she was pretty sure, this weird ache in her chest would diminish.

Until then, she'd fake it.

After all, she had always been a good liar.

Hopefully crying herself to sleep at night wouldn't become a regular occurrence. It had taken all the tricks she knew from her days of hang-overs and hopelessness to get the puffiness around her eyes to diminish.

When Piper had walked into the bathroom and saw her holding cold spoons from the freezer on her eyes, she didn't say anything.

Possibly she just thought it was something Hannah was doing out of vanity.

How pitiful was that? That she actually preferred her sister to think of her as appearance-oriented instead of having to talk about how fucking *sad* she was.

She turned around and stopped short as Johnny's frame filled the doorway of the small supply room.

Damn, he was gorgeous.

He handed her a tidy bundle of cords. She took it and hung it on the only empty hook.

"Shawn is trying to teach Piper how to play drums," he said with a wince.

"Is that what I hear?" Hannah replied. "I thought a marching band was falling down the stairs."

His crooked smile made her heart hurt just a little.

Not too much.

Just enough to remind her she had one.

He opened his mouth like he was going to say something and then stopped. His dark eyes narrowed slightly and he opened his mouth again.

But again, nothing came out.

"What's up, Johnny?" she asked, really hoping it wasn't going to be some pandering nonsense.

"You're truly incredible. You know that, right?" His earnest tone and the specific words he'd chosen to say caught her off guard.

Suddenly the supply room felt rather small.

"So are you, weirdo," she replied with a grimace.

He closed his eyes and sighed heavily. "No. You don't get it." He opened his eyes and pinned her to the spot with his intense stare. "I know you said you've left all this behind."

By "this," she was pretty sure he meant the recording studio and all that it involved.

"But..."

He reached up and ran a hand through his hair.

"But what?"

At first she thought he was just going to thank her for not bailing on Shawn. But with the nervous energy rolling off him, she was beginning to think it was something else.

"Ah, this is harder than I expected."

She frowned. Nothing could possibly be more difficult than what they had already worked through together.

"You're overthinking it," she stated.

His eyes darted to hers.

"Just say it," she encouraged softly, the ends of her mouth tugging into a smile.

He stared at her lips for a beat and then relaxed his shoulders.

"I would like you to work here. With me. Be my partner."

That…

Was not anywhere in the realm of what she'd been thinking.

"Seriously?" she blurted without meaning to.

He rubbed his forehead with one hand. "Look, I know, okay? I know all the reasons you'd not want to do it. It's a risk, it's not something you've ever talked about wanting to do. But…" He huffed and fixed his gaze right on her. "You're amazing as a producer. I've watched you squeeze gold from a ball of mud on multiple occasions. And, maybe this is the most important part, you seem to really enjoy doing it."

Hannah stepped back, a little blindsided by the idea.

Johnny rubbed his jaw with the hand that had previously rubbed his forehead. Yeah, he was nervous.

She couldn't blame him.

He was basically asking her to come out of retirement when she had made it very clear how she was done with all of that.

"I've thought about it a lot. You could use a pseudonym on everything. No one here knows anyway, and they're used to producers having multiple identities to keep straight."

"How long?" she asked.

He jerked his chin back. "How long? As long as you want."

"No, how long have you been thinking about this? You said you've thought about it a lot. How long?"

Johnny's face went carefully blank.

"Why does that matter?"

Because she needed to know if this was a real thing or if it had just occurred to him last night.

Was this because he felt sorry for her?

"How long?" she repeated, keeping her tone even.

It was one thing for him to be disgusted with her. That, she understood. Fuck, she was disgusted with herself. It made sense, it added up.

But being offered a part of his life as an act of pity was something she was *not* interested in.

She was a big girl; she could hold her own rejections without someone needing to "soften" the blow.

The longer he stood there not speaking, the faster her mind worked to getting her riled up.

Oh no, ugly emotions were rising.

Defensive, angry, disgusted emotions.

Weren't they friends? Hadn't they just discussed how important they were to one another?

If having friends meant they wouldn't tell her the truth in an effort to "spare her feelings," she didn't want any part of it.

Rock the boat, baby.

"You could have just told me," she threw out accusingly.

His eyes widened and he opened his mouth to protest, but she was over it.

Whatever.

She'd told him something incredibly personal and difficult last night and he couldn't even be straight with her about how it had made him feel.

Pushing past him, she left the supply room in search of Piper.

She followed the sounds of chaos into the live room.

Johnny caught up with her.

"Hannah!" he barked, grabbing her elbow.

She whirled around, disconnecting them.

"Don't touch me, dude," she warned.

He blinked and shook his head. "O-okay. You wanna tell me what's going on?"

To his credit, he really did appear gobsmacked.

But she was too hurt and angry to stop, so she had one option before she said things she couldn't take back—and that was to leave.

"I think that if you use that big brain of yours, you'll figure it out."

She turned around and used two fingers to motion at Piper to get going. "Time to head out."

"Hannah, seriously," Johnny kept trying. "What the hell is going on? Just talk to me."

She took a deep breath and pressed her lips together, refusing to look at him again. She didn't want to see his stupid handsome face, and his dark puppy dog eyes, and his stupid, stupid lies.

"Is this because of what you told me last night about having h—"

She whirled back around, ready to straight tackle him if he finished that sentence in front of Piper.

He must've realized his mistake, because he faltered, eyes shifting nervously to Shawn and Piper watching silently at the drum kit.

"Uh," Johnny cleared his throat. "What you told me about the jalapeños?"

Her lip curled and she crossed her arms over her chest.

Really?

Seriously?

"Because I haven't fully processed that information yet," Johnny went on, his expression pained.

"What's there to process, Johnny?" Hannah shrugged. "You know what jalapeños are, right?" she asked, being a snot.

He cocked his head to the side, unamused.

"Yes, I know what jalapeños are," he spat her attitude right back. "But I had to do some research last night about what happens when you have jalapeños on your taco!"

She waved her arms to the sides. "You're either okay with jalapeños on the taco or you're not. It's not that difficult of a concept. Most of the time there are no jalapeños, and they're pretty easy to avoid. But I get it if even being in the same room as the jalapeños is something you want to avoid. I just wish you'd *say* that."

"I don't want to say that because that would be a lie! I was up all night long, Hannah! I haven't slept in almost forty-eight hours. You can't just drop something like that on a guy and expect him to already have all the answers!"

"I asked if you had questions!" she retorted.

And yes, they were both shouting, but not angry shouting. It was more loud speaking. A detail that Hannah noticed and it only fueled her...*excitement?*

Oh geez, she was really screwed up if having a passionate argument with Johnny thrilled her instead of making her want to run for the hills.

Stupid, stupid, stupid.

"Yes, but I had questions that I didn't think you'd be able to answer." He held up a hand and counted on his fingers. "One, what if jalapeño juice gets in my eye? That doesn't sound great, does it? Two, if I ended up with jalapeños on my burrito, what would that be like and what are the next steps? Three, how the hell am I supposed to tell you that I really don't give a shit about the jalapeños when you are so very obviously sensitive about it?"

She jerked her head back, silent.

Out of the corner of her eyes she saw Shawn hustling Piper out of the live room.

Yeah, that was probably for the best. Their metaphor was pretty transparent.

She rubbed at the center of her forehead with her fingertips.

"What?"

Johnny's head dropped back and so did his shoulders. "C'mon, Hannah. It's not like you make any of this easy."

"Excuse me?" She bristled. "I am very direct. You're the one who sidesteps things."

He glowered at her.

"You want me to be direct? Is that it?"

"As long as it doesn't kill you," she said, just throwing the sass around like confetti.

"Okay." He ran his tongue over his teeth and bobbed his head. "You make it impossible to not love you."

Her heart stopped.

And her mouth went slack and also dry.

He shook his head and rolled his eyes to the ceiling. Then he turned those honest eyes on her and continued casually.

"And believe me, I tried." His lips twitched as he scanned her face. "You keep trying to throw these little grenades at me, like it'll make a difference. You call it being direct?" He scoffed. "Nope. You're cagey and guarded with that heart of yours, and I get it. Because I've seen it. I know what it's capable of."

He ran a hand over his mouth and she braced for more.

"When did I start thinking about asking you to be my producing partner? Um, like day three of recording with Sunshine."

Her stomach wobbled and she tried to swallow, but her mouth was still too dry.

"What did you think I was trying to tell you last night when I sang you Sir Paul fucking McCartney?" The exasperation on his face had her heart beating heavy.

The fact that he'd used the f-word wasn't lost on her either.

"I thought that's just what we do. We use music to communicate what we're feeling…" She trailed off as she heard the words out loud.

Oh, shit.

"Yeah. We do. We both do it. You put your heart into music and I have been right there, ready to catch every single drop."

Oh, fuck! Shit, fuck.

"You love me?" she asked, not sure she was understanding what he was saying. What if she was misinterpreting this entire thing?

He nodded, eyebrows lifted. "Kind of a lot, if I'm being honest." He licked his lips and took a small step toward her, then stopped. "But I wasn't planning on telling you."

"Why not?" she asked, truly confused and curious.

"Because, Hannah, people have been telling you bullshit your whole life to get something from you. I wanted to *show* you. I didn't care how long it took. I had faith we'd get there."

Her heart was murmuring its own devotion to Johnny through her chest and she flexed her hands at her sides, trying to keep her head on straight.

This was dangerous.

He was saying a lot of things and she liked them. But he was right, she'd learned that words couldn't be trusted.

But…" His eyebrow arched as he went on. "You brought up the herpes last night, and I realized our heads were in different places."

He slowly closed the gap between them and stopped a foot in front of her. He reached for her hand and she let him. He held it in both of his, and the connection warmed her, bringing that now familiar security she felt when she was close to Johnny.

He studied her face seriously.

"I thought you wouldn't want me," she said, her voice raspy with shame.

"I know," he replied. "I didn't know how to tell you that was ridiculous."

"I'm broken, Johnny," she said with a small hiccup, sounding pitiful and weak, and she *hated* that.

He cupped the side of her cheek and ran a thumb over her jawline. "Nope."

"I could hurt you."

"Okay."

Okay? He was just fine with that? Who was this man?

"You're not the villain you think you are, you know."

He just dropped that little bomb. So casual, like he was remarking on the weather.

"I will do anything to capture that wild heart of yours. I don't care how long it takes or what ways you try to push me away. I see you. And I'm coming for you."

CHAPTER TWENTY

THAT'S WHERE YOU TAKE ME

HANNAH

"So..." Piper drew the word out and Hannah braced for what she knew was coming.

She was kind of surprised that it had taken the entire drive across town for Piper to say something.

"Even though you and Johnny were yelling at each other last night, we're going over to celebrate Shawn's birthday?" She turned those piercing blue eyes on Hannah. "Won't that be weird?"

"It probably will be," Hannah agreed.

"Then why are we going?"

"Because it's Shawn's birthday."

It's not like it had been Hannah's plan to do things this way. She hadn't even considered involving herself in Shawn's birthday. But Sarahi had texted her and so had Shawn, asking her to come.

And damn the unexpected, she wanted to go.

Shawn had become very dear to her, especially after working with him all day yesterday.

Unwillingly, uncharacteristically, she'd become invested in the young singer.

And his brother.

But that went without saying.

Didn't it?

She still hadn't been able to reconcile all the things he'd declared to her yesterday.

Less than twenty-four hours since he'd just casually used the L-word on her.

Like any respectable adult, Hannah had immediately left the premises.

Yes, she'd run away.

But she hadn't wanted Johnny to *know* she was running away. So she'd told him she needed "space" and its super annoying companion "time."

Bullshit, bullshit, bullshit.

And Johnny, being Johnny, had given her exactly what she'd requested.

Did he know she'd be here tonight?

What would she do if he took one look at her and realized how not worth it she was?

None of those things mattered, she supposed as she slid out of the car and tucked her hands into her pockets.

Piper slammed the door and took off for the front of the house, way more comfortable at Shawn and Johnny's aunt's house than she was.

They'd only been there once, but she'd enjoyed it. Sarahi and her sisters were fun. The family had made her feel welcome.

But, even the warmest welcomes could wear out.

Hannah swallowed down her small spike of anxiety and glanced around the cold, quiet neighborhood. She imagined for a moment that this could be a regular thing. That being invited to family parties and celebrations might be a part of their future. Something Hannah knew Piper deserved.

A real life.

Not the hiding in plain sight one she had been cursed with the day Hannah had inherited her.

"I knew you couldn't stay away from me."

Hannah glanced up to find Johnny standing in the open doorway. The glow from the interior of the home splashed warmly onto the front steps and walk, beckoning her to come in. Her expression smoothed when their eyes met.

"Hey," she said, sounding stupid to her own ears.

She also didn't deny his statement, because what was the point?

She didn't want time and space.

She just wanted to be with him all the time.

His lips tugged up on one side, like he could read her thoughts, and it did funny things to her insides.

She made it to the doorway, and he didn't move to let her in.

Instead, his little half smile grew a fraction.

"Glad you made it," he said, and then he dropped his voice. "Auntie made tacos."

"You're kidding," she replied, eyes round.

All he did was grin and step aside to let her in.

Without thinking about what she was doing, she reached out and swatted his abs as she walked by him. He caught her hand in his and gave it a squeeze. She felt, rather than heard, his chuckle as he closed the door behind them.

And that quickly, her anxiety dissolved into a memory.

Johnny took her coat and hung it up for her.

Then, he took her hand, and she let him.

It happened so naturally she didn't even realize it until later that night when she was alone in bed. All night, when given the chance, Johnny had a hold on her.

Laughter and conversations piled on top of one another filled the dining room as she entered.

"Hannah!" many voices declared, and she made her way around the room, giving hugs and receiving cheek-kisses from nearly everyone. Johnny's finger was hooked into the back pocket of her jeans.

And she didn't mind it.

Any of it.

After dinner, after singing, after cake, Hannah found herself on the stairs.

The same place she'd sought refuge on her first visit. Though refuge seemed like the wrong word.

Johnny was behind her, his knees framing her body, his hands on her shoulders, making casual circles with his thumbs where her neck met her back. They faced the large living room, where Ana and Piper had divided the family into teams for Charades.

Or a version of Charades that Hannah had never played before.

Shawn took a seat on the stair beside Hannah and glanced at her and Johnny, a smile tugging at his mouth.

"Did you hear about Shatface?" Shawn asked.

Hannah ran her tongue over her teeth to keep from outright grinning.

First of all, Shatface? Fucking brilliant.

Secondly, she'd heard.

Happy birthday, kiddo, she said inside.

If Johnny ever asked, she would tell him.

But he was the only one allowed to know that Hannah was the reason that Shatford had been investigated. No one else needed to know that little bit of petty revenge that Hannah had managed to arrange.

Not that much had to be done.

She'd simply decided to be the final straw for all the things Shatford needed to be held accountable for.

"The best part of her being fired is my application to be a tutor was approved. I can officially take on ESL students instead of sneaking around the study halls."

"Shawn!" Ana called, waving him over for his turn.

Shawn bounded off the steps.

Johnny removed his hands, only to wrap his arms around her and rest his chin on her shoulder. "Did you have something to do with that?" he asked in her ear.

She leaned back into him and made a small affirmative sound.

He chuckled before brushing his lips along the shell of her ear. "Mmm, I like you." His deep voice was a caress along her spinal column.

Hmm.

Maybe they needed to talk about reality for a second.

It was all well and good being wrapped in the arms of a veritable storybook hero. But that couldn't last forever.

Right?

Keeping her eyes on the activity in front of them, she tilted her head to speak to him.

"Your family is pretty amazing," she stated the obvious.

He grunted his agreement, waiting for her to continue.

"Someday I could be found out, you know." She felt his body grow still around her. "And then it could—it would—ruin all of this. I will destroy their peace."

The truth of what she was saying hung heavy in between them, and a small ache in her heart started to make itself known.

"They didn't ask for that life. The same as Piper. Or you and Shawn." She wanted to be ignorant to her own choices. She wished she could be blind to the consequences and the baggage that came along with who she was.

But she couldn't.

"I care about you too much to let that happen."

Johnny let her go and shifted to sit on the same step she was on so he could look her in the eye.

Which he did.

"Do I get a say in any of it?" he asked seriously.

She frowned because she wasn't sure what he meant.

"I know the risks, Hannah," he said softly. "I know who you are and who the world thinks you are. And I'm telling you…" He held her eyes with his. "You're worth it. Whatever happens, I'm in it with you."

Her heart tumbled and fell and splashed right into his messy love.

How had a miracle found her when she hadn't even been brave enough to hope for it?

"And this family." He lifted a chin, indicating the loud voices outside their quiet conversation. "They really are amazing. They can handle it."

That was an easy promise to make. But not so easy to keep.

"What are you guys talking about?" Mia interrupted them, leaning over the banister.

Hannah hadn't noticed her approach, so she had no idea what Sarahi's sister had overheard.

"Are you talking about Hannah being Ashton James?"

Hannah blinked and Johnny blinked right back at her. Both of them equally shocked into silence.

Johnny recovered first. He cleared his throat and frowned earnestly at Mia. "What are you talking about?"

"Please," Mia scoffed. "We've known the whole time. Sarahi recognized her at basketball registration."

The room seemed to tilt and Hannah's stomach dropped to the floor.

Too many thoughts swarmed her mind, fighting for relevancy.

Had they told anyone? Of course they hadn't told anyone. Alex would've found out. Why hadn't they said anything? No one had signed an NDA. She would never be able to afford to pay off the entire family; it would bankrupt her. Not that it mattered; she'd figure it out.

Her thoughts stilled when Johnny applied pressure to her knee. She glanced up and found is brown eyes calm and confident.

"Mia, have you told anyone?" Johnny asked.

Mia snorted. "Right. Like that's gonna happen."

"Wait. Why didn't you say anything?" Hannah asked.

Mia's eyes bounced between Johnny and Hannah, and for the first time in the conversation, she looked guilty.

"Because…" Mia's voice trailed off and her gaze went beyond Hannah to a point behind her.

"Because I told them not to."

Aunt Carmen stepped into the conversation and Hannah swiveled on the step to face the older woman.

"I don't understand."

Carmen's eyes, brown and soft and so like Johnny's, examined Hannah in a way she wasn't sure she'd ever experienced. It felt…maternal.

"Because you have the look I did when I came to this country for the first time. The look of a woman running for her life."

Hannah's heart squeezed and she inhaled a choppy breath.

"You will always have refuge with us."

Hannah couldn't respond. Her mouth had dried up.

Carmen smiled softly and transferred her gaze to Johnny. She nodded once and then hooked an arm through Mia's, leading her away.

And leaving Hannah and Johnny alone.

Still unable to speak, Hannah slowly shook her head at Johnny, wishing he really could read her mind. And maybe he could, because he choked on a laugh and then slid close to her side, putting an arm around her shoulders. She leaned into him and closed her eyes.

Did she deserve their acceptance and protection? No.

Did she deserve their kindness and understanding? No.

But maybe it wasn't about deserving.

Maybe it was bigger than that.

Who was she to tell people what they could and could not decide for themselves?

Piper's loud laugh drew her attention and she smiled at how bright and happy her sister was.

Living in secret had had its purpose.

But the purpose had been fulfilled.

She needed to speak to Quinn because she was done standing in the way of everyone's happiness.

Including her own.

* * *

The lights came up and they were brighter than she remembered.

Smoke swept over the floor before her and swirled lazily in the multicolored beams pointed directly at her.

Hannah squinted against the brilliance. She held a hand up to shade her face, but it didn't help.

The sequins on her dress caught her attention and she looked down.

Hadn't this dress been ruined years ago?

Maybe it had been repaired.

She pulled the hem through her fingers, watching the glint and sparkle shift and fall.

Her stomach ricocheted with familiar butterflies, and her earpiece crackled in her ear.

It wasn't working again.

She tugged it out and let in dangle over her shoulder.

All she could hear was her breath and her heartbeat—loud, loud, louder.

Sweat trickled from her hairline, down her temple, and dripped from her jaw.

A hand touched her right elbow and slowly slid light fingers down her forearm to her hand. She turned her head to see Johnny there.

His eyes on her.

His fingers reached hers and he laced his with hers, pressing their palms together.

In her left hand was a microphone.

She glanced back at Johnny, who was standing by her side, shoulder to shoulder.

He wasn't distracted by the lights and the smoke. He kept his attention on her.

She looked up and there was no ceiling, only stars. A black, black sky with pinpricks of light.

Taking another labored breath, she stepped forward to her mark and brought the microphone to her mouth.

Hannah sat up in bed, sucking in a breath big enough to make her dizzy.

The gray light of morning peeking through her curtains revealed her quiet bedroom in the condo where she'd resided for eighteen months.

She wasn't on a stage in a stadium.

No bright lights.

No smoke.

She glanced to her right and the empty bed beside her.

No Johnny.

Shaking off the dream, she swung her legs out of the bed and headed into the bathroom.

She turned on the shower and stepped inside.

Of all the families in all the world she could have stumbled into, it had to be one that understood her motivations.

When she'd said goodnight to Johnny last night, she'd kissed his cheek.

And when she closed her eyes while hugging him, she saw her next steps laid out in front of her like a freshly paved road.

She knew exactly what to do next.

She finished in the shower, wrapped a towel around her torso and one around her head, went back to her bedroom, and sat down on the edge of her bed, facing her closet.

And stared.

Picking out what to wear felt like a bigger deal today.

Should she wear something sexy?

To work?

Bleck, no.

But neither did she want to dress boring.

Not today.

Johnny made her want to be…something.

Something closer to herself.

The sensation that accompanied that want was like electricity traveling between her brain and heart on a relay.

He made her unafraid to be whatever it was she was cursed to be.

After two years of sobriety and never stopping, never taking a break, in her fight to be *better*, she'd started to realize there were parts of her that weren't going to leave.

Her big mouth, for one.

But he seemed to be okay with it.

She stood and started picking through the choices in her walk-in closet.

The night they'd danced in his kitchen and she'd told him about getting slapped and subsequently fired, he'd laughed.

He'd laughed so hard and deep, she wanted to be able to make him laugh like that forever.

He hadn't chastised her or scoffed or looked disappointed.

She would never be polished and sweet and shiny. No matter how hard she worked at it, she'd always have rough edges and a sharp tongue.

Johnny deserved better.

She rubbed the back of her neck as tension pooled there.

Because even though Johnny deserved better, she still wanted him.

And wasn't that just the most selfish thing ever?

Classic Hannah.

But he knew.

He knew most of her bad. He knew what she was capable of.

And he stayed.

Johnny wasn't an idiot. He was smart. Careful with his time and attention. He didn't waste energy on things that he didn't want or need.

He was the first person she could remember being able to tell the truth to without needing to apologize after.

With Johnny, she felt…safe.

Safe to be herself, and safe to explore who she wanted to be.

On that thought, she grabbed a pair of distressed skinny jeans, a sky-blue silk camisole, a white sweater with a deep V-neck, and her black leather jacket.

* * *

JOHNNY

"Nikki, I don't know what you want me to tell you." Johnny sighed. "It was a good deal. I took the risk."

"They're junk, Johnny. Every single one," Nikki hollered over her shoulder as she trudged back down the hall, box of broken pedals in her hands, probably headed to the dumpster.

"I guess sometimes things are too good to be true," he muttered to himself.

"Talking about me again?"

Johnny turned around to find Hannah standing in the doorway of the live room. Black leather jacket draped over an arm, white sweater slipping off one shoulder, tight jeans, black heeled boots. No glasses today, her raven hair loose and slightly tousled.

Damn.

That hair of hers.

It was like animated Disney princess hair. Thick and luxurious and shiny.

He'd never wanted anyone the way he wanted her.

Her beauty was a dangerous kind of intoxication.

The more he drank her in, the more lost he became.

And he didn't care to be found.

She was all passion and danger.

A fire that began on the surface and went all the way to the core of who she was. The kind of heat that could keep him warm, winter after winter.

"What are you doing here?" he asked, trying to appear casual. He stuck the pencil he'd been using behind his ear and tucked the clipboard under his arm.

"I was offered a job?" She narrowed her eyes playfully.

"A job?" He rubbed his jaw. "I think I would have heard about that."

She bit her bottom lip in mid-smile while rolling her eyes.

He lifted his chin toward the control room upstairs. "Let's talk in my office."

She slid her eyes that direction before moving.

He closed the door behind them and set the clipboard down on the edge of the soundboard.

"You look amazing today," he finally declared. "It needs to be said. You're..." He inhaled deeply and held her gaze. "Hard to resist."

"Resist?" she repeated with a curious smile.

"You must know how I feel about you," he replied, his voice rough. "It's not a small thing."

Her lips parted as the smile slipped from her face.

They stared at one another for a long minute.

"Johnny," she whispered softly.

And his whole world hung on that small breath.

"I came to talk business," she said after a beat.

He nodded. Obviously, that had been her purpose, but he wasn't going to play coy with her either. Never would she be able to look at him and say she didn't know how he felt about her.

"I want to be your producing partner. But I don't just want to work here for the helluva it. I want to buy in." She took a seat on the stool by the soundboard. "I want to own a percentage. I'll need to see your profit and loss statements, and then we can discuss what's fair and what you want from me."

One side of his mouth ticked up and he crossed his arms over his chest. "Really. You want in on this dump, huh? Is that all?"

She grinned and it hit him right in the chest.

"I have a list of demands, but let's just work on one at a time."

He arched a curious eyebrow.

"What about living in ambiguity?"

She barked a laugh. "I think you mean anonymity."

"Sure." He shrugged.

"I think it can be managed. I have a meeting with my landlord later to work out the details."

"You're serious?" he asked, feeling something shift in his chest. He was pretty sure it was his hope trying to get to the front of all other emotions.

Her happy expression faded and she swallowed.

"If you're comfortable with it."

He frowned, trying to figure out why he wouldn't be comfortable with it. This was what he'd been wanting.

"Johnny, I'm a lot of things. But I'm not someone who can offer you a peaceful life. There's always going to be something just around the corner. I have no way of predicting who or what might come crashing through the door. I don't know if that's a future you'd want—"

"It is," Johnny stopped her.

"It might be really chaotic at times," she told him what he already knew.

"Hannah Lee," he said earnestly. "You and me? We make our own peace. Together."

She nodded, her eyes getting bright. He must've said the right thing.

"I will give you my best," she promised.

His heart broke at that. Did she really not know how much that was?

"That's more than you realize."

She took a deep breath and drummed her fingers lightly on her thighs.

"We're still talking about working together, right?" she asked hesitantly.

He nodded, a faint smile tugging at his lips. "Obviously."

She pressed her lips together and his smile grew.

Clearing her throat, she stood. "I have another meeting to get to, then." She slid her hands into her back pockets. "If we have an agreement, that is."

"I'll get the P&Ls together. Maybe we can discuss the details soon?" He tilted his head. "In a more private location?"

She nodded, but her gaze was on his mouth.

"Call me later?" she asked, still staring.

"Is there something else you want to talk about?" he asked, moving a step closer.

Her eyes bounced up to his and she blushed. "Uhh, I don't think so."

He took another step, watching as her pupils dilated. "You sure? You look like you have something important on your mind."

"I was remembering something is all." She spoke quietly, her voice husky.

Was she thinking of the time they'd kissed in the library and how it had set his soul on fire? Because he thought about it constantly.

"Stop looking at my mouth," he commanded, taking another step closer.

"I'm not looking at your mouth," she lied, voice dropping to a velvety rasp.

They were less than six inches apart now.

He slid his right hand under the heavy fall of her hair and ran his thumb along her jawline. He settled his left hand lightly on her hip and pulled her a fraction closer.

She tipped her head back and parted her lips, her eyes on his.

He glanced at her mouth and back to her eyes. "I like your sweater," he whispered, millimeters from her lips. He flexed his fingers against the soft fabric. The white with the sky-blue underneath made her eyes look like twin blue flames.

"I like your everything," she whispered back.

A rumble sounded from deep in Johnny's chest.

He wasn't sure if he made the noise or if his heart spoke for him.

But either way, it was hard to miss. Her eyes widened and those fiery blue irises looked right through him.

He kissed her slowly, first her bottom lip, then her top. Taking turns with each of them. Her lips were soft. Otherworldly. He had thought he'd romanticized their kiss in the library, but no. This couldn't be exaggerated. It couldn't even be described.

It had to be experienced.

The way her mouth responded to his, with pressure and pause. Taking, giving, tasting, *enjoying*.

Another rumble came from his chest and he spread his fingers over the back of her scalp, his hand at her ribs splayed wide. He needed to touch as much of her as possible.

Her tongue slid into his mouth and he bent her backward, pressing their bodies together. She arched into him, her fingers in his hair. Her nails gently scraped his scalp, and the sensation traveled down his spine.

He broke away from her mouth and stared down at her bright eyes and flushed cheeks.

"Maybe we can talk about that later?" he asked.

His body screamed at him to keep going, to spread her out on the leather sofa and explore every delicate inch of her body.

It had been a long time since he'd felt so overwhelmed by desire. He was a grown man, not a hapless teenager, helpless to hormones and inexperience.

But touching Hannah was an adventure all its own.

"Sure," she replied breathlessly. "We can talk about that later."

He displayed his appreciation by nipping the soft column of her throat with his teeth. She sucked a breath, and her body jolted in his arms.

He pulled her close to his chest and righted both of them. She rested her cheek on his pectorals, and he knew she was listening to his heart come back to a decent rate.

It didn't embarrass him. She should know what she did to him.

After a minute, she stepped back and tucked her hair behind her ears.

"So…you'll call me later?" she asked, sounding less certain than he expected.

"Oh, yeah," he replied with a cocky smirk.

She rolled her eyes, but it was just an act. Then she gathered her coat and left.

And Johnny couldn't wipe the grin off his face for the rest of the day.

* * *

HANNAH

If Quinn and Alex were surprised that she was there before them, they didn't show it.

And truthfully, Hannah needed the extra minute alone.

Because this was a big fucking deal.

And while she was positive these were the next steps to take, it was terrifying.

But she'd learned these past years of running from ghosts and building the life she wanted, the fear was temporary.

She had shown up for herself again and again. She'd proven to herself that she could do the important work.

But it wasn't about her anymore.

And it was that thought that had her excited for the next stage.

"Remember when I first came to you and you suggested a decoy?"

Quinn's eyes sharpened on her. "Are you ready to consider the original plan I drew up for you?"

Alex took his customary seat on the lone stool in the freight elevator and opened his laptop.

"How certain are you that it would really work?" She had to ask. In the two years of these clandestine meetings with these two weirdos, they had never lied to her.

Or betrayed her.

"I'm very certain," Quinn replied smoothly. "May I ask what changed your mind?"

Johnny's face entered her thoughts and Hannah smiled.

"Mr. Torres?" Quinn guessed.

Hannah glanced up at his slightly amused tone.

"Am I being stupid?" she asked him.

Asking Quinn this question was different than asking her therapist. Her therapist would try to be objective and she'd never call anyone stupid.

Hannah knew Quinn wouldn't hesitate to call an idiot out.

"I think…" Quinn took a thoughtful breath. "Sometimes we find someone. Or they find us. And there is a rescuing on both ends. And when that happens, people like us"—he dipped his head at Hannah—"will do what we must in order to protect those we love."

That's what this was all about, wasn't it?

Johnny and Shawn and the rest of their family had restored her faith in love.

And hope.

And loyalty.

"So, this decoy…" Hannah's palms began to itch and she squeezed them into fists.

Alex turned the laptop around, and a photo of a woman who looked nearly identical to Hannah appeared on screen. She was stepping into the back of a limo, her sunglasses aimed directly at the camera.

"Oh, wow," she breathed. "Who is she?"

"I feel it would be best if you never had contact with her. And I chose her for this assignment myself. She would be a member of your full-time security team. Which you will have from now on."

Hannah cringed. She had wanted Piper to have as normal of a childhood as possible.

"My people are incredibly discreet. It sounds immense, but all we're talking about is a decoy and an undercover teacher at Piper's school. No one will even know. Not even Piper."

That sounded better than being followed around by armed guards.

"There's also the matter of Johnny's family." Hannah coughed a short laugh. "They, uh, they've known who I am the entire time."

She waited for that information to sink in.

Within seconds, Alex was typing furiously.

"And I want to buy into Johnny's studio. I want to stay here and make music and live my life...and be happy." Declaring her desires out loud lifted a weight from her chest. "But I need to know they'll be safe while I do that. Not just Piper. Johnny, Shawn, and everyone else."

Quinn's lips twitched. "I think we can manage that."

"You're absolutely sure your people can be counted on? I don't have a great history of people having my back. Even when I paid them to."

Quinn exchanged a look with Alex, who shrugged. He narrowed his cool gaze at Hannah. "Who was disloyal? Your manager?" he asked sharply.

What was it with this guy? Was he part mind reader, part spy, part asshole? A trifecta of dickery?

"He was just the tip of the iceberg," Hannah admitted.

Alex was still typing.

Quinn exhaled through his nose.

"Your decoy is ready. She'll be in LA by the end of the day, and the new narrative begins," Alex declared, sounding satisfied.

"That fast, huh?"

"I've had this plan in place for nearly two years," Quinn said, sounding only the slightest bit irritated with her. "It's going to work."

Hannah felt his declaration settle in her bones.

"I believe you."

CHAPTER TWENTY-ONE

BRIGHTEST MORNING STAR

HANNAH

When the window to the concessions opened, there was already a long line of women waiting.

Hannah spotted Johnny instantly and her heart fluttered.

He was in another Henley today. Black. Damn, he looked good in a Henley. It hugged his muscular shoulders and lean torso, tapering into a tight waist. His denim-clad lower half couldn't be seen from where she was sitting, but she knew what it looked like. His jeans were probably the same soft, well broken in ones he always wore. The left back pocket more faded than the right because it was where he kept his wallet.

"Doesn't it bother you that those women drool over him?" Sarahi asked, obviously seeing where Hannah's attention was pointed.

Hannah hummed. "No. He's very attractive. It's the closest most of them will ever get to that kind of gorgeous. Let them look."

It wasn't until she felt Sarahi's stare on the side of her face that she realized what she'd said out loud.

If Sarahi had been fishing for information on what Hannah felt for Johnny, that had been pretty clear.

Sarahi snorted. "If they were looking at my husband that way, I'd have to cut them."

Something about the way she'd said that with her beautiful accent and so matter-of-fact had Hannah laughing.

"Well…" Hannah sighed as her laughter settled. "I guess I'm not a jealous person. Protective, yes. But not possessive."

Sarahi humphed.

Hannah knew that her casual remarks to Johnny's cousin implied they were more together than they had established. At least, formally.

The rest of their week had moved quickly.

Hannah had spent every day in the studio with Johnny. Most of the time they were discussing business plans, minority ownership, and expansion.

They also took breaks to make out sometimes.

And when Johnny hinted at wanting to spend some more quality time together, sans the interruptions from Nikki and the other two engineers, Hannah reminded him that she had a twelve-year-old to think about.

That was usually the bucket of cold water they both needed.

But she did want to speak to him alone. She hadn't quite found the right way to tell him about her new security plan orchestrated by Quinn and Alex.

Which seemed to be working *very* well.

Hannah and Piper had Googled *Ashton James* last night and already the decoy had made splashy appearances in key locations around Hollywood. The tabloids were eating it up.

"Ana asked if Piper could spend the night tonight," Sarahi broke into Hannah's thoughts. "She's not allowed to have slumber parties anymore after the last debacle. But I said I would make an exception for Piper since she's family."

Hannah's heart squeezed.

"Really?" Hannah asked.

Sarahi nodded, a secret smile on her lips. "Maybe you can make plans with someone?"

That wasn't subtle.

"I think that's an excellent idea," Hannah replied, her stomach fluttering.

Her eyes went back to the hot guy working the counter.

She watched Johnny be kind and patient with every person in line. Behind him, Shawn hustled, filling orders.

Okay, maybe she felt a little possessive.

Because they felt like they were *hers.*

Her people, her little family.

When had that happened?

She stood and made her way down the bleachers. Johnny spotted her coming around the court and his gaze felt heavy on her.

He didn't look away, even as he finished an order and handed someone their change.

She got in line, fine with waiting her turn.

The line moved forward and she flashed him a smile. His eyes watched her mouth and then bounced up to her eyes. His expression open.

"What can I get for you, beautiful?" he asked, the endearment rolling off his tongue easily.

The woman who'd been in the line before her snapped her head over quickly and scanned Hannah up and down.

Hannah ignored her. She put her elbows on the counter and leaned toward Johnny. He mirrored her actions, his lips tipped up on the sides. Their faces were only inches away from each other.

"Piper is going to a slumber party tonight and I was wondering if you had plans for dinner?

His eyebrows lifted in interest. "Mmm, are you making something delicious?"

She tilted her head to the side with a flirty smile. "Always."

His smile grew and his gaze dropped to her mouth, her shoulders, her chest, before flicking back up. "What time is good for you?"

Any time. Now. A minute from now. Just be in my space again.

But instead she said, "Five-ish."

He reached for a strand of hair near her face, wrapped it lightly around his finger, and gave it a gentle tug. It may as well have been connected to her heart because that's where she felt the pull. "It's a date."

* * *

"Are you and Johnny going to get married?"

"What?" Hannah dropped her straight iron and almost burned her neck.

Piper stuck her head in the bathroom.

"Why would you ask that?"

"Because you loooove him," Piper said teasingly.

Hannah snorted but didn't argue.

"Marriage isn't always the best choice for everyone, pipsqueak."

"Ana's mom said that if Johnny didn't marry you, then he was a moron who didn't deserve to have offspring."

Hannah nearly choked. That sounded like Sarahi.

"We haven't discussed it," she said around her laughter.

"You have a date tonight, right?" Piper came into Hannah's bathroom and sat on the ledge of the bathtub. "Just ask him if he wants to get married." The tween shrugged. Like marriage was akin to asking someone if they liked pink lemonade.

"I do have a date tonight," Hannah confirmed, turning off the flat iron. She'd fixed her hair and done a very subtle smokey eye. She couldn't remember the last time she'd been on a date. Not that that said much, considering her functional blackouts.

But she was going to remember this one.

The knock on the door signaled that Damon was there to take Piper to Ana's.

"Do you have all your stuff?" Hannah asked, following Piper to the door.

"Yes. I even double-checked."

"Are you sure?" Hannah didn't want to have to get any intrusive phone calls for something silly, like a toothbrush.

"I'm sure." Piper opened the door and Damon stood ready.

"Let's go, bodyguard man." Piper waved a hand and trudged out the door.

Damon dipped his chin at Hannah and followed the source of most of her headaches down the hall.

Hannah closed the door and took a deep breath.

Okay.

Piper was safe. She was with people she trusted and she was whip smart.

Hannah could do this.

She checked the dinner in the oven—pork chops with roasted apples. Then she set the table and lit a bunch of candles. Like, a fuck-ton of candles. Just candles everywhere. Only the ones on the table were actual fire, though. The rest were LED. She didn't want to risk burning the place down. That would definitely be a mood killer.

Checking the clock, she realized she was nearly out of time.

She went back to her room to change into the dress she'd picked out earlier. She hadn't wanted to wear it in front of Piper because of its revealing nature.

It was a black lace mini dress with an open back. It had a high neckline in the front, sleeveless, and fit her body perfectly. She slid on black stilettos to go with it and then looked at herself in the full-length mirror in her bedroom. And tried to calm her racing heart.

Maybe Johnny would think she was being too presumptuous.

It wasn't that she expected they'd be intimate, but if they were, she wanted to be prepared in all the ways.

That included shaving everything, lotion, perfume, and condoms.

She glanced at the nightstand beside her bed, where the brand-new box of prophylactics was housed.

"This is stupid," she muttered, and hurried to the closet.

She'd asked him over for dinner. This was too much for dinner.

A knock stopped her forward momentum and she grimaced.

"Mother*fucker*," she hissed. She stepped toward the doorway, then doubled back to the closet and back again. "Oh, Hannah, you little idiot," she muttered, choosing to answer the door.

She would just own her mistake and they'd laugh about it, and she'd change into sweats or something to make up for it.

She opened the door and stopped breathing.

Johnny was in a suit.

Holy hell.

A nice suit was like lingerie for men.

Black pants, black jacket, white shirt.

The shirt was unbuttoned by at least three buttons, revealing dark chest hair.

His hair was combed and styled back, and the dark scruff on his face highlighted his jaw in a very lickable way.

Okay, Johnny had always been attractive. But at what point had he become drop-dead gorgeous? Had she just been too focused on her own damn issues that she hadn't been able to fully appreciate the masculine perfection in front of her?

"Hannah Lee James," Johnny said in his smooth, deep voice. "You plan on being the death of me?"

She glanced up to catch his heated gaze.

He crossed the threshold and she backed into the condo. He caught the door with a hand and closed it with a shove.

His eyes roamed over her, up and down and back again.

"You look good, Johnny," she was able to finally speak.

He shot her a crooked smile and it sent tingles through her body.

"Just trying to keep up, babe," he murmured, taking one of her hands. He brought it to his mouth. "You're stunning," he said against the back of her fingers. And then he kissed them.

Soft, warm, lingering lips on her fingers.

Those tingles shot through her stomach and down her thighs.

Never had anyone kissed Hannah there before. And now she hoped Johnny would always be the only one.

She forced a swallow in her suddenly dry throat. "Are you hungry?" she asked.

He let go of her hand and looked toward the kitchen and the set table. "I could eat," he replied. He turned slowly around in the condo, taking in all the candles and dim lighting.

Hannah hoped she didn't look disappointed when she went to the oven and put on her hot mitts.

She had invited him over for dinner.

They should have dinner.

They had all night for everything else.

That thought had her smile returning.

"I have news," she said, excited and apprehensive about telling him Quinn's plan.

"Oh?"

She took out the pan of pork chops and apples and set it on the stove top. She put the hot mitts aside and felt Johnny at her back.

He moved her hair to the side and trailed a finger down her bare spine.

"Damn," he hissed, and the sound hit her low in the belly.

She didn't move as he slid his fingers up and down her spine.

Warm breath puffed on her shoulder blade and she stopped breathing. Lips trailed kisses along the back of her shoulder to her spine.

"What's your news?" he asked, stepping back.

She took a stabilizing breath. Had she ever been so enamored with a man before? No.

His gentle nature, his steadfast approach to life and love.

Safe and sexy in one.

It was a wild notion and it called to her.

She turned around and clasped her hands under her chin, unable to hide her excitement.

"God, you're cute," he said with a smile that reached his eyes.

"I've decided to embrace the decoy life." Saying it out loud felt incredible. "'Ashton James returned to LA this week to establish her new, quieter lifestyle."

Johnny's expression turned thoughtful, then confused, then it hit him. His eyebrows lifted and his gaze sharpened on her face.

"Which leaves me free to live the life I want."

His eyes bounced between hers, questions lurking in those dark brown irises.

"I mean, it's still possible for hiccups along the way, but the new security measures should help mitigate any real danger. To me and Piper, obviously, but also to you and Shawn and the rest of your family." She swallowed, his silence making her nervous.

He stepped forward and cupped her jaw, sweeping his thumb along her lower lip.

"What do you want for your life, baby?" he asked, voice rough.

She knew what he was asking. And he was going to make her say it.

"I want to make music again. Specifically with you. I want to be around to help Shawn with whatever he ends up doing. I want Piper to be happy and safe." She blinked slowly and bolstered her heart for its next big leap. "I want you."

“Me?” he repeated, his thumb made another sweep of her lip.

Hannah nodded, her heart racing. “I love you,” she whispered, feeling more vulnerable and exposed than she ever had before.

“You love me?” he asked, his face dipping to hers. His other hand went to her hip and tugged her closer. She pressed her palms against his chest but not to push him away.

“More than you know.”

His exhaled against her lips and she felt tension drain from his body.

Then his mouth landed on hers, tender, slow, with increasing pressure. A question, a hopefulness, infused every delicate movement of his mouth.

Hannah smoothed her hands over his shoulders and twined them around his neck. His arms wrapped around her, bringing their bodies together.

She slid her tongue against his lips and he opened his mouth to greet her. Electricity shot down her spine and thighs, sending tingles through her body.

Her head dropped back and his mouth met her neck in open-mouth kisses.

Slow, slow, slower.

Hot, hot, hotter.

His hands smoothed over her sides and gripped her hips, holding her to his hard body. She raked her fingers through his hair as his mouth nipped at her neck and followed the nips with soft kisses.

“We don’t have to eat right now,” she offered hopefully.

His sexy chuckle rumbled through her body, making her weak.

She let her greedy fingers travel to the exposed skin at his chest.

“We don’t have to do anything you don’t want to do,” she said, trying to keep her entire body from catching fire.

This was tricky for her.

He was successfully turning her on with very little effort on his part. But she couldn't forget that she was damaged goods. She would take what he was willing to give, but she couldn't expect—

"I want to," he cut her off with a kiss. Tender, hot lips nibbled at her own.

"I'm—" She swallowed and tried to focus. His hands kneaded her hips and her butt, turning her insides into molten lava.

"I'm on an antiviral. I've never missed a dose. And I have condoms in my room."

This probably wasn't sexy talk. Even though it had done nothing to dissuade him from licking a trail along her jaw and sucking her earlobe into his mouth.

"Okay," he murmured, acknowledging her words.

"There's still a risk, though." She sucked in a breath when one of his hands slid down and his fingers curled around the hem of her dress, hiking it up slightly.

"I know the risks," he said, sucking gently on her pulse point. "I've read all about it. I've made my decision. You just tell me when."

"When," she breathed when he licked her earlobe one more time.

Johnny's hands on her hips spun her around and he walked them both toward her room. Once there, he removed a small foil package from his pants pocket and set it on the nightstand. Then he returned to her.

Her gaze lingered on the condom for a moment.

He'd brought his own.

Something about that small fact had her heart soaring.

A small but immovable truth took hold in her heart: she was going to enjoy worshipping this man for the rest of her life.

* * *

She covered her eyes with her hands and giggled uncontrollably.

"You okay?" Johnny asked, sounding amused.

"Ask me again when I come back to earth," she replied.

He chuckled and sat up on the edge of the bed. "I'll be right back." He stood and headed for the bathroom.

Hannah took a deep breath and stretched all her limbs, loving the way they tingled in the aftermath. She pulled the covers back and crawled under the soft comforter.

Johnny came back into the room and she curled around a pillow as she watched his naked form in the candlelight.

"You're super hot," she said.

He laughed as he joined her in the bed. He curled his lean, hard body around hers from behind and rested his chin in the space between her shoulder and neck.

"How are you feeling?" he asked.

"Hmm, euphoric."

He chuckled and pressed a kiss to her shoulder.

"Can we do that again?" she asked hopefully.

"Whenever you want," he promised easily.

She hummed happily and he snuggled in closer to her.

Her thoughts turned inward and she tried to ignore them. Turning in his arms, she faced him.

Seeing the expression on her face, he smoothed her hair back and kissed her forehead.

"What's going on, baby?" he asked.

Baby. She could get used to that.

"What if this is a bad idea? Us, I mean."

"Tell me why you think that?" he replied, sounding unbothered.

"Because I'll hurt you," she responded sadly.

"You will?" he asked, sounding surprised.

She rolled her eyes. "C'mon, Johnny. Be serious about this."

"I am." He wrapped his arms around her and pulled her close. "Who says you'll hurt me?"

She stared into those dark brown eyes. Eyes that had become the closest thing to home she had found outside of herself. Fear and uncertainty clawed at the back of her mind, trying to take over her happiness.

"What if it's in my nature?" She lifted a shoulder and let it drop.

He studied her face for a beat. One of his hands rubbed a circle on her back between her shoulder blades.

"We might hurt each other," he said, his voice deep and easy. "I think that's the risk humans take when they fall in love. It's in all our nature. We just have to choose better."

She swallowed, her heart still lodged in her throat, making it difficult.

"I care about you so much," she confessed. "I didn't…" She struggled with this part. The vulnerable part of honesty. It was one thing to be honest about all her sins. It was something else to be honest about her heart. "You were unexpected," she finally finished.

"So were you."

He found her hand and brought it to his lips. Turning it over he kissed the palm, his mouth soft and warm.

Something big and electric moved through her chest.

It was all right there in his eyes and in his arms. An emotion too large to hide from.

Maybe she'd fallen for him years ago. Or maybe she'd only stumbled.

Knowing that he'd seen the best and worst of her had her feeling like he knew her better than anyone.

Was that stupid?

Because it felt stupid.

But it also felt incredible.

"I really don't have to pretend with you, do I?" she asked, more thoughtful than anything.

He cracked a grin on one side. "I'd like to see you try to pretend anything."

She slanted a look his way. “Oh, am I so transparent?”

“No,” he replied instantly. “Not transparent at all. But you don’t leave the people you care about guessing how you feel.”

“These days, I have a very small circle.” Images from the past flickered through her mind. But they’d become blurry. “I’m careful about who I let in.”

She pursed her lips, thinking of Shawn and all his ambition and talent. He was still at the beginning of everything.

“Sometimes I still get so mad at myself. Mad that I let the wrong people into my life. And let them be so close to me, you know? My own manager was just a shit-stirrer. He’d pay photogs to show up when I was drunk at places. And then put on a theatrical display of trying to protect me.” She rolled her eyes, tasting the old disgust in the back of her mouth. “And I trusted him to have my back?

“Or my assistant? That girl…” She shook her head and let out a heavy sigh.

Never, in all the time she’d been away from the game, had she spoken about the little things that still got to her. The small details of the life that had never really belonged to her.

“She would take video of me and sell it. She informed on me to Terrence. She used my name to get access to all the best clubs and restaurants. She played the game *really* well. Those two deserve each other.”

Hannah batted her eyelashes to signal her annoyance.

“He’s her manager now. She’s her own brand. More popular than I ever was. Has her own reality show.”

She watched recognition dawn on Johnny’s face.

“Holy crap,” he muttered.

“It’s gotta be way easier to produce and execute the drama on your own show instead of trying to catch it live,” she muttered, chest tight.

She swallowed and nodded, looking away as her cheeks flamed hot.

Why did shame still sting her? She wasn't responsible for them or their choices. She was only responsible for her own.

She knew that from a logical standpoint. But her sore heart would still occasionally beat a guilty rhythm.

"I want to be grateful for the experiences that I've had. I know it hasn't been awesome, but I learned a lot. And there is gratitude there. And I hope someday I can go straight to gratitude without a pit stop at shame and guilt." She nodded, conviction settling softly into her bones.

Yeah, that's what she wanted.

"Can I ask you something?" he asked.

She smirked. It was such a common question between them now.

"You said…back then, back when we first met…that you had to get rid of me anyway…"

He didn't finish the question because it wasn't necessary. She could hear it in the tone, see it in his eyes.

"Because I would have run away with you," she said softly.

Johnny lifted an eyebrow.

"If you'd have asked, I would have said yes. I would have run and never looked back." She licked her bottom lip, letting her tongue linger for a moment on the thought. "I needed to save you from everything that I knew I was."

It was something she'd been over in her head multiple times since she'd remembered. The very fact that she hadn't remembered him was confusing. Because if he was as important as the startling memory implied, how had she forgotten?

"I was on a very clear path. I knew what I wanted, and you represented the opposite. You were freedom and love and goodness…and I knew you wouldn't look at me the same way after a while. And I didn't want to have to face that."

She snorted and tipped her eyes to the ceiling. "I must've locked you away somewhere where I couldn't feel guilty about it."

Maybe that was a stretch, but it was the only thing she could come up with.

If she'd been trying to explain to anyone else, she wouldn't have been so candid.

"You will always be safe with me," he promised, reading her mind. "Teammates, remember?"

Her lips tugged up on one side.

"And you were right," he continued in that smooth, self-assured, easy way of his. "I would have gotten you to run away with me." Then he winked.

He rolled onto his back and she adjusted beside him, resting her head on his pectoral. He wrapped an arm around her shoulders and held her hand to his abs with his other.

"I think," he began, that deep, easy voice sounding even better with her head on his chest. "One of my favorite things about you is how soft you are for those you care about. Piper, Shawn, me…Your giant heart opens up and you tuck us all inside."

She closed her eyes and melted into him with his words.

"My mom was a drunk," he confessed quietly.

She stilled, heart racing with his words.

"Not until we moved here, though. She didn't really want to leave Honduras. She wanted to stay and be with my—" He swallowed. "With him."

Johnny took a deep breath and let it out slowly, like it was holding all of his residual confusion and frustration.

"I tried to get her sober. I used to get up in the middle of the night and dump all the bottles down the drain. Or I'd hide her purse from her and pay the bills myself. She was that out of her mind."

Hannah squeezed her eyes shut as her nose began to sting.

"When she got pulled over for driving drunk, I was relieved. I thought it might be a wake-up call. But that's when I learned she had never renewed her visa."

Hannah moved her hand on his abs to make slow circles, needing to offer him comfort, even if it was more than a decade too late.

"All these years I've never stopped wondering why we weren't enough for her. Her kids, you know? I know moving to a new country and starting over wasn't the easiest thing, but she wasn't alone. Why couldn't she be happy with us?"

Hannah pushed up on an elbow and gazed down at Johnny, her instinct to protect him fierce. "It wasn't you."

He held her gaze, shadows of old hurt moving in his eyes.

"Johnny, I can say with one hundred percent certainty that it had nothing to do with you."

"I know," he replied roughly. "But not until you."

He smoothed her hair back along her temple and ran a finger down her jawline.

"I don't think you'll ever know how much of me you've healed just by being you."

Her heart took flight, spreading wings she had no idea existed. Immediately, her body felt light and free.

He must've sensed the internal change in her because those gorgeous lips of his twitched. "I love you, Hannah Lee."

He said it like a promise.

Like it was just something that he was going to do no matter what she said or did.

A peace settled in her and she blinked at him, letting go of the "what ifs" and "what abouts."

"So, we're just gonna do this?" she asked with a teasing smile. "Just be in love with each other and see what happens?"

His smile grew with her words and her heart raced.

"You love me?" he asked, tilting her chin slightly and drawing her closer.

"Like you wouldn't believe," she murmured over his lips before sinking into a dizzying kiss.

This was her life now.

Not Life Before.

Not life in between.

This was life worth living.

And she'd never been more hopeful or excited for the present.

EPILOGUE

ONE YEAR LATER

BREAKING CELEBRITY NEWS

Ashton James, pop music's former bad girl, just dropped a new album titled Better.

A year ago, CelebX broke the news that Ashton James had returned to Southern California to claim her crown. Keeping a low profile, rumors swirled around the It Girl as she worked on her next project.

At midnight, a new album began popping up on music platforms all over the world.

CelebX has reached out to Ashton's people for comment. They promise a statement will be arriving later in the week.

First listeners have taken to social media to proclaim this album her most complex and genuine. With fifteen tracks of brand-new material, it appears she had a hand in crafting every song.

Already hitting number one in multiple countries, is this the return of the Queen we've all been waiting for?

CelebX will update this story as more information is provided.

The Motherfucking End

ACKNOWLEDGMENTS

Writing can be such a lonely occupation. I am grateful for the amazing people in my life that kept me going with their love, friendship, belief, and inspiration. Without them, this story would not exist.

Penny, Fiona, Brooke and the other Smartypants Authors. None of this would be possible without each of you. Thank you for your encouragement, your jokes, your persistence, and your talent. You lifted me up and kept me going when it felt like too much. I hope I can return the favor someday.

The It Girls of the Early Aughts. This story took much inspiration and creative liberties from the tabloids printed during the early 2000s.

Misterwives. You released an album while I wrote this story that became half of my entire playlist. Thank you for that.

Taylor Swift. You released an album the same day. That was the other half of my playlist.

The Johnnys. I was new at school and you let me sit by you at lunch. Just because I didn't speak Spanish didn't stop you from adopting me into you little family. Thank you for the friendship and teaching me how to swear in Spanish.

Scott Colby. Always. Forever.

My readers. Your messages of encouragement and the gift of your time means more than you can know. Thank you for inviting me into your lives. I am honored.

My betas. Thank you for your patience, kindness, and truth. Thank you for loving these characters the way I do. Thank you for not abandoning me when I was driving you crazy with multiple rewrites. You're the real MVPs.

Jo. Thank you for your patience and persistence. Without you I would be lost. Your friendship only continues to mean more to me over the years. Your humor, your grace, your heart — you have no idea how invaluable you are. Tell Pete 😉

Jamie. I can't imagine life without you and don't want to try. Without you my life would be bleak and unfunny. You are brilliant and beautiful and I'm keeping you forever so stop trying to get away.

Kellcie. You believe in me in a way that I don't understand. And I'm humbled by it. Thank you for your friendship.

Annie. Please, for the love kibble, stop barking. I know you're spoiled and I know it's my fault but please let me finish this and then we can go play.

Kati. Peaches. My life took a very happy turn when you entered it. I can't picture adventures without you there beside me. Let's go on another one.

AJ. Your countless phone calls and never ending encouragement mean more than you realize. Thank you for your stories and inspiration and your steadfast belief in me. I hope someday I can deserve it.

Sarahi. Your heart and your beauty shine brighter than the sun. I'm so thankful you are a permanent part of my life. Thank you for sharing your stories and wisdom with me. Thank you for loving my brother. He's at his best when he's with you. We all are.

Bria. Thanks for talking me off the ledge numerous times. All the laughter, pep talks, and good advice. You are incredible and talented and I hope I get to be a part of your life forever and always.

Zack. Thank you for believing in me. For your wisdom and insight. But most of all for your friendship. It has been and remains the most important of my life. I love you an appropriate amount.

Charlie. My joy. My gift. Being your mom is the greatest pleasure of my life. I love you even when it annoys you. That's when I love you the most.

Charles. Captain Awesome. Cap. My love. My heart. Without you there would be no stories to tell. You teach me about love and romance every single day. Promise not to stop when I say "when."

God. Thank you for this. For them. For all of it. Everything. Thank you for making me. And for continuing to make me, again and again. My cup runneth over.

ABOUT THE AUTHOR

Heidi writes stories that she hopes will inspire her readers to take their hearts on one more adventure.

She still lives in the Black Hills with her alarmingly handsome husband, their fearless child, and a rather large and spoiled dog.

She is fueled by her unwavering and perfectly normal devotion to Dave Grohl and coffee.

And a whole lotta love.

heidih.net

Email: heidih.writer@gmail.com

Find Smartypants Romance online:

Website: www.smartypantsromance.com

Facebook: www.facebook.com/smartypantsromance/

Goodreads: www.goodreads.com/smartypantsromance

Twitter: @smartypantsrom

Instagram: @smartypantsromance

OTHER TITLES BY HEIDI HUTCHINSON

Double Blind Study Series:

Learn to Fly

In Your Honor

Tectonic

Deepest Blues

The Hope That Starts

Brand New Sky

Into the Night We Shine

Matter of Fact

Soaring Bird Series:

Like the Back of My Halo

Sushi and Sun Salutations

Puppy Love and Peanut Butter

In Between Series:

In Between the Earth and Sky

In Cold Mud Series:

Stubborn Hearts

Crossover with Bria Quinlan:

Things That Shine

www.heidih.net

ALSO BY SMARTYPANTS ROMANCE

Green Valley Chronicles

The Love at First Sight Series

Baking Me Crazy by Karla Sorensen (#1)

Batter of Wits by Karla Sorensen (#2)

Steal My Magnolia by Karla Sorensen(#3)

Fighting For Love Series

Stud Muffin by Jiffy Kate (#1)

Beef Cake by Jiffy Kate (#2)

Eye Candy by Jiffy Kate (#3)

The Donner Bakery Series

No Whisk, No Reward by Ellie Kay (#1)

The Green Valley Library Series

Love in Due Time by L.B. Dunbar (#1)

Crime and Periodicals by Nora Everly (#2)

Prose Before Bros by Cathy Yardley (#3)

Shelf Awareness by Katie Ashley (#4)

Carpentry and Cocktails by Nora Everly (#5)

Love in Deed by L.B. Dunbar (#6)

Dewey Belong Together by Ann Whynot (#7)

Hotshot and Hospitality by Nora Everly (#8)

Love in a Pickle by L.B. Dunbar (#9)

Scorned Women's Society Series

My Bare Lady by Piper Sheldon (#1)

The Treble with Men by Piper Sheldon (#2)

The One That I Want by Piper Sheldon (#3)

Hopelessly Devoted by Piper Sheldon (#3.5)

Park Ranger Series

Happy Trail by Daisy Prescott (#1)

Stranger Ranger by Daisy Prescott (#2)

The Leffersbee Series

Been There Done That by Hope Ellis (#1)

Before and After You by Hope Ellis (#2)

The Higher Learning Series

Upsy Daisy by Chelsie Edwards (#1)

Green Valley Heroes Series

Forrest for the Trees by Kilby Blades

Seduction in the City

Cipher Security Series

Code of Conduct by April White (#1)

Code of Honor by April White (#2)

Code of Ethics by April White (#3)

Cipher Office Series

Weight Expectations by M.E. Carter (#1)

Sticking to the Script by Stella Weaver (#2)

Cutie and the Beast by M.E. Carter (#3)

Weights of Wrath by M.E. Carter (#4)

Common Threads Series

Mad About Ewe by Susannah Nix (#1)

Give Love a Chai by Nanxi Wen (#2)

Key Change by Heidi Hutchinson (#3)

Educated Romance

Work For It Series

Street Smart by Aly Stiles (#1)

Heart Smart by Emma Lee Jayne (#2)

Lessons Learned Series

Under Pressure by Allie Winters (#1)

Made in the USA
Monee, IL
11 October 2021